Date Due

OCT 26 1987		
OCT 26 1987		
FEB 09 1989		
JAN 24 1992		
FEB 10 1992		

THE
PORTENT

THE
PORTENT

MARILYN HARRIS

G. P. Putnam's Sons   New York

Library of Congress Cataloging in Publication Data
Harris, Marilyn.
    The portent.

    I. Title.
PZ4.H3145Po [PS3558.A648] 813'.54 80–13751
ISBN 0–399–12506–X

PRINTED IN THE UNITED STATES OF AMERICA

Let not men say
"These are their reasons—they are natural"
For I believe they are portentous things.

—Shakespeare

Biochemical systems exchange matter with their surroundings all the time. They are open, thermodynamic processes. This is the secret of life. It means that there is a continuous communication not only between living things and their environment, but among all things living in that environment.

—Dr. Lyall Watson

Omnipresence means there is no boundary between life and non-life, that therefore all things are in essence alive.

—Guy Murchie

All are but parts of one stupendous whole, whose body Nature is.

—Alexander Pope

We tend to think of ourselves as the only wholly unique creations of Nature, but it is not so. Uniqueness is so commonplace a property of living things that there is nothing at all unique about it.

—Dr. Lewis Thomas

All things are full of Gods.

—Thales

Prologue

May 6, 1951

There was no real cause for alarm yet.

From where he had fallen, he could see through the second-floor window onto the dirt road below. Not that there was anything much to see except the heavily rutted tracks, two sagging structures across the way, the weed-infested ruins of three others, the wind spiraling dust fingers into the air, and to his left, the jagged horizon line of mountains and the end of the day. Night . . . Dark . . . Damn!

"Claire!"

His cry echoed about the abandoned loft and returned to him in the form of fine grit which filtered down through the gaping hole in the roof. Fearing further collapse, he twisted his head about and tried to look up, and for his troubles suffered a sharp pain in his left ankle at the precise point where the timber had fallen, pinning him. A searing bolt of new pain shot up into his hip and suggested the wisdom of nonmovement.

With no choice but to oblige, he rested the side of his face on his arm and muttered, "Claire," and wondered how long it would be before she realized he was missing.

Not long, he was certain. They had left the trailer and jeep alongside the road about an hour ago. Two hours? She'd spied some purple flowers growing along the high ridge. Jess had called after her that he was going to explore the little ghost town and had watched her for a few minutes as she'd scrambled up the steep incline, fascinated by the sculptured movement of tight blue jeans over a beautifully formed ass. He'd started to call her back. It *was* a honeymoon.

His discomfort and apprehension eased by the distraction of sexual energy, he tried again to pull his leg free of the heavy timber. No use. A grim thought occurred. Was the ankle broken? No. Inside his boots he could wiggle his toes. Then all he would need, once freed, was an ice pack and Claire's loving ministrations.

"Claire!"

As he shouted again, he looked down on the road below, thinking he'd seen something, a flash of color, movement . . .

"Claire! Up here. Can you . . . ?"

But it was nothing, merely a cloud passing over the dying sun. He struggled a moment longer, fighting panic. Hell, he didn't even know where they were. This godforsaken place wasn't even listed on the map.

A gen-u-wine ghost town, Claire, he had announced, a high plateau tucked into the folds of the mountain . . . untouched by human hands . . .

"There's gold in them thar hills. . . . Reach for your gun, Sheriff, this here is Jess Conrad James—"

Shit—

"Claire!"

In spite of the rigid posture necessary to accommodate the pinned portion of his leg, he reached out for the sill of the low window and tried to drag himself free.

He heard an ominous creaking beneath him, the old floorboards beginning to bend like half-cooked spaghetti.

He froze. That was all he needed, for the floor to go, plunging him and the half-fallen roof into the dusty room below. He'd need more than tape then. . . .

He held still. The floor grew steady. There was no real cause for alarm yet. It was only a matter of time before his bride of two weeks came and found him.

You're a lucky bastard, Jess Conrad, back from Korea and into Claire Heller's bed. . . .

Could she lift the timber? Of course she could, with his help.

"Claire?" What in the hell . . . ?

He closed his eyes to accommodate a wave of mild nausea, the canned-tamale lunch objecting to his predicament in its own way.

The party's o . . . ver . . .

. . . time to head back to Evanston and a few years of G.I. Bill, a graduate degree, a baby or two wedged in between Biology 415 and Physical Anthropology 403, a reassuring and predictable route which would, with luck, lead to a position in a small liberal-arts college, Claire, president of Faculty Wives, their children bright, healthy, curious. How modest were his dreams. Yet after the ordeal of Korea, it was all he wanted. . . .

8

"They are coming up the hill, sir. Heavy casualties. I don't think we can hold them."

NO!

For several minutes he tried to discipline his mind with objective data.

The survival abilities of several species is superb: the Cameroon toad and the hog-nosed snake both play dead, and the most accomplished death feigner of all is the American opossum, Didelphis virginiana, which has a remarkable fixed-action pattern to call on.

He pressed his forehead into the rough floorboards and thought quite rationally that he would give the entire $93.35 in his wallet for a beer. An overwhelming thirst had come from somewhere. Those canned tamales? . . .

The windowsill was a good eight inches beyond his reach. The fallen timber was immense—now, where would you find timber like that in the U.S. today?—twenty feet in length, two feet in diameter. Still, he should be able to dislodge it, at least enough to slip free.

But after a second, third, and fourth effort when nothing had happened but an increased sense of his ankle being crushed, he gave up and lay motionless, one hand outstretched, palm down toward the elusive windowsill.

Rain?

With the first splattering of moisture, he didn't even bother to look up. Immobility has high survival value. . . .

"Claire?"

Another drop . . .

Dusk and clouds look the same. Who would have thought rain? The sun had blinded them earlier in the day.

Immobilization can be induced by constriction, disorientation, fear . . .

Bingo! All three. The jackpot.

Damn it!

"Claire! Help . . ."

The force of his voice dragged his head upward as another drop of moisture spattered against the back of his hand.

Jesus!

His hand was red-splattered. Blood? When had he hurt his hand? He had not hurt his hand. His hand was intact.

He twisted his head toward the hole in the roof. Through the jagged opening he saw the sky. Blue with tints of dark purple. Not a rain cloud in sight, though admittedly his sight was limited.

Another drop.

A wound was bleeding. Not his. . . .

All right. Just a minute—an animal, a squirrel, chipmunk on the roof, caught in the cave-in as well, flying timber, a crushed or severed paw . . .

He approached reason very stealthily yet irritably. Some damn thing was bleeding on him.

"Anybody up there?"

9

He held still, listening. The wind answered.

Oh, Christ, what had happened to their plans for the evening? Durango by nightfall, the luxury of an eight-dollar motel room and a hot bath, maybe even an inexpensive restaurant meal . . .

Have you noticed, Jess, how canned food all begins to taste the same?

As his neck ached from the awkward twisted position required to look up, he turned about.

Catatonia, catalepsy, thanatosis, action inhibition . . . Could he move, and his mind was willing him not to?

Then do it! It was only a matter of sending the message from the brain to the pinned leg. Only a matter . . . What had lured him up to this abandoned loft in the first place?

Curiosity killed the cat. A hint, a clue as to what the two-story structure had been used for. A saloon? A general store? An assayer's office?

Look at this old pick! And this horseshoe! We picked them up on our honeymoon. No, we took the back roads. Show them those purple flowers, Claire, the ones you pressed in the . . .

Do it! Ignoring the elusive windowsill, he positioned his hands directly beneath his chest, pausing for a brief inspection of the blood on his right hand. Then, like a paraplegic, he tried to concentrate all his energies into dragging his body forward, a massive effort which resulted in exactly nothing except quivering shoulder muscles, a distinct ringing in his ears, and a bird's-eye view of the room below through the cracks in the planks which formed the floor.

After several minutes of labored breathing, the brain messengers started out again, running the gauntlet from cortex to calf muscles, an army all racing downward with a simple message: Move, damn it!

Suddenly, in the room below, a shadow crossed his line of vision. Disoriented, the brain messengers broke rank. There was someone down there. Call out for help, you idiot!

The effort ceased. With one eye he tried to track the shadow through the crack. Where was the substance? All shadows had substance.

Who? He wasn't alone. Claire? No, it wasn't Claire. Why no? Just no. They weren't alone. She was in trouble too. That's why she wasn't looking for him. The brain messengers were running amok.

In the sepia-colored room below, filled with dusk and no clues, he saw a moving something which had yet to materialize. . . .

You were lucky, young man. They were armed and dangerous. Broke out of state prison a week ago. Playing possum was the best thing you could have done. Yessiree. No trace of the missus as yet. I'm sorry, but we'll keep lookin' . . .

Not footsteps, though he turned at an angle that the human spine had never achieved before and looked toward the narrow steps.

Quiet. Don't move.

Still no footsteps, though a cramp knotted in his lower spine, a fist-hard vise of objecting muscle. Straightening made it worse, and with one blurred eye he looked through the crack into the room below and saw . . . nothing.

10

He held still in spite of the contracting pain, searching as far in all directions as the one-sixteenth of an inch would permit.

Move now! There was nothing, had been nothing except his own body coming between the sky above and the room below. *He* had cast the shadow.

No real cause for alarm yet. . . .

Summoning energy he didn't know he had, he extended his hand toward the windowsill, felt for and found a beveled edge and dragged himself forward, hearing in the process an ominous creaking of wood both above and below, but heard as well the timber shift, only inches, but it was enough.

Ignoring the pain, he looked back and carefully eased his foot loose and watched with held breath as the timber immediately fell back, making noisy contact with the loft floor.

A little amazed at how easy it had been after almost an hour's struggle—two hours?—he propped himself up in a sitting position, keeping a watchful eye on his left foot as though it were an errant child who had wandered too far and had now returned to its parent.

It hurt like hell. Sprained, no doubt, though not broken. Crisis over. Panic behind him. Still gasping for breath from his recent effort, he looked up toward the hole in the roof. The blood had stopped, though he was sorry for whatever small animal he may have injured in his careless trespassing.

He shivered. Fear, apparently, had kept him warm. Then, feet, move! With caution, aware now that the ancient structure was as fragile as a house of cards, he started up, using the windowsill for support, his right leg supporting his body weight until fully up, when he tested the strength on the left foot.

Jesus!

As the bruised ligaments objected to one hundred and seventy-six pounds of body weight, he sat heavily on the sill, extended his left leg out in front of him, and shouted,

"Claire!"

He looked down through the window and tried to see to the edge of the high meadow where they'd left the jeep and trailer. While he couldn't see, he knew it was there, less than five hundred yards, within the range of a human voice, particularly since there was nothing to compete with that voice except the blowing wind.

"Claire!"

Why in hell didn't she hear him? Could he make it back to the jeep unaided, and if he could, could he drive, and if he couldn't, could Claire drive? The jeep had whined all the way up, had fought the heavily rutted cow path, had squeezed through the narrow rock canyon walls . . .

Listen!

He looked up. There was something on the roof. The injured chipmunk? He focused on the jagged hole with such intensity that his eyes blurred. The sound, a scurrying, ceased. He spied, hanging down, a piece of splintered timber about the height of a walking stick.

With the intention of pulling it loose and fashioning a makeshift crutch, he pushed off from the windowsill and commenced a laborious hopping, hearing threatening reverberations, the old wood objecting to pressure in the same way that his ankle had objected.

11

Standing directly beneath the place where the timber had fallen, he reached up and with little effort pulled the wood crutch loose, and though it was full of splinters, still it served the purpose, and leaning heavily on the awkward peg-leg, he wasted no time in gaining the top of the stairs.

He learned quickly how to accommodate his ankle and maneuvered his way down the narrow passage, ducking his head, still fearful that the whole damn place was on the verge of collapse.

On the ground floor with the door about thirty feet ahead, he suffered a twinge of anger. The public should be warned.

Unsafe. Do not enter except at your own risk.

Would that have kept him out? Hell, no. He took a final look at the large dusty room which he'd explored at length before the stairs had lured him up into the loft.

A general store, most likely, the place where those early settlers had come for human contact to discuss the latest blizzard, yesterday's avalanche, the various whims of nature which undoubtedly had made their lives an adventurous hell. Where were their descendants? Obviously no one had chosen to stick around.

There was plenty of evidence that the settlement once had been fairly prosperous. The structures were large compared to the other abandoned mining towns they had visited in Colorado. Tent cities, most of the others had been. But this one had started out with permanence in mind. Then why wasn't it listed on the map?

As the questions turned in his mind, he realized that it had been these same questions which had lured him into his recent predicament.

Not again, thank you. He was smart enough to know that he'd been lucky. The ankle hurt like hell, but at least he could move it. His one goal now was not the solution to the mystery of the past, but the location of his bride and the devout hope that between them they could navigate their way back down that goat path which they had wrongly interpreted as a road, find civilization by nightfall, where under the soothing influence of a hot tub and a good steak they could laugh about the melodrama of the afternoon, and ultimately, in delicious and prolonged lovemaking, ease pain and court forgetfulness.

He took a last glance about the crumbling interior, feeling in a way that he had become part of the myth of the place, and saw through the back window a portion of the mountain which seemed to stand guard over the ruins. Adjusting the makeshift walking stick to serve as a third leg, he hobbled toward the door and felt an unseasonably cold blast of dust-filled air sting against his face, and bowed his head into the new discomfort.

Spitting grit, and temporarily blinded, he stepped out onto the heavily rutted road, amazed at the power of erosion. Either that or those first intrepid settlers had dragged cannons up and down their main street.

Damn! It was like the curb-walking he used to do as a kid, one foot up, one down, the whole process made even more difficult by the pressure inside his boot, an ominous sign that the foot was swelling.

He increased his speed as much as he dared, and felt peculiarly old, as though the last few hours had drained some vital supply of energy. Looking up into the wind, he searched the road ahead. The walk into town had seemed

12

so short. Now he couldn't even see the trailer and jeep, and of course it was asking too much of fate to let Claire appear.

He stopped for breath—damn altitude—and to clear the blowing dust from his eyes and realized that he felt a need to get his bearings.

What the hell—bearings! He'd walked in a straight line into the old settlement.

No panic! Simple! He'd not noticed the road rising or falling. Obviously he had walked up a slight incline. Two hundred yards would see him to the crest, where he'd look down on the familiar trailer, the trusty jeep, World War II vintage.

In spite of the discomfort, he increased his speed, occasionally forgetting the function of the walking stick and putting partial weight on his ankle, cursing aloud now as it occurred to him that it might interfere with their lovemaking. What the hell, there were other positions. . . .

He smiled and vowed that as soon as he found her, he could (A.) make a bid for her pity, (B.) scold her gently for not coming to his rescue, (C.) coax her into the trailer, (D.) talk her out of those tight-fitting jeans, (E.) . . .

Hallelujah! There it was, exactly as he had thought, the jeep and trailer obscured beneath a subtle rise of land.

"Claire!" As he shouted her name into the wind, he looked up at the sky and saw fast-moving clouds that seemed to collide with each other. Something to do with the altitude perhaps, atmospheric conditions, a storm coming. Hell, that's all they needed.

"Claire!"

As he hobbled down the incline, he tried to brace himself against the face-jarring pull of gravity. Why didn't he remember this incline? If he'd not been able to see the trailer from the ruins of the settlement, why had he been able to see the ruins from the trailer?

Well, he'd figure this one out later. For now, his ankle was swelling inside his boot, a storm was brewing, and he wanted to get down that one narrow road and to the highway to Durango before nightfall. He'd had enough of wilderness.

When he was about thirty feet from the jeep and trailer, he called for what he hoped would be the final time. "Claire? Are you here? I could use an arm . . ." He held his position, listening, somehow wanting her to see him. He could use a little wifely pity now.

"Claire, please, I need . . ."

The wind scooped up new dust and threw it at him. He bowed his head and leaned heavily against the hood of the jeep and saw the grille splattered with dead bugs.

Not back yet. That was apparent. Annoyed, he looked across the high meadow, dark green velvet dotted with white, yellow, and purple wildflowers. But no sign of Claire.

He lifted his vision to timberline, to the stand of uneven trees growing along the high ridge, fir, pine, aspen, then beyond that to the craggy stone face of the mountain itself.

If she *were* in trouble . . .

He gripped the walking stick as though to strangle it. He was not exactly in

13

condition to launch a search which could cover everything including the face of the mountain itself.

Take it easy! No cause for alarm yet, though in increasing anger he limped around to the driver's seat, flung open the door, and planted his hand, palm down, on the horn. As the tinny siren resounded above the wind, he pressed harder, as though extra effort might make a difference.

Oh, Claire, where are you? Please come . . .

Against the onslaught of his accelerating pulse and the increasing discomfort which was now creeping up his leg, he tossed the walking stick aside and eased into the driver's seat, carefully lifting his leg after him, and pulled the door shut.

The warmth felt good, reminding him that he'd been cold. He bent over, the better to see the scene beyond the bug-splattered windshield. He wasn't aware that he was shivering until he heard his teeth chattering, and quickly he reached into the backseat for his army jacket, souvenir of Korea, and saw her matching one, courtesy of army surplus, and thought with new worry that she must be cold as well.

As he dragged the heavy khaki jacket up front, he saw the scattered debris of their three-week trip; the dog-eared and poorly folded road maps that had guided them on their odyssey from Illinois to their farthest point, Phoenix, Arizona. California had beckoned, but they had chosen the isolation of the Rockies instead.

In the cramped quarters of the driver's seat, he slipped awkwardly into the jacket, patted the chest pocket, found a Lucky Strike package with two cigarettes, tapped one on the steering wheel, launched a search in the opposite pocket for his lighter, took a long drag, and felt instantly a soothing of anxieties.

She'd be back soon, clutching her purple flowers, breathless, her face flushed with color, telling him everything she'd seen and heard and felt.

Lord, but he loved her, had loved her since that first time when he'd seen her on campus five, six years ago.

Momentarily lost in memories of the beginning, he flicked the cigarette ashes onto the floor and longed to straighten his throbbing leg and again bent low and searched the vista beyond the windshield.

Not only was there nothing, but he discovered now that he couldn't even see the stand of trees on the high ridge. They had been swallowed up in a fast-falling dusk. By his estimate there was about half an hour of daylight left.

In a rapid, angry movement he took a final drag on his cigarette, opened the door and flicked the butt across the road, and again flattened his palm against the horn, performing a kind of wild and witless Morse code, two longs, two shorts, one long.

The outburst left him curiously breathless. Not enough air. He leaned across to the opposite window, his line of vision starting low, then systematically making its way up the mountainside, brought forcibly to a halt by that band of blackness which appeared to cut the mountain in half. Green was still visible on this side, and the rubble of stone that marked the regions above timberline on the other. But all light was gone from that central sector. Even the shapes of trees were no longer distinguishable.

14

My God, where could she have gone? Although he tried not to, he remembered his earlier premonition that she was in trouble.

For a moment he rested his elbow on the steering wheel and gnawed at his thumbnail. Beneath the nail he tasted grit and with the tip of his tongue found a splinter in the fleshy part of his thumb and remembered his recent struggle in the collapsed loft, the timber shifting suddenly. Foot freed.

Could something like that have happened to her? Injured? Seriously? The thought produced his first genuine siren of alarm. No one knew where they were. Their last contact with the world had been the phone call to her parents two nights ago. Someplace in New Mexico. They'd camped out. She'd made a pot of chili . . .

They'd stopped at a Texaco to gas up before heading into the mountains. They'd followed Highway 160 for a while, had turned off at a place called Valenco . . .

Where are you going?

Someplace where I can make love to you for an uninterrupted twenty-four-hour period.

Quickly he reached into the backseat and shuffled through the road maps, found Colorado, and flattened it against the steering wheel.

In the diminishing light, he found the Continental Divide, Red Mountain Pass, down to Valenco, there, and they'd turned left out of Valenco. Or had it been right?

What matter? No matter. They were somewhere in the middle of that dark green square inch on the map where nothing was marked, nothing visible, no friendly red dot suggesting a town, no squiggly red line representing a road.

Somewhere in that square inch his wife was gathering purple flowers while he sat cramped in the jeep, hurting, hungry, cold. . . .

Easy! Alarm was permitted, but no panic, please. She was capable, intelligent, and responsible. She'd take no foolish chances and had a good instrument of intuition.

The thought provided him with minor comfort, though simultaneously he flattened his hand against the horn, and above the continuous siren, glanced directly ahead through the front window and instantly removed his hand as though the horn had become hot.

What in the . . . ?

The road *was* flat. With complete ease he could now see the entire abandoned settlement, the collapsed structures on his left, the one partially standing on the right. There was no hill, no incline, the road was flat.

He sat blinking at the optical illusion. Perhaps he had merely . . .

Perhaps hell!

With a jerk he threw open the door, and howled aloud at the first step and drew his knee up to his chest, and for a moment performed a bizarre dance in an attempt to accommodate the pain.

His recovery was aided by large doses of adrenaline and an equally large desire to get the hell out of this place. He retrieved the crude walking stick which he'd dropped beside the jeep and made his way to the back, where, buried under the debris of empty potato-chip bags and old newspapers, he

15

found the flashlight. Carefully he crawled over the coupling which connected the trailer to the jeep and confronted the vast, slowly darkening meadow and the black band beyond.

"Claire? Claire, can you hear me!"

Of course she can't hear you, you jackass. Go and find her. Now!

Half-stumbling, he made his way down into the culvert which separated the rutted road from the meadowland. Logic was a helpful tool, informing him that if she were anywhere in the knee-high grass, she would be visible to him. But since she was not visible, then she must have wandered up as far as the ridge of trees.

A quarter of a mile? More? Less? It was impossible to tell. With every step reminding him of his partially numb leg, he started the laborious trek upward, fighting gravity, wind, encroaching darkness, and pain. After ten minutes he had to stop for breath. Whereas earlier he had been cold, now he was over-warm and sweating heavily. And hallucinating. The rippling grasses on all sides began to resemble water, as though he were wading across a waist-deep lake instead of high, dry land.

But the effort was the same, a solid force pushing against him, transforming every step into a battle won or lost, the black ridge seeming to come no closer.

About forty-five minutes later, under the duress of his weight, the walking stick broke, a sudden malevolent snapping, as though it too had joined forces with the inhospitable terrain.

You will not reach the top, you bastard. . . .

I will.

Limping, half-crawling, acquiring an indifference which allowed him to ignore the lack of oxygen, he clawed his way higher and higher, lacking now the energy and breath to call her name aloud, but thinking it with each exertion: Claire, Claire . . .

When he was less than fifty yards from the ridge of trees, and confident that he could go the rest of the way, he flattened himself in the grasses and heard his pulse, rapid and irregular, his heart on the verge of exploding, and rewarded himself with a moment's rest, though he knew that was all he could afford, for dusk had become night, and the dim eye of his flashlight was as nothing confronted with total darkness.

He'd never known night to descend so fast. By his estimate it wasn't six o'clock yet. Raising himself on his elbows, he pushed up the sleeve of his jacket and tried to focus on the face of his watch in spite of the stinging sweat and read . . . *two-twenty?*

. . . and the watch was new, a wedding gift from Claire. Two-twenty—about the time they'd discovered this place. No need for additional panic. Obviously damage had been done when the timber from the roof had fallen on him, or maybe . . .

Weary of thinking, he dragged himself with renewed effort to a sitting position and stretched his left leg out—the pressure informed him that the boot would have to be cut off—and saw far below the toy-sized jeep and trailer, looking out of place and intrusive in the uninhabited, night-shrouded landscape.

Well, Claire certainly wasn't down there, but somewhere behind him, out of sight in the trees, or beyond. No, she wouldn't be so foolish as to attempt the rock face of the mountain itself.

But at this point, lacking confidence in her degree of foolhardiness, he pushed up to his knees, propelled himself the rest of the way with his good foot, and, half-dragging the other behind him, turned on the flashlight and sent the feeble eye of light ahead, observing that the beam did not as yet even reach the trees, let alone penetrate them.

If the light was anemic, perhaps now his voice would not be. "Claire!" he shouted. "For God's sake, where are you? Claire?"

Listen!

Scrambling, he took the last twenty yards, impervious to everything save the sound of faint hissing, as though someone nearby had tried to form the name "Jess" and had managed only " . . . ess."

With the first step into the trees, he felt a new, deeper chill, and drew the collar of his jacket up about his throat. Pausing to adjust his eyes to darkness, he lifted the flashlight and sent its weak beam deep into the stand of timber. From the road it had appeared to be a narrow band at timberline. Now he discovered that he could not see through to the other side.

"Claire? Where . . . ?"

There it was again, a faint " . . . ess." He turned rapidly in all directions, the flashlight beam bouncing wildly off every green-black tree. He experienced a tingling, vibratory sensation across his face, and took a step backward, only then aware that he'd walked into a large spiderweb. After a few moments of spastic flailing, he determined that the spider was no place around, though he continued to beat at the air.

Then he was moving again, in no particular direction, a brief sortie to the right, which revealed nothing except the darker cavern of the woods, then to the left and more of the same, and at last he held still, trying to rely on his sense of hearing.

Silence. Nothing moving. Not a bird call or a cricket.

"Claire? Can you hear me?"

" . . . ess, go . . . 'ack . . . "

The thunder that beat in his ear was his own pulse.

"Claire? Where are . . . ?"

Flailing his way through the density of trees, he moved straight toward what he was certain was the sound of a voice.

The beam of the flashlight preceded him by about four feet, illuminating a limited and monotonous world of spruce and fir and thick-trunked aspen, no variation, not one alteration in color, texture, light.

"Claire, answer me if you—"

" . . . back."

He heard it distinctly, and not too far away.

"Claire, call out again. I can't find—"

Suddenly, in his haste, he stumbled. His dragging foot caught on a protruding root; the sensation was as pronounced as if someone had reached out and grabbed his ankle. As he fell heavily forward, his leg twisted again, a burning sensation accompanied by the crack of a bone. The flashlight, in his violent descent, became dislodged as both hands moved out to break his fall.

For a moment all he could do was press his face into a moldy rot of fallen needles and dead leaves and wait out the pain. He'd done it this time. He knew it. No mere bruise, strain, sprain, whatever. Every nerve in his body was sending out sirens of alarm.

"Claire . . ."

Weakened, his voice fell back on him in a useless whisper, and as the first wave of pain diminished into blessed numbness, he raised his head, leaves clinging to his face, and saw the flashlight, hurled about ten feet ahead, its beam seeming to grow fainter.

"Claire . . ."

From this prostrate and weakened position he was on the verge of pulling himself forward when the faint eye of light seemed to turn and focus on the trunk of a large tree.

Through eyes dimmed with pain, he saw a variation, a piece of worn blue denim blending with the brown mottled bark, saw a shoulder, the angle of a cheekbone, lips . . .

"Cla . . ."

He tried to speak her name, but could not, and instead lowered his head and tried to clear his eyes and clear his mind as well of the macabre illusion. Shadows and circumstances were playing tricks on him. That was all. At least he'd found her. Jesus, they'd talk about this for days to come, though who back in Evanston would believe them?

Once more. Slowly he lifted his head and tried to blink his eyes into focus. And saw it again. And knew enough to hold still. And knew enough not to cry out.

Her features were still visible, though quickly disappearing, the imprisonment complete, her head held high, a brown scale moving liquidly over her mouth.

". . . ess . . ."

Frozen in horror at what his conscious mind was recording and rejecting, Jess clawed at the wet earth.

"No!"

Somewhere outside him he heard a man's voice raised in a solitary reverberating scream which echoed endlessly across the side of the mountain, an indecipherable sound of terror and protest.

All structures were changing. The order of everything was being altered. Even the male scream decomposed into the incoherent whimperings of a child with an injured foot, a shattered mind, and a head of solid snow-white hair. . . .

1

Tomis, Colorado—May 19, 1981

"My merry-go-round," Vicky pronounced with insistent four-year-old pride of ownership, and lovingly placed the toy within inches of Sarah's toe-less tennis shoes.

"You betcha." Sarah smiled down over the clothesline, a bit saddened that the most remarkable phenomenon to date in her daughter's young life had been a sleazy merry-go-round which she'd seen last summer in an equally sleazy parking-lot fair in front of the Safeway in Durango. Who would have thought the simple classic ride would so totally capture the child's imagination? Now Vicky saw merry-go-rounds everywhere. Last Christmas Hal had found this inexpensive miniature reproduction, which for the past five months had gone with Vicky to bed, to the bathtub, to the table, to Inez's . . .

"Hey, where're you going?" Sarah called out, looking up from the merry-go-round.

"To say hello to the mountain," came the piping though diminishing voice. Shades of Hal again. Every morning, Hal glanced out of the kitchen window to "say hello to the mountain." Monkey see, monkey . . .

"Vicky, don't go too far! Did you hear me?"

Too far! How far could those four-year-old legs go? As Sarah reached into her carpenter's apron for additional clothespins, she edged the merry-go-

19

round to one side with the tip of her toe and concentrated on her intrepid daughter, clambering up the high meadow.

"Copper! Wake up and earn your keep," she scolded sternly, nudging the sleepy Irish setter lying at her feet. "Go on! Go watch after her."

The dog opened one heavy eye, begrudgingly dragged his carcass about twenty feet away to the edge of the garden, and collapsed again, as though drugged by the high bright sun and crisp thin Colorado air.

"Terrific," Sarah muttered, and squinted after the bright pink jacket which was now bending over in the tall grasses in close examination of something.

At that moment Vicky waved at her, and she waved back and again shouted, "Not too far. We'll have our sandwiches when I finish . . . "

For some reason she knew that Vicky hadn't heard her over the whistling wind. No matter. She'd be through here in fifteen, twenty minutes; then she'd lure her back with the small hamper of peanut-butter-and-jelly sandwiches and a bag of Fritos.

She took a last look after her dark-haired, fair-skinned daughter, then turned back to the clothes basket. Quickly she inserted three clothespins into her mouth, bent over the basket of clothes, and was just lifting out a heavy damp bedsheet when she felt a sharp pain in her lower abdomen.

As she gasped for breath, the clothespins fell from her mouth while with her left hand she tried to soothe and support the growing fetus inside her.

"Easy," she whispered as the discomfort diminished. Even then, with her hand pressed against her protruding belly, she could feel the flailing. A foot, probably.

"All right. I agree. Enough bending and lifting for a while. Sorry I disturbed your nap."

She dropped the wet sheet back into the clothes basket and glanced over her shoulder at Copper, lying in an obscene belly-up position of total relaxation. About fifty yards up the meadow, she saw Vicky methodically gathering a small bouquet of wildflowers.

"Then why not us?" she said to the infant in her womb. "Five minutes, and back to work. What do you say?"

With one hand caressing her belly in a soothing gesture, she looked at the log bench which Hal had fashioned for "sitting and drinking in the peace," and chose instead the natural incline beyond the path where the grasses were tall and uncultivated and soft.

With the awkwardness of her seven-month pregnancy, she lowered herself to earth, unmindful of the flowered print cotton dress which slid above her knees in the process. Before she lay back on her elbows, she pushed off her tennis shoes and raised her knees as far as the protrusion would permit, and luxuriated in the sensuous feeling of bare feet in cool grasses.

The baby kicked again. "Easy," she soothed. "Not long now," and fished through her carpenter's apron for the small pearl-inlaid opera glasses which for some reason that morning she'd retrieved from her dresser after she'd made the sandwiches.

Suffering a peculiar sense of embarrassment, she glanced over her left shoulder in the direction of the high ridge. After four years in Tomis, most everybody else was accustomed to the remote presence of the "Mountain Man." Why wasn't she? She'd spied on him almost daily those first two years. And worried about him.

How does he live, Hal?

That's his business, wouldn't you say?

Yes, she'd agreed. With everything. Still, after four years . . .

From the distance, and even without the aid of glasses, she saw the curious clearing, a dilapidated trailer, the carcass of an old vehicle—World War II jeep, Hal had said—and the most bizarre of all, a large crude structure of wood and stone, primitively constructed and vaguely reminiscent of an Indian tepee.

And she'd seen *him* as well, from a distance, four, maybe five times, Tomis' very own Mountain Man, bent, white-haired, walked with a pronounced limp. On occasion she'd seen him puttering about his garden, tending his chickens, one goat as far as she could make out.

As her neck began to ache from its awkward angle, she placed the opera glasses in the grass beside her. Now she needed a pleasant vista, and commenced a slow scan of the high meadow above the town, as pristine and as perfect as it must have appeared on the first day of creation.

With one exception; and she smiled, finding even the exception pleasing, that distant sleek blue-and-white helicopter, Bell 222, property of Dr. Roger Laing, who had descended from the heavens only a few hours ago, unscheduled—Roger never did anything on schedule—and who at this very moment was in the back room of Hal's restaurant holding a mysterious meeting with Hal, Brian, and Mike. What it was all about, she had no idea. She thought it peculiar that he'd not even taken the time to come up and say hello. But hopefully he'd come to stay for a few days, and now there was the evening to look forward to, and apparently something urgent was in the wind, and she'd forgive Jolly Roger anything, that bright charming eccentric from Evergreen who had adopted Tomis as his second home—or had Tomis adopted him?— and whose driving goal and greatest delight was the collection of rocks of all sizes, all shapes.

Roger Laing was an original. The world wasn't ready for more than one. He had appeared that first arduous summer in his battered and beat-up black Mercedes and had lent them a hand, an arm, a back, and moral support when they had sorely needed it.

A biologist and anthropologist with degrees from Princeton and Stanford— he said he'd wanted to see if they think differently at opposite ends of the country—he had served on the faculties of four major universities until 1968, when he had fled the halls of academe . . .

. . . you see, they always insist that science is based on man's view of himself as a curiously limited creature trapped in a purely physical universe . . .

. . . and had returned to his native Denver and the bosom of a family who had had no economic worries since Grandpa Laing had carried the first wagonload of gold out of Cripple Creek in 1891. Roger then had retreated to the family "cabin" in Evergreen, a small, picturesque community about thirty miles out of Denver, and had founded CUSP—Committee for the Under-

21

standing of Short-lived Phenomena—a select international community of rogue scientists who studied and explored such unscientific subjects as pendulums and electromagnetic fields and ley lines.

Lord, the stories Roger Laing could tell! Sarah thought back to last Christmas. For three weeks, most of December, they had been snowed in, the road impassable, and for three weeks Roger had held them spellbound with accounts of the various phenomena which the committee had been called upon to investigate during his years at CUSP. Spooky tales, although he had reminded them that magic is but an unexplored power of the mind, and the occult, or *occultus*, simply means hidden knowledge.

There had been the case of the boy in West Texas who one day had started speaking gibberish which, upon investigation, had turned out to be the language of a remote South African tribe. And there was the case of the two old-maid sisters from Portland, Oregon, who had told their rabbi that they felt they had reason to be afraid of their rosebushes. Six days later their bodies had been found at opposite ends of their garden, covered with deep and multiple lacerations, as though massive thorns had been dragged across them.

Last winter, with the wind whistling about the corners of Hal's Kitchen, that macabre tale had scared the daylights out of her. Now it sounded merely fanciful, clearly the product of Roger's massive imagination.

Still staring at the helicopter, Sarah saw the man effortlessly in her mind's eye, that ageless, slightly rotund bachelor who had enlivened and enriched their lives at all-too-short intervals during the last four years.

Suddenly it occurred to her that Vicky did not know that Roger was here. Vicky adored him, and this might be a way to lure her back down to the safety of the garden.

Looking in the opposite direction, she focused on the spot where she'd last seen Vicky.

Gone!

"Vick . . . "

There she was, just rising up out of the tall grass. Sarah kept her anchored in her sight for several minutes and really wished that she would come back. Since last year and the death of young Kent Sawyer, the "perfect freedom" of Tomis had held slightly less appeal for her. Still, she didn't want to become "that kind of a mother," not with a second child on the way.

So she took another reassuring look at the bright pink jacket, then tried to clear her mind and ease the tension in her neck by looking straight down on the town itself, feeling the pride she always felt when viewing it from a distance, keenly aware that she and Hal, almost single-handedly, had rescued it from the oblivion of dust and time four years ago.

Well, in all honesty, not single-handedly. There were six of them, the Fox Fire Kids, that's what they called themselves, that hardy band of three couples, gloriously displaced in the Colorado Rockies from the Boston area.

It had started in the summer of '75, when Hal, with a brand-new law degree from Boston University, had suddenly and mysteriously decided he really didn't want to practice law, not in Boston, not in Massachusetts, not on the East Coast. This intelligent and precise man had filled the air of their Back Bay apartment for days with such vagaries as, "I want to build something, I want to discover something that needs me as much as I need it, I want to . . . "

Mildly bewildered—his Beacon Hill mother still had not recovered—Sarah had watched, speechless, as he'd closed their apartment, bought an expensive jeep with four-wheel drive, liquidated the major portion of the sizable portfolio which his father, also a Boston lawyer before his death, had left him.

Still reeling from the spectacle of a rational man gone suddenly irrational, Sarah had said good-bye to the Commons and China House and Filene's and had watched the landscape beyond her window change from the crush of traffic and poisonous fumes of the eastern megalopolis to the rich and rolling farmland of the central United States.

Their first destination was to have been her parents' home in San Antonio—she'd been a history major at B.U. when she'd met Hal Kitchens. Both of them had just been coming down off the high of the late sixties, the muddled nightmare of Chicago, Selma, and assassinations. They merely had been two more college-educated refugees, hungry to remake the world or create a new one.

They'd never made it to San Antonio. The Rocky Mountains had seduced them, and a wrong turn on the highway from Valenco to Durango had led them here, to this sad, abandoned little ghost town which had been slipping quietly into oblivion since the turn of the century.

No cry of "Eureka!" had announced their discovery. Rather, Hal had methodically taken the better part of one day to explore the heavily rutted "main street," the two crumbling structures and the weed-covered ruins of three others, the magnificent juxtaposition of Mt. Victor rising high above the plateau, the alpine freshness of the air, the colorful carpet of wildflowers in the high meadow.

What's that up there, Hal?

Our very own Mountain Man, that's what.

Our?

She'd known then, and was not opposed to the idea, to the challenge of a life-style that placed more value on community than on career. In the midst of this beautiful earth, Hal's irrationality had suddenly seemed perfectly rational. Such a place deserved preservation, rejuvenation.

They had spent a week in the courthouse in Durango. It had been surprising how few of the natives even knew the settlement had existed.

Ain't nuthin' on Mt. Victor . . .

Hal's New England accent had put off a few of the locals. But the county surveyor, a wizened little man with horn-rimmed glasses and a string tie, had gone back with them to the mountain, had agreed that there was "sumpin' on Victor," had returned to the basement of the old courthouse, and three days later had found a solitary musty document confirming the establishment of a settlement of public lands in 1892 named Tomis. Why Tomis? George Tomis? Charlie Tomis? No one knew.

Since the last recorded deed of ownership had been for silver mining in

1892, Hal had struck a bargain with the county for a fair assessment of back taxes and had bought outright 250 acres encompassing the heart of the "town" and a modest border on all sides for limited expansion.

That night in the American Legion hall, which housed Durango's leading Mexican restaurant, over the best *chiles rellenos* Sarah had ever eaten and too many margaritas, Hal, with a glow on his face that had nothing to do with either the chili sauce or the margaritas, had lifted his glass and announced, "We're home."

The next morning they had headed back to Boston to see to the completion of certain business affairs and to enlist carefully selected help in the form of Kate and Brian Sawyer, close friends from Brookline with a pale, chronically ill eight-year-old son named Kent. It had not been too difficult to persuade them that the mountain air might do Kent a world of good, and Brian's engineering degree from MIT would be of enormous help.

Also on their list of friends to seduce were the Dunnes—Mike, a boyhood friend of Hal's and an internist at Mass. General who was fast drinking himself to death, and his wife, Donna, a pretty dark-haired Canadian from Toronto who sensed that they were in trouble but had no idea where the thorn was lodged. Both families had been ripe for transition, and both had jumped at the opportunity for a "new and different world."

Deep in memory, Sarah dragged herself back to the present and looked more closely down on the realization of the dream. There it was, nestled like a lost jewel in the green velvet folds of Mt. Victor. Tomis, Colorado, year-round population, fifty-seven, but growing slowly and ballooning last summer with tourists to over one hundred, the camping area on the edge of town filled with jeeps of every size and description, backpackers, campers, a delirious horde, all searching for original fabric, and finding it in Tomis.

Suddenly she shivered and remembered her sweater, knotted about the handle of the picnic hamper about twenty feet away. She stared at it for a moment and decided that getting up was too much trouble, and rubbed her arms, grown fleshy in her pregnancy, and knew she'd put on too much weight, but what the hell. . . .

With the summer season just starting, and after the birth of the baby, she'd take it off. As she rubbed her arms, she felt of her rough elbows and stopped one hand in motion and stared at her short nails and saw a healing burn from the broiler on top of her right hand, working hands, and she wondered whatever had become of that slightly vain, self-centered woman of four years ago.

Gone! And good riddance, annihilated in the backbreaking labor of that first summer, when, aided by the Fox Fire books and large amounts of their own daring, the six of them had built three simple log cabins, had dug sewage lines and buried septic tanks, had fashioned a dowsing rod, and had determined that young Kent was the most sensitive, and had ignored the jeers of the drilling crew when Kent had instructed them to drill . . . there—at a spot on the edge of town just below the high meadow. Ninety feet later the crew had struck water.

Sarah smiled. Oh, Lord, it had been fun, a massive sense of adventure and discovery marking every hour of every day, all three men growing beards—

24

Hal still sported his—she and Donna and Kate relieved for the first time in their lives of the need for makeup and hair curlers and dryers.

But it had been Sarah herself who had provided them with their most exciting adventure. On that final trip back from Colorado to Massachusetts, in some friendly Holiday Inn, she had conceived Vicky. At first she'd tried to keep the pregnancy a secret, fearing that it would interfere with Hal's dream. But after he had caught her vomiting three mornings in a row, the secret was out, and on February 24, 1976, squatting on a blanket spread before the fire in their cabin, with the wind howling and snow beating a gentle counterpoint against the windowpanes, inundated by an almost mystical feeling of support and love, with all five of them in constant attendance, she had gripped Hal's hands, and after twenty minutes of mild discomfort, Vicky had slipped effortlessly from her womb. They had named her Victoria, the feminine version of the mountain in whose shadow she was born.

Hal had stretched out beside her after first placing at her breast the tiny blood-smeared infant.

"Tomis' first citizen," he had whispered.

Never had she known such feelings, every sensation heightened as though a layer of skin had been removed and had left all the nerve endings vulnerable and exposed and receptive.

It had been merely their own version of paradise that first year, every crisis met and conquered.

The first citizen of Tomis? Where was she?

Quickly Sarah swiveled about, a moment's panic rushing over her as she searched the meadow for the bright pink jacket. There she was. About fifty yards higher up the mountain.

"Vicky! Come on back, now. That's far enough . . . "

As she called, she felt the force of the wind blow her voice in the opposite direction, back down toward the town. She'd have to go and get her. No easy feat with the baby still kicking against her belly.

"Vicky!"

The child was either deaf or impervious to a mother's call.

Time to retrieve her. Too much sun was bad for the child. Vicky had inherited Hal's dark hair and transparent skin. The high May sun of Colorado could burn her. Sarah and Donna had long since adjusted to it, acquiring a perpetual tan which they wore winter and summer. And of course Kate didn't go out anymore, and thus the sun was not a problem.

Half-raised for pursuit of her daughter, Sarah felt a peculiar breathlessness and sank slowly down into the soft grasses, her eye moving down to the town, beyond Mr. Hills's "new-old drugstore," to the small grove of aspen below the main road, the white picket fence just barely visible from this angle and this distance.

After the power lines had been strung in '77, they'd thought they had everything they needed. How wrong.

Kent Sawyer had disappeared on June 12. The five of them had searched and called for two days. Then Hal had taken the truck and gone into Durango for help. For seven days Sarah and Donna had cooked for the search party of over thirty men, had tried to comfort Kate, who in the last days of her agony had simply taken to sitting in the rocker on her front porch, her eyes fixed on the high ridge, on the Mountain Man's trailer.

On June 19 Hal had found Kent, though he'd not brought the body down immediately. Instead he'd come back for Mike, and the two of them had gone back up to timberline.

"An animal," Mike had pronounced simply, and had refused to let either Brian or Kate see the body of their son. The search party had been thanked and dismissed, and a cemetery had been hastily planned. Kent had been buried on June 20, the day before his ninth birthday. Mike had given Kate a shot of something, and she'd not regained full consciousness until two days after the burial.

As though by tacit agreement, none of them had ever spoken of it again, the first deception, the first illusion in paradise. It needed to be talked about, and for a few days Sarah had tried to question Hal.

What kind of animal? What was the condition of the body?

But Hal had said nothing, and Mike had gone on a three-day binge in Durango, and Brian had aged visibly as he'd tried to comfort Kate, who alternately had raged against the mountain and knelt before her son's grave and talked to him as though he could hear and would respond.

Strange, how all of them had overlooked the need for a cemetery. Now there were five other graves to keep Kent company. One was old Mrs. Marshall, who along with her retired army-officer husband had established a small general store last year to accommodate the rapidly increasing summer tourists.

Hal had sold the land to them at a bargain price, and they'd both been an asset to the community, Mrs. Marshall with her curly gray hair and kind ways, and Tom, who with surprising imagination had recreated a rough-hewn version of a turn-of-the-century general store complete with pickle barrel and a wheel of cheddar and three deep freezers large enough to store a year's supply of meat and produce for the "year-rounders," thus eliminating the many trips down into Durango, particularly during the winter months, when the road was impassable.

A heart attack, Mike had said of Mrs. Marshall's death, brought on by the high altitude and the labor of summer; and again with love they had dug a new grave and had clustered in support around Tom, hoping he'd decide to stay. He had.

Three graves belonged to members of the blasting crew whom Hal had hired in the summer of '78 to widen the narrow road which cut a tortuous path up the mountain to the town itself. Young men of Mexican-American descent, they had been on their way to the job when their pickup had blown a rear tire and the truck had careened off the road and plunged down the side of the mountain, exploding in flames, the bodies burned beyond recognition.

The contractor, out of Durango, had said they were itinerants working for a day's wages, and a grim-faced Hal had ordered them buried in Tomis' cemetery and then had stood constant watch over the job until the road had been widened and guardrails placed the last ten dangerous miles of the ascent into Tomis.

The sixth grave belonged to a young girl, a runaway, they had discovered

26

later, who while in the company of her traveling companion had overdosed on Quaaludes. They had been camping on the edge of town.

The parents had been located in Pittsburgh and had refused to claim the body, so they had buried her beneath a simple stone next to Mrs. Marshall. The young man had disappeared in fright.

Thinking on death, Sarah shuddered.

It's bound to happen, Sarah, as the town grows.

But did they want Tomis to grow? And how much? And how long could they control it before it became as overcrowded and pretentious as Vail, or as artificial as Central City, or worse, as polluted and poisonous as Denver.

Without warning the idyllic day turned sour and she looked down on the top of their restaurant—Hal's Kitchen—a large log-cabin structure erected around the core of their first cabin, where at this moment the meeting was going on with Roger Laing. What *was* it about? He'd called the men together and they had gone into an immediate conference.

Now Sarah was curious to know what was going on. From where she sat she saw smoke curling from the chimney. With the lure of a generous salary and the promise of private lodgings, they had managed two summers ago to coax Inez, Durango's best Mexican cook—hell, the best Mexican cook in the world—up to Tomis. A slim, middle-aged, dark-haired second-generation Mexican-American, Inez Fuentes was the unofficial matriarch of the little town. Amazing, how many people took their problems to her, both summer and winter folk. Her level black eyes and serene face spoke of a wisdom beyond the capacity of most mortals.

Suddenly Sarah remembered. Inez had gone into Durango today to interview for summer help. Who was doing the cooking? Hal did it on occasion, but certainly he was well-occupied with Roger. Probably it was Joyce, Inez's assistant, a peculiar young woman of Mexican-American descent, as silent and cold as Inez was warm and talkative.

Suffering a sudden sense of her own neglected duties, Sarah sat up with the intention of making up for lost time and took a final look at the pretty miniature town below, just emerging from a normal winter of over three hundred inches of snow. The architecture was a pastiche of fanciful Victorian ornamentation, weathered and aged planking, comfortable log cabins, steep tin roofs, tall paned windows that distorted reflections—a town of uneven lines and miraculously even tempers, mildly cockeyed front porches, smiling doorjambs, window boxes filled with geraniums and fuchsia and ivy, hand-cut picket fences. The men in winter gathered around the coal stove at Tom Marshall's store; the schoolage children—there were about twelve of them now—cut a tunnel through the snow walls to Mina Murdoch's front-parlor schoolroom.

Dear Mina. Sarah remembered well *her* arrival two years ago with the bright announcement, "I've a degree from Sarah Lawrence, one from Columbia, thirty-one years of teaching experience, and perfect health, yet the state of Colorado says I'm too old to teach. What do you say?"

Hal had put it best when he said he'd give anything to be a boy again and on the receiving end of that rich mind and fertile imagination.

So there it was, Tomis, a small island of refugees from the twentieth century, looking for a quieter, simpler pace of life, a place nearer to nature, a place where doors could be left unlocked, where at the first call for help, everyone came running. And they were not exclusive. Anyone was welcome so long as they left their twentieth-century egos and drives at the foot of Mt. Victor like so much unnecessary baggage. The point of it all, then and now, was to nurture community, to restore the original fabric of the place. And that they had done with admirable and stunning success, with only a few bad moments along the way.

Mildly annoyed by her propensity for wool-gathering, Sarah angled her heavy body about, ready for the ascent. In the process, her hand brushed against the opera glasses which she'd taken from her apron. Quickly she glanced up toward the high ridge, adjusted the lenses, and started a slow track up the side of the mountain, everything grown uncannily large under magnification, until at last she saw the weather-beaten trailer, a massive rock propped beneath the hitch to keep it level, equally massive stones under all the wheels. There were two small windows which appeared to be blocked out in some way.

Slowly she eased the glasses to the side and found the husk of the jeep; it appeared to have been completely dismantled. Only the shell remained. Below the jeep she saw a small garden plot, the earth appearing newly turned, as though he were getting ready to plant. And beyond that was a flimsy-appearing wire fence which contained a dozen or so chickens, a crude chicken house, and what appeared to be a toolshed.

Where was the goat? Usually the goat was tethered in this same clearing. But all she saw now was the scattering of stumps which suggested that timber had been cleared years ago, possibly to erect the curious structure which loomed large over all, that off-center pyramid with a tree growing out of the top, the trunk concealed within the structure itself.

She held the glasses steady on the baffling scene. She'd heard some of the O'Connell kids talking about him. A few brave ones claimed to have ventured within a few hundred yards of the place. The most dramatic rumor, spread by the kids themselves, was that he was the Devil, complete with supernatural powers, and that he was capable of turning any trespasser into stone.

Last winter Rene Hackett, wife of Jerry Hackett, who ran Tomis' only service station, had complained that Lucy, their fourteen-year-old daughter, was having recurrent nightmares about the Mountain Man and suggested that, come spring, a delegation of men should go up and rout him out.

Of course there was no way that Hal would permit that, and apparently Lucy's nightmares had ceased, and Rene was now fully occupied with her spring garden.

Again Sarah focused the glasses and made a slow track across the whole settlement.

Suddenly she stiffened. Through the magnifying lenses, near the wire fence, she saw him, tattered, worn boots, mudcaked, soiled khaki work trousers with both knees out, a worn and ripped army jacket, his shock of white hair wind-touseled, and his face obscured behind a set of field glasses which, as best as she could tell, were focused directly on . . . her.

Quickly, guiltily, she lowered her own glasses and felt her heart accelerate.

28

He'd never done that before, never spied back on her. Suffering a burning blush on her cheeks in spite of the cold wind, she looked up at the high ridge with her bare eyes and saw nothing except the vague outline of what she knew was there.

She'd have to tell Hal about this, though she could well imagine his answer.

So he's giving you a taste of your own medicine, uh? Leave the poor bastard alone, and he'll leave you alone.

Still, she *was* curious, and slowly lifted the glasses again, intrigued that they were connected by an umbilical of reciprocal curiosity.

But halfway up the high meadow she found a splotch of bright pink, saw Vicky scrambling higher than she'd ever gone before, moving with four-year-old energy and determination in a direct line to where the man stood.

"Vicky!" The first cry was little more than a whisper. "*Vicky!*" The second was a scream which burned all the way up her throat and for all her efforts was blown back into her face by the strong downward drafts coming from the top of the mountain.

Then she was scrambling as much as her overweight and awkward body would permit, reaching out for support. By her estimate Vicky was still about a hundred yards from the dilapidated wire fence.

"Vicky! Come back!"

But her screams were useless, and halting only long enough to accommodate a sharp pain in her side, Sarah again lifted the glasses and saw a flash of red fur cavorting alongside the child.

Copper! Hurriedly she wet her lips and tried to whistle. Hal had spent the winter teaching the dog to obey. If she could call Copper back, Vicky would follow.

But her mouth was dry, and she'd never learned how to put her fingers between her lips and make the ear-shattering whistle that Hal could produce.

Hal! She must get Hal. He would . . . But then she'd have to take her eyes off Vicky, and that she could not do.

Again she lifted the glasses and saw that while her daughter's progress was slow, it was steady, those short legs devouring the distance step by small step.

Then Sarah was running, one arm cupped in awkward support beneath her belly, wasting precious energy in the repetitious cry of "Vicky, come back," knowing that the child couldn't hear, but crying out anyway.

Oh, God, make her turn back, please. . . .

"Vicky!"

After less than thirty yards, painfully breathless, the stitch in her side exploding into continuous knife pricks, she halted again, her dried lips still mindlessly repeating her daughter's name. Her hands trembled as she lifted the glasses, moving past the bright pink jacket up to the man himself.

God, no . . .

She saw that he'd laid aside his field glasses and was now shouldering a rifle, his weathered, oddly featureless face obscured behind the butt as he sighted down the barrel.

"Vicky!"

Her high-pitched scream exploded inside her throat at the precise moment the shot rang out.

She was incapable of holding the glasses steady, and drew them back down to the pink jacket in a shuddering, erratic movement: Vicky, still upright, Vicky peering in curiosity up toward the high ridge in the direction of the shot, Vicky at last reversing her position and running, terrified, back down the high meadow.

She was crying, but then, so was Sarah, who dropped the opera glasses into the grass, and in spite of the objecting pain in her womb, ran to retrieve her daughter.

2

For the first time in over three years, Hal Kitchens was ready to kill for a cigarette. All of the tension . . .

Those antitrust briefs should have been ready yesterday. Now, when in the hell can you have them? . . .

. . . and pressure . . .

So you're Harold Kitchens' son, uh? Well . . .

. . . had returned.

As the stunned silence in the room pushed aggressively about him, he leaned back in the chair and peered through the partially open door which led to the large dining room, the cash register, and the cigarette machine.

One. How would it hurt? Not one package. One cigarette.

No! Quickly he caught himself in time. He'd worked too hard to break the habit, though he'd put on a ton of weight in the process in spite of the backbreaking labor of the past four years.

Hal dried the palms of his hands on his jeans and tried to talk his system out of its need for nicotine, and looked up at Roger Laing, who had just dropped a bombshell in their midst from which they might never recover.

Someone had to repeat the word, haul it out in the open, test it on the air. Perhaps Roger was mistaken, though after a four-year friendship, Hal knew that was a weak hope. Roger Laing was never mistaken.

31

"Mining? Here?" Hal asked quietly, hoping for an immediate refutation.

Instead Roger Laing hoisted his large six-foot-two frame out of the chair opposite the table, strode the length of the room, and stared out of the back window, which gave a perfect view of Mt. Victor. With his face turned away, he nodded, and a second later, words followed. "Yes. I'm afraid so. At first I couldn't believe it myself. But I've just spent three days in Denver and two in Durango, and—"

"Well, why in hell hasn't somebody bothered to tell *us?*" Hal exploded, his anger dragging him forward in his chair. "What did they intend to do? Just dynamite around us, or under us?"

Regretful of the outburst, which he knew would solve nothing, he saw Roger turn slowly back from the window, a look of deep commiseration on his face. For the first time in four years, even Roger Laing seemed strangely wordless, and for a few additional minutes a communal state of shock compounded the silence.

Hoping to find comfort, if not safety, in numbers, Hal looked about the table at the other three men seated with him. To his left slouched Mike Dunne; from time to time Hal saw his head nod disjointedly, as though he were fighting sleep. And losing. No wonder. He'd been up all night delivering a baby in the camping area, a young couple from Nebraska having a last fling before parenthood tied them down.

"They is tied now," Mike had joked as he'd shuffled, unshaven and hollow-eyed, into the meeting about half an hour ago. He'd tried to sustain himself with five cups of coffee, but the caffeine was having absolutely no effect.

Hal wondered now if Mike had even heard Roger's grim announcement. Should he awaken him? Why not? It sure as hell concerned him as well as everyone else. As he reached out to shake Mike's arm, he heard a curiously muffled and distant pop, like the backfire of a car or the report of a gun.

He looked up at the other men, their expressions mirroring his own. He met Mike's glazed eyes and looked beyond Mike to Brian, who dragged himself to the edge of his chair, and beyond Brian to Tom Marshall's burr haircut, his weathered face displaying the greatest curiosity of all.

"What was that?" Hal asked.

"Pop goes the weasel," Mike joked sleepily.

"Sounded like a car," Brian said, still listening.

"Car, hell," Tom Marshall said quietly.

They waited for the mysterious sound to come again. And when it didn't, Hal saw Brian shrug massively and settle back in his chair. At the same time, Mike awkwardly adjusted himself as though in search of a more comfortable position to sleep. Only Tom Marshall continued to sit with a taut, listening ear.

Nothing, Hal decided. Certainly nothing compared to the enormity of this new problem about which they knew nothing and about which they must know everything if they were to survive.

In a new mood of relative calm, with all anger and panic safely repressed, at least for the time being, Hal invited, "Come on, Roger. Tell us everything."

Slowly Roger Laing returned to the table, as though he knew he must speak, yet dreaded it. Hal had never seen him so hesitant and grim. Usually everyone in Tomis associated the arrival of Roger Laing with an unscheduled holiday, a time to toss over chores and routine, to gather in Hal's Kitchen over endless pots of coffee and listen to the fascinating stories of an articulate and brilliant man, accounts liberally laced with humor and wisdom, that rarest of combinations, a natural-born storyteller recounting the incidents of an extraordinary life.

Now there was nothing of the *raconteur* on Roger's face as slowly he withdrew his recently abandoned chair and sat heavily, rings of perspiration staining his khaki workshirt in the cool afternoon.

As he began to speak, his voice was totally without inflection, and he appeared to be talking to the surface of the table rather than to any of the men present.

"I heard it first about ten days ago in the lobby of the Brown Palace in Denver, of all places," he said, looking up briefly, as though enjoying a small irony. "A friend from the Colorado School of Mines asked me for information on the new mining activity taking place on the Western Slope." He shrugged and lightly shook his head. "Of course I thought he meant Crested Butte and Mt. Emmons. . . ."

Hal listened and saw in his imagination the picturesque little town about ninety miles to the north that had waged such a valiant battle against the destruction of their village and mountain by Amax Incorporated, a multinational mining corporation who had discovered 165 million tons of molybdenum a thousand feet below the surface of Red Lady Basin. Crested Butte had lost, or was in the process of losing. The result would be the rampant destruction of more than a thousand acres of prime wilderness.

"But your friend," Hal asked tentatively, "wasn't talking about Crested Butte?"

Roger shook his head. "No. He mentioned Mt. Victor—"

"Shit," Mike muttered, apparently more awake than Hal had thought.

"So I began checking," Roger went on, "and because of the public outrage resulting in numerous delays at Crested Butte, this new group is moving with greater . . . circumspection." His delivery of the word converted it into an obscenity and provoked a protest from Brian.

"Circumspection or concealment?" he demanded. "Like Hal says, what right do they have to haul ass up here, send out survey teams, and put into effect a full-scale mining operation without—"

"They have the law for one thing, Brian," Roger said firmly.

"Law?" Hal exploded, feeling himself to be on familiar though neglected ground.

Again Roger merely nodded. "Remember your law history," he scolded gently. "The mining law of 1872, when Congress voted to give away the minerals on all public lands—"

"Eighteen-seventy-two?" Mike parroted. "I know the bums are notoriously lazy, but surely there have been revisions of the law since 1872."

"None," Roger said with awesome certainty. "The 1872 act confirmed the principle that gold or silver or any other mineral belonged to the person who

33

found it. It prescribed a minimum of paperwork and a fee of two-fifty to five dollars per acre to establish possession, not only of the ore but of the land over it. It set the 'claim' area at twenty acres but prescribed no limit on the number of tracts to which one person or company could lay the claim. . . ."

As the bleak facts were trotted out, Hal remembered them all too well, never dreaming that the dusty archaic words of a leather-bound lawbook would one day kill his dream.

Slowly he turned sideways in his chair, as though from that enclosed position he could more easily dodge the facts.

Roger went on. "Although the mining industry has changed drastically in the last one hundred years in terms of size, economic concentration, and technology," he said, staring at the palms of his hands as though the words were printed there, "defenders of the 1872 law continue to insist that it protects the individual 'small miner.' "

Suddenly he sat up straight in his chair, as though the ancient inequity had to be confronted directly. "But the solitary old prospector with pick and shovel and mule has been replaced by massive corporations. Modern open-pit mines can be miles across, and high-technology exploration equipment probes thousands of feet into the earth." He laughed, a sound which had nothing to do with good humor. "In 1872, a legal concept such as 'access' meant one crude pack trail. Now it means a network of bulldozed roads—"

"Christ," someone whispered. Hal couldn't tell who. He felt in a curious way as though Roger's word had paralyzed him. He knew everything and yet he knew nothing.

"Who?" he asked simply, looking up. "Amax again?"

"No," Roger replied, a portion of anger gone from his voice, replaced by apology. "CMC," he said. "Century Mining Corporation."

"Multinational?" Hal asked.

"Yes."

"What are they after?"

"Molybdenum."

Mike stirred. "Translate for a simple Boston boy."

Roger obliged. "It's a metallic element used primarily as a hardener of steel for jets and cars, engines and Arctic pipelines, stainless steel and even the lightweight frame of your ten-speed bike—"

"I gave up bikes when I was fourteen and had mine stolen," Mike muttered.

"Unfortunately, hundreds of thousands of others haven't—"

Suddenly Brian left his chair and moved through the door which led into the large dining room, as though he were leaving. Abruptly he stopped and looked back. "Is it big?"

Roger nodded. "The free world's third-largest deposit of molybdenum, estimated to be worth over three billion dollars."

"Bingo!" Mike said.

For a moment everyone held their various positions, the despair manifesting itself now in a kind of lethargy, as though merely knowing the size of the enemy rendered them impotent.

Tom Marshall, who more than any of them continued to give at least the

34

impression of considering the matter—years of army life could do that to you—sat up in his chair as though at attention and asked, "Precisely what does it mean—to us, I mean?"

Roger glanced at him as though for the first time here was a question which was not so easy to answer.

"That's what I've been trying to find out for the past week," he admitted wearily. "Information of any kind is hard to come by. Clearly they would prefer to avoid the national attention and outrage provoked by Crested Butte."

"Did they hope to conceal it from *us* as well?" Mike asked acidly.

"No, they will contact you, when it suits them."

"And when will that be?" Brian asked, still halfway out of the door.

"Wait a minute," Tom Marshall interrupted with dwindling patience. "My question first. What precisely does it mean to us, to Tomis?"

Hal looked up in time to see Brian Sawyer retreat back to a near chair. Without warning, an image of young Kent Sawyer passed before Hal's mind, an unfortunate image of the boy's mutilated body. Struggling under a new weight of guilt, he missed the first part of Roger's reply and heard only, ". . . so I'd say it would be limited at first, perhaps three hundred workers taking core samples, running metallurgical and engineering studies, constructions of roads of course over which the heavy seismograph equipment would have to be transported. Ultimately, when the mine is in full swing, it could mean as many as three thousand construction workers—"

"Three thou . . ." Hal tried to repeat the words and couldn't.

"—not counting, of course," Roger went on, "dependents, the families of all those men. At Leadville, the creation of the mine added twenty thousand to the population in the first year."

The dream *was* dying. Hal could feel it in himself, in the shocked silence of the others. Everyone who presently resided in Tomis had come here to escape the very confusion which Roger had just spelled out. Hal thought despairingly of the boom-town atmospheres of other Colorado towns, the insidious, uncontrolled growth, the artificiality, the greed.

While he was still trying to deal with these horrors, Roger went on, full-voiced now, as though it was time to present everything and face it.

"I feel you should know something else," he said, encompassing all four men with a single glance. "The problem with mining molybdenum is that it constitutes only about four-tenths of one percent of the ore in which it is found. The remaining 99.6 percent of the rock has to be disposed of somewhere. It is a process, literally, of tearing down a mountain from the inside out, hauling it piece by piece to a mill, extracting the moly, and dumping the remains in tailing ponds. The mining corporations make no apology for the method. It's the only way. Unfortunately, a mountain can't be put back together again."

Hal bowed his head into his hands and rested his elbows on the table. The silence was broken only by Brian muttering something under his breath which sounded dangerously like *"Fuck them."*

With the persistent naiveté of a child, Mike grumbled, "It isn't fair. We've busted our asses to create a place which suits us. We've poured our money,

35

our sweat, and on occasion our blood into the creation of Tomis. Now a bunch of goddamned corporate assholes come along and—"

He was interrupted by Tom Marshall, whose initial question apparently had not been answered. "I repeat," he said, strangely calm, "what precisely does it mean to us? What are their intentions? To start dynamiting, without a word, in the hope of driving us away?"

Hal looked up, interested in the answer. Roger didn't reply immediately. For a moment he stared at Tom as though debating with himself whether to reply or not. Finally, "I'm not sure," he admitted. "I can give you my opinion, if you wish . . ."

"Which is?" Mike urged.

"It would be my guess that they have no desire to drive you away. From what little I could learn in Denver, all of the core-drilling and feasibility studies have taken place on the other side of the mountain, which would indicate that the mother lode is beneath the northern slope of Mt. Victor."

"I . . . don't understand," Brian confessed for all of them.

Again Roger obliged. "I suspect it would suit them very well if Tomis were to remain intact and functioning, a ready-made community less than five miles away from the center of their activity, available to their crews complete with a store"—and he nodded toward Tom Marshall—"a restaurant, a doctor"—and this time Mike won the nod. "In fact, I wouldn't be too surprised if you received offers soon to expand all your facilities, add new services, enlarge the existing ones." He paused, then added, "Of course, all this would be generously financed with mining money. They might even offer to fix Main Street properly . . ."

As his voice dwindled into an apology, Hal glanced at Brian and Mike, their faces upturned, though blank, their minds clearly moving along with his to the mystery of Tomis' main street, an artery which had required fresh blacktop every year for the past four and which would require it again this year.

Something below there that don't take too kindly to gravel and hot tar, the contractor from Durango had pronounced. *Never seen such buckling.*

And buckling there had been and buckling there was now, thick heavy ridges of earth pushing up every spring. Jerry Hackett down at the service station loved it. He made a small fortune every summer on split mufflers and new shock absorbers.

But Hal's interest was drawn back to the table by Tom Marshall, who now sported a rather incongruous grin. "Bucks," he said patly. "If I understand it correctly, the mining presence would mean bucks for all of us."

Roger nodded. "Indeed it would. Every business on Main Street would feel it. Miners' wages are high, and Tomis would be the logical place for them to spend it."

Fearful of this new complication, and seeing the town divided by greed and the promise of riches, Hal snapped, "I don't think that's a primary consideration, Tom."

"Isn't it?" Tom countered. "You can speak for yourself, Kitchens. But you have no right to speak for all of us."

Slowly, reluctantly, Hal abandoned his argument. No, in all honesty, he

36

couldn't speak for everyone. For example, Rene and Jerry Hackett had come here for the first time three years ago as summer visitors. They had liked what they had seen, had detected a safe haven in which to raise their precocious and rapidly developing daughter, Lucy, and seeing the lack of a service station, they'd gone back to Nebraska, sold everything to their name, and had returned in September dragging a large U-Haul trailer behind their beat-up Chevy. Hal had given them enough land for a service station and a sizable plot for a house and garden. Jerry had promised to pay him back in small monthly allotments. They did well in the summer months, but how would Jerry Hackett react to the promise of a winter bonanza as well?

And there were others, most of whom had gambled their life savings on a small piece of Tomis because they liked what was going on here, or rather what was not going on here, which was hysterical growth and runaway population.

"No," Hal conceded quietly, "I can't speak for all, but—"

"Hal, wait a minute."

Annoyed, he looked down the table at Tom Marshall. The man shook his head and began nervously to rub the back of his neck. "I . . . was just thinking. We probably shouldn't be so hasty in our condemnation." His hand moved up and commenced rubbing his burr-top in a self-comforting gesture. "Well, what the hell? This *is* a damn important decision."

A little disappointed at this break in their ranks, Hal sat back in his chair. "Then I'll speak for myself," he began, doing nothing to soften the harshness in his voice. "I would rather see Tomis sink back into the wilderness than to submit it to wholesale commercialization. If we'd wanted discos and singles bars and trendy restaurants, we would have settled elsewhere with a lot less effort. Instead we came here—"

"Right on," Mike muttered on one side.

"He speaks for me as well," Brian said, and pushed back in his chair as though again ready to leave.

Only Tom Marshall continued to sit in a position of rigid military attention. "Look, there's no need to make a decision now, is there?" he suggested hopefully. "In fact, I propose a town meeting. Let everyone know what's going on, talk it over with the women. I can't believe that they would object to just a tad more civilization, some nice shops and maybe a beauty parlor, a nice little alpine tearoom where their bridge club could meet for lunch . . ."

Hal shook his head slowly, even as Tom talked, seeing Sarah in his imagination, and Donna, and poor Kate. They had never been bridge and beauty-salon women even back in Boston. And four years of hard work, of minor and occasionally major deprivation, had thoroughly removed all their shiny, false twentieth-century patinas and had rendered them indescribably beautiful and natural, with their tanned faces and clear eyes.

"I'm afraid you're guilty of another error in judgment, Tom." Hal smiled. "Our wives, even more than ourselves, would object to the proposition of too-rapid growth."

"Why don't you ask them?" Tom challenged quietly.

Roger Laing, who had been strangely passive for the last few minutes, stood up as though sensing the break in ranks and feeling the need to heal it.

"Tom's right on one score," he said. "A decision does not have to be made immediately. And I suggest that you do call a town meeting, as it will affect everyone in Tomis." He stood behind his chair now, resting his crossed arms on the back. "And I suggest further that a few of us go back into Durango tomorrow. I was given two names in Denver—Paul Jeffries and Frank Quinton. One is the chief surveyor and the other's in charge of hiring. Yesterday I was unable to locate either of them. If we could talk to them, see how rapidly they intend to move, determine just what their intentions are . . ."

Following this rather sensible proposal, no one spoke immediately, as though good sense was incapable of altering their frustration and apprehension. Mike stirred first, aimlessly dragging the tip of his finger through a small puddle of spilled coffee. "Meeting or no," he muttered, "I have the distinct feeling that we have just been screwed."

Brian stood up and stared down on them all, and in his gaunt, hollow-eyed expression Hal felt a ton of new guilt come crashing down on him for the death of Ken Sawyer. He and Sarah and even Mike and Donna had invested only labor and money in the creation of Tomis. But Brian and Kate had made an investment of flesh and blood.

"All right," Hal said with dispatch, trying to dispel the guilt. "I'll call a meeting *after* we go into Durango. Maybe then we will—"

"I've got to go home now," Brian said abruptly, looking over his shoulder into the deserted dining room, which led to the door. "Kate's waiting."

"Go ahead," Hal urged kindly, knowing the afternoon ritual as did everyone in Tomis. The only time that Kate Sawyer ever ventured out of the house was to visit her son's grave.

In spite of his declaration to leave, Brian stopped in the door. "Is there . . . anything we can do to stop them?"

Hal looked hopefully back at Roger, who was still bowed over the back of his chair. "You mean as far as keeping them out altogether?" he asked softly.

Brian nodded.

Again Roger hesitated before answering. "Well, there's the historic-preservation people, who contacted you last winter. They didn't make a hell of a lot of difference at Crested Butte, but if we could build a fire under their inspection, and if they find Tomis 'authentic' enough, it might help if you could get yourselves declared a historic site."

"Try again," Mike urged cynically. "Somehow I don't think that the Century Mining Corporation would be unduly intimidated by the historic-preservation people who go about nailing little bronze plaques to doors and trees."

"They are more powerful than that," Roger insisted.

"Still, try again."

"Well, there's the Colorado River Process . . ."

"A bunch of damn bureaucrats," Brian muttered.

"True, but they might hear us—"

"What do you want to bet that their pockets have already been lined with CMC money?"

"Perhaps," Roger admitted in a tone of defeat.

"What else?" Brian asked, Kate and his son's grave momentarily forgotten.

In an attempt to take the heat off Roger, Hal stood. "What about the U.S. Department of the Interior?" he suggested.

"What about it?" Mike asked.

"Oh, hell, I don't know," Hal exploded. "Remember, this just came down on us as well as you. We'll need some time to—"

Mike's voice moved slowly into the echo of his anger. "They've got us by the balls, Hal, and both you and Roger know it."

"Then how about an economic boycott?" Hal suggested, the idea just occurring. "They'll have to build their own bloody town, because Tomis will be closed to them."

"Wait a minute," Tom Marshall interrupted angrily. "I thought you were going to call a town meeting, let everyone decide. You're talking like it's a foregone conclusion we ain't gonna play ball with them."

Slowly, reluctantly, Mike nodded. "He's right. You first have to convince everyone on Main Street that money is evil, particularly mining money."

As the awesome weight of defeat settled over the room, Hal walked to the back window and stared up the winding gravel path which led to his house. His and Sarah's. Damn! Why now? *Why,* after four years, just when they were all beginning to lean back and enjoy the fruits of their labors, a quiet, special community isolated most of the year by geography and unfriendly climate, a place of trust and fellowship, with most of their physical needs taken care of, and all their spiritual ones.

"We should have bought the whole damn mountain," Mike muttered in an inaccurate postmortem. It would have made no difference. The archaic mining laws would have taken care of that.

Brian stirred, lifted his head, and looked directly at Hal. "What about sabotage?"

At the quiet suggestion, Hal blinked, amazed at its source. He noticed Roger slowly straddling his chair, a clear look of amazement on his face as well.

"Why not?" Brian persisted. "The first equipment will have to come up our road. For a project the size of the one Roger has just described, they'll require crews of workers and machines, an occupation army." He paused and studied his hands. "So . . . many things can go wrong. I'm not saying it will stop them, but it might slow them down and give us time to—"

Predictably, Tom Marshall exploded. "What you're suggesting, Sawyer, is breaking the law, and I for one don't want no part of it."

Hal glanced toward Mike and saw the same stunned expression. Brian apparently saw it as well. "Well, why in the hell not?" he insisted. "They obviously have seen no reason to apprise us of what's coming. Clearly the element of surprise is a large part of their strategy. If it hadn't been for Roger, we would simply have looked up one day to see the road lined with semis and trailers and trucks carrying seismographs. Too late then to do anything but cooperate or get off the mountain."

Suddenly he stood, the normally soft-spoken manner gone, replaced by a depth of emotion which was all the worse for the cold way in which it mani-

39

fested itself. "I will not leave here," he said, "and neither will Kate. We can't. Not now. And neither will we be driven out by what we came here to escape from in the first place."

At the door he turned back, and in spite of the distance, Hal saw a thirty-five-year-old man who looked sixty. "It's that simple," he concluded. "I don't think any of us are prepared to stand by and watch them take it from us."

Then he was gone, leaving Mike and Tom Marshall staring gape-mouthed after him, and leaving Hal to digest the frontier mentality which had insidiously invaded the back room of his restaurant.

"Strap on your six-guns, partner," Mike joked softly. "The bad guys is a-comin'."

"Do you think he was serious?" Tom Marshall asked, still shocked.

"In a word, yes." Mike grinned.

"Sabotage?" Tom repeated. "It's . . . breaking the law."

Mike nodded and shoved his hands deep into the pockets of his jeans jacket. "If I had to choose between the bureaucrats and corrupt federal agencies and a few sticks of well-placed dynamite, I'm afraid I'd choose the latter."

"You're not serious?" Tom challenged.

"If they're not serious, I'm not serious," Mike laughed and ambled through the door. He called back, "It's good to have you with us again, Roger, despite your shitty news. I'm heading for home, Hal. I always get hornier than hell when I'm tired. We'll talk later."

"Mike!"

Hal tried to call him back, annoyed that after a twenty-year friendship, he still couldn't always tell when Mike was joking.

But he was gone. And of course he had been joking, and Brian as well. True, they'd shed much of their excess civilized baggage over the last four years. But at base they still were products of their century. Not one of them was equipped by nature or training or inclination to carry out a reign of sabotage.

At last Tom Marshall made a move to leave, his stern face lined with new censure. "I've got to get back to the store," he said gruffly. "But let me remind you, Hal, this is a matter for the town to decide, all of us. I for one wouldn't object to a full cash register twelve months out of the year, and I know a few others who wouldn't object, either."

Hal nodded and glanced across at Roger, who still sat straddling the chair, his face a mask safely concealing his opinion of everything that had been said here.

"Do you hear me, Kitchens?" Tom Marshall demanded from the door. "You got no right to do anything until—"

"I hear you, Tom," Hal nodded wearily.

"Well, I just wanted to make sure. No offense . . ."

"No offense."

Tom nodded, at least temporarily reassured. "Good to see you again, Roger," he added, though his voice sounded strained.

Then he was gone, and only two remained, confronting each other over the debris of old coffeecups and spilled sugar.

Roger stirred first, standing up from his awkward straddling position, slowly shaking his head. "I'm sorry," he apologized. "I probably should have spoken first to you alone . . ."

"No need. The rest would have learned about it sooner or later." Now he looked directly up at Roger with the most pressing question of all. "How fast do you think they will move?"

Roger shook his head and stretched a kink out of his back. "I can't say, Hal. Information is so hard to come by. It's as though phantoms are running the operation. I do think it's important that we go back into Durango tomorrow . . ."

Hal nodded. "Of course."

Abruptly the shrill ringing of the phone interrupted the new silence. Hal glanced through the door toward the cash register, waiting for Inez to come and answer it. On the third ring, he remembered belatedly that Inez was gone today, into Durango, in search of summer busboys.

"Damn," he cursed on the fourth ring, and started hurriedly up, banging his shins on the table leg in the process, rubbing the throbbing area as he ran awkwardly through the empty dining room, and at last retrieving the phone on the eighth persistent ring. "Hello?" he shouted into the receiver, slightly breathless from his short sprint.

At first he heard nothing but static, as though the electrical impulse was having difficulty making it over the mountains.

"Hello?" he called again, and glanced back toward the door which led to the small back room, and saw Roger Laing peering after him.

"I'm sorry. I can't hear you," Hal shouted into the receiver, having heard a dim voice at the other end of the static. "Could you speak up? I'm afraid we have a bad . . ."

Then the static subsided and he heard clearly a male voice, impersonal, an operator, distinctly not American, asking in a clipped British voice, "Dr. Roger Laing, please. I'm trying to locate Dr. Roger Laing. Could you—?"

"Just a minute. He's here," Hal said, and held out the phone to Roger who still stood framed in the far doorway.

"It's for you," Hal called. "Someone's managed to track you down."

With a look of surprise, Roger started across the dining room, his hand already extended toward the receiver while he was still a distance away.

The transfer made, Hal retreated, curious as to the nature of the call, clearly transatlantic, though there was no mystery there. Roger had friends and colleagues all over the world.

As the initial exchanges were made, Hal moved away from the area, not wanting to give the impression of eavesdropping. But what the hell? They were in the room alone. It was difficult not to overhear.

As he aimlessly straightened ashtrays and salt and pepper shakers on the tables, he heard Roger's voice explode in extreme pleasure. "Percy? Is that you? Where are you calling from?"

There was a pause, and Hal looked back to see him cradling the receiver with both hands, as though to reinforce the connection.

"Yes," he heard Roger say. "I've been away from Evergreen for several days. Did you call there first?"

He smiled at the reply. "Ah, yes, good efficient Patty DeNunnzio . . ."

41

Hal recognized the name, Roger's secretary of long standing. Apparently someone had tracked him down through Miss DeNunnzio.

"Well, what is it, Percy?" Roger asked, settling on the low stool behind the cash register. "Nothing wrong, I hope. Are you well?"

Hal continued to wander through the empty tables, overhearing every word and struggling against mild resentment. *He* needed Roger's undivided attention. There were a million persistent questions concerning the mining threat, strategies to be laid, courses of action to be explored. And what if the rest of Tomis voted to cooperate with the mining corporation, and what if . . . ?

Abruptly he looked back to the place where the phone conversation was taking place, intrigued by Roger's prolonged silence. Someone was talking long and hard on the other end.

Suddenly he saw Roger rise from the stool as though the force of the information coming from the other end of the receiver had literally lifted him to his feet. When he spoke, Hal noticed a marked difference in his voice, hushed, disbelieving.

"Are you certain, Percy?" he demanded. Apparently without waiting for a response, he spoke rapidly. "How many times did you test them? And under what conditions? And how can you be so sure? Remember how many times in the past we have been mistaken."

Giving up all pretense of detachment, Hal sat quietly at a table mid-room and openly listened. Something momentous had happened somewhere. What, he had no idea.

"When did you send them?" Roger demanded now, his voice brisk. "Did Miss DeNunnzio say they were there?"

Alarmed by the look on Roger's face, Hal sat up.

"Percy, are you absolutely certain?" Roger demanded again, then quickly soothed, "All right, all right," as though someone was getting tired of being challenged. "Of course." Roger nodded. "Of course, yes, immediately. And I'll call you just as soon as I . . ."

With sinking spirits, Hal suspected that something had just displaced the mining threat in Roger's mind. Or perhaps they were connected?

No, no way. What could a call from England have to do with the imminent destruction of Tomis and Mt. Victor?

From where he sat, he heard a flurry of last-minute promises and instructions. Someone was to wait until he contacted them again. There was mention of calling a committee together, a cryptic though brief discussion of the need for absolute proof and secrecy, then finally the words he dreaded most.

"Yes, Percy, I'll leave immediately. And don't worry. I'll call you just as soon as . . ."

Hell! Hal turned sideways in the chair, trying to deal with his disappointment. The emissary of bad news was apparently on the verge of splitting, his attention distracted by some long-distance announcement of greater interest. What in the hell were *they* to do?

"Yes, Percy. I'm glad you called, of course. And don't worry. Maybe you're wrong . . ."

Puzzled, Hal looked back toward the phone. Apparently it was to someone's advantage to be proved wrong. Well, it was of no consequence to him or

Tomis. The threat facing them was clear and well-defined, a mismatched David-and-Goliath struggle, one small town against a multinational mining corporation and the preservation of a way of life which they all had worked so hard to achieve.

Lost in his own thoughts, he didn't even hear the receiver being returned to the hook. Only when Roger spoke directly to him in that excited tone which had marked the entire conversation did Hal look up.

"I'm afraid I have to leave, Hal, to go back to Evergreen," Roger said with rushed apology.

"So I gathered."

"I won't be gone long," Roger added, already moving toward the kitchen and back door. "And I'm sure you know I wouldn't leave if I didn't feel it was important."

Hal nodded. He *did* know that. Still, he was curious. "May I ask?"

"No. Not now," Roger said, not unkindly but firmly. "It's an . . . experiment, the results of twelve years of my labor and a lifetime for Percy Forrester, my colleague in Cornwall. He claims to have discovered new and significant data. If it's true . . ."

Hal had never seen the man so distracted, his eyes blinking rapidly as the force of his intellect tried to deal with the mysterious phone call. Obviously there would be no stopping him. The best Hal could hope for was the promise of an early return.

"You won't abandon us altogether, will you?" he asked quietly, still seated at the table.

From the kitchen door Roger looked back with comforting reassurance. "You know better than that. And I may return as early as tomorrow morning if . . ." He broke off. "At most it will be three or four days."

"What if—?"

"Nothing will happen before I return. I'm confident of it. If it does, give me a call immediately."

Hal nodded and started slowly to his feet. The least he could do was walk with him to the helicopter. "Sarah will be disappointed."

"Tell her to keep the guest room intact."

"I will. Still, I wish . . ."

"We'll figure out something, Hal. I promise."

Apparently the vague and hasty reassurance from the kitchen door was about all that Roger could muster. As he fished hurriedly through his pockets for keys, he added, smiling, "Brian's idea might not be completely without merit."

"Sabotage?" Hal asked, amazed.

"Let's call it a stalling action. Whatever, we'll discuss all possibilities at length as soon as I return."

Then he was out of the door and moving across the gravel driveway and the high meadow beyond. He walked backward for a few moments, stopping once to pocket several rocks which had caught his eye. In the familiarity of the gesture, having watched him gather rocks for the last four years, Hal softened, feeling deep affection for Roger Laing in spite of his disappointment. Roger would be collecting rocks on Judgment Day.

43

Now he heard him call out to him, "Tell the others what happened. Try to get your town meeting together as soon as possible. A consensus would be helpful."

Hal nodded to everything, and followed after him to the edge of the drive, still feeling curiously abandoned in spite of Roger's reassurance.

Then there were no more exchanges, and he saw Roger scrambling up the slight incline to his helicopter. In a remarkably short time the rotors stirred sluggishly into action, causing a displacement of air and dust, and a few minutes later the sleek helicopter lifted off, whipping the high grasses as though they had suddenly become liquid. Through the side window he saw Roger lift his hand in a brief salute before he turned his attention to the control panel before him.

A marvel of twentieth-century technology, the helicopter made little more than a purring sound as it ascended over the high ridge. It was Hal's guess that no one in Tomis had even heard the sudden departure. He held his position, still fighting feelings of abandonment, until the helicopter was a speck on the northern horizon, heading for Gunnison, Colorado Springs, and ultimately, Denver.

Slowly he turned back toward the restaurant, his hands shoved in his pockets, feeling a new chill in the wind. Sarah *would* be disappointed, as would everyone else who had looked forward to an evening of Roger's company.

Well, what the hell. He *had* promised to return as soon as possible, perhaps as early as tomorrow morning, three, four days at the latest. For now, there was nothing any of them could do but wait and hope that Century Mining Corporation did not move on them immediately.

In the face of this new and bewildering problem, Hal moved slowly into the warmth of the kitchen, having already decided that the sacrifices they faced were too great. Was there time to launch a nationwide campaign on the abuses of the mining laws? Whether they could succeed in preserving Tomis depended on whether their message got through. But there was so little time. . . . Yet the alternative would be the boom-town syndrome which already had destroyed the social fabric of many Colorado communities, the rampant growth which had spawned increased crime, alcoholism, drug use, child abuse, mental-health problems, the nightmare gallery that was life in the latter half of the twentieth century for most people.

At that moment he heard a familiar noise, the trusty, percolator gurgling of Inez Fuentes' ancient VW bus. He went quickly to the side window, in time to see the vehicle pull into the gravel driveway behind the restaurant. From where he stood, the rear of the bus seemed filled with bobbing, craning heads. As Inez crawled down from the driver's seat, he saw the side door opening and saw four strapping Mexicans pour out, all in their late teens, he would guess, dressed in skin-tight T-shirts, one proclaiming "Pancho Villa Lives," another, "The Grateful Dead," and all stretching their well-formed muscles after the cramped ride up from Durango and eyeballing the back of the restaurant, the mountain, everything.

Well, his summer busboys had just arrived, though to the man they looked street-wise, capable of far more than simply jockeying baskets of dishes about. Where in the hell had Inez found them? The state reformatory?

44

Puzzled by his alarm at such ready manpower, he decided that he'd meet them tomorrow. Inez knew what to do with them. For now he hurried through the restaurant, heading toward the front door. He would circle around the other side, thus avoiding them.

Like Mike, he was in sore need of an interval alone with Sarah, though not for sex—he'd already done his bit in that department. But she had to be told what had happened, the new threat which hung over all of them, reducing their efforts of the last four years to an existential joke.

He took the gravel path running, looking ahead to the pretty cabin which stood alone and removed from the town in a grove of large spruce and aspen.

Sabotage?

He felt as though he had unwittingly become a part of the land's mythology, all the ancient conflicts, ancient warfare; dry-land farmers versus cattlemen, red men versus white, mining corporations versus refugees from the devastation of civilization.

Through the thick trees he caught a glimpse of the implacable stone face of Mt. Victor, rising to dizzying heights above Tomis' plateau.

As his boot struck the first step of their cabin, he called out in need of reassurance, "Sarah! . . ."

3

She heard him coming and quickly blew her nose and prodded the smoldering log in the stone fireplace into fresh flames in an attempt to dissipate the perpetual chill of the cabin, which in its protective shelter of trees never knew the full rays of a warming sun.

Her hands were still trembling, but she mustn't let him see. She considered switching on one of the lamps, but changed her mind. The shadows of late afternoon suited her.

Why she felt it necessary to hide her fear from her husband, she didn't know. But for the last four years the pioneer mentality had invaded all of them, infecting even poor Kate, who had never shown honest grief over the death of her son.

As she stood before the fire, charting his progress up the gravel path, she stared at the poker in her hand and thought angrily that if something happened to Vicky, they all would be treated to one hysterical bitch.

She dropped the poker with a clatter and glanced toward the small hallway which led to Vicky's room. Sleeping now, after Sarah had coaxed a half-cup of chicken-noodle soup down her, constantly reassuring her that she was all right, that the "bang" had not been intended to hurt her. *Bullshit*. She'd rocked her to sleep in the old Boston rocker, almost undone herself by the sight of tears still clinging to those long dark lashes, the manner in which the child had clung to her merry-go-round even in sleep.

46

Terrific! Nothing like the trauma of being shot at to make a four-year-old's day. Well, she was in complete agreement with Rene Hackett now. They would have to rout out the Mountain Man, whoever he was, whatever his problem. The number of children in Tomis was increasing annually. Indeed, one of the drawing points of their little town was that it was a place where children could explore and investigate their environment in complete safety. Now, what safety, with some nut on the high ridge with a rifle and the willing ability to use it?

She heard his step on the stairs and counseled herself to stay calm, and heard him call her name, and did not answer until he was standing in the door, a fully bearded dark-haired man who made terrific love, who had given her one and three-quarters children, and who had led her away from reassuring civilization into the excitement of creating a new world.

Apparently rendered sightless by his rapid transition from sun to shadow, he stood framed in the door for a moment and called again as though he hadn't seen her. "Sarah?"

"Shhh. Vicky's sleeping. I'm here. By the fire."

"Why in hell is it so dark? Turn on a—"

"No. Leave it as it is for a while."

He closed the screen door behind him, then pushed the inner door closed and predictably stubbed his toe in the thick brown rag rug she had made that first winter, and headed toward the kitchen. "Wait right there," he called back. "I have news."

So do I, she thought grimly, and listened to the familiar sound of the refrigerator door opening, the snap of the top of a Coors, the door closing, and there he was again, wiping the excess beer out of his beard from a thirsty first swallow.

Unfortunately they both started to speak at once.

"Vicky was shot at today—"

"I'm afraid we have real trouble—"

Apparently her message was the most potent of the two, and registered on his face in an expression of shocked disbelief. "Vicky was . . . wh-what?" he stammered.

Not waiting for her repetition, he slammed the beer down on the table and took the hall running.

Sarah closed her eyes and sank heavily into the rocker and stared unseeing into the fire. Again she could track his actions without seeing him, his progress in Vicky's room.

A few minutes later she heard the bedroom door close quietly, and he was standing across the room from her again, the shocked expression replaced by a degree of puzzled relief.

"What . . . did you say?" he asked, retrieving his beer and coming forward until he stood directly before her where she sat at the fire.

"I'm afraid you heard correctly the first time," she said, pleased with her degree of calm. "We were hanging up clothes. Vicky was playing in the meadow above the garden . . ." She paused before confessing, "I found him through the glasses."

47

"I thought you weren't going to spy on him anymore."

"Good thing I did today," she snapped, the facade of calm cracking. "I saw him, Hal," she went on, keeping her voice down. "I saw him staring back at me, then I saw him with a rifle, saw him take aim and fire directly at Vicky and Copper."

At the recreation of the nightmare, she leaned back, her hand gripping the arms of the chair, and rocked rapidly back and forth.

With her eyes closed, she was aware of Hal's hand, still damp from the can of beer, covering hers. "Good Lord," he muttered, and somehow she wanted more.

"Where's Copper?" he asked, looking about for the Irish setter that was his pride and joy.

She shook her head, still rocking. "I don't know. I didn't see him come down."

Suddenly he stood. "You mean you just left him?"

The rocker stopped. "My God, Hal, as soon as I got my hands on Vicky, I . . ."

But she never had a chance to finish. She watched as he hurried to the door, flung it open, and commenced a series of ear-splitting whistles.

Damn! He was sure to wake Vicky, and she hadn't begun to talk herself out. Over the high-pitched whistles and his cries of, "Come on, Copper, come on, boy," she leaned forward and tried to rise, with the intention of telling him to keep it down.

But her bulging middle refused to bend, and she clawed for a few moments at the arms of the chair and finally surrendered to it, and at the same time his whistles and shouts ceased.

"You shouldn't have left him," he scolded, closing the door again. "We made him a house dog last winter while he was a pup. Now we just turn him loose to all that out there and expect him to fend for him—"

"Hal!"

Her voice was low, but the tone clear. Finally he shut up about the damn dog, retrieved his beer, and sat on the arm of the sofa opposite her.

"I'm sorry," he muttered. "It's not been a good day for anyone, has it? Don't worry about Copper. I'll go looking for him in a minute."

"Have you heard one thing that I've said to you? Your daughter was shot at today—"

"—and missed."

Shocked, Sarah could only stare at him.

"Well, what other method does he have for warning people to stay away?"

"How about words?" she suggested acidly. "And I don't think he intended to miss."

"Of course he did. A man like that owes his existence to his skill with a gun." He reached behind and grabbed Vicky's bright pink jacket, which she'd dropped onto the sofa. "Was she wearing this?"

Sarah nodded.

"And you don't think he could have hit this target if he'd wanted to?" He tossed the jacket back onto the sofa and took another swig of beer. "I heard the shot," he confessed, his voice falling, "from the restaurant. I thought it was a car backfiring."

She shook her head, not quite trusting herself to speak yet. She'd thought earlier that she might have to restrain him from taking off for the high ridge alone instead of gathering the help he needed first. "No," she said, "no car backfiring, merely your daughter serving as a target for a demented bastard."

"You should have been watching her more closely," Hal said flatly. "That's his territory up there, and this is ours. As far as he's concerned, we are the intruders. He had the mountain all to himself before we . . ."

Still unable to believe what she was hearing, Sarah again started the laborious trip upward, thinking somehow that if she were on her feet, either she would make sense or he would.

While she was still struggling, he drained his beer and muttered, "I'm afraid our true problem does not reside on the high ridge."

At that moment, Sarah was aware of someone else missing, someone whose good sense and rational judgment she'd counted heavily on in this new crisis.

"Where's Roger?" she asked.

"Gone."

Stunned, she looked up. "Gone? Where? He just got here."

Hal shook his head and studied the empty beer can. "Well, he's gone now. Back to Evergreen. Something urgent. There was a phone call. Hell, who knows anything where Roger's concerned? He said he'd be back as soon as possible, maybe tomorrow."

Disappointed, yet trying to mask it, she asked, "What brought him here so unexpectedly? He seemed . . . worried. What did he say?"

"What didn't he say?" Hal muttered. "Ever hear of CMC? Century Mining Corporation?"

"Mining?" she parroted. "No . . ."

"You will," he murmured, pacing off the room.

Sarah watched, bewildered, as his black mood deepened and spread. She'd frequently seen him like this back in Boston, caged, impatient, brooding. But not here. "Hal, what did he say? Please . . ."

Just as she was about to ask again, he strode to the back door and called out, "I'm going to look for Copper. I'll be back."

"Hal, wait, please . . ."

But he didn't.

Maybe it was for the best. Both of them were suffering from a bad case of nerves. Anyway, she would hear his news soon enough, and from the manner in which he was angrily climbing the path, it might be nice for a while not to know.

Roger was coming back. That was good. Roger could distract them with his blustery laugh and tales of the absurd. And whatever threats were out there would be dissipated in the rush of summer traffic, and in time she might even manage to forget that her daughter had been shot at today and she would

49

simply have to remind herself that whoever the Mountain Man was, he was to be pitied for his loneliness.

For now, the baby was doing flip-flops in her belly, and in an attempt to ease him as well as herself, she stretched awkwardly out on the sofa, drew up the afghan that Kate had made for her that first winter, and thought ahead to her delivery in mid-July.

4

Donna Dunne made love with her husband twice in forty-five minutes, and when his erection and ardor showed no signs of diminishing, she pushed gently against his chest and suggested, "Put it to bed, Dunne, and you do the same."

He nuzzled her breast; his voice came out muffled. "You know that delivering babies always makes me horny, all that nice pelvic activity."

She closed her eyes in his hair and felt his tension building again and thought that since they had arrived in Tomis four years ago, he'd changed little. His compulsive-addictive personality was the same as ever. He had simply substituted sex for booze. Which was okay. At least he couldn't get falling-down drunk on sex.

As he pushed deeper inside her, she waited patiently for his release, and it came in a miraculously short time, accompanied by a shudder and a sudden relaxation which caused him to slump upon her.

"Enough?" she asked, and ached to straighten her legs and escape to a hot shower.

He raised up and grinned down on her, a few strands of brown-gray hair plastered to his forehead. "For now," he said. "Thanks. . . ."

As he rolled off her, she eased her legs downward. "Too bad you can't enter some sort of contest," she joked lovingly. "Three orgasms after a night's work must be some kind of record."

51

"Not a bad idea," he said, one hand still playing with her nipple. "We could call it the 'Tomis Summer Sex Festival,' public copulation in front of Hal's Kitchen, and the winner gets to spend twenty-four hours alone with you. . . ."

She watched his hand as it covered her breast, kneading. "You'd do that to me?"

"Sure, since I'd be the winner."

"Your hormones are screwed up."

"Speaking of screwing . . ."

As he pressed against her, she quickly rolled to the edge of the bed and felt grit on the wood floor beneath her bare feet and saw the abandoned vacuum sweeper, her activity when Mike had come in and picked her up and carried her to bed.

"Where are you going?" he protested, reaching out for her, and missing.

"I have to go to Kate's. I promised . . ." She looked back and saw his mood change as she knew it would. The mention of Kate Sawyer was capable of doing that. Still gazing at him in silence, she was sorry that she'd brought the subject up. The expression on his face was the same drained look which four years ago would have spelled a bout with the bottle.

"I'm sorry, Mike," she said, "but I do have to go. Kate always expects one of us, either Sarah or me . . ."

He nodded quickly, as though he really didn't want to hear about it, and with small-boy modesty drew the sheet up over him.

"Did I ever tell you," he began on a burst of enthusiasm, desperately trying to recapture the abandonment of unlimited sex, "about my intern friend who once said that the best time to have sex with a woman was right before she delivered?"

In mute apology for having radically altered his mood, Donna held her position on the side of the bed, prepared within reason to let him talk himself to sleep. It wouldn't take long, and she was curious to know what had happened at the restaurant with Roger Laing. Kate could wait a few minutes.

"How so?" she said, sensing a bizarre tale.

"Well, why not?" He grinned. "A little anesthetic, the legs strapped neatly apart, the cervix alive for the big moment . . ." He laced his hands behind his head. "My friend claimed to have done it five times."

Genuinely shocked, she asked, "What about the nurses, the others in the—?"

"They thought it was hilarious."

"That's sick."

"The husband caught him on number six, removed a few of his teeth. The last I heard, he was selling State Farm in Seattle, Washington."

She started up from the bed, heading for the shower, when he reached out and drew her back, one hand caressing the side of her face in a gentle reprimand. "You should know better by now. Don't believe half of what I ever tell you." He paused, his manner sweet. "Believe this, though. I do love you. . . ."

She kissed him in chaste, sisterly fashion, not wanting to awaken sleeping dragons.

52

Still he held her arm. "Are you happy here now, Donna?"

An ominous "now" it was, reminding her of her endless bitching four years ago, her repeated threats to leave both him and this godforsaken place. How impossible it had been to try to explain to her parents in Toronto why her American-doctor husband had turned his back on a promising Boston career for the wilds of Colorado. She still hadn't explained it to them, and wasn't certain that she'd explained it to herself. All she knew for certain was that she did love him, then and now, that he had been in the process of killing himself, and that their sex life had been zero. She also knew that there wasn't enough money in the world to make her go through that first godawful year again.

"Yes," she said at last, smoothing his brow, sensing the beginning of sleep.

"Then do me a favor, will you?" he slurred, his eyes growing heavy. "Throw those damn pills away and let's have a—"

"Oh, Lord, Mike, haven't we discussed that enough?"

"No, we haven't. Why don't you want a child? Sarah's certainly doing her part—"

"Good for Sarah."

"We're settled here now. Vicky is flourishing. It's a perfect place for—"

"What about Kent Sawyer?"

Again without meaning to, she bluntly brought the conversation to a painful halt. "Go to sleep, Mike. I'll see you later," she said softly, and this time left the mussed bed with such speed he couldn't catch her. At the bathroom door she looked back, aware of his eyes upon her. In an effort to send him off to sleep with happy dreams instead of brooding ones, she cracked, "You just dig pregnant women, that's all. And stay away from Sarah Kitchens or it will be Hal who knocks your teeth out."

Without waiting for his response, she slipped behind the door and closed it, still feeling his eyes upon her. As she confronted the small cubicle of their bathroom, she was aware of her heart beating unnecessarily fast. Belatedly she remembered that she had forgotten to ask him about the meeting this afternoon.

Well, later. What she had never confessed to Mike, or anyone else for that matter, was the fact that in many ways this place frightened her. Its isolation during the winter months for one, the creep who lived up on the high ridge, the curious sounds coming from no place that she sometimes heard in the middle of the night, the changes that had come over them all in the last four years, increased sexuality, ravenous appetites of all kinds, a wilderness, as though the civilizing effects of their past lives had been merely a thin veneer.

Still leaning against the bathroom door as though to barricade it, she knew that she was as guilty as the rest of them. How radically her standards had altered. At some point her compulsion for cleanliness and order had gone out of the window. No longer were bed linens changed every other day. She did well to do it every other week. And the vacuum sweeper had been a Christmas present from Mike two Christmases ago and was now passed among the three families. . . .

She smiled and shook her head. If you can't beat 'em . . . But the truth

53

was, she'd give her right arm for a splash of neon, for a single expanse of pavement that did not mysteriously crack every spring, for her charge account at Jordan Marsh and two tickets to a pre-Broadway opening at the Shubert.

She drew back the shower curtain and turned on the hot water full blast and waited for the steam to build up, and looked out of the small bathroom window at the calendar picture of high mountain peaks, and thick green velvet stands of fir and pine. She pushed open the casement window and took a deep breath of fresh mountain air and felt herself impaled on her own dilemma.

It *was* beautiful here, a rich sense of community enhanced with every newcomer. She'd never thought it possible, the ease with which they all had become friends, not just the original Fox Fire Kids, but the rest of them as well, Tom Marshall, and dear old Mina Murdoch, and Jerry and Rene Hackett, all intrepid souls who'd pawned all earthly goods in order to purchase a small square of the dream.

Well, if they could survive, she could, though it did scare her sometimes, the vastness, the aloneness and isolation. . . .

About fifteen minutes later, her skin tingling from the hard scrubbing, she wrapped a towel around her and cautiously opened the door.

As the pent-up steam billowed past her, she glanced toward the bed and saw Mike asleep, the sheet drawn up to his chest, his arms relaxed over his head.

Hurriedly she scooped up her jeans where Mike had dropped them on the floor, and her brown flannel shirt with the ripped sleeve. Hopping into one leg, she drew the jeans up and caught a glimpse of herself in the wavy bureau mirror. Still naked from the waist up, she buttoned the jeans effortlessly and indulged in a moment's pride as she viewed her slim waist and well-formed breasts. Poor Sarah, lumpy and misshapen.

It might be fun to tell her of Mike's bizarre account of rape in the delivery room. Good for a squeamish laugh or two. Of course, Sarah wouldn't have to worry. No delivery room for her. Like a classic earth mother, she'd given birth to Vicky in their cabin after a scant twenty minutes of labor. But as for Donna . . . No, thank you. No babies, please. Maybe later. . . .

Dressed, she pulled on her loafers, ran a quick brush through her straight long black hair, and walked hurriedly through the living room. She was late, and Kate would be more upset than usual. As she went out the front door of their cabin, which had been built on the ruins of one of the original structures, she saw Mike's sign, wood-burned into a square of highly varnished knotty pine: "WE DUNNE IT—DONNA AND MIKE, M.D."

She touched it lovingly on its standard. He was so proud of that sign, though with the addition of the "M.D." their living room in the summer months resembled a clinic. In fact, last fall Mike had converted the storage room into a small examining room.

She didn't mind. She loved the flow of people with their safe minor complaints, bellyaches, splinters, headaches from the altitude . . .

As she started down the walk toward Kate Sawyer's house, she felt remarkably good, her body alive with the lingering sensation of her orgasm, the cool

54

breeze and hot sun alternately warming and cooling her, pristine little Tomis all around her, the unique houses seeming to smile as she passed.

Beyond her house she ran her hand along the smooth round timbers which early this spring the men had constructed to corral Runaway Creek, a normally lazy little stream which meandered through the town. She looked over the edge of the timber embankment into the creek itself, which was running fast and hard with the spring thaw. Every year up until now, the creek had flooded the town, thus necessitating the reinforced-timber embankment. It was a crazy creek, surfacing at some points, then disappearing underground. Roger Laing claimed that once, as a boy, camping on the mountain, he had followed the stream to its source, a natural spring almost at the very top of Mt. Victor.

My, but she *was* dawdling today. Kate probably wouldn't speak to her, but how long was this period of mourning to go on?

Lacking an answer, and a little ashamed that she'd even posed the question, she thought again that she should be on her way. But the rapidly tumbling white water seemed to have a mesmerizing effect on her, reminding her of a mad dog she'd seen as a child growing up in Toronto. The white foam was the same. Two firemen had come out and shot the dog.

Standing this close to the torrent, she could feel the spray and could feel as well the vibrations of its powerful tumbling descent, and above the roar she just barely heard a voice behind her, shouting, "It's running fast, isn't it?"

As she turned, she saw a broad white apron first, then the broom in his hand, and at last his face, rather bony and stiff from years of army discipline.

"Tom . . ." She smiled. "It does seem to be running faster than—"

Suddenly his expressionless face altered. "Look out!" he shouted, and lifted the broom handle toward her and appeared to be starting forward, when she felt something touch her from behind, only a light touch at first, though as she turned to see for herself the cause of his alarm, a black scratching something entwined itself in her hair with incredible power, and at the same time she felt a slash across her face, and still there was more entanglement, something which felt like claws raking across her shoulders and down the back of her shirt, and as she flailed against its unexpected power, the scratching increased, a many-armed black skeletal monster who seemed determined to pull her into the rushing stream.

She heard her own screams and was aware of Tom Marshall shouting, "Hold still, Mrs. Dunne. It's caught. Just hold . . ."

With her head down in an attempt to protect her eyes, she was aware of his struggle to free her, something pulling painfully on her hair now, her scalp burning, her face twisted in terror.

Though he'd told her to hold still, her movements were spastic, her mouth dry as she continued to feel pressure and strength coming from a source that should possess neither pressure nor strength.

"Tom, help!" she screamed, and as he bent closer over her from behind, she felt herself pinned against the embankment, her head jerked forward at a severe angle, the top half of her body suspended over the angry stream, something still pulling at her.

At last the tension broke with a crack, and looking up, she saw a large dead tree, blackened, its stiff limbs extended into macabre angles, rush rapidly downstream.

Tom Marshall hovered behind her, concerned and breathless. "Close call, that," he panted. "Are you all right?"

For several moments Donna couldn't reply, and clung to the embankment for support. Her legs were trembling, her face and neck and hands burning from repeated scratchings.

"Mrs. Dunne? It's all right now. It's gone. . . ." Tom was now standing beside her, staring down the creek, where the large tree was still bobbing crazily about, a monstrous dead thing.

"Here, you better come into the store and sit down," he offered kindly, trying to turn her about. "Never seen anything like that in my life. I saw that thing rising up like . . ." He shook his head. "Come on, Mrs. Dunne. It's over. You had a nasty scare, that's all. Shall I call Dr. Dunne for you?"

At last the dead tree disappeared around the bend in the creek, and Donna closed her eyes and tried to calm her nerves. "No, T-Tom, I'm f-fine," she stammered, afraid to let go of the embankment for fear her legs would fail her. She still could feel the pulling sensation against her scalp, and now for the first time she felt something wet running down the side of her face and reached up and found blood.

Tom saw it as well. "It's not bad," he soothed. "But you should get some disinfectant on it. You wait here and I'll go get Dr.—"

"No!" She shook her head and dabbed again at the cut. "It's all right, Tom. Mike's sleeping. Don't bother him. He was up half the night—"

"Still, you should—"

"I'm on my way to Kate's. She'll have—"

Rapidly he shook his head. "I just saw the Sawyers heading for the cemetery about a half-hour ago."

So! Kate *had* lost patience. Well, it was all right. Brian should be the one with her anyway. Donna and Sarah went with her only when he wouldn't or couldn't go. Still, she would have to apologize. . . .

As she felt the warm trickle of blood running down her chin, she fished through the pockets of her jeans for something to stanch the flow. Four years ago she wouldn't have been caught dead without a clean handkerchief. Now? Nothing.

"Here," Tom offered, digging beneath his apron and producing a small package of pocket Kleenex.

Smiling her thanks, she took one and dabbed at the cut on her face.

"Come on, Mrs. Dunne. I'll walk you home . . ."

No, she didn't want to go home, because she wasn't absolutely certain that she could make it, though the distance was less than seventy-five yards. How embarrassing it would be to faint from an entanglement with a dead tree.

Feeling childlike because of Tom's close scrutiny, she looked about for a near harbor. Across the street she saw Hal's Kitchen, lights on in the rear, Inez back from Durango and getting ready for the evening meal.

There was her safe harbor, and she ventured a first tentative step away

56

from the embankment, and though her knees were still shaking like jelly, they did manage to support her.

Pressing the Kleenex to the cut, she backed away. "Tom, thank you. I don't know what I would have done—"

"It was just a dead tree." He smiled reassuringly, picking up his broom where he'd dropped it. "It was the force of the water that—"

"I know." She said. "Thanks again." She waved the packet of Kleenex at him. "I'll pay you back later."

She turned about and made her way carefully across the cracked blacktop, raw earth showing in a few places. It was murder on tires. They would have to have it resurfaced before the summer traffic got too busy.

At mid-street she hesitated. She could still feel it, that awful pulling sensation, and the blood from the small cut on her face seemed to be increasing. Three sodden Kleenexes . . .

As she started up the steps to the restaurant, she noticed her arms for the first time, long red ridges on her skin, one on the left arm beginning to show a trace of blood.

Dear God! She'd never felt such power.

Clinging to the railing, she pulled herself up the three steps and pushed open the door and got a good strong whiff of chili peppers and onions and corn tortillas. She stood by the cash register for a moment and glanced back toward the swinging doors which led to the kitchen. She considered calling out, then changed her mind. Someone would appear soon.

For now she considered it a major feat that she had made it to a table. She pulled out a chair, and sat, her fingertips damp with her own blood.

As she tried to draw one steady breath, she lifted her head and felt something still entangled in her hair. She dropped the Kleenex and sent one hand up and found a piece of gnarled, blackened wood. Grimacing, she removed not only the twig but several strands of hair as well, and dropped both onto the table as though they were hot, and stared at the small piece of wood where it lay like a solitary finger.

It was while she was trying to forget the pulling sensation that she heard the swinging doors creak open.

"Inez," she called out eagerly, looking up.

But it wasn't Inez. Instead she saw four young Mexican men. From that distance and in her state of mind, they looked identical, like cutouts, uniformly dressed in jeans and white T-shirts, their long black hair hanging to their shoulders, their eyes fixed on her in what appeared to be hostile suspicion.

Aware of herself as spectacle with her bloody face and mangled hair, she managed a smile in an attempt to put them at ease. "Inez—is Inez around? Tell her that Donna Dunne is here and would like . . ."

But no one moved. All four boys continued to stand just this side of the swinging doors, which were still swinging, the creaking hinges providing the only noise.

"Inez . . ." she tried again. "Do you know where Señora Inez is? I need . . ."

57

Still no reaction except for a subtle moving together, as though they were closing ranks. The one on the far right smiled.

Oh, hell. Enough! She knew Inez was in the kitchen. She could hear someone moving about. In no mood to be put off or intimidated, she stood with effort and began to make her way through the clutter of tables, heading toward the kitchen door and the line of four who now blocked it.

"Inez! Are you there?" She raised her voice in an attempt to penetrate over those blank faces, which she noticed now were no longer blank. All four expressions were identical, their eyes moving slowly down the front of her shirt, lingering in the area of her breasts.

Embarrassed, she looked down, and only then discovered the top two buttons of her shirt undone, her cleavage clear for all to see.

As her embarrassment and anger increased, she grabbed the front of her shirt. "Inez!" she called again, and receiving no answer, backed slowly away from their eyes. In her retreat she collided with a table; the force of the collision sent an ashtray across the smooth Formica top. As it shattered to the floor, she looked up to see them all grinning at her.

"Bastards!" she muttered beneath her breath, and was just heading toward the door when she heard a familiar voice. "Who is it? We're not open yet. Five-thirty. Come back—"

"Inez!"

As she looked toward the kitchen, she saw the slim dark-haired woman who mothered them all staring at her from over the swinging doors. "Is that you, Donna?" Inez called out, squinting into the semidarkness at the front of the restaurant. Seeing that it was, and apparently catching a glimpse of Donna's bloodied face, she pushed through the doors. "My Lord," she gasped as she drew near. "What in the name of . . . ?"

Inez put her arm about Donna's shoulders and assisted her to a chair. She shouted something in Spanish to the four boys. At last Donna saw them move; two went back into the kitchen, one turned on the light switch, and the fourth headed toward the serving table at the rear, where pitchers of ice water and glasses were awaiting the evening trade.

More than ready to be "taken care of," at least for a few minutes, Donna said nothing and fought back a burning behind her eyes, the residue of fear and embarrassment.

After making certain that everyone was dispatched on various errands, Inez wiped her hands on her apron, dragged a chair close, and leaned forward with onion-fragrant hands in horrified examination of Donna's face. "What happened?" she asked softly, her commiseration doing little to check Donna's tears.

With a self-deprecating laugh, Donna announced simply, "I tangled with a dead tree. In the creek. It . . . seemed to want to take me with it. . . ."

From the puzzled look on Inez's face Donna knew that nothing she had said made a great deal of sense.

"Where's Mike?" Inez asked sternly, as though to suggest that Mike's absence was the cause.

"Sleeping," Donna replied. "He delivered a baby last night out at the camping area. I was on my way to Kate's, and . . ."

At that moment one of the boys placed a pitcher of water and a glass on the table. Somehow he looked less threatening now. Then two others emerged from the kitchen, one carrying a small battered first-aid kit, the other protesting something in rapid-fire Spanish. No wonder they hadn't understood her.

In her efficient manner, Inez poured a glass of water and offered it to Donna, then snapped open the first-aid kit and began to look over the contents. All four boys had regrouped a distance away and were staring again.

"Who are they?" Donna whispered.

Inez looked over her shoulder, saw the silent audience, and again erupted in a continuous stream of Spanish that sounded like sleet striking a window. Accompanying her verbal commands with broad gestures, she sent the four running, two toward the flatware bin, where they commenced setting the tables for dinner, the other two disappearing into the kitchen.

"Troublemakers," she snapped. "At least, they were down in Durango. But they'll cause no trouble here. I've warned them, they'll toe the mark . . ."

As she withdrew a bottle of Bactine spray, she used it as a pointer and gestured toward the two boys setting the tables. "That's Phillip and Carlos, and the other two are Pete and Juan. The sheriff in Durango gave them their choice between working here for me this summer or going to the reformatory."

Terrific. Donna kept wary eyes on the two working at the far end of the restaurant.

"They're good boys, though," Inez added, "just bored, like kids everywhere, but I plan to keep them busy. Now, lean close and let me see how deep that is. I still don't understand—a tree, you say?" She removed the top from the Bactine, reached for a paper napkin, dunked it in the pitcher of water, slipped her other hand behind Donna's neck, and drew her close.

As she gently wiped away the blood, the cooling sensation of the water felt good. Donna concentrated on the silver crucifix around Inez's neck, the nailed Christ done in graphic detail.

"Not deep," was Inez's diagnosis. She angled Donna's face toward the light and squirted the Bactine three times.

No sensation, only a pungent medicinal smell and a good sense of being safe.

"There," Inez pronounced at last, gently pressing a large Band-Aid into place. "Tell Mike I'll send him my bill. Now, are you all right?"

"Fine, and thank you. It was the strangest thing—"

"Well, I've got to get back to work," Inez interrupted, gathering up the scattered items and stuffing them back into the first-aid kit. "I've been gone all day, and Joyce has the kitchen in a mess. You want to come back and have a cup of coffee while I—?"

Donna shook her head. "No, I was on my way to Kate's. I'd better . . ."

Inez's face suddenly went slack. Quickly she crossed herself, snapped the kit closed, and started up from the table. "Will you and Mike be in for dinner?"

"I don't know. He was sleeping when—"

59

"You'd better come. Fresh sopopillas in the oven . . ."

"We'll see."

Then she was gone, and Donna was left at the table with the smell of Bactine blending repulsively with the smell of onions and peppers. Dinner. She'd made no plans. Maybe she could drag Mike back for . . .

Suddenly she looked up, feeling eyes on her, all four boys staring.

She stood with such force that the chair almost clattered over backward. She hated to be critical, but she wasn't certain that Inez had made the right decision in bringing them here. She could just hear Rene Hackett, who was convinced that every male in Colorado had received news of fourteen-year-old Lucy's virginity and had launched a concerted campaign to alter it.

At the door she took a last look backward. The four were still watching her. She felt goose bumps and quickly closed the door behind her. She once considered crossing over to the embankment, where she could hear the rushing white water, but she changed her mind and increased her step down the cracked main street, feeling threats all around her.

5

In the ungodly silence of the little cemetery below Tomis, Brian Sawyer leaned against the white picket fence and noticed the absence of bird sounds, the absence of all sound save for Kate's soft voice as she sat cross-legged in the grass beside Kent's grave.

Whenever possible, Brian tried to avoid these afternoon "visits" with their dead son. Though he was ashamed to admit it, on more than one occasion he had hidden in the back of Tom Marshall's store, or feigned some job that needed doing, dead timber cleared, a fence mended, *anything* to avoid what was going on now. Usually Sarah or Donna came with her. But the steep walk down was difficult for Sarah now, and today Donna had been late for some reason, and in his anger over the afternoon meeting in Hal's Kitchen with Roger Laing, he'd gone straight home, where a very agitated Kate had been waiting, insisting that they go now, as Kent would wonder where she was.

He shoved his hands into the pockets of his khaki work pants, beginning to feel the chill of late afternoon. "Kate, come on, now. Let's go home. A bowl of hot soup would be . . ."

From where he stood near the gate, he saw not one alteration in her position, heard no break in her voice as she continued to address the carefully tended grave and small headstone as though it were capable of response. "Do you remember that time, Kent, it was your ninth birthday party and we took

61

all your little friends to Nurembaga Park and we rode on the merry-go-round and your horse was the largest because you were the birthday boy . . ."

Christ! Abruptly Brian turned his back and grasped the picket fence. Beyond the crest of the hill, he saw the valley spread out in panorama below him. In the opposite direction he saw the implacable stone face of Mt. Victor, and perched precariously in between on the small plateau was Tomis, a dream gone sour.

It couldn't go on. For either of them. He should have listened to her right after Kent's death, when she'd begged him to take her away. Then *he* had been the one who had insisted that they stay, something to do with the need to acknowledge grief and face it.

Not once in the last two years had she shown the slightest inclination either to acknowledge her grief or to face it. In fact, to the contrary, Kent seemed more alive to her now than when he had been alive, and any mention of leaving Tomis was met with stony refusal and ultimately she fell into complete silence and he always ended up talking to himself.

As her voice droned on behind him, he heard a quality that he'd heard more and more often of late, a singsong, demented tone, as though she had lost complete contact with this reality.

"Dad will be home soon, Kent, and then we'll start the fire. Yes, you can hold your own stick, but keep the marshmallows away from direct flame or they will burn."

In an act of discipline he closed his eyes and tried to close his ears as well and vowed to give her five more minutes. Then bodily, if necessary, he would take her home, though for all his efforts, he knew he would simply transfer her to that damnable straight-backed chair near the window, where she sat from morning to night, knitting endless afghans. There were thirty-two in the trunk in their bedroom now.

Angrily he pushed through the gate and walked a few yards beyond, still hearing her voice, that awful tone. In desperate need of distraction, he imagined that he was surveying from where he stood to that far peak across the valley. He closed one eye and looked past an imaginary stave toward the distant point. The second stave should go . . . there, the first blotting it out, and the third . . . there. Yes, he could do a straight line clear across the valley.

Big deal! Stone Age man could do that, the legions of priest-surveyors who marked out the ley lines which crisscrossed the earth and with which every engineer was familiar.

The distraction over, he glanced back into the cemetery. She'd moved up to the headstone and was now embracing it, her fingers caressing the carved letters: "KENT SAWYER   JUNE 21, 1969–JUNE 12, 1978."

She had kept the birthday cake in a box until it had turned hard and rocklike. The Scrabble set was still wrapped in birthday paper on his dresser alongside the bow and arrow. Brian had finally talked her into giving the new set of World Books to Mina Murdoch for use in her one-room school.

But everything else remained the same, his room filled with odd souvenirs picked up during his adventures, a rusted horseshoe, an old pick, mute evidence of the first settlers, countless rocks with unusual stratifications.

62

Could a boy wish for a more magnificent playground?

Yes! Something in the "playground" had killed him, though to this day Brian had no clear idea what. Hal had found Kent's body, but he hadn't told anyone but Mike. All Brian had seen and heard was the sealed coffin and the angry suggestion from Hal that it remain sealed. For everyone's sake.

Behind him he heard Kate's droning voice cease. He looked back and saw her on her hands and knees in prayer, her head bowed, her hair more gray than brown, her arms pitifully thin beneath her windbreaker, and for a moment all his anger and resentment and confusion blended and he ached to take her in his arms and carry her away from this place, not just this cemetery, but this *place*. The dream was over, finished. Didn't they all know that? Before the summer was over, the mine would be in full swing. There would be bulldozers working five miles east of Tomis. Hal's Kitchen would be inundated by an army of strangers. A tent city would spring up beyond the meadow. New businesses would come in, bars, hamburger stands, the kind of women who followed large construction crews.

Embarrassed, he looked away from his wife at prayer, thinking of the two-story white frame house in Durango. *Mrs. Underwood's Boarding Rooms.*

My girls are clean. All that I ask is that you wear this to see that they stay that way.

Good quality. Lamb skin. Didn't interfere with sensation. He had caught himself masturbating in the bathtub, and self-disgust had led him to Mrs. Underwood's. It wasn't difficult. Someone needed something from town at least once a week, and Hal always let him go, as though he knew.

He felt a dangerous load of guilt blend with his grief and anger, and in a sharper voice than he might have wished, he called out, "Come on, Kate. I'm freezing. That's enough. Let's go."

But it was as though he'd said nothing at all. She was still kneeling, though her back was to him now and she was bent over, her shoulders moving rapidly, as though . . .

No! He took the gate running and grabbed her from behind and pulled her to her feet and saw her hands covered with dirt, a small indentation of raw earth at her feet where she'd been trying to dig down to her son.

"He wants out," she sobbed, struggling against his restraint.

"He's dead, Kate. Come on, Let's go home. . . ."

As he angled her about into the position of an embrace, she went limp in his arms, not fainting or losing consciousness, but simply an unresponding female body, her eyes slightly glazed with a residue of tears, her mouth slack, a thin stream of spittle slipping from one corner, her dirt-encrusted hands limp at her sides.

"Kate?"

But there was no response. Gently supporting her, he led her through the gate of the cemetery and prayed that Main Street would be deserted. God, how he hated the looks of pity.

"Come on, Kate," he urged. She struggled briefly for a backward look. As he propelled her deadweight back up the steep hill, he searched his mind for an excuse to go into Durango tomorrow.

6

In spite of the grim nature of the meeting, Sarah loved the bustle of life that was now filling Hal's Kitchen. The day after Roger Laing had told them of the mining threat, Hal had decided it was time to hold an open forum, apprise everyone of what was going on, and try to arrive at some sort of plan and consensus. Roger was still absent, though Hal had waited for him all day.

Now, as the large dining room continued to fill, she felt her attention torn between Vicky on her right, who was placidly coloring in her circus coloring book—since the shooting incident, the child had been too placid—and Donna Dunne on her left, who still bore the scratches from her humorous encounter with the dead tree.

"You say you were accosted by a dead tree, my dear?" Mike had teased her in his best W. C. Fields imitation. "Nothing worse than a craven, over-sexed tree."

Seated in her customary awkward position a distance from the table, Sarah saw Inez angle her way through the kitchen door balancing an enormous tray of coffeecups. According to Hal, coffee would be on the house, everybody would have to pay for his own Coors, and the hard-liquor bar would be closed.

As she rubbernecked about, it all somehow reminded her of the political meetings of the sixties, their blind adoration of Gene McCarthy, their equally

64

blind loathing of Richard Nixon. In those innocent days, they all thought he had done his worst in his treatment of Helen Gahagan Douglas.

"That's pretty, Vicky." She smiled, admiring the bright merry-go-round which the child had colored. "Remember what I told you and try to stay within the lines."

Wordlessly Vicky picked up the black crayon and made an enormous circle which covered the entire page, merry-go-round and all.

"There they are," Donna whispered, poking Sarah's arm and nodding toward the four boys whom Inez had hired for the summer.

"I know." Sarah nodded, a little annoyed at Donna's persistence. "I've met them. I've even talked with them. They're harmless."

Suspicious, Donna leaned back. "They don't speak English. How could you have—?"

"Inez translated," Sarah answered, keeping an eye on Vicky. Under the duress of surprising strength in that pudgy four-year-old hand, the black crayon had just cracked in half.

"Not so hard, honey," Sarah said. She picked up a blue crayon and demonstrated in light feathery strokes how it was to be done.

Curiously, at that moment she recalled Donna's account of Mike's tasteless tale about rape in the delivery room. Over coffee this morning, she'd had to deal with that bit of tacky nonsense. With a surprising degree of insensitivity, Donna had laughed, then had scolded Sarah for losing her sense of humor. It was not the sort of joke that a woman in her seventh month could find amusing. Still, there was no cause for alarm, for there would be no delivery room for Sarah. This new baby would arrive effortlessly, with Sarah surrounded by love and in her own bed. Forget the obscene story. Don't dwell on it.

Donna was still whispering something on her left, but Sarah's attention was now focused on her daughter. She'd not told anyone but Hal about the shooting incident the day before, and even he had refused to take it seriously, his attention divided among the missing Copper, the still-missing Roger Laing, and the threats of Century Mining Corporation, which was the cause of the meeting tonight.

"Belly up, boys!" came a raucous male voice from behind, and Sarah glanced back to see Jerry Hackett swigging a dripping can of Coors, the excess running down both sides of his mouth and into his beard. He seemed in high good spirits, but then Jerry always was.

Now in his flat Southwestern voice he was informing everyone within earshot that it was "gonna be ripe pickin's this summer. I predict it. They's already twelve jeeps out at the camping area, and it ain't even June yet."

This announcement won a cheer from several of the men standing about the coffee table. Looking backward, Sarah caught Inez's eye and winked, and as she turned back around, she saw Donna, still focused on the four Mexican boys, who hovered about the swinging door which led to the kitchen.

"They're harmless," Sarah soothed, patting her hand, and was just about to refocus her attention on Vicky when suddenly she felt something, a peculiar vibration, beneath her feet. She saw the crayons on the table begin to move, as though someone were gently shaking the table legs. She looked up, wondering if anyone else had noticed it. Apparently not, and when she looked back down, the crayons were motionless.

Strange. Though perhaps not. Hal's Kitchen was full and still filling. Then too, Inez had complained a few days ago about the motor in the large walk-in refrigerator.

Vibrations. Overworked motor. Problem solved.

"Here, Vicky, try this one," she quietly suggested, disliking the vacant stare on her daughter's usually vibrant face. As Sarah flipped to a clean page in the coloring book and positioned it in front of the child, she heard Donna say in a shocked whisper, "Good Lord. Look at that! Did all that happen last winter?"

Sarah looked toward the door and saw Lucy Hackett, Rene and Jerry's fourteen-year-old, although tonight she bore little resemblance to a pubescent teenager. Garbed in a skin-tight T-shirt which said "Make Me Happy," the letters undulating across the twin mountains of her breasts, she was clearly braless; everything moved when she did. Below her waist, the scenery was fascinating. No longer lost in the worn jeans and shapeless flannel shirts and mackinaws of winter, she now sported a pair of black shorts which revealed every crease and curve of her tight young body.

"You'd think she'd be freezing," Sarah whispered, feeling a chill in the air in spite of her own bulky knit sweater.

"Well, if she is, she won't be for long," Donna muttered, and Sarah watched as every male eye near the door altered in some way as the young girl passed among them. Old Callie Watkins from the hardware store did a clean classic double-take. Walt Gibson just gave up and looked in the opposite direction, though the tips of his ears burned beet red.

Sarah giggled and quickly concealed it as she saw the young temptress heading their way. "Hi, Lucy," she called when the young girl was within earshot. "Where's your mother?"

Around the gum-popping, Lucy said, "She wasn't feeling very well, Mrs. Kitchens. She told me to come and listen."

"Well, why don't you sit with us, then," Sarah invited, and motioned toward the empty chair next to Vicky.

"Hi, Vicky," Lucy said, and dragged the chair close. "Whatcha doing?" and for a moment the little girl lost in the woman's body won out, and she reached for a handful of crayons and began expertly to color a fresh page.

To Sarah's pleasure, Vicky seemed delighted and leaned forward with as much interest as she'd demonstrated for anything during the day.

Behind her, Sarah was aware of a cessation of voices around the coffee table, a notable absence of male voices, as everyone, including Lucy's father, continued to watch as though mesmerized.

"Oh, boy," Donna muttered.

"Shh," Sarah whispered, not wanting to embarrass Lucy. In an attempt to distract Donna's attention as well as everyone else's, Sarah leaned up in her chair and peered toward the end of the room, where she saw Hal in close conference with Mike and Brian. Why didn't they call the meeting to order and get on with it? Apparently they were waiting for everyone to settle and get talked out, although after the confinement and isolation of winter, that

66

could take all night. There was a good sense of fellowship in the room, neighbors meeting for the first time without the heavy confinement of winter garments, a pronounced sense of victory that all had survived another winter. Sarah had noticed it every year they had been here, almost a spring ritual of jubilation, winter endured and defeated. Garden plots being planned. Tom Marshall was swamped with orders for seed and fertilizers. Once again the natural progression of life would continue.

In a reflective quiet moment, feeling the baby turn inside her, Sarah marveled anew at how acutely she felt everything here, every emotion, every response heightened. She *did* love it.

"Sarah! Look who just came in."

It was Donna again, apparently keeping a close watch on the door.

Sarah glanced up, surprised, then quickly urged, "Go get her. Hurry! I bet Brian doesn't even know . . . "

The object of their focus was Kate Sawyer, who had just entered the dining room, her perennial knitting basket on her arm, and who now stood looking out over the crowded room as though she'd inadvertently wandered into a gathering of strangers.

Sarah watched as Donna made her way through the crowded area around the coffee table. Kate continued to stand by the door, one hand now moving nervously over her throat. It hurt just to watch, as Sarah recalled her long and treasured friendship with Kate Sawyer. Back in Boston, scarcely a week had passed without the two families getting together; Durgin Park, Jimmy's Harborside, Kate always laughing, her head filled with a hundred projects.

Dear God, where had that woman gone?

Donna had been waylaid halfway to the door by Mina Murdoch. Sarah leaned up and tried to catch Kate's eye. She looked so lost.

Then Donna was moving again, taking Mina with her, the short plump little woman filling her ear with something urgent.

At last, contact.

Mina had stopped talking, obviously seeing the reason behind Donna's haste. Both women appeared to say something to Kate, who responded with a faint smile. Sarah saw Donna point in her direction. As Kate looked this way, Sarah waved and smiled and motioned for all three to come.

As she turned back in search of an empty chair, Lucy thoughtfully spoke up. "I can hold Vicky on my lap, Mrs. Kitchens, if you want."

As the three women drew near, Sarah belatedly realized she needed more than one chair. As she started laboriously to her feet, Mina called out a smiling protest. "Keep your seat, Sarah Kitchens," she scolded. "I just wanted to say hello, then I'm going to sit down front. Do you think Hal will let me say something before the meeting starts?"

"I'm sure he will, Mina, just tell him . . . "

Mina's gaze fell disapprovingly on Lucy Hackett. "Good evening, Lucy," she said, a new sternness in her voice and manner, the schoolmistress strong within her. "You missed your French lesson this morning. Terri O'Connell said you were ill, but you don't . . . look ill."

"I had the cramps," Lucy announced bluntly, not looking up from the coloring book. "Mama said I could stay in bed."

67

Mina flustered red at the announcement and covered her embarrassment with the stern warning, "Then we'll have double vocabulary tomorrow."

"Yes, ma'am," Lucy said, still not looking up.

Mina stared down at the young girl a moment longer, the censure clear on her face. Then briskly she said, "Well, I'll leave you ladies. Quite exciting, isn't it, when we all come together like this."

As the plump, cheery little bird continued to back away, she collided with the next table and rapidly turned about in greeting to Callie Watkins and his wife and two friends who were visiting them from California. As introductions followed apologies, Sarah motioned for Kate to come and sit in the chair on her right, leaving the other chair for Donna.

Still wearing that expression of complete bewilderment, Kate eased slowly down.

"What a pleasant surprise," Sarah whispered, reaching for one cold hand, trying to dislodge it from the basket and failing. Beyond Kate, she saw Lucy look up in mild alarm. *The crazy woman . . .*

"I came down to see you right before dinner," Sarah went on. "But no one was there. Were you . . . ?"

"I'd gone to see Kent," came the soft reply. "He said he was very cold." Slowly the cold hands started fumbling through the basket of knitting, and withdrew a half-completed pale blue afghan.

Feeling helpless, Sarah looked toward Donna for direction, moral support, guidance, anything. But there was no help there. In fact, in Donna's face she saw her own desolation mirrored. How was it possible to know a woman intimately for over fifteen years, best friends in every sense of the word, and not now know how to reach her?

As the clack of the knitting needles started up, she dismissed the unanswerable question and took solace in the fact that Kate *had* appeared tonight, apparently without Brian's assistance. And that was something.

Sarah drew a deep breath. And felt it again, a barely perceptible vibration.

"Do you feel anything?" she whispered to Donna, who was seated sideways in her chair, watching Kate's knitting needles as they flew back and forth through the blue yarn.

"Feel what?" Donna asked.

"The floor shaking. Put your feet flat . . . "

Donna gave her a curious look, then straightened about in her chair. "What am I supposed to feel?" she asked.

"Never mind," Sarah whispered, at last seeing Hal break away from his endless conference with Brian and Mike. Anyway, it had stopped again, though one solitary red crayon was rolling across the table as though of its own volition. She saw Lucy reach out and pull it back and give it a small maternal pat as though commanding it to stay still.

"Ladies and gentlemen, if I may have your attention, please . . ."

As Hal's deep voice boomed out over the noisy restaurant, Sarah relaxed into her chair for the first time. In a curious way, the evening had already worn her out.

"Come on, folks, let's settle down. . . . A few announcements," Hal was

68

saying now, "before we get to the main business of the evening. First, a personal one . . ."

Copper! Why in hell hadn't she waited for the dog yesterday? Because her daughter was being shot at.

" . . . he's a good dog, but just a pup, and if you all would keep your eyes out for him, I'd really appreciate it."

A small rustle of sympathy broke the silence. Someone near the front said, "I saw a black-and-white terrier the other day, but I think he belonged to a camper."

Hal nodded. "Copper is a setter, as you all know. I'm sure he'll come back, but . . ."

As his voice drifted off, Sarah felt a second pang of guilt. She should have waited for him.

"Now, Mina would like to say a word," Hal went on, stepping back from the table and motioning Mina forward.

Mina had put on too much rouge tonight, or else she was blushing under the weight of all those eyes. Donna once had said that Mina Murdoch was Tomis' very own Emily Post. Somehow, with her neat lace curtains and lovely antique furnishings collected from her travels all over the world, she kept them all relatively proper, kept the wildness down and the banner of civilization flying high. Dear polite, refined Mina.

Now she smiled demurely. "Thank you, Hal, and I'll only take a minute. I know there are more pressing matters at hand . . ." Daintily she cleared her throat, and in the sleeve of her pretty voile dress Sarah detected the edge of a white lace handkerchief.

"Two items, really," Mina began, her musical schoolteacher's voice sailing gracefully out over the crowded room, which was now totally silent with respect, as she'd effortlessly reduced them all to schoolchildren.

"I need to have a list of all those parents who want their children to have summer tutorials," she began. "I realize this wasn't necessary last year, but our little town *is* growing. I'm more than willing to schedule as many as possible, but I must know in advance. So please see me after the meeting and . . ."

Suddenly she stopped speaking. Into the unexpected silence came a deep and distant rumbling. Everyone heard it, and Sarah saw heads swiveling in bewilderment.

"Thunder." Mina smiled reassuringly. "And wouldn't a gentle rain be good for all our gardens?"

As voices rose about her, Sarah tried to listen. It hadn't sounded like thunder. Too prolonged, too . . .

"Now, for the second item," Mina went on as the rumbling diminished, "and then, Hal, I'll give them back to you. I'm going to establish a small lending library in my home this summer. I thought it would be a nice service for our summer guests as well as one we all would enjoy during our long winter months. I will make available my personal library and would appreciate it if you all would scour your bookshelves for editions that you don't prize too highly. No first editions, please. Paperbacks would be good, and any and all literature suitable for children that you may have—Golden Books, picture books, books on nature, that sort of thing. I'm most intent upon establishing a children's corner. Respect for literature is perhaps the greatest gift we can give them."

This sentiment was rewarded with a polite scattering of applause, and Mina concluded with a simple plea, "So bring me all your books and I'll take full responsibility for cataloging and shelving them, and Tomis will have a full-fledged library, and that, in my opinion, will be a glorious accomplishment."

A second round of applause accompanied her back to her chair, with Sarah heartily contributing. The Tomis Library. Leave it to Mina. Last summer her pet project had been the Tomis Historical Society and she had begged people to bring in any artifacts that they had found in their various explorations about the town and mountain.

"Someone was here before us, you know," she had announced at a town meeting. "What we must do is build as solid a link as possible with those who preceded us. We don't even know where our name came from, now, do we? Well, we must work on that."

Sarah looked quickly up, remembering. Tomis! Before summer's end, Mina had pronounced the word with a faint Eureka cry in Hal's Kitchen. The faded red binding of the old book had squealed as she'd flattened it open, the better to read.

Before the Metamorphosis had received its final polish, Ovid was suddenly expelled from Rome, on some charge that was never made explicit, and ordered to live a life of exile at Tomis on the Black Sea Coast.

Hal and most others had laughed. Colorado was a far cry from Rome.

Still, Tomis! There you are. Perhaps one of the early settlers had been sent into exile—on some charge that was never made explicit.

"Do you suppose she wants dirty books for the Tomis Library as well?" Donna whispered slyly. "I have a few tucked away."

Sarah smiled distractedly. Vicky was growing restless on Lucy's lap, and Lucy was displaying a bit of restlessness herself, having found the four young Mexicans who were lounging near the kitchen door. Over the top of the swinging doors, Sarah saw Joyce's blank face. It was amazing that after two years in Tomis, everyone knew so little about Joyce. Inez had told her once that Joyce was the daughter of a cousin, that she had had rough beginnings, that she'd been dismissed from school after the sixth grade as being mentally retarded and what was Inez to do?

Disturbed by how much the vacancy in Joyce's face resembled Kate's, Sarah dragged her attention back to her daughter, who was struggling to get down from Lucy's lap.

At the same time, Lucy stood and began making her way through the tables, heading predictably toward the kitchen doors. The four boys suddenly stood at attention as those unrestrained breasts drew nearer, challenging "Make Me Happy."

"Trouble," Donna muttered under her breath as the boys followed Lucy out into the kitchen and the swinging doors swung shut behind them.

"All right," Hal announced full-voiced from the far end of the dining room. "Now, let's get down to business. I suspect that everyone knows what we are

70

here for, but in the event someone doesn't, let me state it as simply as possible. Our good friend Roger Laing was here yesterday and brought a distressing rumor, the possibility of a large mining development on Mt. Victor by an outfit called Century Mining Corporation. It seems they have discovered a sizable deposit of molybdenum and, according to Roger, they may want to use Tomis as their base of operation."

He paused as though expecting a response. There was no response, but everyone appeared to be listening intently.

"Now, I'm sure I don't have to tell you what effect such a development would have on Tomis. I've spent the last twenty-four hours exploring every legal avenue available to us, and I'm sorry to have to admit that there aren't many. I'm afraid the best we can do is to delay them for a while by filing for a hearing with the Colorado Department of Natural Resources and perhaps even taking our case to the U.S. Department of the Interior—"

"What *is* our case, Kitchens?"

Sarah sat up. The voice had come from behind. It sounded like Jerry Hackett, and it sounded hostile as well. She saw her surprise mirrored on her husband's face.

"Our case?" he repeated, and shrugged. "That's why we have met tonight. We've worked hard, all of us, to nurture our community. All they will do is exploit and ultimately destroy it."

"Still, it could mean bucks."

"Yes."

Jerry Hackett again. Sarah turned around and saw the man standing defiantly before the coffee table, beer in hand.

"Yes, it would mean bucks," Hal concurred. "It would also mean a transient population, a crime rate perhaps, overcrowded facilities, a boom-town atmosphere. I don't have to point out what's happened in Leadville or any number of other communities in Colorado. Correct me if I'm wrong, but it seems to me that we all came here because we cherish certain values which we felt were slipping away from us in our old communities. Well, it may only be a matter of time before we are forced to say good-bye to them again."

"What do you suggest that we do, Hal?" This voice was near and belonged to Callie Watkins, whose bald head shone like an eye in the crowded room.

Unfortunately, Hal hesitated, and in the vacuum, voices rose in confusion and discussion.

Get 'em back, Hal, she thought nervously. This is not the time to confer with Mike and Brian.

"All right, you asked what we can do," he shouted, trying to regain their attention. "First, we have to make certain that we have a majority opinion. As Tomis would be the nearest town, we stand both to profit and lose."

Again the voices rose in confusion and debate.

"Come on, now, all of you," Mike shouted. "This isn't the time for gabbing. What Hal here was referring to was a rumor, merely a rumor, that's all."

Without warning, Donna rose, her female voice sounding unnaturally thin and high after the male voices. "Mike, Hal, all of you," she called out. "Why don't you share the rumor with us? Just tell us what Roger Laing told you. I think we all need to know what—"

71

"Right on!" someone shouted behind them.

As all three men looked up in surprise, Donna sat down, a faint look of remorse on her face, as though belatedly aware she might have said the wrong thing.

"Come on, Vicky," Sarah whispered, trying to reach beneath the table for the child, trying simultaneously to keep an eye and an ear on what was going on. But Vicky eluded her grasp and scooted to the far side of the table, wholly out of Sarah's view.

"Do you want me to get her?" Donna offered, seeing the dilemma.

Quickly Sarah shook her head. Hal was on his feet again, his normal, bearded, bearlike appearance reduced in some way. For a moment, he looked like what he was, a born and bred city lawyer playing pioneer.

"Well . . ." He faltered, displaying an uncharacteristic lack of leadership. "I'm not certain what it will gain us to discuss rumors at this point."

"The mine isn't a rumor, Hal."

This female voice spread both silence and mystery over the room. Sarah angled about in her chair and saw Inez Fuentes behind the coffee table, her face lifted toward Hal, a pitcher of cream in her hand.

She went on, her voice clear though filled with quiet apology. "I hope I didn't speak out too soon," she murmured, "but I heard about it yesterday when I was in Durango. They've been hiring crews there for several weeks now. My uncle told me—"

"What?" Hal interrupted. "What did he tell you?"

"That it was all set, that they were going to mine Mt. Victor, that they'd found a moly load worth three billion dollars, the largest in Colorado."

Dear God, no, Sarah thought, seated sideways in her chair, her head turning from one end of the room to the other as she tried to determine the accuracy of Inez's words and tried equally hard to digest the stunned look on all three men at the head table, a state which was rapidly spreading through the entire room.

Jerry Hackett, who was supporting the rear wall and nursing a fresh can of Coors, asked tentatively, "You don't mean here, do you? All that's goin' on over to Crested Butte—"

"No, Jerry, my uncle said here. Tomis. Mt. Victor." Slowly Inez placed the pitcher of cream on the table, a look of apology on her face. "I'm sorry," she said to no one in particular. "I . . . suppose he could be wrong, but . . ."

As her voice drifted off into the general stunned silence of the room, Sarah looked back toward Hal and Mike and Brian. Surely they would refute it.

But if Hal had any reassurance to offer them, he gave no indication of it and was again conferring in private with Mike and Brian, the three of them literally turning their backs on the crowded room, the people taking advantage of the vacuum by talking nervously among themselves.

Sarah bent over and saw Vicky beneath the far edge of the table, and saw something else, a spreading wetness on her light blue playsuit, an ominous dark blue between her legs.

"Oh, no," Sarah muttered, and tried again to reach for her child. But the

72

obstacle of her belly would not permit it. "Donna, would you get her for me? I have to take her home."

"Why? You can't leave now."

"She's wet her pants."

At this announcement Donna bent over to see for herself. "No harm," she soothed. "At least you know that's taken care of for a while."

"She's going to stink . . ."

"What's going on here stinks. No one will know the difference. I think you'd better stay."

A typically nonmother statement, Sarah thought, and though she loved Donna, she hated her slim waist and firm breasts and flat belly and freedom and ignorance over what contained urine could do to a baby's tender skin.

Still, maybe she was right, and the rising confusion in the room begged to be watched. Resignedly she tossed a crayon onto the table, saw it bounce once, then vibrate as though someone were shaking the table legs. Vicky?

"All right," Hal shouted, a peculiar tone of anger in his voice. He had to shout it three times before he finally got them settled down again. "Tomorrow Brian and I will go into Durango and see what we can find out. Until we have at least rudimentary facts, there's not a damn thing we can do."

"I say let 'em come," Jerry Hackett called from the rear.

"No!" came another voice from the far left.

"Wait a minute," Hal shouted, both hands raised. "Let's try to be orderly."

At that moment a flurry of voices erupted from the kitchen, accompanied by a scuffle of feet and Inez's voice, outraged "Go on! Get back there where you belong, you hear?"

Lucy Hackett came stumbling through the swinging doors, her pretty, petulant face even more petulant, the white T-shirt slightly askew.

Hal stopped speaking as all heads turned toward the disturbance. Just over the top of the swinging doors Sarah could see four heads of black hair grouped close together, as though for protection.

"You see? I told you," Donna whispered. "I bet they weren't doing the Mexican hat dance."

Suddenly Inez's face appeared over the top of the doors, then with equal speed disappeared, taking the four heads with her, leaving an angry trail of Spanish in her wake as she herded them deeper into the recesses of the kitchen, leaving poor Lucy to withstand the stares of the entire room.

Embarrassed for the girl, Sarah considered going to her. But at that moment she heard Jerry Hackett's angry footstep as he retrieved his overripe daughter and propelled her rapidly toward the door.

"Do you suppose she was going to take them all on?" Donna whispered. "Oh, to be young again . . ."

With the slamming of the front door, the incident was over except for a tremor of nervous giggles, a few men whispering together, and poor Hal holding his legal pad, his purpose shattered into a million pieces.

"As I was saying . . ." he called out, and gave up. He wasn't going to be saying anything for a few minutes, until the tittering and giggling ceased.

73

Sarah glanced toward the kitchen door. Not a sign of Inez or the boys.

"What a fiasco," she muttered to Donna, sensing that Hal would never regain their full attention. A few of the men began to drift back toward the coffee table on the pretense of refilling cups, but in reality seeking eyewitness information from those who had stood the closest to the little melodrama.

Despair increasing, Sarah closed her eyes and felt a dull but persistent ache in the top of her head. Nothing was going to be accomplished here tonight. It was as though the room was filled with children who had been confined too long by winter and now all they wanted to do was giggle and gossip. Well, Hal would simply have to try later.

"Come on, Vicky," she called out, extending her hand beneath the table, at last making contact with her daughter. Not until Vicky was standing before her did she see the tears, very silent and very large, that were spilling out of those dark eyes.

"Vicky, what is it?" she asked, alarmed, drawing the child close.

Donna saw the tears and bowed close with the same inquiry. "What is it, honey? Did something scare you?"

In an attempt to wipe away the tears, Sarah felt the child's forehead. She was on fire with fever.

"Oh, God, Donna, she's burning up," Sarah whispered. "As soon as this circus is over, send Mike up, would you?"

Gratified by the look of alarm on Donna's face, Sarah drew her daughter to her and was just leaning upon the table for leverage when she felt it again, stronger this time, a vibration of massive proportions.

"What in the . . . ?"

She glanced at Donna. Thank God. There was a look of alarm on her face at last. She'd felt it as well. Suddenly, all about, Sarah heard a sharp cessation of voices, the entire room falling silent, everyone looking about in bewilderment.

Vicky was crying openly and pressing against Sarah as though she were trying to find an entrance back into the safety of her womb.

"What . . . is it?" someone called out near the front of the room.

Still the vibrations increased, accompanied now by a low rumble. Sarah joined the voices of alarm. "Hal, what . . . ?"

"Everyone! Hold your position," he shouted, and she saw Mike and Brian on their feet beside him.

Someone else near the front of the room was crying now, and over the bending, twisting heads, Sarah saw Mina leave her chair and move unsteadily to the someone who was terrified.

Sarah gripped the edge of the table, her hand and arm shaking along with it. Clasping Vicky to her, she caught a glimpse of Kate Sawyer, whose placid face showed not the least sign of alarm.

Suddenly, "Get down!" Hal cried out. "Everyone, flat on the floor!"

Sarah shoved Vicky under the table, thinking: Earthquake? No, not possible. Tornado? There was no storm. As she reached back for Kate, she saw that Donna had beat her to it and was now bodily lifting the woman from her chair and practically falling across her as she forced her onto the floor.

Nearby she heard someone praying, but the droning voice was soon oblit-

74

erated in a deafening roar, the sound of a thousand trains, all heading out of control toward the restaurant. Vicky was sobbing and trying to say something, but Sarah couldn't hear a word. It was as though the child had gone mute or she herself had gone deaf.

Halfway beneath the table, she looked up and saw the massive wagon-wheel chandelier swinging like a trapeze. The outlines of every table and chair blurred. Every solid line and angle grew fuzzy. The entire restaurant was moving rapidly up and down.

Terrified, she enfolded Vicky in both arms and pressed her head down. The roar was still increasing, this solid building in the grip of a force shaking them as a terrier shakes a rat.

"Donna . . ." She couldn't even hear her own voice, and prayed silently, wondering if she would die here, with Vicky in her arms, separated from Hal, never understanding what . . .

As the roar reached the pain level, she lowered her head and thought of her parents and heard a crashing of timber and smelled smoke. The lights flickered. Women were screaming. The light went out, and all was dark. And silent.

For several minutes no one moved, no one spoke. She wasn't certain if the new trembling was coming from her or Vicky.

Suddenly the lights flickered on again, and still no one moved. She'd never heard such a silence, not merely an absence of sound, but an absence of pulses and heartbeats.

A chair scraped. Someone whimpered. A woman's voice called out, "Kent?" She saw Donna stroking Kate's hair. "It's over," she soothed.

Slowly they all began to move, gingerly testing legs, arms; pulses resumed. She heard a voice, Hal's, she thought, call out, "Is everyone all right?"

Sarah looked up at the ceiling and saw the wagon-wheel chandelier motionless now. Then she was aware of someone kneeling beside her and heard Hal's voice, up close. "Are you . . . ?"

"I'm all right, and so is Vicky. What . . . ?"

"I don't know. Wait here."

"No, let me come—"

"*Wait here!*"

As Hal rushed out of the door, accompanied by several men, Sarah grabbed Vicky's hand and with Donna's help made it to her feet.

Apparently no one else in the restaurant had heard his command, and in residual fear all rushed the door, causing minor congestion, a few of the women supported by their husbands, all shaken.

"Get Kate," Sarah ordered, "and let's get out of here." Ignoring Hal's command, she started toward the door, Vicky in tow, Donna and Kate bringing up the rear. The crowd didn't seem to be moving, as though, once on the sidewalk outside, all had been stopped in their forward progress.

Seeing the bottleneck, Donna took the lead. "Move along, please," she called out, and slowly the congestion broke up and they made their way down the steps and out into the night. Concerned for Vicky, Sarah was looking down and thus barely heard Donna's first gasp of, "Dear God . . ."

Then she saw it as well, looking eerily large and deadly in the faint glow of

75

the streetlamp, a massive boulder the size of two cars resting right in the middle of the street.

"Fire!" someone shouted, and the single cry stirred them into movement. Sarah pushed her way to the side of the restaurant and saw flames shooting from the rear of the storage house behind the restaurant and saw in the firelight the path the falling boulder had cut, a wide swath down the side of the mountain, flattening everything in its way, trees, their garden, the clothesline, apparently missing their house by mere feet, flattening the storage house, and crashing finally between Callie Watkins' hardware store and the restaurant.

Lacking a fire department, the men quickly formed a bucket brigade which stretched between the fire and the back of Callie Watkins' store. About twenty minutes later the flames were extinguished and a ghostly layer of smoke covered everything, causing Sarah's eyes to burn, everyone to cough while still staring at the enormous boulder.

She caught sight of Hal, his face grim and blackened, the sleeve of his shirt torn. A curious lull set in after the small fire had been brought under control; then a few of the men approached the boulder cautiously, as though it were still capable of doing damage.

Clasping Vicky to her, Sarah found a safe harbor near the corner of the restaurant and looked about for Donna and Kate, but in the confusion they had become separated. She nodded to a few faces and agreed that it had been a close call. If the path of the boulder had been a mere twenty feet to the right, everyone crouching beneath the tables would have been crushed.

"Mama, I want to go home," Vicky whispered.

"Yes," Sarah comforted, though she continued to watch as the men approached the boulder, Hal and Brian moving around it on the left, Mike and Tom Marshall and several others going right. Completely obscured, they disappeared on the other side.

Sarah waited along with everyone else, feeling herself drawn to the near-tragedy. Twenty feet to the right, and they all . . .

In the silent waiting, she looked back up the side of the mountain. In the four years they had been here, they had never suffered a rock slide. Why now?

"Let's all go home," she heard Mike shout, a peculiar crack in his voice. "Everyone home. It's all over."

Why was he angry? And where were the other men who had disappeared behind the boulder? At the extreme left edge she saw Hal and two others bent over in examination of something. Still Mike continued to bully them. "Go along with you. Nothing more to see. Please, go home, all of you."

But as though by tacit agreement, no one moved, except to inch slowly toward the boulder itself, as though they knew there was something of interest on the other side that was being kept from them.

No, thank you, Sarah thought. She'd had enough for one evening, and as she was debating with herself whether to lead Vicky up by the still-smoldering storage shed or take the long route on the other side of the restaurant, a woman's shrill scream punctuated the night. She turned back and saw through the small crowd to Kate Sawyer, who was tearing at her hair with both hands, her eyes fixed on something beneath the boulder, her screams a continuous siren now, attracting all, including Sarah, who arrived last and pushed through the stunned crowd and stopped and roughly shoved Vicky behind her, belatedly wishing that she'd followed Mike's command and her own instinct to leave.

A man's arm and the top of a shattered skull were visible beneath the boulder. The skull had split open. She covered her mouth with her hand.

"For God's sake, get out of here," Hal whispered fiercely.

Someone was weeping. Sarah looked up to see Lucy Hackett, mascara-tinted tears staining the "Make Me Happy" T-shirt.

"He . . . he just stood there," she sobbed. "He pushed me out of the way, and then he . . . just stood there. Oh, get him out, please, Mr. Kitchens. Please make him stand up. . . ."

Sarah saw Brian trying to calm Kate and lead her away. Hal looked helplessly down at Jerry Hackett crushed beneath the boulder, as though he were seriously trying to oblige Lucy. Donna clung to Mike's arm and hid her face. Someone was praying, "Mary, Mother of God, have mercy . . ."

"Go get Rene Hackett," someone whispered.

No! screamed a voice inside Sarah's head. Don't get Rene Hackett. She mustn't see this.

No one should have to see this.

7

Disliking the feeling of "being in charge"—Brian and Hal had waited until the road crew arrived, then they had gone into Durango to see what they could find out about the mine rumors—Mike Dunne sat at his kitchen table and wished that Donna was with him. She was baby-sitting with Kate Sawyer in Brian's absence.

It was going to be one of two things, he thought, staring wearily at the cup of cold coffee before him. Either two plugs of cotton for his ears or a raid on the bottle of Chivas Regal buried in a tin box behind the wood bin.

Suddenly he shoved the coffee halfway across the table, spilling it, and stared dejectedly down at the brown puddle. No! The battle had been too hard. Four years of sobriety.

Would the jackhammers never cease?

Late last night, Hal had called Durango for a block and tackle to remove the boulder.

Ain't no block and tackle on God's green earth large enough to remove what you've jes' described.

A crew of four armed with jackhammers had arrived at midmorning and were literally having to dismantle the boulder piece by piece. Also last night they had dragged Jerry Hackett free, had buried him early this morning, and since then Mike had seen a constant stream of people: headaches, nausea, nerves, nightmares . . .

He'd been up all night for two nights in a row. What the hell! He might as well be back at Mass. General.

Wearily he reached for the sponge on the counter and soaked up the spilled coffee and stared at the tuna sandwich which Donna had left for him before leaving to relieve Sarah with Kate.

For a moment the room seemed to whirl about him. A small shot of Scotch would steady it.

No!

He rose unsteadily to his feet and made his way into the small examining room. Primitive and limited, it was all he wanted: a single examining table, a locked cabinet containing a few basic drugs, a goodly supply of tape and bandages, one stethoscope, one blood-pressure unit, and a large amount of compassion and understanding of human nature.

But people were bound to fall apart when mountains came crashing down upon them without warning. Fear had moved in. And grief.

Absentmindedly he straightened the white sheet, slightly soiled from his last patient, the old man who was visiting Callie Watkins, an uncle or someone from California. He'd thought his heart was beating too fast, and it had been. Mike had given him a tranquilizer and had advised that he get back down to sea level as soon as possible.

One shot! How would it hurt?

Rat-a-tat-tat-tat-tat-tat-tat . . .

Damn!

His nerves seemed to be jumping in time with the jackhammers, and he stretched out on the examining table and stared straight up into a single strip of white neon. He closed his eyes and let his arms hang limp off the side. Physician, heal thyself.

Donna . . .

Donna would ease the pain in his head. Donna would keep him away from the bottle in the wood bin. And what did Brian and Hal hope to find out in Durango? The truth of the matter was, they all were in a state of bloody siege and their dreams for Tomis were dead.

He had talked briefly, privately, with Inez Fuentes after Jerry's burial. With eyes red and swollen from weeping, and clutching her rosary, she had at first tried to avoid his question, then she had whispered, "CMC is what my uncle called it, Mike—something . . . I can't remember . . . Century, that's it, Century Mining Corporation, and they aren't coming in, Mike. They're here!"

Shit!

His anger dragged him up to a sitting position, his legs straddling the table. He glanced at his watch. Six-twenty-five. How long would Hal and Brian be gone?

The top of his head throbbed. He jerked open the drawer and shook out two Vanquish, tossed them back into his throat, and swallowed hard. A shot of Scotch would have done as well. Better.

One shot! No one would know. And he could control it this time. Hell, his supply was limited. Tom Marshall carried a few bottles of California wines, but for Chivas Regal, you had to go all the way into—

"Mike?"

As though he'd been caught in the act, he whirled on the voice coming from the front of the house and cursed whoever it was who had lacked the decency to knock, and instantly withdrew the curse as he saw Sarah Kitchens' bulky figure come into view, Vicky in hand, both of them wearing the same worn, frightened expressions which were epidemic in Tomis today.

"You busy?" she inquired from the door, looking about the small examining room as though someone else might be in the room with him.

"No, no," he said too eagerly, and wished that Donna would let him get her pregnant, and realized that out of all of Tomis' limited population, the sight of Sarah Kitchens pleased him most.

"You sure you're not . . . ?"

"No," he reassured her. "Just fighting my demon, and I can use all the help I can get."

He charted the rapidly changing expression on her face; first alarm, then concern, then compassion, and as he bent over to scoop Vicky up in his arms, he saw the uneven hem of Sarah's cotton dress, saw her bare legs, and realized how seldom the men in Tomis got to see bare legs anymore. All the women wore jeans except for Sarah, who had outgrown hers about two months ago.

"How's my girl?" He grinned up at Vicky's sober face. The child had seen everything the night before.

"She's running a low-grade fever, Mike," Sarah began, "has been since . . ." She broke off. It didn't require too much effort to fill in the blank. "I meant to have you look at her last night but . . ."

Interesting, how effortlessly he understood everything she wasn't saying.

"I know," he answered her silence. "Come on," he said to Vicky, placing her on the examining table and feeling a fever with his bare hand. Around one hundred was his guess. "Is she eating?"

"Not much, not even her favorites."

"And what are your favorites?" Mike asked, tickling the child beneath the chin before he unbuttoned her shirt and slipped it off her shoulders. Her color wasn't good, a gray pallor to her skin. "She's . . ."

" . . . four," Sarah said.

"Good God," Mike muttered, warming the stethoscope in the palm of his hand, recalling Vicky's birth, the singularly most beautiful ritual he'd ever seen. "Okay, Vicky, come on, let Uncle Mike see what's going on inside that pretty little chest. All right?"

The child made no response, had made none since Sarah had brought her in.

Alarm increasing, he closed his eyes and listened to the heartbeat. Perhaps a little slow. . . .

"Has she been sleeping well?"

"Too much," Sarah worried. "Long afternoon naps, and she seems to be tired by six o'clock."

He moved to the opposite side of the table and fully expected Vicky to swivel after him. Most children did, apparently feeling the need to keep him in sight.

80

Vicky didn't move. As he placed the stethoscope against her back, he noticed her ribs, clearly visible. Too visible.

"What are you feeding her, Sarah?"

"Anything she wants."

He nodded and heard that slowed heartbeat again, but that was understandable if she'd been sleeping a great deal.

He concluded the superficial examination and encountered no problems until he tried to peer into her throat. Then Vicky objected to the throat swab.

"Come on, Vicky, open wide. . . ."

But the child reached out for Sarah, who was there enclosing her daughter in her arms and making Mike's job impossible.

"Do we have to do that, Mike? She hates it."

Annoyed, he snapped, "If there's something wrong with her, we had better find out . . ."

Reluctantly Sarah released Vicky and tried to turn her about. But the child was whimpering now, repeatedly begging, "No, Mama, please. I want my merry-go-round," leaving Mike feeling like the Grand Inquisitor.

Helpless, Mike shrugged as Sarah looked pleadingly at him over the top of Vicky's head.

"If it's a throat infection," he said, "she should be on antibiotics, but of course I can't determine that, can I, without looking?"

"Maybe later, Mike, please . . ."

Outside and down the street, the jackhammers were still at work. Again his pulse seemed to be keeping time with the driving, staccato rhythm.

"Will it ever stop?" Sarah murmured, finding her own comfort in one of Vicky's curls, twisting the baby-fine dark hair around and around her finger.

"A drink *would* help," he said expansively, only half-joking, until he saw the look of alarm on her face.

"Just kidding," he reassured her. "But I do have a stash."

As her look of alarm increased, he laughed. "All alcoholics have stashes, Sarah. Didn't you know that? It's part of our rehabilitation."

"I don't—"

"Of course you do. In order to fight the devil, we have to keep in close proximity to him. Daily denial." He grinned, loathing the words. "How can we deny ourselves something that isn't a clear and present temptation?"

"Does . . . Donna know?"

"Hell, no, Donna doesn't know, and don't you tell her," he added sternly. Sorry now for having contributed to her lousy state of mind, Mike changed the subject. "Come on. I'll walk you home."

"What about . . . ?"

As she cupped her hand about Vicky's head, indicating that the need for help had not been assuaged, Mike offered, "Bring her around tomorrow. Maybe she'll . . ."

As he looked closer at Vicky, he saw, incredibly, that she'd fallen asleep, half-propped up against Sarah, her legs curled relaxed on the examining

81

table. It was only early evening. In the past, energetic little Vicky had been the last dog to die, so to speak.

"You say she took a nap this afternoon?" he asked, raising his voice over the blasted jackhammers.

Sarah nodded. "I woke her up when we left Kate's. She slept all afternoon."

Seeing the worry in her eyes as she eased Vicky down onto the table, Mike skillfully hid his bewilderment. "Well, I'll take a closer look at her tomorrow. Whether *she* wants it or not," he added pointedly. "It's probably nothing. After the confinement of winter, it could be . . ."

Not knowing what it could be at all, he shifted the focus of attention to the predominant bulge beneath Sarah's dress. "And you—how are you feeling?"

"Very pregnant," Sarah said, managing a faint smile. "This one is so active," she added, smoothing her hand over her stomach. "Sometimes I wonder if he's going to wait another two months." She looked self-consciously down at her bulging midsection. "When do you think they'll be back?" she asked, worried.

Feeling the need for movement, he turned to the sink and began to wash his hands. "Hal and Brian? Probably late tonight. Maybe they'll stay until tomorrow if they find out something . . ." As his voice drifted, he shook off the excess water and reached for a paper towel.

"Things are changing, aren't they, Mike?"

Still turned away, he heard the desolation in her voice and moved to dispel it. "Well, we don't know anything for sure yet, do we?"

"They are," she said. "And there's not a damn thing we can do about it."

"Let's wait and see," he comforted.

"Did Hal tell you that Roger Laing was coming back?"

For the first time he looked across at her, pleased by the news. "When?"

"As soon as possible." She shrugged. "Something urgent called him away, but he said he'd be back."

"Well, that *is* good news. Crazy Jolly Roger," he mused.

Sarah reached behind and rubbed the small of her back. Obviously the weight of the pregnancy was beginning to take a toll of her spine. "Did Hal tell you about Vicky?" she asked, still rubbing her back.

Blank again. Not wanting to cast Hal in the role of negligent father, Mike said nothing and let her speak.

"About the gunshot?"

He blinked at her. "The . . . what?"

She nodded. "Yesterday. We were hanging up clothes, and Vicky was playing in the meadow above the house. I was . . . busy," she went on softly, "and when I looked up, she was heading for the high ridge. The bastard took a shot at her."

"Who?"

"The creep who lives up there."

"Are you certain?"

82

"Of course I'm certain, Mike," she insisted. "I was there. You sound like Hal."

"All right," he soothed, a little amazed at this revelation. In the four years since they had lived in Tomis, the "Mountain Man," as they all called him, had fascinated and puzzled them. But they had never seen him close at hand. They had never invaded his privacy, or he theirs. Why now, after all this time, would he suddenly take a shot at a child?

"It could have been a . . . hunter, you know."

"Hunting what?" she demanded, full-voiced over the maddening staccato of the jackhammers still plugging away down the street.

Mike shrugged as he realized that he had no valid rebuttal. There was no game in the area, no deer, no elk, no bear, not even a decent rabbit.

Aware of her close scrutiny, which suggested that she knew he had no reply, he smiled slyly. "Well, Roger Laing can't be right all the time," he said, referring to Roger's explanation two, three years ago when they had first confronted him with the mystery of a gameless mountain region.

The foraging patterns of animals are established in their nerve cells. Centuries of evolution have programmed them to feed in a certain locale. Tomis simply is not on their prescribed route.

He met her gaze and retreated. "Oh, what the hell, Sarah. I don't know. I can't believe he really intended to hurt her."

"Who do you suppose he is, Mike?" she asked quietly.

"God, who knows?" he said, pushing away from the counter. "Someone even more fed up than we were, I imagine."

"How does he live?"

Again, no answer, only the realization that the man had never been seen on the streets of Tomis, though Callie Watkins swore he saw him once in Durango, a limping white-haired old man who smelled to high heaven. But then, with a half-dozen vodka martinis in him, Callie Watkins could see anything.

"Come on," Mike said with renewed energy, "I'll walk you home. I suggest that you get her into her own bed," he added, motioning toward the sleeping Vicky. "Let's see what a good night's sleep will do for her."

On the porch, he held the door for Sarah, then let the screen door close noisily behind them. No lock or key. Neither was necessary in Tomis. He watched as Sarah leaned heavily on the banister and waddled down the three short steps. The extra weight worried him. She might not have such an easy time of it this go-around.

"Are you okay?" He could hear her labored breathing after the mild exertion.

She nodded and waited on the sidewalk, clearly drinking in the blue-gray peace of early evening. There still was a good nip in the air, as though winter were reminding them to enjoy the grace and ease of spring while they could.

Mike paused beside her. It *was* beautiful, a hundred shades of blues and greens, the high meadow dotted here and there with yellow and white flowers. By mid-June it would be a solid carpet. Then he looked on up to the high ridge and the stand of massive fir and pine and aspen, some of the largest ever seen in Colorado, according to Roger Laing, and higher still to the stone face of Mt. Victor, rising fourteen thousand feet above sea level, a perfectly formed mountain, as though the Divine Creator had said: This is the way a mountain should be.

"Mike! What's that?"

Sarah stood a few steps ahead of him and was now pointing up. Her voice no longer reflected either awe or peace. From where Mike stood, she appeared to be pointing up at the Mountain Man's clearing.

"What?"

"Look! Up there. Don't you see it?"

Then he did. "Good Lord," he muttered. "When in the hell did that happen?"

A light. There was a single light where before there had always been darkness at the very summit. At first he thought it might be a reflection of the sun, an optical illusion. But as he shifted Vicky in his arms and squinted up toward the heights, he saw that it *was* a light, a single very powerful beacon.

"What does it mean?" Sarah asked quietly, pushing close to him.

He knew damn well what it meant. And so did she. "It means power lines," he said. "It means something's going on on the other side."

He was aware of Sarah shivering in the early-evening cold. "Come on, let's get you two home," he ordered, and started to lead her out into the street, then changed his mind. The damn crumbling blacktop was dangerous to walk on. In the semidark, she might stumble.

So he kept to the narrow sidewalk though it meant they had to walk Indian fashion, and as he propelled her into the lead, he noticed that she seemed incapable of taking her eyes off the mysterious light. "Every night I look up at that mountain through my kitchen window, Mike," she said over her shoulder, "and I've never seen that light before. This is the first time—"

"Watch your step," he suggested sternly.

As they drew near to Tom Marshall's store, they stared out at the enormous boulder which rested placidly in the middle of Main Street. It had stopped short of totally occluding the artery. Cars could still pass on one side if they "broke speed and inhaled," as Hal had put it. As far as Mike could tell, the jackhammer crew had chipped away less than one-fourth. The rubble now rested to one side of the mother rock. He had hoped they could bring in a crane and totally remove it by tomorrow. Now he wasn't so sure.

"Well, it *did* miss us," he said, as much to comfort himself as Sarah.

"It didn't miss Jerry Hackett," she said in what sounded like just barely controlled anger. "Someone's been working up there," she went on. "You said so yourself. The light . . ."

"Take it easy."

"Why?" she demanded, facing him. "How are we to know that that boulder wasn't purposely dislodged?"

"Oh, come on, Sarah . . ."

"Well, it's a possibility, isn't it?"

Yes, it *was* a possibility, but one he didn't care to think about.

As they started up the path, Sarah seemed deep in brooding, the substance of her thoughts clear. *Someone could have dislodged it on purpose.*

84

"Take it easy," he cautioned again as he heard her panting from the climb.

At the bottom of the steps which led up to the porch, he stopped. He really didn't want to go in, and now tried to awaken Vicky so she could take the steps under her own power. But the child was totally out of it, as though she'd been drugged.

"I'll carry her inside," Sarah offered. "You go on. Donna will be waiting. Kate's been difficult today. Her tranquilizers aren't working."

"Are you sure you'll be all right?"

"Of course," she scolded, lifting Vicky from his arms, angling the child onto her hip.

"Hal will be in shortly," he called back. "I'll send him right home."

"Yes, please . . ."

"You're sure you're—?"

"I'm fine, Mike."

He waved and started back down the gravel path, not wholly convinced that she was, that any of them were.

"Jesus," he whispered, cursing the world for going so totally sour and unpredictable, and speeded up to a trot toward Kate Sawyer's house.

8

To Brian's whistled accompaniment of "Raindrops Keep Fallin' on My Head," Hal shifted the gears of his jeep for the first steep incline which led to the high plateau and Tomis. After the frustrating dead ends of the afternoon and early evening, the abrasive air felt good.

"Come on," he muttered as the old jeep growled at the incline. "You've done it hundreds of times before. You can do it again."

In his mind, Hal traced the route home, the only route home.

That isn't a road at all, someone had said. It's an obstacle course.

Right! Hal grinned. The old jeep was purring good now. Back on familiar terrain. It had been the boredom of the flatland that had upset it.

"So you found out exactly nothing?" Brian asked, apparently cheerful after his visit to Mrs. Underwood.

Well, the way Kate behaved, Hal couldn't blame him.

"Hal?" It was Brian again, the chill air blowing his thinning hair every which way. "Did you find out anything?"

"No," Hal replied at last. "A big fat zero."

"This Quinton guy never showed?"

"Not while I was there. I don't know. Roger will be here in a few days. Maybe he'll know something more." He sat up straight and gripped the wheel with both hands. "How's Kate doing, Brian?" he asked, changing the subject.

He could feel the plunge in Brian's spirits. For a moment he didn't answer, but continued to stare out of the window, face averted. "She needs psychiatric attention," he said flatly, a twinge of anger in his voice. "I believe we all are aware of that."

"Then get it for her," Hal urged. "Take her into Denver. Stay there for the summer. You can't go on like this, either one of you."

Brian looked at him, a strange, almost accusatory look for killing the glow left by the visit to Mrs. Underwood's, for reminding him of what was waiting for him in Tomis.

"She won't leave," he said, "and I think you are aware of that as well—"

"Look, I'm just trying to help."

He hadn't meant to offend him. Or had he?

About a half-mile farther was his estimate to the series of three tricky turns leading to Tomis. No trick to it if one approached cautiously, shifting gears and applying the brake all at the same time. Three men had died at the first turn, the road crew who had come up to blast a wider access through the canyon walls.

No skid marks. Not one sign that they had made any effort to reduce speed.

Guardrails now. No need for it to happen again. Look at them. Good strong barriers of reinforced steel . . .

"Come on, Hal, slow down." It was Brian, leaning up in the seat.

"Goddammit, look for yourself," Hal exploded defensively, pointing at the speedometer. "It's thirty and dropping."

"Thirty my ass."

They were going faster than thirty, and Hal knew it too. Broken speedometer? And how was it possible to "race" up this incline? He took his foot off the accelerator altogether and expected the jeep to respond with the sudden drag of diminishing power.

But it didn't.

"Hal, what in the hell . . . ?"

Hal was pumping the brake now as fast and as hard as he could, refusing to believe the lack of resistance, his boot making solid contact with the floorboard. Brakes gone?

"Christ . . ."

"What is it?"

"What do you think it is? Hang on!"

In the faint yellow light of the dash, he saw the speedometer still climbing, forty, forty-five, fifty . . .

His foot was off the accelerator.

In an effort to stem his rising panic, he looked ahead and saw, thank God, the first curve no place in sight, the narrow blacktop stretching straight ahead before them. At least he had about a half mile more to try to bring the jeep under control. Brian was sitting sideways in the seat now, one arm propped on the dash, his face reflecting more than mere tension.

"The brakes, Hal," he shouted. "For God's sake, put on—"

87

"What do you think I'm trying to do?" Hal shouted back, his right foot now in perpetual motion, pumping up and down, nothing happening except the speedometer still rising. Fifty-three, fifty-five, sixty . . .

"Turn off the ignition," Brian ordered, his voice scarcely recognizable.

But Hal was afraid to take his hands off the wheel. The jeep was vibrating badly now, a curious internal shuddering, as though it too were objecting to the duress of its own speed.

Suddenly Brian reached over and flipped off the ignition. *The motor was still running.* Hal could feel it beneath the hood.

"What in the . . . ? Get ready to jump," Brian cried.

"Jump?" Was the man insane? At this speed?

"Don't move," Hal ordered, still wrestling the wheel, trying now to push the gears into reverse. Of course he'd strip hell out of them, if it worked. But he had no choice.

And neither did the gears. They growled. He smelled smoke, but nothing altered their speed or the one-eyed beam of light bouncing crazily about the road ahead, which still stretched before them in one straight black shimmering line.

No! Too much was wrong. The curve was near. He knew it. He'd driven the road too many times before. The straight expanse was all behind them now. Memory and instinct told him the first curve should be straight ahead.

Then where in the hell was it?

"Hang on!" Hal shouted, prepared to turn the jeep, now registering sixty mph, into the sheer rock wall on his left if necessary.

"What are you—"

"Hang on!" Hal cried, and hesitated a moment longer. He didn't know what it was that was stretching before him, imitating the road. An optical illusion? Something to do with the one headlight? Whatever . . . The fact that there appeared to be a road now where none existed would have to be dealt with later. And if there was no curve where memory told him there should be a curve, then they would crash at sixty-five mph into a solid rock wall.

The black needle was bouncing about in the vicinity of seventy now.

"Hal . . . ?"

With all his strength, he gripped the steering wheel and jerked it sharply to the left. As he lowered his head against the inevitable crash, he saw what appeared to be a blinding white light. When he least expected it, his right foot, still pumping the brakes, felt resistance, the brakes catching and holding, the scream of tires laying down rubber, both men hurled forward in collision with the windshield, a shattering of glass, a mysterious roar, as though they were in a wind tunnel. Then silence. . . .

Hal heard a wheel spinning somewhere, but at first could not readily move from his sprawled position over the steering wheel.

"Brian?"

No answer.

Something was beginning to throb in his chest, and slowly he eased himself back off the wheel. Broken ribs? No, just bruised, though his neck hurt like hell.

"Brian?"

He started to reach across, then changed his mind. Beyond the shattered windshield to the right, he saw . . . nothing. A black abyss—meaning a portion of the jeep was on the road, but at least one wheel, the right front, was dangling in space.

Then Brian stirred, groaned. One arm lifted.

"Hold still!" Hal ordered. "Dammit. Hold still."

"What . . . ?"

"You're all right," Hal soothed. "Just don't move until I . . ."

Until he what? Got out of the jeep and left Brian's weight to send the jeep toppling onto the rocks far below?

"What is . . . ? I'm bleeding."

"Cuts," Hal said. "Give me a minute."

From where he sat behind the wheel, he looked out of his side window. He'd been right. If he'd turned five seconds earlier, he would have been more right. They were in the curve, at least part in.

He leaned carefully up. The jeep swayed. *Freeze!* Why had the road appeared to stretch straight ahead? Someone traveling here for the first time would have . . .

No skid marks. They had left not a trace of skid.

"Hal, come on, I have to move. I'm bleeding all over the—"

"Okay, just a minute." Again he tried carefully to lean forward. Three wheels on, one off, was his estimate. All right. They were alive, they had that in their favor. It was just a matter of . . .

"Brian, I want you to . . ." *What?* " . . . ease over, and I mean *ease,* you hear?" With one hand on his own door handle, Hal extended the other toward Brian. The jeep shifted again.

"Wait!" Hal shouted. "Freeze!"

Caught in a half-turn, Brian froze, his face toward Hal for the first time. *God!* Blood everywhere, dripping down his nose into his mouth . . .

For a moment they stared at each other.

"I think we have one wheel off—"

"Christ!"

"Hold on. What I want you to do is to try to ease over, as close as you can get . . ."

"Now?"

Hal nodded. Slowly he leaned back, locating as much weight as possible on the left side of the jeep. Brian was now easing up in the seat, blood dripping onto his hands. The jeep seemed to be holding steady.

"Come on," Hal urged, reaching behind for the door handle. "Okay, we're going to move together," he whispered, as though to raise his voice would cause a dangerous imbalance. "I'm going out the door, and you're going to slip behind the wheel. Can you do it?"

Brian nodded. Lord, he looked terrible, blood coursing down over both eyes. Scalp wounds, most likely. Had a way of bleeding like hell.

Slowly, carefully, with held breath, Hal eased his door open, an inch at a time, filling the cavity with his own body, angling over, all the time keeping a close eye on Brian, who was following after him.

89

One leg out. And down. Solid ground. Thank God. "Come on, we're going to be okay, Brian. Take the wheel now and . . ."

As Brian reached up, the right-front side of the jeep sank lower. "Easy," Hal warned. "Don't turn the wheel, just use it for . . ."

Hal freed his other leg, yet clung, monkey fashion, to the side of the jeep, using his full body weight for ballast, softly urging Brian, "Come on. We're about there. . . ."

A moment later, as Brian half-fell through the door, Hal jumped free. The front of the jeep slid down another several feet, then stopped, perched precariously half on, half off the side of the mountain.

"We did it!" He grinned and looked down on Brian where he lay beside the road. "Here, let me take a look," he said, kneeling beside him, gingerly pushing aside the blood-soaked hair where it lay plastered to his forehead. He looked back into the jeep for material of any sort, then stood up and stripped off his shirt. Brian objected, "I'm all right, really. Just cuts . . ."

Hal paid no attention and ripped the back of the shirt into strips and squatted again, dabbing gently until he found the source of bleeding.

"Lie still, damm it," he muttered as Brian tried to twist away from him.

"Is the jeep . . . ?"

"I don't know. I'll look in a minute." As he explored the blood-soaked hair, he finally found it, one major laceration directly above Brian's forehead.

"Jesus, that hurts."

"Sorry, old buddy. Good thing you got a hard head. You're not dizzy or anything, are you?"

"I said I was fine. Let's just get the hell out of here."

As Brian pulled himself to a sitting position, Hal ordered, "Here, put your hand right here. Hold it tight. It may stop the bleeding."

He folded the shirt into several thicknesses, flattened it over the general area of the laceration, then placed Brian's hand atop it.

Shivering, he reached into the jeep for his windbreaker and slipped it on over his bare chest. His hands were sticky with Brian's blood. A few stitches from Mike, though, and he'd be fine.

"All right," he commanded. "You just sit there and let me take a look . . ."

Making certain that he did not touch the jeep, he eased down onto the shoulder and around the hood. Cold as hell. Wind picking up. Yes, there it was as he had suspected, one wheel hanging off, the jeep angled into the crushed guardrail.

Dear God, thank you for the guardrail. Without it, they would have . . .

"Hal!"

He stared a moment longer at the free-floating wheel. If the guardrail held, it might not be too difficult to ease the jeep back onto . . .

"Hal? Where are you? Someone's coming."

He looked up, surprised, into the darkness, altered only by the dim yellow spill of dash light coming through the open door. Quickly he pulled himself back up to the road and saw Brian, still seated, his hand clamped atop his head, the other pointing down the road, where some distance below, Hal saw two faint eyes of headlights.

Who could it be? Who cared? It was help, and they could use some.

For several moments both men watched the car as it progressed to the first turn. Sometimes it disappeared from sight altogether, following the contours of the earth, only to reappear, heading straight for them.

"Diesel," Brian muttered. "Listen . . ."

Hal nodded. It was a big car, the headlights on bright, blinding them, drawing nearer. Someone lost?

"Sit still," Hal ordered, stepping up onto the road.

As the chugging grew louder, Hal drew his windbreaker together and zipped it. He lifted one hand to his eyes in protection against the overpowering headlights, which now blinked twice, once to normal, then back to bright. Apparently the driver had seen them.

He heard the car break speed, still wondering: *Who?* This road led to only one place. Tomis.

"Can you see who . . . ?"

"Not yet." No choice now but to close his eyes against the glare of headlights, and it was while his eyes were closed that he heard the car as it began to brake, and smelled diesel fumes and heard the chugging vibrations of the powerful engine as it was brought to a halt.

Quickly Hal stepped to one side out of the glare of lights and saw a sleek black Olds Regency Ninety-Eight and heard the whir of an electric window.

"You're in trouble," a man's voice shouted over the noisy engine, a peculiar statement of fact more than a question.

Hal drew close to the window and bent over. "I'm afraid so. I was wondering if . . ."

"Of course."

As the man switched off the engine, Hal stepped back from the car. "My friend here is injured, though I don't think it's serious."

"What happened?"

In the residual spill of lights from the dash and headlights, Hal saw a tall lean man in a dark business suit step out. He appeared to be about sixty, was tieless, the top two buttons of his shirt undone. There seemed to be something wrong with his left coat sleeve; it hung awkwardly down, obscuring his hand, as though the sleeve were too long, or . . .

"We tangled with the guardrailing, I'm afraid," Hal joked, trying to lighten the tension. "I don't know. Do you have a rope? Maybe if we could attach . . ."

But clearly the man wasn't listening, and now entered the glare of his own headlights and stooped down before Brian. "Here, let me take a look," he offered kindly. "I've had some medical training."

Hal looked down where the examination was taking place and in the direct glare of headlights saw . . . Good grief! The man had no left hand. No wonder the coat sleeve had . . . Hal stepped closer, making eye contact with Brian, who obviously had seen the lack as well, the withered, slightly pink

91

stump which the man was wielding as expertly as though there were a hand attached, using it to push back Brian's blood-soaked hair.

"Glass," the man said. "One deep laceration, three smaller ones that I can see. You've got some slivers that should come out."

Without missing a beat, he reached into his inside pocket and withdrew a clean white handkerchief and wiped the blood off his stump. "Will it drive?" he asked, looking up at Hal, referring to the jeep.

"Uh, yes . . . no . . . I don't know. The brakes were acting up," Hal stammered, still fascinated by the withered stump and the man's expert manipulation of it.

"Then may I suggest that we leave it?" the gentleman said, rising. "I assume we're all going in the same direction. Tomis. I'd be happy to . . ."

Hal concurred, and belatedly offered his hand. "Kitchens," he said, "Hal Kitchens. And the one bleeding over there is Brian Sawyer."

The man nodded, still wiping his stump, and extended his right hand. "I'm Frank Quinton," he said cordially. "Come on, now, let's get your friend to a doctor. I assume there is one in Tomis? . . ."

Quinton? Frank Quinton? Century Mining Corporation? The man he'd waited for all day in Durango? The enemy himself?

Hal did well to nod.

9

Nothing in the world more beautiful, Sarah thought as she stood on her back porch at seven in the morning, looking first toward the high snow-spotted peaks which ringed Tomis' plateau, then down to the still-sleeping town, smoke curling out of Inez's chimney, one or two smoke trails farther on down the street.

She lifted her face to the perfume of early-morning air and smelled the scent of pine, wildflowers growing nearby. Quiet. So quiet.

With her foot she nudged the carton forward, half-filled with well-worn Golden Books, one dog-eared set of a children's encyclopedia. *Our Magic World,* read the cover on top.

Well, Mina would appreciate them for the "Tomis Library," and Vicky wouldn't miss them, although last night, refreshed from her nap on Mike's shoulder, she and Sarah had spent the evening hours waiting for Hal by going through the books, and then with typical childish perversity, Vicky had wanted to keep them all. Now Sarah sat awkwardly on the three-legged stool, ready to sort through this last carton before she handed them over to Mina.

Hal. . . . The sweetness of the morning was made sweeter by a faint surge of thanksgiving. It could have been so dangerous. And poor Brian. Mike had worked past midnight stitching him up.

Faulty brakes, according to Hal, though he'd not said much more. He'd seemed more concerned with getting Mr. Quinton settled, had even routed Polly Whiteside out of bed at midnight and had talked her into opening one of her guest rooms. A widow from Chicago who had thrown in the towel after three muggings, Polly had arrived at Tomis two summers ago, had clipped a few of her dead husband's coupons, and had built a lovely mock-Victorian house on the west end of Main Street and opened five guest rooms to the summer trade on a first-come, first-served basis.

Reluctantly—Polly had claimed nothing was ready for the season—she had taken in Mr. Quinton, and Hal himself had guided the big black Olds around the boulder in the middle of the street and had waited to see that Mr. Quinton was comfortably settled.

They were to meet and talk sometime this morning, but Sarah was certain they both would sleep late. He'd seemed nice enough, Quinton had, quiet. No left hand. Wonder what . . .?

To work, she ordered herself. She wanted to get these books to Mina first thing, before Vicky woke up. Then she had a load of wash to do. Maybe she could get Hal to hang them up for her. She didn't like to go up to the garden anymore.

Garden! What garden? Everything had been destroyed by the progress of the boulder. Hal had restored the clothesline before he had gone into Durango. For the rest of it—the lawn furniture, the garden plot neatly laid out for spring planting, a few early-blooming flowers—it looked as though a bulldozer had passed through at top speed.

Sarah pushed open the screen door and half-dragged, half-carried Vicky's red wagon to the bottom of the steps. As she walked, she called the roll for Tomis. Across the way was Tom Marshall's store, then the new embankment for Runaway Creek . . . . Poor Donna. Then there was the Billingslys' house, a nice older couple, he a retired CPA, she a wizard with African violets. Good Methodists, they ached for a small church. No one else shared their ache.

Next were the Charters, then Ned Wilson's Hot Tub Emporium, and across the way was Callie Watkins' hardware, and then the Hillses' "new-old drug store," and down the way was Mike and Donna's pretty house of Swiss Alpine design, "Heidi's House," Donna called it with just a hint of derision.

And back on Sarah's side was Cobb's Laundromat—during the summer months one of the most popular places in Tomis—and next to Cobb's, the Allegros' Treasure House, a gift shop where Ellen Allegro could display her moderately good mountain landscapes and Jason could exhibit his really excellent metalwork sculptures.

Next was Rene and Jerry Hackett's house, Rene's now. Poor Lucy . . .

Next to them were the Drivers, with three children, and the O'Connells, with five, all faltering Catholics in every area except bed, and the Lewises with two children. "Kiddie Row," they called this part of Main Street. And beyond the Lewis house, the second break for Runaway Creek, where it metamorphosed from underground to surface. And then there was Mina's place, looking like a doll's house.

Everything that Mina owned seemed to shine brighter than anyone else's.

94

Sarah stopped to rest her arm from its backward angle pulling the wagon and looked admiringly across at Mina Murdoch's. It would qualify for the cover of *Better Homes and Gardens,* the archetypal mountain cottage, an antique spinning wheel, a *real* antique gracing the front porch, its tray filled with red geraniums which seemed more vivid than anyone else's. The white lace curtains seemed whiter, the lace finer, the steps brushed cleaner, the two green wicker chairs greener.

Coming, Mina, she thought eagerly, lifting the wheels of the wagon over a bad spot in the road. Is tea on? She hoped so. Somehow Mina always made her feel less mediocre, less accidental, less mortal.

She pulled the wagon to one side near the bottom step, placed her hands near the small of her back in an attempt to stretch a kink out of her spine, and for her efforts received a good solid kick from the infant inside.

"Mina?"

As she started slowly up the stairs, she sent her voice ahead, a little surprised that Mina hadn't seen her yet and come out in greeting. She generally took her breakfast tea on the small table in the front room by the window.

"Mina? You there?" Sarah called softly, seeing the front door pushed to, but not completely closed. Of course she was there. Where else would she be? Well, she could be out walking. . . .

"Mina?"

She stared at the partially open door and briefly debated whether she should knock or just go in. Knocking seemed so formal, and how many times had Mina marched intrepidly up Sarah's gravel path, gained the porch, and announced herself in the living room?

Slowly she pushed open the door, just wide enough to peer around the corner into the shadowy interior, no lights burning. From where she stood, she saw the lovely rose velvet settee, another antique, dark mahogany furniture, the eggshell-colored walls covered with lithographs from her travels.

Sarah stepped halfway through the door and started to call again, when suddenly she heard voices, very quiet, more than one, male voices, or so she thought, coming from . . .

She glanced toward the heavy rose velvet drapes which separated the living room from Mina's bedroom. Sarah had never seen the bedroom, had had no cause to see it. Her visits to Mina always took place either on the porch, or in this room, or in Mina's broad sunny kitchen through that door.

But she had always assumed the bedroom was behind those heavy drapes, and now she was certain that Mina was in there—with someone else . . . several someones.

Hell, what should she do now? Who in Tomis, what man or men, would be up at this hour, and what business would take them into Mina's bedroom?

For a moment she clung to the door while the debate raged. Advance? Retreat? Call out and let them know she was there? Step aside and knock loudly, or proceed to where the drapes had been partially drawn and see for herself?

Acknowledging and dismissing her role as a nosy, prying bitch, she moved silently across the room, her steps padded by the soft Oriental carpet beneath her feet.

Too late to retreat, and not really wanting to anyway, Sarah stopped less than two feet from the drapes and angled her vision through the inch-wide crack and saw . . .

Candlelight? It was dark except for a flickering pale glow which seemed to emanate from the floor. A candle, yes. Several candles.

Peering closer, she blinked in an effort to clear her eyes and saw two of the boys that Inez had brought up from Durango, and from the sound of male voices coming from beyond her range of vision, she assumed that the other two were here as well, concealed behind the drapes. And seated cross-legged on the floor in a dark flowing robe, her eyes closed, head lifted, was . . .

Mina?

Sarah held perfectly still, failing even to breathe for a few seconds. When she did at last draw breath, she smelled something pungent, sweet, sharp, like incense or . . .

Transfixed by the unorthodox scene, yet wholly baffled, she tried to make words out of the hum of voices. But it was impossible. All she heard was the deeper register of the boys, punctuated now and then by Mina's musical voice.

Suddenly embarrassed, she stepped back in an attempt to execute a speedy exit, and unfortunately collided with a low table adorned with a pot of African violets.

The pot slid, the table scraped, the hum of voices fell silent. "Who's there?" she heard Mina call out.

Quickly, though not as nimbly as she might have wished, Sarah hurried back to the front door. In a full and only slightly quavering voice she called out, "It's me, Mina. Sarah. I've brought you some books." As she talked, she slipped out of the door as though she'd just arrived.

Too much time passed before Mina answered, confirming Sarah's suspicions that she'd interrupted something. What?

The voice came at last, less musical than usual. "Just a minute, Sarah."

While she waited, Sarah turned away and stared, unseeing, at the antique spinning wheel filled with bright red geraniums. Across the street she saw Doris O'Connell emerge from her house with a broom and start sweeping her front steps. Sarah waved. Doris waved back. From somewhere she smelled the good odor of coffee brewing. Tomis was beginning to stir.

Hurriedly she glanced back toward Mina's front door, thinking she'd heard a step. Damn! How embarrassing! Why had she come so early? And why hadn't she knocked? And what in the hell was going on in . . .?

Suddenly the door opened and one of the Mexican boys appeared.

"*Buenos días, señora,*" he muttered, and walked directly past her, his hands shoved into his jeans pockets, his shoulders lifted against the morning chill.

A moment later two others emerged, and said nothing, did not acknowledge her in any way. One jumped from the porch, ignoring the three steps altogether; the other bounced jauntily down, and both ran to catch up with the one in the lead. Amazing, how identical they are, Sarah mused, same physique, same costume of worn blue jeans and white T-shirts, same long black hair, same . . .

A sudden noise at the door drew her attention back, and there stood number four, although this one looked a bit worse for wear. He appeared to cling to the doorframe for a minute. His eyes looked heavy, as though he were sleepy or ill, and his T-shirt appeared twisted, one side hitched up, revealing a smooth flat abdomen.

Finally he pushed away from the support of the door and stumbled past her. He was barefoot. Baffled, she watched him down the steps, saw him almost collide with her wagon of books. He appeared drunk, or stoned.

She might have watched them all the way up Main Street except for the pronounced feeling of eyes upon her, this time coming from the door behind her. She looked over her shoulder and saw Mina, though it was a Mina she'd never seen before, that plump aging face without life or expression, a cold look of nonrecognition.

Before such a look, Sarah foundered. She'd seen such expressions before on strangers' faces in Boston, zombielike, transfixed.

"I'm . . . sorry," Sarah murmured, moving away from the expression. "I . . . obviously came too early. Books . . ." She smiled idiotically, pointing toward the red wagon on the sidewalk. "I'll come back later."

She had taken two steps down toward the sidewalk when the old, familiar Mina returned in the shape of that melodious voice, all warmth and hospitality and now just a tinge of apology.

"Sarah Kitchens! Get yourself back up here. What a lovely early-morning surprise. Come on! Right now!"

Still hesitating, Sarah glanced down the street. The boys were gone. "I . . . didn't mean to . . . interrupt . . ."

"You interrupted nothing," Mina said with mock sternness, stepping all the way out onto her porch, grasping the long velour robe about her. "Now, come on in," she insisted hospitably, "and leave the books. We'll get them later. And how typically thoughtful of you to answer my plea so readily."

There was no resisting her, and Sarah really didn't want to. It was just . . .

"Come!" Mina ordered, walking all the way to the steps and grasping Sarah's arm as though to drag her bodily back into the house. "I'll put on the teakettle, then you must tell me exactly what happened last night. The boys said there had been an accident of some sort, Hal and Brian, I believe they said. Oh, do tell me it wasn't serious, but of course it wasn't, or you wouldn't be out and about so early. It's lovely, isn't it, hearing a spooky tale when one already knows the conclusion."

Throwing resistance to the wind, Sarah walked with her back across the porch and into the living room. The heavy drapes which led into the back room were pulled tight now, she noticed, though there still was a peculiar odor in the air, mingling with the faint scent of burned-out candles.

"Come on into the kitchen," Mina urged, grasping Sarah's arm with fingers which felt like ice. "I don't know about you, but tea and toast would hit the spot, don't you think?

"I know what you're doing," she added in singsong fashion as she filled the teakettle with water. "You're wearing yourself out searching for an explanation—"

"No, not—"

"Yes!" Mina laughed, placing pretty china teacups and saucers on the table, leaning close, her face flushed. "All right, cross your heart and hope to die, stick a needle in your eye," she chanted playfully. "I'll confess my secret if you'll make it your secret as well."

Not certain that she wanted to hear the confession, Sarah protested, laughing, "I don't know what you're talking about, Mina, Now, about last night, there *was* an accident, not serious, but it—"

"I have a weakness," Mina interrupted, lifting her eyes heavenward, her brown-spotted hands clasped upon her breasts. "Oh, several, really." She giggled. "But only one that we need to talk about now."

"Mina, please, it isn't—"

"I adore good grass," she said quietly. "You know, pot, marijuana, whatever they're calling it now. I really do. I've smoked it off and on for over thirty years, long before it was fashionable or rebellious to do so, in those early days when the only place you could get it was from a black jazz musician. There isn't much in this world that can't be solved in a dark room with good music and a reefer."

Stunned, though amused, Sarah ducked her head to hide a smile. It hadn't been incense at all. How could she have forgotten the odor so easily in four years? A stoned schoolmistress. Terrific! Again she almost laughed.

"I saw the boys," Mina went on, the need to "confess" apparently strong within her, "passing a joint the other night behind the restaurant. We struck a bargain," she concluded brightly. "I'll teach them English this summer if now and then they'll share their stash with me. Of course, we have to do it early, before they go to work."

The whistling teakettle drew her back to the stove and left Sarah feeling sheepish. Mystery solved. Big deal!

"Here you are." Mina smiled, placing a steaming cup of tea before her. "You won't tell, will you? I mean, there are a few in Tomis who might not understand . . ."

Relieved, Sarah laughed outright. "No, I won't tell, and I certainly won't tell Hal, because he may feel compelled to join your early-morning tutorials. He studied for most of his bar examinations under the unique influence of Colombian Gold." She felt herself beginning to relax after her earlier alarm. This was the old Mina, intelligent, charming, distracting.

"Now, what are we going to do about this mining threat?" Mina pronounced broadly, draining her teacup, refilling it, and gesturing to Sarah to help herself.

Taken slightly off-guard by the direct and unanswerable question, Sarah shook her head and stirred a spoonful of sugar into her tea. "I haven't had a chance to talk to Hal yet. I don't know what he found out in—"

"I'm afraid there's not going to be any stopping them," Mina interrupted. "Inez told me that her uncle said the first trailers would be arriving in a day or two to house the survey crews. The heavy machinery will arrive shortly thereafter. First ground is to be broken in three days."

Three days! Sarah hadn't heard that, and she was certain that Hal hadn't either. She bowed her head and caught a partial reflection of her face in the shimmering tea. It was like hearing the date of an invasion. "Oh, Mina . . ." she mourned, and could not articulate her specific grief.

Suddenly the early-morning quiet was shattered by a familiar sound, the jackhammers at work again, chipping away on the boulder, reminding her of hazards all around, the mysterious light which she and Mike had seen atop Mt. Victor, Hal's peculiar reticence about his trip to Durango, Vicky's new lethargy, not one bright spot on her mental horizon regardless where she looked.

Mina's smile faded. "The mining people," she grumbled, stirring her tea, though she'd put nothing in it. "How nice it would be if the earth just swallowed them all up."

A bit excessive, that. Sarah smiled. But then, why not?

"Has Copper come home yet?" Mina asked, reaching behind to the counter and withdrawing a pack of cigarettes. Strange. Sarah had never seen her smoke before.

"No," Sarah replied, watching the flame of the match as it caught on the cigarette. "I didn't know you smoked."

"I don't generally." Mina shrugged. "I just keep them around in case I feel the urge. Most spinsters are known for their lack of bad habits. But what are we but our bad habits? They make us feel alive, don't they?"

A bit nonplussed by how little she knew of the woman she thought she knew intimately, Sarah nibbled on a corner of her toast and thought she really should be getting home. "Brian and Hal had a close call last night," she said, standing. "Brakes failed on the first curve."

"Lord have mercy," Mina gasped sympathetically, stopping at the top of the stairs. "Are they all right?"

Sarah nodded. "Thanks to the guardrail. Brian went through the windshield. A scalp cut. Mike patched him up. They had to leave the jeep."

"And Jerry Hackett gone," Mina mourned, as though somehow the two incidents were connected. "I must go and see Rene today. I'm sure you know she's going to need all the help we can give her. That slut of a daughter isn't going to help her any."

Shocked by the designation, Sarah looked up, wondering if she'd heard correctly. But Mina rushed past her, spying the carton of books, leaving a musical trail of, "Oh, how lovely! What a marvelous time the children will have with these. You are too generous, Sarah. What about Vicky? And our little friend in there who has yet to emerge?"

Quite unexpectedly she reached out and grasped Sarah's stomach. "Do you suppose he's lost his tail yet?" she whispered, grinning, her teeth up close in the brightness of morning a hideous yellow, her breath no better, her face a network of fine lines.

Embarrassed and a little put off, Sarah tried to move away. But Mina held her fast, slipping one arm around Sarah's waist, the other hand encircling the globe of her stomach in an intimate gesture. "That was why I was always afraid to have a child, you see," she whispered, still holding Sarah fast. "I just knew I would give birth to something . . . hideous—a serpent, something which faltered coming up the ladder of evolution."

Suddenly frightened, Sarah protested, "No," and pulled away.

"Are you all right, my dear?" Mina inquired, concerned. "I meant nothing by it. Surely you . . ."

Across the street, two of the O'Connell children called out, "G'morning, Miss Murdoch, Mrs. Kitchens."

Still alarmed, Sarah backed away, unable to respond. Mina returned the greeting with a cheery "Good morning, children. Don't forget, ten A.M. History and geography." She looked back toward Sarah. "Please, my dear. Are you sure . . .?"

"I'm fine," Sarah said quickly. "I must go now. Hal . . ."

"Of course, and how can I ever thank you for the books. They will be put to good use, I promise."

As Sarah turned away, she closed her eyes briefly, then opened them to chart the hazardous footing. *A serpent, something which faltered coming up the ladder of evolution.*

Do you suppose he's lost his tail yet?

Nerves on edge. Something was gaining momentum. The fetus inside her was going crazy, thumping one side of her womb, then the other.

While she was still several yards away from the boulder, she crossed over to the sidewalk which led in front of the restaurant. Damn! She'd forgotten to stop at Tom Marshall's. Well, later. She'd come back with Vicky. Vicky always enjoyed the big glass jar filled with penny candy.

For now all she wanted was to go home.

As she stepped up onto the sidewalk in front of the restaurant, the noise was deafening. She could feel the vibrations beneath her feet. To her right, she saw movement behind one of the red checkered curtains of the restaurant.

She looked in that direction, ready to wave at Inez. But it wasn't Inez. The boys were peering at her through the window. There were three of them, their black eyes following her, the lower part of their faces obscured behind the café curtains.

She started to wave, then changed her mind and hurried around the corner of the restaurant. Although she refused to look, she knew they were still watching her, through the side window now, as though they were tracking her.

She bent into the incline.

Sometimes I wonder if the human mind was really made for thinking.

Hal, please be awake, she prayed, and tried to run the rest of the way, but the gravitational pull of the steep incline wouldn't let her. With each step forward, her legs grew heavier, her body more cumbersome.

"Hal!" she called out, in need of help, and received no answer.

10

From her crow's-nest bedroom—Daddy always said she could look down on the whole world—Lucy Hackett peered out of her window into the street below and saw Sarah Kitchens leaving the bitch Murdoch's house.

She liked Mrs. Kitchens. She was kind and always talked to Lucy like she was a human being. As for everyone else in this miserable town, including the fucking bitch across the way . . .

Shivering, Lucy dropped the curtain and scrambled back beneath the covers, listening. He should have been here by now. Eight-thirty, she'd said, knowing her mother would be safely gone by now. And he'd agreed. Well, she couldn't wait all morning.

Above the bed on the opposite wall, John Travolta smiled down on her. And next to him was a huge poster of Captain Kangaroo. But it hurt too much to look at Captain Kangaroo, so she focused on John Travolta for a moment. Then she leaned over the side of her bed, wiggled her hand in between the mattress and the springs, and withdrew a small metal tin of Bull Durham Tobacco. No Bull Durham now—it contained four joints which Carlos had given her in exchange for letting him feel her breasts the day Daddy had been buried.

She sat up in the middle of the bed, legs crossed, and carefully lit one, thinking as how she'd fry bacon later to get rid of the smell. Funny taste for grass. She inhaled deeply and held it, her lungs burning. She swallowed hard and coughed until her eyes watered and held the joint the way she'd seen them hold it.

Nothing! No big deal. She tried again, another heavy drag. Hold it. Shit, it burned like hell. But she swallowed hard and listened carefully, thinking she'd heard something downstairs.

What if her mother had forgotten something and come back? Quickly she licked her fingers and pinched the end of the joint, put it back in the tin, and stuck it under the mattress. Her mother would skin her alive if . . .

"Mom? That you?"

Still seated in the middle of her bed, she waved her hands frantically about, trying to disperse the lingering smoke. The room seemed unsteady.

"Mom?" She reached in the opposite direction toward her dresser and snagged a spray bottle of Charlie, knocking several other bottles over in the process.

Over the hiss of the spray, she listened. Crap! What if Carlos had been here? What if they had been getting it on pretty good . . . ?

"Mom? Is it you?"

As the rooms below gave back silence, Lucy's finger froze on the spray top. She closed her eyes, the better to listen, and felt like she was floating.

No one? Maybe she'd better check to make sure. No! She was getting as freaked out as her mother.

I tell you, Jerry, he comes down at night, that Mountain Man. I've seen him. He passes right by the bedroom window. It isn't safe for Lucy . . .

Slowly she drew a deep breath and tried to steady the world, and relaxed back into the bed.

Look, Princess, wanna see Captain Kangaroo?

Seated on her father's lap, the brownish-pink very smooth head emerging through his zipper . . .

Shhhh! Don't tell your mother—Captain Kangaroo's cold, Princess. Let him in. He's free-e-e-ezing . . .

She lay perfectly still in the middle of the bed, not bothering to wipe away the tears. Captain Kangaroo had made her feel so-o-o-o good. Suddenly she moaned.

Before Daddy had died, she'd almost talked him into leaving Tomis and going back to Omaha. The night before he'd died, after the light had gone out in her mother's bedroom, he'd come up to Lucy's room to play Captain Kangaroo, and he'd promised her then that if he could make a killing this summer, and he thought he could, then maybe, just maybe, they'd go back to Omaha for the winter.

Slowly she raised up. Now they'd never leave. Her mother had insisted that she and Lucy could run the filling station.

Like hell!

She glanced at the clock on her dresser. Five till nine. Hal's Kitchen. That's where Carlos was. She was off the bed, shivering slightly in her baby-doll nightgown, moving toward the door, where she saw three doorknobs, the watermelon wallpaper swimming in liquid white and red and green on either side of the wall.

· What in the . . . ? Quickly she reached out for the support of her desk. Steady! It was that shit he'd given her to smoke. He didn't have to do that. She had picked him special out of all four as being the best one to play Captain Kangaroo with. He didn't have to . . .

A moment later she had steadied herself against the desk. She looked over her shoulder toward the door. One doorknob. The big fat melons were anchored securely in mindless repetition, their crawly vines reaching over into the next panel, and the next, and the next. . . .

Moving more slowly now—he wouldn't go away—she gained the door and opened it and started down the steps in a sedate manner.

"Carlos?"

Midway down the steps, she called ahead, her eyes focused on the kitchen and the closed back door. Bending over, she saw a figure through the glass. The door was unlocked. Why didn't he just come in?

"Carlos? It's open. Come on . . ."

She eased down another step, still keeping her eyes on the glass in the back door. Someone was standing there just out of sight. She could see a shadow.

"Carlos, come on . . ."

She flung open the back door, expecting to see him. But there was no one there. Shivering, she looked to the right of the porch, thinking maybe he was playing a trick on her. He was the nicest of the four, laughing all the time, making jokes . . .

"Carlos?"

She heard something. With one hand still on the screen door, she looked out over the backyard, past Daddy's toolshed, the empty drums in which he was going to plant strawberries this summer. Over there was something, behind the drums, about thirty feet away.

"Carlos?" It *was*, but what in the hell was he doing over there? Maybe he had seen someone and decided to hide.

She shivered. It was kind of exciting, kind of like doing something real wrong, not just playing Captain Kangaroo.

Suddenly she stepped back onto the porch and spied Daddy's rain slicker hanging on a nail. She slipped into the cold rubber fabric and wrapped the excess around her, her arms lost in the oversized sleeves. There! At least she was covered.

Barefoot, she went out of the door and down the steps and looked carefully both to the right and to the left. No sign of Mrs. O'Connell or any of the kids. She did hear a distant refrain of a rock song on Terry O'Connell's transistor. But that went on all the time. Surely Carlos hadn't been freaked out by a radio.

She looked in the opposite direction, into the Allegros' backyard. Nothing but the junk pile of scrap metal that Jason used to make his "art." Art, my ass, Daddy had said.

Nothing there either. Then what in hell had spooked Carlos?

"Hey," she called out softly. "Who you hiding from? The coast is clear."

From where she stood in the middle of the yard, she could see his white T-shirt, the top of his head, but she couldn't see his arms. He looked like he'd fallen into a hole or . . .

"Carlos? What . . . are you doing? It's all clear. Come on, now, let's . . ."

She made her way slowly around the barrels, then stopped. She stood motionless, though her heart was beating too fast. She started to call his name again, but could not. He was visible from only the waist up, the lower portion of his body sunk in earth. And he was sinking lower, ever so slowly, as though the ground were sucking him in. His arms were . . . gone, caught in the press of earth. And his head was slack against his chest, though he looked up once at her with wide, distended, fearful eyes.

"*Cristo* . . ."

. . . was what she thought he said. Then the ground began to shift, and he slipped down to his chest and lifted his face once more, pleading, "*Dios* . . ."

Her first impulse was to run, but she couldn't do that, couldn't leave him. *Help him!* Help how? And what had happened? What . . . ? She stood rooted in horror and heard a soft sucking sound and saw his eyes close, one shriek clawing raw from his throat.

At last she rushed forward, grasped the neck of his shirt, and tried to pull him free—and up close saw blood forming in the corners of his mouth. As he slipped from her grasp, the shirt tore in her hands and she saw him in earth up to his chin now, like a bodiless head, his mouth open, though fast filling with mud, his eyes fixed on the sky, until they too were covered with earth, the soft moist dirt appearing liquid, shimmering, then growing hard again, solid. And quiet.

Lucy could not move. In paralyzing shock, she stared at the smooth still earth. "Car . . ."

For a moment the paralysis extended to her mind and nothing moved there, no knowledge of who she was, where she was, what she had witnessed. She'd suffered nightmares in the past. Then it was just a matter of waking herself up and hearing Mama bang the pots and pans about, and hearing Daddy cuss at the cold and the deep snow.

She dug her fingers into the palms of her hands until the nails bent back to the quick and hurt. The pain caused her mind to stir. But nothing else altered, not the solid earth or the hideous vision which had burned itself into her brain, the equally terrifying sucking sound, his face slipping from sight, then silence.

She blinked down at the solid earth, and shuddered so hard she bit her tongue. Then she fell to her knees and began to claw at the earth.

About a half-hour later she had dug down a little over a foot. Her fingers were bleeding. Her face was splattered with mud where she'd tried to wipe away the tears. And she had found . . . nothing.

She lifted her face to the sky.

"Daddy!" she screamed.

11

"Mr. Kitchens? I was told I might find you here."

Deep in thought, Hal looked up from stirring his coffee and saw first the amputated hand, the stump a pale pink edged in darker brown, as though the flesh had been imperfectly drawn over the wrist bone and sewn together.

No shame. In fact, the sleeve of the navy-blue cardigan had been pushed up to the elbow in a macabre display.

"Mr. Quinton," Hal said, easing his vision past the stump and on up to the man's face. "Please, sit down," he urged, his eyes struggling to stay on the man's gaunt face. In daylight he looked terrible, a yellowish pallor to his skin. "I . . . was going to let you sleep in for a while. It was a late night . . ."

Since Quinton was saying absolutely nothing, Hal talked on. "Would you like breakfast? You must be hungry. Inez makes the best *huevos rancheros* in the Southwest. You need an asbestos-lined stomach, however, but if you would care for . . ."

All the time he was talking, Quinton was drawing out the chair opposite him with complete ease and deliberation. He was a rather distinguished-looking man, actually, except he was bone-thin. Ill? Recovering . . . or succumbing?

"Yes." Quinton smiled pleasantly. "Eggs sound good. Shall I . . . ?"

"No, I will. Inez!" Hal shouted, sending his voice through into the large dining room, where he saw Inez at the cash register, putting in new tape.

Occasionally one of the Mexican boys would intersect his line of vision, carrying dirty dishes from the breakfast trade, setting up for lunch.

He saw Inez wave at him, indicating just a minute. "I trust you slept well," Hal asked.

"Very well." Quinton nodded and said nothing more.

Now, as he looked about at the back room of the restaurant, Hal saw him focus on the stack of invoices which were to have been Hal's morning work.

"My office, I'm afraid," Hal explained weakly. "I seem to do all the bookkeeping here. Of course, sometimes in summer we do need it for the overflow."

My God, why was he rambling on so? Obviously Quinton didn't give a damn what he used the back room for.

Now he saw the man lean back in his chair, cross his legs—tailored gray flannels—pale blue silk shirt beneath the dark blue cardigan. Still perfectly at ease.

Nervously Hal stacked the scattered invoices, mostly from the wholesale suppliers in Durango, and pushed the books aside. There would be time later . . .

"Ah, Inez." He smiled, motioning the woman to come in. "This is Mr. Frank Quinton. With very little effort I've talked him into sampling your *huevos rancheros*."

Beyond Quinton's shoulder, he saw Inez's normally cheery face cloud. "Little effort for you, maybe," she grumbled. "I'm shorthanded this morning. One of my boys failed to show."

"Please?" Hal smiled. "And a pot of fresh coffee would be nice."

Without a word, Inez left the doorway, and left as well a strong feeling of imposition.

"What happened out there?" Quinton asked at last, gesturing toward the street and the sounds of jackhammers, like a gigantic dentist's drill.

"A rock slide," Hal said, eager to end the awkward silence. "First time in four years. A man was killed."

"You can't blame us." Quinton smiled. "We've not done any blasting yet."

A curious comment. It had not occurred to Hal to blame them, which brought him back to the initial dilemma of this baffling meeting.

"Your wife seemed . . . upset this morning," Quinton said, moving rapidly from one baffling subject to another.

Unable to make the transition, Hal foundered. "My . . . wife?"

"Mrs. Whiteside directed me to your home," Quinton explained. He had not altered his position since he had sat down, a man of minimum movement. "I went up there first, thinking to find you. Your wife said you were here. She seemed upset."

"As I'm sure you noticed, she's . . . pregnant," Hal said vaguely. "About a month and a half to go. Our daughter has not been well . . ."

"I'm sorry."

One of the Mexican boys appeared at the door, tray in hand, bearing a

106

steaming coffeepot, cups, saucer, flatware, a paper place mat with red and green sombreros in each corner and "Hal's Kitchen" printed in bold red print across the front.

Outside there was a break in the jackhammers. In the new and heavy silence, Hal felt even more embarrassment. "We are hoping they can move the damn thing today," he said feebly. "Too large to be hauled off without first breaking it up."

Quinton nodded as if he knew all that, and for the first time made direct eye contact with Hal. "How's your friend this morning?" he asked. "I trust he was taken care of."

"Yes. Mike Dunne is a doctor. He's patched almost all of us up at one time or another. Superficial cuts, that's all. A couple of stitches . . ."

"What *did* happen? Last night. I should think you would be very familiar with the road."

"Last night . . ." Hal shrugged, wondering how long they would encircle the heart of the matter. "Brakes, I guess," he said vaguely, not wanting to complicate the already tense encounter with the nonsense of mirages and optical illusions. He would save those mysterious items for Roger Laing.

Where in the hell was he? Hal had spent half the night trying to call Evergreen and Roger Laing and had been unable to get a line through.

"Yes, brakes," he repeated. "That's all. Should have had them checked before we left." He laughed in a self-deprecating manner. "Broke the first rule of safety in mountain travel. Have brakes checked regularly." He paused, reached for the coffeepot, and filled his cup. "Unfortunately, it was the owner of Tomis' only service station who was killed in the rock slide."

"How long have you been here, Mr. Kitchens?" Quinton asked, shifting only long enough to recross his legs, his mutilated arm still prominently displayed.

"Four years, going on five," Hal replied. An innocent question. A time-passer.

"What brought you here?"

A bit more difficult, that. "There were six of us initially," Hal said, stirring sugar and cream into his coffee, struggling for a simple explanation. "We . . . wanted something else—better," he concluded ineptly.

"Better than what?"

"Than what we had."

"There wasn't anyone here when you came, was there?"

"No. Public land. We had to search like hell to find the platted deed at all. Eighteen-ninety-two was the only date we could come up with. Apparently there was a small settlement then, a silver camp, probably, or gold . . ."

"Silver."

Hal looked up, surprised by the certainty in the man's voice.

The Mexican was at the door again, this time carrying a fragrant platter of *huevos rancheros*, the eggs scarcely visible beneath Inez's hot sauce.

"There you go." Hal smiled. "Eat up, and I'll stand by with the fire extinguisher."

The poor attempt at humor was lost on everyone as the boy left immedi-

107

ately and Quinton angled the platter around with his stump, picked up the fork with his right hand, and commenced eating rather meticulously, mixing egg yolks with hot sauce, the pointed stump resting beside the platter as though to steady it.

For several moments nothing happened in the back room but the consumption of food. "If you'll excuse me . . ." Hal muttered, having no pressing errand, but embarrassed to be staring. He walked outside into the sunlight.

"Hey!" He saw Bobby O'Connell pedaling his bike down the street, trying to avoid the potholes. Fifteen, red-haired, freckled. Andrew Wyeth's *Young America.*

" 'Morning, Mr. Kitchens."

"Bobby, would you do me a favor?"

"Sure!"

"Would you go find Dr. Dunne for me? Tell him I'm waiting for him here. It's kind of important."

"Sure thing, but I think he's busy right now, though. My mom had to take Lucy Hackett over to see him. I was just on my way to get Mrs. Hackett . . ."

Hal stepped closer to the edge of the sidewalk. "What's the matter with Lucy?"

The boy did a quick gesture, encircling his fingers about his ear. "Mama found her digging a hole in the backyard. Really freaked out. Bad grass, if you ask me."

The boy pedaled away to the other side of the street, his bike wobbling as it encircled the boulder, his cheeks flushed with excitement and the nip in the air.

Bad grass! Mina Murdoch had tried to tell him a few months ago that the kids were getting it from somewhere. He'd not believed her. Where in hell would they get grass up here? Still, people *did* go into Durango, and kids went with them, and there were plenty of young people around in the summer, passing through, camping out . . .

"Hal, your man is waiting . . ."

He looked back toward the restaurant to see Inez calling to him.

"Thanks," he muttered, touching her arm in passing, "for everything."

"Who is he?" she asked, a clear look of censure on her dark features.

"He's with the mining corporation."

She held the screen door for him. "If I'd known that, I'd have seasoned his eggs with bug spray. Who bit off his hand?"

Hal smiled and said nothing, looked across the dining room into the small back room where Frank Quinton sat, statue-still, facing away from them.

"What happened to your other boy?" Hal asked, trying to give the impression of sharing her problems.

"You tell me," Inez snapped. "When I do lay my hands on him, I'll send him packing back to Durango. From what I can make out from the others, he had a date with Lucy Hackett. Can you imagine?"

Dr. Dunne's busy with Lucy Hackett. Bad grass, if you ask me.

Christ! Troubles, line up and take a number.

He hurried past the empty tables, keeping his eye on the erect head and

108

shoulders of Frank Quinton. "Shall I call out the fire brigade?" he quipped as he entered the room, spying the empty platter.

"They were very good," Quinton said without looking up. "Thank you. Now, what did you want to see me about, Mr. Kitchens?"

Hal took a deep swig of cold coffee. "I think you know," he said, deciding to match the man's mood and to hell with social amenities.

"Were you looking for me yesterday in Durango?"

"I was. What do you want here, Mr. Quinton?" Hal asked bluntly, all the backed-up problems beginning to push against him.

"Here? Nothing."

"What's going on up the mountain? We've heard rumors."

"Of what?"

"Mining exploration."

"No exploration, Mr. Kitchens. That was ten years ago."

"Then what?"

"Mining."

The word so flatly delivered brought the already strained conversation to a halt.

"Crested Butte," Hal muttered finally, thinking of the small Colorado town not too far away that had waged such a valiant war against a multinational mining corporation.

"Nothing compared to Mt. Victor." Quinton was caressing his stump now, his lean, spatulate fingers moving in a circle over the rough pink top. "Frankly, I was surprised to find you here," he added.

"Why?"

"I was here ten years ago, and it was wilderness."

"As I said, we only arrived . . ."

Quinton nodded. "And you've had no . . . trouble before the recent rock slide?"

"Trouble? I don't . . ."

"Do you realize, Mr. Kitchens, that you have built your little town on one of the major ley lines in the Northern Hemisphere?"

"A major . . . what?"

"A ley line, one of the most powerful I've ever seen."

"I'm . . . sorry, Mr. Quinton. I haven't the faintest idea what . . ."

"They crisscross the earth, parallel lines of great magnetic force, generally between one and two feet apart. But here in Tomis is the most powerful type, an aquastat, *two* sets of parallel lines, like two railway tracks running parallel."

As the words spilled out, Hal was aware that he was crouching, harboring his cup of cold coffee as though it were the only object in the room which made sense.

"How many times have you had to run new blacktop out there?" Quinton asked, angling his head toward the front door and the street beyond.

"Three. Four, counting this summer."

"And why do you think the rock slide stopped in the middle of the street? Why didn't it go on down the side of the mountain? The momentum was certainly great enough to carry it to the valley floor."

109

Hal gaped, sensing the man would answer his own question. And he did.

"It was stopped, Mr. Kitchens, by a powerful electromagnetic field, as though a giant hand had reached up . . ."

In a bizarre gesture, he held up his stump at the exact moment he said "gigantic hand." For a moment Hal saw him staring at his amputation as though seeing it for the first time and hating it. An expression crossed his face—Hal couldn't tell what—and then it was gone.

"Because of this, Mr. Kitchens, CMC has put off the development of Mt. Victor, on my recommendation. Now we have no choice. The world's supply of moly is limited. If we don't develop the mine, someone else will. I'm sure you can understand that."

"You make it sound as though it's a foregone conclusion, Mr. Quinton," he said.

"It is, I'm afraid. Crews could be coming in as early as the next day or two."

"We have no recourse?"

"I didn't say that. I'm sure you know all the avenues for litigation. You can tie us up, at most, for a year, maybe two."

"But in the end, it will do no good?"

"It never has. I'd be lying if I gave you false hope."

Somehow Hal sensed in the man a tone of apology.

"It will be the death of Tomis, you realize that, Mr. Quinton."

How calmly they were speaking of such matters.

"I do. It will be the death of Mt. Victor as well. Unfortunately, we have all the power, Mr. Kitchens, from the archaic mining laws to technology to professional lobbyists to corrupt and shortsighted politicians. They all play their parts on cue, and the result is a perfectly orchestrated rape of the land."

There was more than apology in his voice now. Something else. Disgust? Anger?

Hal pushed back in his chair. "Tell me precisely what it means, Quinton. I suspect you know everything. . . ."

For the first time, a hint of a smile crossed the skeletal face. "Not everything, though perhaps a bit too much," he said quietly. "By the end of summer, fall at the latest, we hope to be mining twenty-five thousand tons of ore daily. The ore will be crushed at the mine site on the northern slope of Mt. Victor and transported via a surface conveyor system to the tailing site at the base of the mountain. There the crushed ore will be processed, producing a molybdenum concentrate of eight pounds per ton. The remaining waste will be dumped into the valley stream."

Runaway Creek!

"Eventually the waste could bury more than a thousand acres of prime wilderness to a depth of at least three hundred and fifty feet."

Hal closed his eyes. He felt sick. Why didn't Inez come and remove the soiled platter?

"Other surface disturbances," Quinton went on in his well-modulated voice, "will include a large network of power lines and the construction of several roads. The power lines are already up. The second impact, of course, will be in personnel. At least three thousand construction workers have been

110

hired to build the mine and a trailer park will soon be under construction. . . ."

As the voice pursued him, Hal stood and walked slowly to the window and saw the three Mexican boys in close huddle in the clearing behind the restaurant.

There was nothing to fight against, dammit!

It was as though the man had verbally emasculated him. And all he felt now in the room was a massive wave of sympathy coming from the most unlikely source of all. Frank Quinton.

No recourse. Three thousand construction workers, the destruction of pristine watersheds, clean air, the dream over. . . .

"No!" Hal exploded, anger turning him about, where he saw Quinton still seated at the table. "No, I think we *will* fight you, Mr. Quinton," he repeated. "We may not win, but we'll give you one hell of a battle."

He had hoped to stir the man to some sort of rebuttal, get him on his feet, find some area of doubt or hesitancy.

Instead: "Good." Quinton smiled. "I was hoping that you would fight."

Baffled, Hal drew close to the table. "I . . . don't understand," he confessed, staring down into the man's noncommittal face.

Slowly Quinton stood, using his stump for upward leverage. "I do my job, Mr. Kitchens. I play my role. I appreciate it when others play theirs. I'm sure it will be a good fight, though neither of us will win it. Someone else will win, someone miles from here, someone we'll never see." With great care he eased his chair under the table. "If you don't mind, now I think I'll poke around your little town for a while. This has always been one of my favorite spots, even though I left my hand in the old man's mouth several years ago, a dire misunderstanding. . . ."

He was at the door now, walking slowly away, head down. He stopped and looked back. "Sometimes I wonder if our whole relationship with the world is based on a misunderstanding. We like to think we have a symbiotic relationship with the universe, but perhaps the universe has never heard of us."

"Quinton . . ."

But by the time Hal rallied, the man was gone. He sat slowly back down at the table, pushed aside the cup of cold coffee, and stared at the chair opposite him.

I left my hand in the old man's mouth.

What in hell had he meant by that?

He propped his elbows on the table and rested his head in his hands.

Ley lines, the most powerful in the Northern Hemisphere.

Shades of Roger Laing.

Call Roger. He could out-Quinton Quinton. He would know what to do.

Would the fucking jackhammers never cease?

Christl!

12

"What happened to her?" Donna gasped, trying to restrain Lucy Hackett on one side of the examining table while on the opposite side Mike tried to strip off the oversized raincoat, blood flying every which way from the girl's injured hands, her eyes wide and frightened, gibberish coming from her mouth.

"Captain Kangaroo Captain Kangaroo . . ."

"Hurry, Mike. I don't think I can hold her much longer," Donna begged as Lucy slipped free from her grasp and raised halfway up from the table.

"Easy, Lucy," Mike soothed, guiding her down again. "I just want to take a look at your hands, that's all."

"No Captain Kangaroo, noroo, noroo, noroo . . ."

"She's hysterical," Donna muttered, and leaned with all her weight against the girl's shoulders. "Can you give her something, Mike?"

Suddenly Lucy screamed and arched upward on the table.

Mike nodded. "Can you hold her?"

"If you hurry."

Donna eased around the table until she was bending over Lucy's head, all her strength angled downward onto the young girl's shoulders.

"Hurry," she called out again as Mike prepared an injection of Thorazine.

"No Captain Kangaroo, noroo, noroo . . ."

Mike pushed up the raincoat sleeve and administered the injection. His hands were slippery with her blood. He stood poised over her, watching.

The dosage proved adequate. Donna could feel the resistance leaving the girl. Her head rolled from one side to the other, the nonsensical sounds stilled.

"A hell of a way to start the day," Donna muttered, gazing down at the front of her robe, now blood-spattered, her hands coated with a mixture of dirt and blood. She leaned over and lifted the girl's shoulders, enabling Mike to remove the coat.

"Oh, my Lord," Donna murmured, gaping down from top to bottom on one of *the* most perfect young bodies she'd ever seen, flimsily covered in a hot-pink baby-doll nightie that wasn't designed to conceal anything.

Interested in Mike's reaction, she looked up from Lucy to find him concentrating on the girl's hands, gently exploring the damage to Lucy's soft dreamy refrain of "Noroo, noroo . . ."

Reassured by his professional objectivity, Donna tried to follow suit. "What is it? Is she badly hurt?"

Slowly Mike shook his head. "It's the damnedest thing I've ever seen. Look, three nails are missing on the left hand, two on the right, and two fingers are broken. It's as though . . ."

Stunned by the diagnosis and aware of the pain Lucy must be experiencing, Donna moved back and commenced stroking her brow in a soothing gesture. "What was she doing?" she whispered, not certain that Lucy couldn't hear every word.

As Mike assembled the necessary materials, he gave the impression of being too busy to answer. "I'm going to give her another shot," he announced, holding the needle up, indicating that Donna was to hold her steady.

But there was nothing to hold steady. Lucy was completely out of it now, her arms relaxed, only her head rolling back and forth, more a self-comforting gesture than anything else. And ultimately even that ceased and she merely stared dreamily up at the ceiling, her lips moving, though there was no sound.

With relief Donna stepped back from the examining table. As she was washing her hands in the sink, she looked down on the soiled raincoat which Mike had dropped onto the floor.

"What *was* she doing, Mike?" she asked again. She'd been in bed when the pounding on the front door had started. It had been a few minutes later that Mike had called for her assistance.

Still no answer, and she looked back to see him at work, cleansing Lucy's hands, then placing them on rubber pads, the flow of blood from the nailless fingers endless.

About an hour later, both hands were bandaged, the fingers set, and Mike raised up as though to stretch a tightness out of his neck and apparently "saw" all of his patient for the first time. "Nice equipment," he muttered, stripping off the bloodied gloves.

Leaning against the counter, her arms crossed, Donna gave him a moment's enjoyment. "Do you have any idea what happened to her?"

Mike shrugged. "Mrs. O'Connell brought her over, said she'd found her . . . digging in the backyard."

"Digging?" Donna repeated, looking down at the bandaged hands. "Digging how? For what?"

Suddenly Mike looked weary. "Beats me," he muttered. "Where in the hell is her mother? Maybe she'll . . ."

All at once Lucy stirred; one leg lifted as though she were going to rise. Her head twisted toward Mike. "Kangaroo," she slurred. "Noroo, noroo, noroo . . ."

"Easy, Lucy," he comforted gently, restraining her. "Stay with her, Donna. I'm going to see if I can find—"

But at that moment the door to the examining room opened, and there was Rene Hackett, her long lean face cast into angles of suspicion rather than alarm, as though, based on experience, she knew her daughter had been bad instead of hurt.

"Rene . . ." Donna started toward her.

"What's she done?" the woman demanded.

"She hasn't done anything," Donna said, taking the woman's arm, feeling more bone than flesh, a little amazed that the ripe, fully developed specimen on the table had emerged from this female cadaver.

"Here, sit down," Donna offered, pulling out the chair from Mike's desk.

"Don't have no time to sit," Rene objected. "One of the O'Connell kids said she was hurt. Now, what happened?"

Helpless, Donna looked at Mike and stepped away. As Mike tried to answer the woman's questions, Donna took a bleak inventory of the woman herself: late forties, perhaps younger, though it was hard to tell. Jerry had always seemed to do the laughing and talking for both of them. Everything sagged. Loose flesh around her chin, nonexistent breasts—where *had* Lucy come by her generous attributes? She was dressed this morning as always in a faded flower-print housedress—Donna recalled her mother dressed similarly in the forties. An oversized army-green sweater, probably Jerry's, appeared to be swallowing her whole, and her hair, nondescript brown, was anchored by the customary hairnet, for what reason, Donna had never been able to determine, for she would have put money on the bet that Rene Hackett had never in her entire life seen the inside of a beauty salon.

". . . not serious, yet baffling," she heard Mike say to the woman who had yet to approach the table where her daughter lay in a state of semiconsciousness, both hands bandaged. "I would suggest," he went on, looking weary for only nine-thirty in the morning, "that you speak with Mrs. O'Connell. She was the one who—"

"Got no business speaking with Mrs. O'Connell about anything," Rene interrupted bluntly.

"But she's the one who—"

"Lucy'll tell me when she gets ready," Rene announced, and drew the shapeless sweater about her and looked for all the world like she was ready to leave.

114

"Mrs. Hackett, just a minute," Mike called after her, first throwing Donna an expression which clearly said: *Help.*

At the door, the woman looked back. "Don't have a minute, Dr. Dunne," she said, rubbing her arms through the sweater, as though she were perpetually chilled. "Got a mess on my hands down at the station. The supplier from Denver come in this morning, and I can't find the keys to the storage. God knows where Jerry Hackett put them, but I—"

"What about your daughter?"

"I thought that was your department."

"She can't stay here . . ."

"Then let her walk home. She ain't no good to me like that."

"She's had two shots. I think she'll need some assistance."

As though watching a slow-moving tennis match, Donna looked back and forth between the two, feeling sorry for Mike, baffled by Rene.

"Aren't you curious, Rene?" she asked, stepping away from the counter and into the exchange. "Perhaps if you talk to her, she'll—"

"Don't need to talk to her," the woman snapped. "Anyway, I know what happened."

In identical responses, Mike and Donna chorused, "What?"

"It's him," Rene said flatly, looking in the direction of the high ridge. "He come down and done something to her. He does things to her all the time. Don't you think that I know it? And Jerry Hackett knew it as well, but would he do anything about it? Will any of you men do anything about it?"

Her voice, speaking nonsense, rose with angry conviction. Donna turned away, weary of the refrain. Mike, apparently less well-informed of the female gossip in Tomis, stepped into the trap. "Who, Mrs. Hackett? Who are you talking about?"

"Him!" Rene repeated fiercely. "Him up on the high ridge."

"The . . . Mountain Man?" Mike asked in an incredulous tone.

"See? You don't believe me. None of you believe me. Well, I'll give you something else to put into your pipe and smoke. He's the one that made that rock out there come crashing down on us, and him's the one that killed Jerry Hackett. But it don't make no difference to you all, now does it?"

For the first time she stopped talking and glanced down on her daughter. If there was an ounce of love in the expression, Donna couldn't see it.

"She used to be afraid of him," Rene went on, pointing down on the drowsy Lucy. "No more. They're friends now. Either she's sneaking out to meet him or he's coming down to meet her. I tell you both, I give up a long time ago trying to make a good girl out of her."

Abruptly she stopped, still looking down on Lucy as though she were the world's greatest disappointment. "She deserves everything she gets," Rene said flatly, "and I guess what you're telling me now is you don't want her in your hair no more either. So . . ."

With remarkable strength she reached down for Lucy's shoulders and propelled her upward to a sitting position; the girl's bandaged hands struck the edge of the table, causing her to groan softly.

"Hey, wait a minute," Mike protested.

115

"I'm taking her home," Rene said. "That's what I'm supposed to do, ain't it? Well, I'm telling you this," she went on, keeping an eye on Lucy, who was weaving about as though she were drunk. "I don't have any time to sit with her. The best I can do is lock her in her room and tend to her tonight when I get home."

Donna started to protest, but changed her mind. In a town the size of Tomis, there was a very thin line between neighborliness and nosiness. Lucy was Rene's daughter, Rene's problem.

With Mike's help, they got the girl on her feet, where she wobbled a moment and would have fallen had it not been for their support.

As the awkward procession started for the door, Donna caught a clear glimpse through the nightgown of a curvaceous ass. "Wait a minute," she called out, thinking what a crowd they might gather, leading the seminude young girl across Main Street to Rene's house. Quickly she scooped up the soiled raincoat and draped it lightly over Lucy's shoulders.

"Thanks," Mike muttered, his eyes brushing over Donna's face, then moving to the ceiling.

"Noroo, noroo, noroo," Lucy began to chant softly as the procession moved through the living room and out onto the porch.

"I really think you should stay with her for a while," Mike counseled as they eased down the front steps. "Maybe when the drug wears off, she'll . . ."

In the massive effort of trying to keep Lucy erect without doing further damage to her hands, he ceased talking. It would have made no difference anyway. Obviously Rene had spent her daily allotment of words.

As they started across Main Street, avoiding the larger ruptures and potholes, Donna fell back and merely watched. She had absolutely no desire to enter that house across the way. Obviously Mike was going the full distance and would at least see Lucy reasonably settled. Well, let him.

On the opposite side of the street she saw Mrs. O'Connell on her front porch, broom in hand. With wry amusement Donna thought what a necessary prop the broom was for busybodies the world over. As Mike, Rene, and Lucy disappeared behind the Hacketts' front door, Donna quickly turned away, but too late.

"Mrs. Dunne?"

She looked back to see plump Mrs. O'Connell waddling toward her, the broom still clasped in her hand. "Is the girl all right?" she called out while she was still several feet away.

"Not right now, Mrs. O'Connell, but she'll recover."

"I've never seen anything like it," the woman gushed, her cheeks flushed from the excitement of the morning.

Just as Donna was thinking she'd cut the woman short, it occurred to her that here was an eyewitness.

"What, precisely, was she doing, Mrs. O'Connell?" she asked.

"Mother of God, I'm here to tell you it was the strangest thing ever," Mrs. O'Connell began, eager to talk about it. "On her hands and knees, she was— out back of their house, behind those old drums that Jerry was going to use for strawberries. Remember?"

No, Donna didn't. "And what was she doing?"

"Digging!" Mrs. O'Connell said with a curious half-laugh which she quickly canceled, as though it were in poor taste. "It took three of us to drag her up. Me, Danny, and Terry. I could tell she was doing awful damage to herself." The woman leaned closer. Donna could smell egg on her breath. "She's not been the same, you know," she whispered intimately, "not since her daddy was killed, may his soul rest in peace. They were just awfully close, a true daddy's girl. . . ."

Donna nodded and crossed her arms against the chill and looked up toward the high ridge and the bare spot at timberline. The Mountain Man's place. *She lets him get at her . . .*

Suddenly she backed away from the still-talking woman. "You must excuse me, Mrs. O'Connell." She smiled. "I'm freezing and I—"

"Of course," Mrs. O'Connell said. "You need more flesh, you do," she added cheerily, "or better, a babe nesting inside."

Donna nodded indulgently. Why did overbred women always want to wish the curse of a child on everyone else? Even Sarah was getting that way.

"I'll talk to you later," Mrs. O'Connell called out as Donna started back to the house.

13

Even from the kitchen, Inez could sense the tension in the dining room. Now and then she left the stove to peer over the swinging doors at the strange assortment of guests. Why in the name of God did every good thing in her life always end prematurely?

"Joyce, we're running short of glasses. No daydreaming back there," she called out to the shadowy female figure bent over the steaming water.

No response, but then, she'd expected none. Mentally retarded, everyone had said. Well, what was she to do? Abandon her?

She needed about four good waitresses, that's what she needed, but then, who would have thought that business would be booming this early in the season? In the past, by mid-May she was only feeding the town, maybe fifteen, twenty per evening.

Now? Again she glanced over the swinging doors and took careful note of the curious all-male clientele, one table of five men she'd never seen before. They looked like hoodlums and had ordered chicken-fried steaks around and five bottles of beer. Phillip had just served them, and no one was doing any talking now. Just slow, steady eating.

Next to them was the road crew, the four workmen who had been trying to move that awful boulder. They were good men as long as she kept the hot-sauce bowls filled. They ate it on everything and then drank tons of beer.

Near the cash register she saw two more newcomers. They had rolled into

118

town about midafternoon in a van with "Century Mining Corporation" printed on the side.

There! You see? Another good thing ending prematurely.

And last, at the table nearest the back room, were Hal and Mike Dunne. Hal had ordered the Mexican dinner, but Mike was just nursing along a cup of coffee. Obviously Sarah was not cooking, and Donna was. She felt sorry for them all. They had worked so hard, too hard, to have all this come down on them. And there was something hopeless about the way they were just sitting, not talking.

Again she cast an encompassing glance over the restaurant, determined that everyone had been served and at least for the moment required nothing else. She stepped back from the swinging doors as Juan angled his way through with a basket of dirty dishes.

There was another piece of unfinished business. The missing Carlos. Probably hitching his way back to town at this very moment. She had warned the boys that life in Tomis was quiet and isolated. How many more would she lose before the month was out?

At that moment Phillip came through the door carrying an empty nacho platter. *"Cuatro."* He grinned.

Table four—the workmen wanted refills, their third.

As she carried the platter to the work counter, she felt peculiarly dizzy and chalked it up to the general tension of the day. And age—that too. She wasn't getting any younger. Who would have thought that by fifty-six she still hadn't found "her place"? Oh, she'd thought she'd found it several times before, with Mr. Fuentes, who'd given her respectability, sixteen years of marriage, and a retarded daughter, then had died of lung cancer.

Of course Hal and Sarah Kitchens had been nice to her, had offered her her own house on a remote and peaceful mountain, with no one around to hurt Joyce, or laugh at her, and, yes, she could bring her "assistant" along. She no longer ran the risk of telling people that Joyce was her daughter.

She glanced toward the dark end of the kitchen and saw Joyce, still bent over the steaming suds. A good girl, really, now twenty-one, never a complainer, never a talker either. Whatever was going on beneath that long ebony hair, she'd never elected to share it with Inez. She was like a silent appendage, had been since the day she was born, with Mr. Fuentes' thick masculine features and strapping physique. The prevailing nightmare of Inez's life was what would happen to the girl after she died. She'd never been able to solve that one.

Where the dishwashing was going on, she heard giggling. "Stop it," she called out to Pete and Juan, who in their idleness were standing behind Joyce, mimicking her movements. "Get on out there," she shouted. "I'm sure there are tables to be cleared."

As the two boys, still grinning, passed her by, she slipped the mitt on her hand, withdrew the platter of nachos, and thrust it at Juan. He took it and almost dropped the hot platter, and with a sense of getting even, Inez saw the pain in his face as he jiggled the platter back and forth, shaking his burned fingers in the air.

"Cuatro," she said with a smile, and handed him the cloth.

As the boys pushed their way through the swinging doors, she saw Phillip just coming through, followed close behind by . . .

"Señora," he whispered, and jerked his head toward two men just approaching the doors.

They were grinning like jackasses, both of them, their business suits looking so fancy and out of place in Hal's Kitchen. She recognized them, the two from CMC.

"Señora," one of them called out, peering over the top of the doors. "We'd just like to pay our compliments to the chef."

"Thank you," she said coldly, and turned back to the work counter.

"I was wondering, might we speak with you for a few minutes?" one called out.

"I'm busy," she said, and tried to pretend to be so, scraping up the excess chips and putting them back into the plastic bag.

"Only a minute, please," the other persisted, starting to push open the doors.

"No," she said sternly. "No one permitted back here but the help." In an attempt to keep them out, she returned to the doors and blocked them.

Beyond the two men she saw Hal, closely watching. "What do you want?" she asked.

"Primarily to compliment you." One man grinned. "I've never tasted better Mexican food."

She nodded and started to turn away.

"Señora, another moment, please. . . ."

"I told you, I'm busy," she snapped.

"Not too busy, I think, to hear us out. You see, señora, we have a proposition."

Again she saw Hal, still watching. Mike Dunne was whispering something in his ear.

Momentarily distracted, Inez absentmindedly rubbed her hands on her apron and thought she'd better get out to the cash register. The platters of chicken-fried steak were almost empty.

"If you'll excuse me," she said, trying to start out the doors, only to discover that neither man would budge. Now they were the ones who held the doors together and grinned down on her. "Would you be so good as to tell us what you are receiving here in the way of a salary?"

"I don't think that's any of your business."

"All right." The man smiled, holding up two manicured hands as though to stay her anger. "Whatever it is, we are prepared to double it."

What in the . . . ?

"You see, señora, we're giving you a chance to join our team. At first, admittedly, the conditions will be crude, a field kitchen to feed our construction workers."

"Not interested," she said, and again started out of the doors and was again blocked.

"Perhaps you didn't understand," the man persisted. "We are asking you merely to name your price, and we are fully prepared to meet it."

For a moment the impasse held. Beyond their shoulders, she saw Hal rising

120

to his feet, his expression one of just barely controlled anger. How dare they try to "buy" her? Didn't they know the word "loyalty"?

"We would take good care of you, *señora*," the man murmured. "Private quarters, quite comfortable, I might add. All you would have to do—"

"Please let me pass," she demanded, pushing against the doors, though her scant weight was no match for theirs.

"We would want you to start tomorrow," he said. "The first of our equipment will be arriving then, and—"

"Look . . ." Inez said, lowering her voice to match theirs, not wanting to signal everyone's attention. As it was, half the restaurant was watching the pushing match taking place at the kitchen doors. "I don't really give a damn what you want or when you want it. What I want now is for you both to clear out of here before . . ."

Something in their expressions had changed. No longer looking directly down on her, they seemed to be staring past her in alarm, to . . .

She looked over her shoulder. "It's all right, Joyce," she soothed, seeing the girl approach, a large butcher knife in her hands still dripping soap suds.

"She'd . . . have a place as well, *señora*," the man whispered, alarmed. "Your . . . daughter, I mean."

Stunned, Inez looked back. Where had they found out about that? No one knew, not even Hal and Sarah Kitchens.

"Get out!" Inez ordered, having seen enough of the grinning jackasses.

"What's the trouble, Inez?"

She peered over the door at the booming angry voice and saw Hal making his way through the tables. No trouble. She didn't want any trouble. "It's nothing, Hal. They were just telling me how much they liked my cooking."

"Taking an awful long time," Hal said, stopping about two feet away from the men.

"Not absolutely true." The man smiled, shaking a scolding finger at Inez. "Actually, Mr. Kitchens, we were trying to hire your cook away from you."

Bewildered and sensing trouble on both sides of the door, Inez looked back toward Joyce and tried to calm her, and at the same time heard Hal, a new strain in his voice. "And what was her response?"

"Oh, it was a temporary no," the man said pleasantly. "But I'm sure she'll change her mind."

"I wouldn't count on it," Hal said coldly. "Now, if you both will be so good as to leave . . ."

"Why?" the second man challenged. "This is a public restaurant."

"No, it's not a public restaurant," Hal replied, a grin on his face which had nothing to do with humor. "It's *my* restaurant, and I order both of you . . ."

As Inez led Joyce to the rear of the kitchen, she tried to remove the butcher knife from her hand. And couldn't. The girl's grip was like a vise, her dark eyes still darting back to where the confrontation was taking place. She saw now that Mike had joined Hal at the door, and heard a heavy nervous silence blanket the dining room.

"We mean to cause no trouble, Mr. Kitchens," one of the men said, still

121

smiling. "All's fair in love, war, and business. We just thought your cook might like to join our team."

Why did every good thing in her life end prematurely?

"Give me the knife, Joyce."

"Also, Mr. Kitchens, I think we should inform you, our first equipment will be arriving tomorrow, several large trailers, earth-moving machinery, nothing very much to speak of at first, though . . ."

Concentrating on Joyce and the knife as she was, Inez did not see the blow. She heard the impact of a fist, and looked up to see one man missing, then Hal disappearing beneath the swinging doors.

Several other men in the restaurant were on their feet now. The road crew started forward into the fray.

But Mike stepped forward and blocked their passage, and the man from CMC reappeared beyond the swinging doors, a small trickle of blood seeping from the corner of his mouth.

"Wise move." He smiled at Mike, withdrawing a handkerchief and dabbing gingerly at his lip. "You see, we could have matched you man for man." At a signal, the five men seated at table number three rose. Dark, swarthy-looking, they moved confidently through the tables, dispersing the road crew without lifting a hand.

"You made the rules, Mr. Kitchens." The man smiled, standing back so the five bullies could move past him to the front door. "All I ask is that you don't forget that. We had hoped to be good neighbors, mutually profitable neighbors, that's all. Good or not, we *will* be neighbors."

From where she stood at the back of the kitchen, Inez couldn't see the cash register. Was Hal going to let the bastards out without paying?

"Wait here," she whispered to Joyce. "Watch her," she ordered Pete and Juan. As she hurried back toward the swinging doors, she saw the road crew settling back in their chairs, their expressions rather sheepish, as though somehow, without lifting a fist, they'd lost the fight. Mike stood close to Hal, his back taut, ready to spring forward at the first sign that further restraint was needed.

And all of Hal's attention seemed to be focused on the cash-register counter.

"Did they pay?" Inez asked, coming up behind him, trying to shift his attention back to more practical matters. "You didn't just let the bums have a free walk, did . . . ?"

As she drew even with him, she saw a crisp new one-hundred-dollar bill resting on the counter. Lord! Not a free walk at all.

"Come on, Hal," Mike soothed. "Simmer down . . ."

But for several moments Hal stared down at the bill, a terrible look on his face, as though he still felt the need to strike something. Quickly Inez slid behind the cash register, punched it open, and slipped the bill beneath the day's meager receipts.

"Are you hurt?" she asked, her heart breaking for him as he rubbed his knuckles. He looked lost, as though at this moment he had no idea where he was or what he was supposed to be doing.

Without a word, Mike stepped forward and turned him away.

Suddenly, from the kitchen she heard a shout. *"Vamos! Vamos! Señorita, vamos!"*

Joyce!

Oh, hell, couldn't the boys do anything right? As she approached the swinging doors at a dead run, she looked toward the end of the kitchen and saw exactly what she knew she'd see, Pete standing on one side of the door, Phillip on the other, the door itself wide open, a rectangle of black, Joyce gone, knife gone. . . .

She grabbed her jacket off the hook by the door and went out into the night to see if she could find the burden that Mr. Fuentes had saddled her with.

All good things end prematurely. . . .

14

Where was Roger Laing? It had been three days now, and not a word. They needed him.

Early the next morning, Sarah stood at her kitchen window and stared up at the high meadow. She *had* heard screams, dammit.

Just the wind, Hal had said.

Not wind.

If it hadn't been for Hal's excited and rather cryptic promise that something of great importance would take place on Main Street this morning, something that would distract her from her seventh-month jitters, she would be perfectly content to spend the entire day inside the house, as she'd spent yesterday, door locked, the two of them, even Vicky responding positively to the quiet and safe seclusion.

Of course Donna had arrived about noon, bringing news of the world. Poor Lucy.

Still in her robe, the remains of Hal's breakfast on the table, Sarah continued to stare up at the meadow. And beyond.

What does the Mountain Man do in the dark, Hal?

Whatever he wants to do.

Not dark atop Mt. Victor, though—that light had burned steadily enough.

Twice last night she'd tried to point it out to Hal, but either he couldn't see it or wouldn't. She'd never seen him in such a state as when he'd come in, angry, excited, constantly rubbing his right hand. *Two can play,* he'd said over and over again.

No breakfast conversation. He'd simply stared at his eggs, with the sense of every nerve tightened.

She leaned farther over the sink and stared straight up at Mt. Victor's stone face. Nothing moved anywhere this morning. Not even a breeze. The wind had blown itself out during the night. Gale-force . . .

"Mama . . ."

She turned toward the sleepy voice and saw Vicky in the doorway, dragging her blanket and merry-go-round with her, nightgown twisted, hair matted, one small fist trying to rub the sandman away.

"Good morning." Sarah smiled. "Trust you slept well . . ."

"Cookie . . ."

"Later," Sarah counseled, following the child's eyes to the cookie jar, filled with the results of yesterday's activities. They'd baked the entire day, sugar, chocolate-chip, a few experimental macaroons which had failed miserably.

"Egg?" Sarah offered.

Vicky screwed up her face, shook her head, and sat plop in the middle of the doorway, thumb in mouth.

"Then cereal," Sarah said, this time a statement of fact, not a choice of options. As she filled the bowl with Rice Chex, she kept one eye on Vicky.

"Come on, honey," she urged, filling a small glass with orange juice. "You eat a good breakfast and we'll both get dressed and go see if they've moved the big rock yet."

"Not hungry," Vicky whispered, sucking her thumb as though she were deriving nourishment from it.

"Of course you are," Sarah scolded, standing over the child, hand extended. "Come on, now," she urged, reaching down for Vicky's hand, seeing a layer of goosebumps on the smooth, tiny arm. "You're cold. You drink your juice and I'll go get your robe."

"Mama . . .?"

"I'll be right back. Let me get your robe. Then I'll have a cup of coffee while you eat your breakfast."

Sarah started out of the kitchen, then stopped and looked back. Looking at the child was like watching a wind-up top which had wound down, and what made it even more frightening was that Sarah could remember the time, just last week, when Vicky would awaken like a wild banshee, a whirlwind of energy and activity.

Now? She might have been a large doll propped up at the kitchen table. Dead, full of dead stuffing, a broken energy circuit, bum batteries.

Watching her, Sarah found herself close to tears. What in hell was she going to do? One child ill, a second on the way. And there too was a new worry. The gymnast inside her had grown ominously quiet.

Move, damn it. One of you.

Robe. Vicky's robe. As she started down the hall, a thought occurred, bringing hope. Maybe Hal would let her go to San Antonio for a while. She didn't like to think of herself as the type who "ran home to Mother." But a change might be good for all of them.

But how would she go? Bus? A day-long bus ride, seven months pregnant, with a four-year-old in tow?

Inside the closet she found Vicky's pink robe, draped it over her arm, and started back toward the kitchen.

As she passed by the living room, she glanced through the windows and saw someone coming up the path. Donna? A bit early for her. She bent down in an attempt to see through the thick shield of pine and fir. It was someone . . .

"Here, Vicky, put this on," she said, placing the robe in the child's lap. Move! Do something! Scream! Yell! "And eat. Every last bite before we go to town."

It was an empty threat. She knew it, and apparently Vicky knew it. The robe slid off her lap onto the floor. And was not retrieved.

Footsteps! "I'll be right back, honey," Sarah murmured. "Please . . . eat."

A knock at the front door. As she hurried into the living room, she saw an outline through the white curtains. Not Donna.

"Inez!" She smiled, pulling open the door, surprised to see the woman here. Breakfast was usually a busy time in the restaurant.

As she started to push open the screen door, Inez objected. "No, I can't stay," she said, looking about the porch in a peculiar manner, as though she'd lost something.

"Is anything . . .?"

"How long have you been up?"

A curious question, as curious as Inez's undone appearance. Generally she was as neat as the proverbial pin. Now she was wearing a soiled apron, and her usually brushed and groomed hair hung in loose strands about her face.

"How long have I been up?" Sarah repeated. "Since about six . . . yes, about a quarter after six. Why? Are you sure you won't come in? Coffeepot's on—"

"No, I can't. I have to get back. I just wondered . . ." Inez faltered, looking behind her now, through the sun and shadow of early morning. "It's Joyce," she said. She crossed her bare arms and rubbed them.

"What about Joyce?"

"I . . . can't find her."

Still holding the screen door open, Sarah pondered the curious announcement. Couldn't find her? Where in Tomis could she have gone? Inez continued, "Last night she ran out of the restaurant and up into the high meadow. I called her, but she . . ."

"Has she ever done that before?" Sarah asked, seeing a mental picture of the tall, gangly, coarse-featured girl.

"Oh, she's run away plenty of times," Inez said, worried, "but not since we came here."

With one ear turned toward the kitchen, Sarah tried to keep tabs on Vicky while at the same time appearing sympathetic and concerned for Inez.

"Well, surely she'll come back," Sarah soothed. "I mean, where could she go?"

"I expected her back this morning," Inez brooded, still rubbing her arms. "In fact, I waited up half the night."

"You must be exhausted."

"And with Carlos gone . . ."

"Where?"

"Oh, back to Durango probably. They're a lazy shiftless bunch, all of them. The only thing they're good at is running from hard work."

"Well, maybe Joyce went back to Durango."

Inez shook her head, dismissing the suggestion. "She hated it."

Sarah was on the verge of asking why, but changed her mind. Instead she offered, "If you're shorthanded at the restaurant, I'll be happy to—"

"No, I can manage," Inez said, as though suddenly embarrassed. "I'm just trying to alert everybody to keep their eyes open. If she's lost, she couldn't find her way home and would need help."

"Of course," Sarah said soothingly.

I did hear screams, dammit.

Not screams, the wind.

"Quite a blow last night." Inez smiled nervously. "I prayed all night that it wouldn't rain. . . . Sarah, are you feeling all right?"

Startled out of her thoughts by the direct question, Sarah murmured, "Fine. Well, as good as can be expected."

"You coming down today?"

"Later. What's going on?"

Inez shrugged and started toward the steps. "The road crew brought up a crane early this morning, biggest thing I've ever seen. If that don't do the trick, nothing will."

She ran up into the high meadow last night.

"Just keep your eyes open, Sarah, will you? She's a good girl, Joyce is. I wouldn't want anything to happen . . ." With a backward wave, Inez started toward the path, head down. She was crying. Sarah was sorry for that.

She closed and bolted the front door and turned back into the kitchen.

"Oh, no, Vicky . . ."

In a makeshift nest on the floor composed of her robe and blanket, the child was curled up, fast asleep.

She'd been out of bed less than half an hour, and she'd slept the night through since nine o'clock the evening before.

"Vicky, come on," Sarah whispered, kneeling by the child, nudging her gently. "Please, wake up. Let's go find Daddy, Mike, Donna, Roger . . ."

Someone!

15

It looked like a massive prehistoric animal with its squat cab body, long cabled neck, and gaping jaws. It was costing him three hundred dollars an hour, but it was worth it, if it worked. Hal looked about at those around him. No one knew what was going to happen except the road crew, not even Mike, who stood to his left in the bright morning sun, his arm about Donna, and not even Brian, who waited on his own front porch about fifteen yards behind them, not too far from Kate, who sat in her rocker, the only one the length and breadth of Main Street who was not watching the circus.

Where in the hell was Sarah?

Hal walked a few steps beyond Mike and Donna and peered up the narrow path across the street that led to their house. Vicky would get a kick out of this, as would Sarah.

What was the matter with her? She was growing as jumpy and as nervous as an old woman. Maybe no more pregnancies for a while. Maybe that was it. They'd flip a coin to see who took the necessary precautions.

"Do you see her?" Donna called out above the scream of the crane.

Hal shook his head. "I'm going to take a run up—"

"No, you wait here. I'll go," Donna offered. Quickly she slipped from beneath Mike's arm, and Hal gave her a grateful look as she started across the street.

The scream of the crane rose as the operator skillfully angled it into position and lowered the steel jaws over the boulder.

Open wide, Hal thought, mentally directing the steel jaws. *Wider!* There.

The screaming ceased, and for a moment all that was heard was the rumbling of the powerful engine.

Mike shook his head. "I don't know," he said skeptically.

"Damn, it had better," Hal cursed. The fucking boulder had burned up two winches. Something *had* to be capable of moving it.

"Come on, come on," he prayed as the crane screamed, the steel jaws tightening about the rock.

Across the way, lined up on the steps of the restaurant, he saw the road crew in their yellow hard hats and orange vests. Good men, all, they'd worked overtime on this problem and had been as turned off as Hal by the Century Mining Corporation boys. The plot of what to do with the boulder was theirs, though Hal had instantly approved.

Twice the crane operator tested the grip of the jaws, tightening the cable, then letting it go slack.

Mike shook his head. "It ain't gonna do it."

"Sure it will."

Once again the cable went taut. Inside the cab Hal could see the man shoving gears every which way. The high-pitched scream reached pain level.

The boulder moved, cleared the ground by about half a foot, then slipped free, thundering back to earth with such force that Hal felt the vibrations beneath his boots.

What in the hell . . .?

Angry, he started across the street toward the cab. But the operator waved him back with an A-okay sign. Obviously he'd just been testing. As Hal rejoined Mike on the opposite sidewalk, Brian came down. "They usually give it three trial lifts," he said. "Just hold your horses."

Hal nodded, reassured, motioning his hand in a gesture of dismissal. Inside the cab, further adjustments were being made, the operator bending low.

"Where are they hauling it to?" Brian asked.

Hal grinned. "Wait and see. You'll—"

"Here they come," Mike interrupted, pointing toward the path to the left of the restaurant.

Hal looked up, pleased. It was Sarah and Vicky. Now everyone was present and accounted for. Crane, do your stuff. . . .

Donna was in the lead, carrying Vicky, while Sarah brought up the rear, her expanding figure lost in a tent-shaped dress of flowered print. Hal watched closely to see that they stayed well beyond the large circle of orange road cones. As they passed the closest point to the crane, he saw Vicky bury her face in Donna's shoulder, saw both women look fearfully up at the awesome machine.

Hal went halfway across the street to meet them, and hurriedly took Vicky from Donna's arms. "Thanks," he said. Then to Sarah he scolded lightly, "What kept you? You almost missed all the fun."

129

The cold expression on Sarah's face momentarily sobered him. Was she mad at him? "Sarah?"

But she took Vicky from him and walked straight on up to the porch where Kate sat knitting.

"She didn't want to come," Donna whispered, apparently as baffled as he. "Is she feeling okay?"

"I don't know," he muttered, watching closely as Sarah kissed Kate on the forehead and settled into the chair next to her and protectively drew Vicky up onto her limited lap and wrapped her arms around her.

"Here we go!" Brian shouted, and the cry drew Hal's attention back to the street, where the crane seemed to be straining forward, the earth again vibrating beneath his feet, this time from the power of the machine as it pitted its strength against the weight of the boulder.

For several minutes the battle raged, all eyes focused on the crane, as with one massive scream the boulder lifted, shifted, lifted again, only inches at first, one foot, then two, the sound hurting his ears, though the sight pleased him.

"It'll hold," Brian shouted, his eyes no longer sleep-glazed.

And it did. Suddenly the godawful scream died. Hal saw the operator lunge at the gears, locking the jaws into place, the boulder now suspended about three feet off the ground. It rocked ominously back and forth in its steel cradle.

Across the way, Hal saw the road crew run down and hurriedly gather up the orange cones.

"Keep 'em back, Mr. Kitchens," one shouted. "We're under way!"

Hal nodded and glanced east down Main Street. "Come on," he said, stirring Mike and Brian into action. "You two take that side. I'll take this. Keep everyone well back."

"Where in the hell are they going with it?" Mike shouted.

"Wait and see." Hal grinned.

Then once again the gears started their high-pitched scream, a different tone this time as the square, squat cab started to reverse itself. The boulder suspended at the end of the long neck swung heavily under the duress of movement. Still the spectacle reminded Hal of some lumbering, cumbersome prehistoric monster, out of its element and somehow in pain.

The large crane reversed its position and finally was facing due east toward the end of Main Street and the single intersection which led down from Tomis to the valley highway below.

Like a flight attendant waving in a plane, Hal ran to a position directly in front of the crane, staying well ahead of the boulder entrapped in steel jaws. Glancing back once toward the Sawyers' front porch, he saw the women—Sarah with her face hidden behind Vicky's hair, Vicky's hands covering her ears in protest against the noise, Donna watching intently, perched on the top step, and Kate placidly knitting. Not one seemed compelled to follow after the parade.

A little disappointed that his audience had been reduced by an important four, Hal shouted ahead to the people standing at curbside. "Move back, please. It might be . . ."

130

But his voice was lost in the whine of the crane, and instead he gestured broadly and saw a few step back, though everyone appeared transfixed by the spectacle.

He glanced ahead and saw the end of Main Street about fifty yards ahead. Mike and Brian stood together at the intersection, which formed a simple T configuration, the horizontal leg continuing on in a heavily rutted dirt road which led around the side of the mountain to the proposed site for the new mine, while the vertical leg formed the twisting blacktop road which led down the mountain to the valley floor and State Highway 5. Any vehicles or equipment that would be moved up to the high plateau would have to pass through this intersection. There was no other way up or down.

Walking backward, Hal waved the crane forward with broad beckoning gestures. Behind, he saw a trail of people, an unscheduled party which, to be sure, had commenced in tragedy but which was concluding with a festive air. He saw several children scrambling up the high embankment which formed the dead end of the highway as it twisted its way up from the valley floor. A few cautious parents tried to call them down. To no avail. They knew, the children. They could smell confrontation in the air.

Then all his concentration was drawn back to the crane. Behind the glass of the cab window, he saw the operator adjusting gears again, trying to hold the weight at the end of the cable steady, all the while manipulating his cumbersome machine into position for the turn.

"I hope to hell he's not going to try to take that thing down the mountain," Mike shouted.

But Hal didn't answer, concentrating on the width of the boulder and the width of the road. From where he stood, it looked to be a perfect fit. Running alongside the crane, he saw the four men from the road crew. One swung up into the cab and started pointing out directions to the operator. There seemed to be a brief debate inside the cab, and at last the crane moved forward into position, facing squarely down the mountain at the exact point where the T-bar of the intersection connected.

"Hal, what in the—?"

Brian never had a chance to complete the question. At that moment the high-pitch scream again splintered the air. The cables shifted and the immense steel jaws lowered the load back down to earth, clung to it for a moment as though loath to let it go, then at last swung free, the boulder perfectly placed.

Suddenly, after almost an hour of shrill screaming and rumbling engines, there was silence. The operator cut all his motors. The steel jaws swung free of the boulder, and the crew's plan was clear for all to see.

The parade following after the crane eased around the now silent machine, assessed the boulder and the blocked road, and stared in growing silence. Then finally someone understood. And laughed. Then someone else, and then another, until it spread like a contagion and grew into cheers and all of Tomis was laughing and applauding and whistling.

Moved by their approval, Hal felt like taking a bow. Brian and Mike were on either side of him now, Mike patting him on the back and grinning like a Cheshire cat. Brian was a bit more circumspect. He eyeballed the road and

131

the boulder, and announced that a small car, a VW or a Datsun, could still pass on one side.

"It's not small cars we're objecting to." Hal smiled. "Let's see a trailer or a semi get by it."

"It won't stop them for long," Brian warned sadly.

Hal agreed. "No, but it sure as hell will slow them down."

A sense of unscheduled holiday had invaded all. He saw Mina Murdoch passing from group to group, exchanging pleasantries, one of Inez's boys in tow, a blanket folded over his arm.

"Well, what now?" Mike asked, viewing the crowd with him. "Shall I run back and get my guitar?"

Hal laughed. "Not a bad idea."

Brian returned from his professional inspection of the boulder and its placement in the road. "Perfect," he agreed. "This will stop them, all right. They ain't going to be happy."

"Let's wait and see," Hal said guardedly, his attention suddenly drawn to the high embankment which looked down on the entire scene. A man stood there, alone, isolated.

"Who is it?" Mike asked, noticing his interest in the solitary figure.

"Beats me," Hal muttered, turning away, his pleasure with himself and the barrier momentarily dampened.

He knew who it was, had recognized him instantly. Frank Quinton.

What in hell was he doing still hanging around?

Hal looked back and saw him again, just standing there, knee-deep in the tall grass of the high meadow, his right arm cradling his handless left, his gaunt tall figure like a black slash against the high blue sky and bright sun.

Shortly before noon a somnambulant mood spread over all. Several women had gone home and returned with blankets and sandwiches. Thermoses of tea and coffee and milk were being passed about. Brian had walked back into town and had coaxed the women out, all except Kate, whom he'd left safely napping on the sofa.

"How much longer, Mr. Kitchens?" one of the road crew called out from his lolling position in the grass near the edge of the road.

Hal shrugged. "They said sometime today. You heard them. If they picked up the equipment in Durango this morning, I'd say . . ."

"They're coming!"

Hal grinned, then glanced over his shoulder. Frank Quinton was still there, standing alone on the high embankment, unmoved, as far as Hal could tell.

The sounds coming up the mountain increased, the scraping of gears shifting, as above the crest of the plateau he saw the first telltale black puffs of diesel smoke.

"Good Lord," Brian muttered. "Sounds like every truck in this end of the state."

"Here they come!" Mike pointed. "Look!"

Just then, coming around the final turn, Hal saw a white pickup with a flashing red light atop and a mounted sign announcing "EXTRA-WIDE LOAD."

Apparently the driver of the pickup had not yet seen the obstruction at the top of the incline, and shifted into low gear for the final ascent, leading the way for an enormous flatbed semi pulling a mobile home the size of three small houses. From the puffs of black smoke visible just over the crest of the plateau, it was Hal's estimate that there were six, perhaps seven other trucks, all moving toward Tomis.

There! At last! The lead pickup had spotted the obstruction at the top of the hill and now slowed, pulling over to the right side of the road, the driver waving frantically out of his window to the monsters following behind him.

"Unless I miss my guess," Mike muttered, "we shall shortly be joined by the two dudes from CMC."

"Presto! There they are." Mike grinned, pointing down the hill to two small figures on foot, both leaning into the ascent. Unable to drive past the obstruction of their own equipment, the two men had been forced to hike up.

When they were less than a hundred yards away, Hal stepped forward. After all, it was his town, his boulder. "Good morning," he called out cheerily to the two red-faced men who were drawing closer.

Coatless, tieless, two spreading rings of perspiration marring their long-sleeved shirts, their shiny shoes dusty from the walk up, they came forward to within about twenty feet of where Hal stood, the smooth P.R. expressions gone from their faces as they struggled for oxygen in the thin air.

"Dammit! What . . .?" The man tried to speak, but obviously there simply wasn't enough air, and for a moment he planted his hands on his hips and let his head hang limp.

Hal didn't know their names. He didn't want to know them. He just wanted them gone. He glanced behind him. Everyone was staring steadily down at the men, and again Hal felt a surge of emotion. Why had it come to this? All he wanted, all any of them wanted, was to be left alone, to create for themselves and their families, not a utopia—they all were smarter than that—but simply their own fabric of life. Whom were they bothering? Had they offended some basic rule of American life that stated that every man must live in fierce and consuming competition with every other man?

"I don't know what you hope to accomplish, Kitchens, by this little trick—"

"Tomis is closed, gentlemen," Hal said quietly. "I tried to make that clear to you yesterday."

"This is a public road," the man interrupted, still dabbing at the perspiration on his face, gingerly avoiding his slightly swollen lower lip, which had connected with Hal's fist the night before.

"No, gentlemen," Hal went on, "the town of Tomis paid for this road, for the widening of it, for the blasting of those canyon walls you just passed through, and for the resurfacing."

"But you're blocking the only access," the second man shouted.

"Then build your own road."

"We can get a court order—"

"Be my guest. But I'd better warn you. The courts move slowly around here. The judge in Durango has been known to take off for a week if the trout are running."

In his brief exchange with one man, he was aware of the second moving behind him. Feeling the need to keep both of them in sight, he stepped back and saw the man staring at the boulder, his focus stopping on the crane and the operator lounging in the cab seat.

"That's state equipment," he accused.

"Right," Hal conceded. "But I have an invoice and a contract that says it's mine for twenty-four hours."

Stymied again, the man circled the boulder, foolishly assessing what he already knew to be true. There wasn't one chance in hell of getting his equipment past it. In the expanding silence, he looked up toward the road. No one moved, no one spoke, a human barrier as intractable as the boulder.

At that moment Hal saw the second man talking with the crane operator. The four members of the road crew were standing nearby, listening. What in the hell was going on up there?

"Brian . . ." he said, motioning him up the hill.

Was money changing hands? Damn! He saw the man reach for his back pocket. "Mike, go see what's . . ."

Suddenly there was a scuffle at the top of the incline. One of the road crew stepped between the man and the operator. He nodded broadly and moved back as Mike and Brian drew near.

A moment later, he came down the incline in angry strides. Without a word, he passed Hal by and motioned for the other man to follow. They stopped about thirty feet away for a brief whispered conference, their agitation increasing, both gesturing broadly toward their own men waiting by the trucks.

Hal looked back as Brian and Mike came up alongside him. "What was going on up there?" he asked.

"CMC made a modest offer of two thousand dollars to the crane operator," Mike said. "One of the road crew kept him honest."

Still the debate raged, and finally the man started off down the hill, his arms swinging angrily as he braced himself against the steep descent.

The second man hesitated, glaring up at them, his face a burnt crimson. "Remember, you made the rules, Kitchens. Don't ever forget that, you hear?"

Hal stood staring after them as the rest of the crowd dispersed. Finally he was alone. Slowly he brought his line of vision back to the high embankment. He wasn't alone. Frank Quinton of CMC was still with him, his expression blurred by distance, though his movements were clear—that maddening, self-caressing gesture of his own mutilation.

Suddenly the man waved at him with his handless arm and turned about and started slowly up into the meadow, moving in the opposite direction from Tomis. He disappeared beneath a small rise of land.

Hal waited. Well, where in the hell was he?

Ten minutes later, still waiting for Frank Quinton to reappear somewhere on the broad face of the mountain, Hal felt weak, his mouth dry, ears ringing.

Don't forget, Kitchens. You made the rules.

16

"More?" Sarah offered, sliding the now cold casserole of macaroni and cheese toward Hal.

"Where in the hell is Roger?" he muttered, shaking his head to the casserole and pushing back in his chair, his mood black and growing worse.

"I don't know what you think Roger can do," she snapped, hurt by the rejection of her dinner. "You know Roger," she went on, going for a lighter mood, anything to offset the tension which now permeated Tomis and which Hal had brought up the path with him about an hour ago. She resented that. She'd had quite enough this morning, that godawful machine, the whole town behaving like hysterical—

"Where's Vicky?" he asked, as though he too wanted to change the subject.

"Where else? Asleep on the sofa."

"Well, that's all right. She had an exciting morning."

"It's not all right, Hal. She had a terrifying morning. What did you hope to accomplish?"

She turned about, more than ready to air everything that was bothering her: her concern for Vicky, her concern for him, for Tomis.

But before his unresponding and glazed face, her impulse died. He looked like a prisoner, as though he were serving a sentence, waiting to be released.

She turned back to the sink, jerked on the hot-water faucet, felt the spray as the water exploded over everything. Of course he would have been happier to remain at the restaurant, where all the "excitement" was going on, or down at the intersection, where Callie Watkins had rigged several large spotlights, casting the already ugly scene into uglier tones of shadow and substance.

But no! Duty! Marital duty had dragged him up the path to his lumpen, misshapen wife.

"Why don't you go on back down to the restaurant?" she snapped over the hiss of the water. "Vicky and I will be all right."

Receiving no answer, she looked over her shoulder and saw him still slumped in his chair, and from the expression on his face, a million miles away. "Hal?"

Dazedly he looked up. "No, I don't care for any more. Thanks."

By nature not designed for self-pity, she turned back to the sink before the stinging in her nose expanded into something sillier.

Mechanically she washed the dishes and thought of her childhood home in San Antonio. Not always blissfully happy. But *safe*. What she wouldn't give to feel safe again!

Dwelling on unknown threats, she raised her eyes instinctively to the beauty of the mountains, always healing, always medicinal. But halfway up, she saw something, the dying sun catching on a plume of red fur, about fifty yards away.

She squinted through the slightly fogged window in an attempt to see more clearly. Gone. If it had ever been there. No! It *was* there. She caught only a glimpse now of a familiar red furry head, bobbling through the high grass, then disappearing.

"Hal . . ."

With the end of the dishcloth she rubbed a clear circle on the window glass and leaned as close as she could. There! She saw him again.

"Hal, look!" she called, trying to stir him into action. "It's Copper. Look!"

He heard. No second invitation was needed, and he was at her side, his head bent to see through the fog.

"Son of a . . ."

Then he was out of the back door and she was right behind him, almost restored by the smile on his face.

"Copper! Come on, boy!" Hal was calling to him, and Sarah found herself grinning at the impending reunion, wondering where the dog had been. Beyond Hal she could see Copper pulling at something in the grass, though he looked up once at the sound of his master's voice.

At some point, the distance between them had lengthened to about thirty feet, though she heard the joy in Hal's voice as he called out repeatedly, "Come on, boy, come on, good boy . . ."

How pleased Vicky would be, Sarah thought as she slowed her pace to accommodate the rough terrain, although, what the hell, if she fell, she'd just bounce.

"Come on, boy, let's go home. Come."

Breathing heavily from her high-speed sprint, she looked up and saw that Hal had come to a halt about fifteen feet from the dog.

"Is he . . .?" she tried to call out.

Suddenly, "Get back," Hal shouted, something breaking in his voice

"Is he hurt?" Sarah called out, still coming.

"Get back, dammit!"

Bewildered by the sudden disappearance of his good mood, Sarah moved a few steps closer, close enough to see the dog clearly, and hear his growling, a low rumbling warning for both of them not to come any closer, and certainly not to try to take away his prize of . . .

"Hal, what is . . .?"

Suddenly both his arms shot out like a traffic cop's. "I said, get back," he shouted.

Something in his tone suggested that she obey, and she was just in the process of turning about when Copper lifted his treasure in his teeth and held it suspended, as though he wanted to show both of them what he'd found, though he was still growling.

What kept her safe at first was the conviction that she wasn't seeing what she was seeing, a head-shaped object with long black hair, the gleam of a cheekbone, severed, half-gnawed neck tendons like red trailing wires, a jaw eaten away, the macabre optical illusion complete as the dog shifted his toy and she saw clearly two eyes, frozen open.

"Oh, God . . ."

"Sarah, please . . ."

She heard a peculiar alteration in his tone, begging her not to see the human head, or what was left of it.

She tried to avert her eyes. Straight up would be a safe direction, to the high white clouds. But she couldn't move. She could smell it now, something close by, and . . .

"Come on, Sarah, I'll take you back."

For a moment she had no idea whose voice that was. It bore no resemblance to Hal's.

Copper shook the human head. A piece of flesh fell from the chin. Then someone forcibly turned her about and waited patiently, his arm about her, while she vomited a steady stream of hot, rancid undigested food.

17

It was dark. She was in her bed, she knew that much, and someone was seated beside her. Not Hal.

"Are you all right?"

Donna? What was Donna doing in her bedroom?

"Vicky?"

"She's asleep, Sarah. You just lie still . . ."

"Light . . ."

There were voices in the distance. She didn't like the dark.

The bed lamp came on, casting a limited glow, and she saw Donna, her hand still on the lamp switch, her face filled with concern. "I didn't mean to wake you up," she apologized softly. "I just wanted to see if . . ."

Asleep? Had she been asleep? And why was she in her nightgown? What had . . .?

"No," she whispered, and covered her face with her hands, and still smelled vomit.

"It's all right," Donna soothed, though something in her voice, like Hal's earlier, suggested that it wasn't.

"Where's Hal?" Sarah demanded, trying to sit up.

"He's in the living room with Inez. Brian and Mike are there too. And Tom Marshall."

Inez.

"Was it . . . Joyce?"

Donna nodded.

"Did Copper . . .?"

"No. Mike said she'd been dead for . . ."

She had to get up. Hal needed her.

"No, Sarah, please, just rest," Donna urged. "There's nothing you can do."

"I want to get up."

Reluctantly Donna stood away from the side of the bed and extended her hand.

Out of necessity, Sarah took it, and together they propelled her to a sitting position, where for a moment every object in the shadowy room danced in triplicate.

"You really shouldn't . . ."

"Did I . . . faint?" She'd never fainted in her entire life, and lacked a frame of reference.

"You . . . passed out," Donna replied safely.

"And puked."

"Yes."

"Hand me my robe."

"Sarah, Hal wants you to stay in bed."

"Hand me my robe."

"You're seven months pregnant . . ."

"No shit."

She stood, wobbled a bit, then blessedly everything grew steady. "What time is it?" she asked, and pulled on the soft velour robe, which only barely snapped in front.

"A little after three."

"In the morning?"

Donna nodded. No wonder she looked tired.

Growing brave, Sarah took a glance in the dresser mirror. As she pushed the matted hair from her face, she asked, "How long have you been here?"

"Hal sent for Mike a little after eight. I came along to help with Vicky and . . ."

"Me," she said bleakly. The dresser chair was near, and she was in need. Weakly she sat. "Donna, I've never seen anything so . . ."

"Don't think about it."

"Don't think about it?" She looked up in mild anger. How could she not think about it? "What are they doing out there?" she asked, looking toward the bedroom door and the living room beyond.

Donna shrugged. "Trying to decide what to do."

"Inez . . ."

"She stopped crying about an hour ago."

Sarah reached the door first and waited for Donna. "Thanks," she whispered, and managed a brief smile, then saw the human head again clamped in Copper's jaws and saw the look of concern on Donna's face and thought of everything they had been through together—and just when they'd thought the worst was behind them. . . .

139

Because it was the natural and necessary thing to do, she found herself in Donna's arms, succumbing to her loving refrain, "It's all right, Sarah. Everything is going to be all right."

Sarah led the way down the hall, though Donna's hand never left her arm, and at their approach she heard the voices cease.

With her appearance in the living-room door, the scene became a tableau. Inez, looking very small and crushed, sat on one end of the sofa, her face hidden behind her hands. Brian was seated on the edge of the easy chair by the window, still sporting a white bandage above his hairline. Tom Marshall leaned against the front door, his customary retired-army-officer bearing obliterated by the occasion.

Mike sat perched on the end of the sofa nearest to her, and looked up and offered the only smile, though as smiles go, it left a lot to be desired. And finally there was Hal standing before the fire, hands locked behind his back, his mood, as always, concealed behind his beard.

And there was one more, lying at Hal's feet, the only pocket of relaxation in the room, Copper, his long gangly legs curled into disjointed angles, the tip of his head pressed against Hal's boot.

"She insisted," Donna said, giving Hal a helpless look.

Sarah ignored them all and moved instinctively to the sofa, to the place of need. "Inez, I'm so sorry," she whispered, sitting beside the woman, her arm about her shoulders.

Inez didn't look up. From the tension in her neck, Sarah knew she was crying again.

For several moments no one in the room spoke. What had they been talking about before she came in? She wasn't a child to be protected and coddled. "What happened?" she demanded of Hal, and saw him turn his back to her and face the fire.

"Mike?" she tried again.

He turned slowly about on the arm of the sofa and managed a succinct explanation. "Joyce . . . She'd been dead at least twenty-four hours is my guess. It wasn't Copper. Some form of . . . strangulation first, then . . ."

"The authorities in Durango should be notified," insisted Tom Marshall, no longer leaning against the door.

"No!" Inez looked up. Her face was dreadful. Eyes red-rimmed, tears streaming. In her hands, Sarah noticed a small silver crucifix.

"Well, what about the death certificate, Mike?" Tom demanded, stepping into the room.

Mike shrugged. "What about it?"

"There's laws that state clearly that—"

"Easy, Tom," Hal soothed, turning back from his inspection of the fire. "We're just talking here, thinking aloud."

"Exactly," Tom said, "and I say that one of us should have left for Durango right away."

"How?" The simple question had come from Brian, reminding them all that the only road out was blocked by the boulder at this end and the stalled seismograph equipment at the other.

· "Well, I say move the damn thing," Tom exploded, clearly uncomfortable with all aspects of law-breaking. "I wasn't so sure we were doing right this morning," he went on. "Maybe none of this would have happened if we'd simply let 'em in."

Sarah looked up, stunned. "Do you think they had any connection with Joyce?"

"Well, she didn't die of natural causes, I can tell you that, Sarah," Tom muttered.

"Mike?" For the second time she turned to Mike for explication.

"Strangulation . . . of some kind, then decapitation," he said to the floor.

Of some kind! What sort of medical opinion was that?

Before she could pose the direct question, Mike went on. "Tom may be right, Hal," he said quickly. "You saw those men in the restaurant last night. They weren't boy-scout leaders. And if that wasn't a threat this morning, I don't know what was."

Sarah looked about the room. More frightening than anything else was the fact that everyone, including Hal, was listening carefully. And not objecting.

"Look, if what you think is true," said Sarah, "then move the damn barricade!"

She saw Mike and Hal exchange a curious glance. Then her attention was drawn back to Inez. "Do *you* want an investigation, Inez?" she asked softly.

"No! No! God, no!" the woman sobbed. She kissed the crucifix, then pressed it against her forehead and again took refuge behind her hands. "Just bury her and give her some peace."

As the sound of deep grief filled the room, Sarah found herself wondering again what specifically had been the connection between Joyce and Inez.

"Are there relatives? Someone to be notified?"

Incapable of speech, the woman merely shook her head.

"No one?" Sarah prodded. "A mother?"

"No one," Inez wept, and lowered her head until her forehead was pressed against her knees, her face wholly obscured.

Sarah looked up at Hal. What more needed to be said?

"All right." He nodded and stepped away from the fire. "I think we should do it now."

"Now?" Just when Sarah thought she'd solved one problem, another presented itself. "At three in the morning? Why?"

"Let them do it," Inez wept.

"Can you stay here for a while, Donna?" Hal asked, moving toward the door, Mike and Brian trailing after.

"Of course."

"Hal, why can't it wait until tomorrow," Sarah begged, trying to rise and failing.

Tom Marshall stepped forward, apparently eager to answer the question. "They don't want anyone in town to know, Sarah. Can't you see that? Some-

141

one else might start asking questions. It's wrong," he said with conviction as the men moved past him to the door. "The authorities should be notified, there should be an investigation . . ."

"Are you coming with us, Tom?" Hal asked from the door.

From where Sarah sat she saw the cold look of resentment on Tom's face. Wordlessly he strode to the door and past the three men, his boots clomping heavily down the steps and into the night.

"Lock the door, Donna, after we leave," Hal said, his voice low.

Why Donna? Was she the only adult present? But as Inez's sobs increased and as the pain in Sarah's back cut straight through to her abdomen, she grasped the sofa and pressed her head back against the cushions to wait out the discomfort, more than willing to let someone else take charge.

With her eyes closed, she saw it again, the long coarse black hair filling Copper's mouth, his teeth clamped over the cheekbone, the dark eyes glassy and distended.

She opened her eyes and saw Donna staring at her from the door.

"Lock it!" Sarah begged.

18

Harve Mullins was having trouble sleeping. Nothing new there. Since the unscheduled birth of the baby a few days ago, he'd been nervous as a cat.

Stealthily, taking pains not to awaken Rita, he slid his feet out from under the covers. He'd check again. No harm in it; still couldn't believe that the pinkish-red infant asleep in the laundry-basket-turned-bassinet was his daughter.

Only a month ahead of time. Most unwomanlike, Dr. Dunne had joked. Harve pushed away from the bed. The trailer creaked. Easy . . .

He looked down on Rita, her long blond hair twisted about her face, her belly nice and flat again. Oh, there would be a lot of finger-counting going on back in Henderson. Married in October, baby born in May. An eight-month pregnancy?

Well, what the shit! He'd do it all over again, though he was sorry for the embarrassment he'd caused his family. But he'd try to make it up—to everyone. *Make what up?*

They'd leave here tomorrow—Dr. Dunne had said it would be all right— for the leisurely drive back to Iowa, then on to the last year at the U. of I, business administration, a good preparation for his dad's drugstore, a constant fitting in of domestic duties . . .

143

A moment passed. Fresh air. Take a leak, then back to bed. It'd be a hell of a drive tomorrow. As he turned toward the door, the trailer creaked again. Shhh . . .

Outside, the cold mountain air made him shiver. The outhouse was about twenty-five yards down the path. What harm in pissing right here? There was no one else about. The old couple from Pensacola had left two days ago. Four backpackers from Oregon had wandered in yesterday, used the water faucet, rested awhile, and had taken off last night. They were probably over the mountain by now.

He unbuttoned his pajamas.

Don't do that, Harve. Why despoil the earth? It's only a short walk.

As he heard Rita's voice in memory, he started off down the path, barefoot, trying to deal with the realization that she was already controlling him. As for spoiling the earth, that filthy shithole ahead was just about as despoiled as you could get.

The dirt path felt packed and cold and damp beneath his feet. Don't need light. You could smell it from here. Dr. Dunne had smelled it as well and had apologized for it. They were going to get someone to clean it up before the summer season got rolling good.

He halted in the dark. What the hell . . .? The damn outhouse should be straight ahead. He could sure smell it. But . . .

He looked about, trying to squint through the shadows. Well, maybe he'd misjudged the distance. He'd better find it soon. Now he felt a crap coming on as well.

For about five minutes he padded down the path, feeling the ground beneath his feet grow muddy and soft. No rain, not today at any rate. Why muddy? As the bottoms of his feet became coated, he cursed and tried to walk to the side of the path and realized that he'd have to wash his feet at the faucet before he went back to bed.

Suddenly he stopped. He *was* on the wrong path. But it had been the *only* path. No need for panic. Just turn around and retrace your steps. What the hell. Neither call seemed so urgent now. He'd wait till morning, till he could see exactly where . . .

He could still smell it, though, stronger than ever, like he was standing right in the middle of it, and now he heard something as well, a rustle like someone was moving through the brush on either side of him.

He stopped and glanced around. "Rita?" he whispered, thinking that maybe she'd followed him. As he started back up the path at an increased speed, his feet, packed with mud, slipped beneath him. Struggling for balance, he extended his arms on either side, like a tightrope walker. The last thing he needed was to fall in this muck. And why didn't he remember it being so wet and slimy a few minutes ago? Had he taken another wrong turn?

Slightly breathless, he looked behind him and saw only the dark shadowy path. Listen! There *was* something moving through the underbrush, something keeping pace with him, stopping when he stopped, moving when . . .

An animal? He hadn't seen any animals about. Okay, enough! Let's go.

And again he was running, his feet sliding, the stench of open sewage rising about him, along with the wind.

But after less than twenty steps in one direction, he stopped, totally disoriented. It was *that* way, behind him. No, he'd come along this way, then . . .

"Rita!"

So what if he awakened her? And the baby. So what if they all had a good laugh later?

Damn! "Rita!"

But the wind had increased to such a pitch that he felt the single name rush past him. Struggling for reason, he told himself that it was simply a matter of staying calm. Everything had an explanation. Sudden mountain storms were not unusual, gale-force winds, sometimes followed by torrents of rain.

As for the slippery underfooting, hadn't Dr. Dunne said that the public toilet was in need of repair and maintenance? Clogged septic tank, ruptured, or overflowing. So! It had ruptured and the sewage was seeping up through the ground. There! Made perfect sense. As for being lost, if he'd just calm down, it would only be a matter of following this one path, for he had taken no turns.

But with the first step, his foot submerged up to his ankle, and with a quick· spastic movement he withdrew it and felt a peculiar suction.

Another step, up to his knee this time, the stench growing worse in spite of the rising wind. He tried again to run and felt a suction all around him, his body weight forcing his legs deeper and deeper.

He screamed, "Rita!" and the ensnaring slime climbed higher.

"Rita!"

Then, up ahead, less than ten yards, he saw it, the outhouse, its single hinged door banging in the wind. Suddenly the poisonous fumes swirled about him, and as he lifted his head in an attempt to breathe, he felt a curious pulsating movement, saw the plain board walls of the shed expand and contract, as though something were swelling inside. It appeared to be pulling itself apart with a nightmarish resonance that joined the wind and resounded in his ear.

The sound boomed massively, and beneath his feet he felt vibrations. In an instant it occurred to him that if he could make it to the solid board floor of the outhouse, he would be all right. Though splattered and stinking, it was still solid, unlike what he was . . .

The earth around him shuddered. He feared falling. "Oh, please," he prayed, and waded ahead, each step requiring more effort than the one before it, the suction growing stronger, the bottoms of his feet feeling battered and bruised.

Not far, four more steps, and he could pull himself up on the door, then swing around and . . .

Suddenly the wind screamed in his ear, the small shed exploded, and he looked straight up into a moving wall, black and slimy in the moonless night, a volcanic upheaval as from all the sewers of the earth.

He lifted his arms in weak protection, something inside the stench pulling

145

at him, the raw sewage moving toward him like a tidal wave, choking off his last cry of terror.

He reached up toward the sky with his right hand in search of something of substance. Then it too was buried. . . .

19

The following evening, Mike Dunne leaned against the counter near the cash register and wondered how long this circus could persist.

From where he stood, he could see Hal at his "desk" in the back room where he'd sat for most of the day, trying to plot the next step in his one-man Alamo.

Laughter erupted at the large table in the corner, where the four from the road crew and the crane operator had passed the day in a pleasant and growing state of inebriation brought on by an endless supply of beer. They were like kids, Mike thought, relieved of jobs they'd probably hated all their adult lives. Now it was whoopee time until the boss-man said otherwise, and precisely when that could come, neither they nor Mike had the foggiest idea.

In the thickening dust, he considered switching on the lights near the cash register, but changed his mind. Through the kitchen doors, Inez was no place to be seen. She had appeared about noon with swollen eyes and had fixed lunch for the road crew. Then she had immediately disappeared, leaving the Mexicans to clean up and telling Hal she was closed for the rest of the day.

Mike considered going home. He should stop by and check on Lucy Hackett, and he wasn't accomplishing a damn thing here. If Donna were home . . .

She said she'd be staying with Sarah and Vicky, if they needed her.

He needed her, but not at Sarah's and Vicky's.

And what in the name of God was that stench? He'd smelled it in varying degrees most of the day, though it seemed to be getting stronger now at evening.

From his own "lookout" at the front of the restaurant—what in the hell else was there to do?—he'd seen a small congregation of men at Tom Marshall's across the way, Ned Wilson, Pete Charter, Ed Billingsly, and Jason Allegro. Mike didn't know what was going on, but he knew they hadn't gone to do their grocery shopping.

For the third time that afternoon Mike spotted the curious Mr. Frank Quinton pacing Main Street, head down, his right hand and left stump clasped behind his back. Of course, he was as much a prisoner as any of them. According to Polly Whiteside, who'd stopped in earlier that morning to inquire about Inez, Mr. Quinton had spent the night on the phone, making endless calls.

Mike closed his eyes and massaged his forehead and came up with a disgusting string of clichés—eye of the hurricane, calm before the storm, it's darkest before the dawn. At the exact top of his head he felt a peculiar pain, sharp, though short-lived, and saw again Joyce's body, decapitated, the most peculiar marks he'd ever seen about her ankles and the flesh of her neck. He had no doubt that strangulation was the cause of death, but strangled with what? And by whom? Someone strong enough to sever the neck tendons and make it a simple matter for Copper to complete the decapitation.

Quickly he looked into the back room, where Hal still slumped alone against the table. Mike suspected that the crude early-morning burial was part of the problem. A lumpy black plastic bag filled with the body of a young girl and dropped unceremoniously into a hastily dug grave at the edge of the cemetery was not the sort of memory that a man like Hal could easily absorb.

"Dr. Dunne? You wanna come and join us?"

It was one of the road crew, lifting a wobbly bottle of Coors toward Mike.

Running out of raunchy jokes? Mike smiled. He had one or two raunchy stories which might amuse them. Still, "No, thanks, but thanks anyway." Shit, if he was going to fall off the wagon, he wouldn't do it with beer, not when he had a brand-new virgin bottle of Chivas Regal.

Fall off the wagon.

You see, alcoholics, what you must learn to do is to take each day like a life . . .

Christ! The humiliation.

Now he couldn't go home, not until Donna was there to keep him honest and sober. As he pushed himself away from the counter, he saw Tom Marshall, Callie Watkins, and Ed Billingsly emerge from the general store, stand close together for a moment, conferring earnestly, then start across the street at a determined stride.

"Hal, there's something that looks ominously like a delegation coming across the street, heading this way."

"Who?" At last Hal looked up with a besieged expression, the shadows

148

about his eyes reflecting the night's activities and the general disintegration which plagued all of Tomis.

Mike craned his neck about and peered again through the streaks of the window and over the heads of the now silent road crew. "Three guesses, starting with the U.S. Army's finest retired—"

"Where's Sarah?" Hal asked suddenly, as though there had been no wife in his recent thoughts.

"Donna's with her," Mike said, alarmed by the distraction on the face that stared up at him. "Here they are, Hal," he whispered, hearing the bell ring as the front door was pushed open. "Hear them out and . . ."

The rest of his advice was lost in the rather martial approach of the three men, who, up close, definitely wore the expressions of a "delegation."

"Tom," Mike called out cheerily, trying to set a rational and light tone. "Inez is—"

"We know where Inez is," the grim-faced man interrupted. "We're not here to eat. We just want to talk."

Reasonable. Mike nodded. "Come on in, all of you."

As the three men pushed into the small room, none chose to sit. Callie Watkins and Ed Billingsly stood stiffly next to the wall, to the man pushing sixty-five.

"Hal, what we want to know," Tom began, clearly the spokesman for all, "is how long this mess is gonna go on."

From where Mike stood in the door, he saw Hal look up, then pick up a pen and tap it lightly on the table. "What do you think we should do, Tom?" he asked with suspect calm.

"What we should have done yesterday," the man replied without hesitation, leaning across the table, reducing the distance between them. "We gotta get that thing out of the middle of the road and let 'em come up. They're gonna come up anyway. It's just a matter of time."

"Not necessarily," Hal said.

"Hell, do you think that rock's gonna stop them?"

"It has so far."

"Well, you heard 'em yesterday. A court order, that's all they need—"

"Don't you think it might be difficult to get a court order providing access to a private road?"

"And in the meantime, what do *we* do?" the man demanded angrily, his two associates nodding vigorously.

Hal smiled, a mistake. "We go about our business as usual."

"How?" Tom exploded, slamming a fist down on the table. "I got wholesalers due up tomorrow, two of 'em from Durango."

It was a weak argument. Hal knew it and Mike knew it. The first lesson they had all learned when they came to Tomis was the primary law of mountain life the world over: Keep the stores replenished. If you use a can of beans, replace it with two, winter and summer. Isolated for at least six months out of the year, the first rite of spring was the restocking of pantries, canned goods, flour, sugar, salt stacked high in every larder. Of course they depended upon Tom Marshall for fresh bread, Twinkies, Ruffles potato chips, and few other dietary marvels of civilization. But as for starving, it was Mike's conservative

149

guess that every family in Tomis could make it through Thanksgiving without losing a pound.

"What are those trucks gonna do?" Tom demanded. "I'm running low now on . . ."

"What?"

"Everything. Cereal, bread, milk . . . yeah, milk. What are the kids gonna do?"

"What are they going to do with open bars on every corner, traffic so thick they can't walk down the street, the air heavy with fumes—"

"Hell, they survive the world over in those conditions."

"Do they? Do they, Tom?" Clearly stirred by his own conviction, Hal leaned forward in his chair. His voice fell. "I thought we were going to make something different here. Sally thought so too, if I recall correctly."

Mike stood listening in silent admiration at this last ploy, the timely reference to Tom Marshall's dead wife, a warm, hospitable woman, as open as Tom was closed.

Now, for the first time Mike saw a discernible wilting in the man's ramrod posture. "Sally's . . . dead," he muttered.

"Yes, but you must have shared her dreams."

"I . . . did, I . . . do," the man stammered, "but . . ."

"Then be patient for a few days, Tom," Hal begged.

"Well, all we want to know is what's gonna happen," the man repeated plaintively.

For the first time, Hal faltered. He looked down as the pen commenced its rhythmical tapping. "I don't know," he confessed, honest if nothing else. The meeting seemed about to disintegrate when he heard the road crew erupt into soft, appreciative whistles, the object of their admiration apparently outside on the sidewalk.

Mike heard a car door slam, heard one of the men mutter, "Crapola. Cotton-pony time."

Mike held his position and kept his eyes on the front door. Someone was coming . . .

"Whew! Stinks . . ." One of the men giggled.

Then there she was, a young girl about eighteen, amply filling a pair of light blue and very smudged shorts, cradling a bundle in her arms, her long blond hair whipped about her face, the face itself a disaster of new tears and old.

"Dr. Dunne?"

He looked closer. Good Lord, it was the young girl from the camping area, the one who'd given birth last week. Embarrassed by the realization that he'd probably recognize her crotch more easily than her face, he made his way hurriedly through the obstacles of empty tables and chairs, the stench growing stronger.

"Rita?" he inquired, smiling, still surprised to see her. He'd thought they had left. The young husband had seemed eager to get home.

Standing less than two feet from her, he saw that the bundle in her arms was her infant daughter. Ill? Why was she crying?

"Come on in," he urged kindly, pulling out a chair.

150

"No," she gasped on a fresh sob. "You have to . . . help me. I can't . . ."

"Of course I'll help, Rita. Is it the baby? Let's have a look."

"No," and she drew back as though fearful he'd take the infant from her. Every time she moved, the godawful fumes swirled about her.

Again he tried to extend a hand of assistance. "Can I get you something, Rita? Coffee? A glass of milk?"

But she drew back a step farther, a solid stream of tears coursing down her smudged cheeks. "It's . . . Harve, Dr. Dunne," she sobbed. "He's gone. He wasn't there this morning when I woke up, and I waited all day and called for him, then the trailer started to . . . jiggle, all crazy it was, and I looked out and . . ."

As fresh tears rendered her incoherent, Mike took the baby, laid back the top cover, and saw the pink smooth face sleeping peacefully through her mother's distress.

He glanced behind to the serving counter near the kitchen door and saw a dozen or so water glasses that had been filled for the lunch trade that had never materialized. He grabbed a glass and hurried back to the young girl. "Here," he urged, "drink this, then you must come and sit down and tell me . . ."

She lowered her hands and revealed the ruin of her face. "Find him for me, Dr. Dunne, please," she begged. "I tried to look, but it's . . . awful out there, can't walk, and it's getting worse, the trailer is tipping, and he wouldn't just leave us, we were going home, and I'm afraid . . ."

As she dissolved into new tears, he looked up to see Hal in the far doorway, the other three men clustered behind him. At their approach, he saw Rita glance up, the sobs diminishing as though she knew she must at least try to pull herself together before total strangers.

"This is Rita," Mike began, "Rita . . ."

"Mullins," she whispered.

"Yes." Mike remembered. "I delivered her baby a few days ago and now she—"

"What is that smell?" Hal demanded, looking about the room toward the kitchen as though that were the source.

"It's . . . me, I'm afraid," Rita murmured, her head down as she assessed her soiled garments. "It's all over the place, everywhere. Oh, Dr. Dunne, please go out and see if . . ."

"She can't find her husband," Mike explained weakly, "and she says that something is—"

"It was making the most terrible sounds," she rushed on. "If Harve is out there . . ."

"What's she talking about?" Hal demanded. Obviously nothing she had said had made sense to any of them, and since it wasn't likely to in her present state, Mike stood with dispatch. Get her settled somewhere, then they'd go take a look. But as he was trying to work out certain logistics, he heard Hal questioning the girl.

"You came from the camping area?"

She nodded.

151

"Is there anyone else out there?"

"No, sir. The Dyers left early yesterday morning and said we should, too. But the baby was fussy, and I told Harve that we should wait."

From where Mike stood behind her chair, he saw the expression on Hal's face. Clearly the camping area had not occurred to him, and apparently the Dyers had left before the road was blocked. It was one thing to barricade the town. It was quite another to prevent tourists from completing their journeys.

Mike waited to see if Hal had any further questions. But when, after several moments, he continued to stare down on Rita Mullins in perplexed silence, Mike took matters into his own hands. "Callie?" he called out to the short, squat man standing behind Hal. "Would you take Mrs. Mullins and her baby down to Mina Murdoch's? Tell Mina to let her wash up, and I'll owe her one."

He saw Callie nod and heard Ed Billingsly offer to walk with them. Mike was grateful for the rather quaint air of chivalry which briefly permeated the room.

"Where . . . am I going?" Rita Mullins asked as the men started to move about her.

"You need to rest," Mike soothed, gathering up the infant and placing it in her arms. "These gentlemen will walk with you, just down the street to a very nice lady's house. You and the baby wait there, and as soon as we—"

"You will find Harve, won't you?"

"Of course, and don't worry. He probably just hiked too far and is at this moment looking for *you*."

In an effort to speed her on her way, Mike hurried to the front door and opened it and stood back as the two elderly men guided her protectively down the steps.

"Don't worry, Rita," Mike called after them. "I'll stop by Mina's just as soon as we know something."

He stood a moment, the door propped open, and watched the three of them head down toward Mina's, each lending her a supporting hand as they made their way across the uneven terrain of Main Street.

"What do you think happened?" Hal asked quietly behind him.

Mike lifted his head and caught a whiff of the lingering stench. He shrugged. "I don't know, but I think we'd better go take a look."

"How? As far as I know, my jeep is still halfway down the mountain."

"We'll take her car."

"All right." Hal glanced toward the table by the window and the closely watching road crew. "You guys be okay for a while? Help yourself to the beer in the cooler, and Inez said she'd be in about six and cook for you."

"Don't worry with us none, Mr. Kitchens," one called out. "First vacation we've had since we was kids."

Mike started out the door, annoyed. Of course Hal had to keep the road crew happy. They were the ones who really controlled the barricade. If the crane operator were to suffer an urgent call of duty, then all would be lost.

"You want to drive?" Mike called out as Hal hurried down the steps behind him.

"No, you drive. I don't even know what we're supposed to be looking for, and I've got to get back soon."

Keys in the ignition. "A missing husband," Mike said, slamming the car door behind him.

As Hal crawled into the seat opposite him, Mike saw the leftovers of the Mullins' vacation: crumpled road maps, a box of graham crackers, picture postcards of the Durango–Silverton train, a box of Band-Aids, and an empty Winston package.

"What if he doesn't want to be found?" Hal asked, tossing the road maps into the backseat.

"Then we won't find him."

"I had no idea there still were people in the camping area."

"Nor did I. I thought they'd left several days ago. They gave me their address to send the birth certificate."

"Is she all right—in the head, I mean?"

Carefully Mike angled the car around the small crater left by the boulder and reversed directions, heading west down Main. "She pushed when I told her to push, if that's what you mean."

As they passed Polly Whiteside's guesthouse, Hal pointed to the big black Oldsmobile. "Have you seen him about today?"

Mike nodded. "He walked off Main Street about a dozen times. Did he ever say where he'd lost his hand?"

"He said the mountain ate it."

Mike nodded, unperturbed. As an explanation, it fit in with the day.

About twenty minutes later, as they were approaching the camping area, Mike felt the tires of the old Chevy object. They seemed to be fighting for traction. Twice he pulled the steering wheel sharply to the right and looked ahead through the windshield and saw the narrow dirt road damp, muddy, and strewn with rocks.

"Look over there!" Hal pointed to the left to a place about thirty yards away where hot steam seemed to be escaping the earth in a small geyser.

Mike tried to glance in that direction, but he had his hands full simply keeping the car on the road. "Don't think we can go much . . . What in the . . . ? Look!"

Through the windshield they saw it simultaneously, a lake of brown slime where the camping area once had been, the continuous hiss of steam gurgling up from the ground in several places, the air filled with foul-smelling sulfurous gases. The once-green glade of thick trees was shrouded in clouds of vapors which concealed everything from view.

They both stared forward in disbelief. Above the gurgling and hissing, Mike heard the car door open. "I wouldn't do that, Hal, if I were you," he warned. "Get back in and let's—"

"I want to see—"

"You can see all you need to see from right here," Mike shouted, beginning to feel the sulfurous fumes burn his lungs.

Hal slammed the door, though he continued to grip the dashboard, on the edge of the seat, his eyes squinting out over the desolate scene. "It's them," he said, his voice low.

"Them?"

"They've ruptured the septic tank."

"The septic tank?" Mike parroted, gripping the wheel, ready to throw the car into reverse. "Fifty septic tanks, maybe . . ."

"It's still coming up," Hal pointed out, the brown slime bubbling less than twenty feet in front of the car.

Harve Mullins! Christ! Where was he?

At that moment, Mike saw it exactly where he remembered it, a silver-colored ridge, flat-topped, about fifty yards away, what was left of the Mullins trailer.

Hal spotted it at the same time. While they were watching, it sank from view. "Let's get out of here," he ordered. "Quick."

Mike shoved the gears into reverse, felt the tires spin aimlessly for a moment, and felt at last the good sensation of traction as the rear wheels found a piece of solid earth and grabbed hold.

He raised his arm to the back of the seat, stepped on the accelerator, and peering behind, guided the car out of the camping area. "Maybe it was a subterranean lake," he said quietly. "Could be." He nodded, agreeing with his own theory. "Heavy sulfur deposits located somewhere deep in the side of the mountain. The vibrations from the rock slide somehow jarred them into activity, disturbed the surface, and . . ."

He felt like an idiot and stopped talking.

"Do you think it will recede?" Hal asked, apparently buying the ridiculous theory.

Mike said nothing and kept his foot poised over the accelerator. If Harve Mullins had been caught in *that* . . .

Mike shook his head and closed his eyes and saw a vision of the trailer sinking out of sight. "Maybe he got out before . . ."

"Let's go."

"The command was what Mike had been waiting for. Without hesitation he backed the car down the road, not trusting the solid-looking shoulders on either side. "What are you going to do?" he asked, at last turning the car about at a small widening in the road. He glanced at Hal and waited for his answer. He was staring straight ahead.

"I suggest we tell no one," Hal said.

"It may be a difficult secret to keep."

"Why? There won't be any campers out here for a while, and nobody from Tomis has any cause to go out."

"What about Rita Mullins?"

For the first time, Hal looked across at him. "I'm afraid she's stuck here for a while. You'll have to help her understand that. Mina will help . . ."

Stuck here for a while. Mike gripped the wheel and wondered why that simple phrase had such an unpleasant ring to it.

"Hal, are you sure you're doing the right—"

"Yes!"

As they approached the edge of town, Mike cranked down his window in an attempt to rid the enclosed car of the noxious sulfur fumes. He still couldn't

154

believe what they had seen. It reminded him of a Dürer or a Blake painting, the work of an artist obsessed with visions of hell.

"Stop here!" Hal shouted as Mike in his preoccupation almost drove past the restaurant.

He brought the old Chevy to a halt beside the new embankment of Runaway Creek. For a moment Hal sat in silence, his hands clasped between his legs. "Will you tell her?"

"Who?"

"The girl."

"What do you want me to tell her?"

"Tell her—"

"I'll think of something," Mike interrupted, having already decided to postpone it for a while. The sulfur fumes had done nothing to ease his head. He needed two Excedrin, a shot of Chivas Regal, and Donna. In that order.

"Are you going home?" Mike asked.

"No."

"Maybe you should. I was hoping you'd relieve Donna."

A look of apology cut through the fog on Hal's face. "I want to make a call from the restaurant first, and I don't want Sarah to hear."

"Who?"

"Roger Laing. He should have been here by now. I want to tell him what's going on, in case they've barricaded the road at the bottom of the mountain."

Mike nodded. That was one small complication he'd not thought of. Tomis might control the top of the road, but someone else controlled the bottom. At the risk of sounding like Tom Marshall, Mike asked quietly, "What *is* going to happen, Hal?"

With the clear intent of avoiding the question, Hal crawled out of the car and slammed the door behind him. "Say nothing," he called through the closed glass. "I'll send Donna home just as soon as I can."

20

Sarah bent over the bathroom sink, spit out the white foamy toothpaste, cupped her hand beneath the water, rinsed, and raised up and stared steadily at her face in the befogged mirror, white foam dripping down her chin.

Behind her in the bedroom she heard Hal insisting quietly, "Well, try again, Operator, would you? And check the number again. I may have given it to you wrong, but I don't think so."

Poor Hal. She reached for the hand towel and wiped her mouth, amazed at his desperate need to reach Roger Laing. What he thought Roger could do, she had no idea. Had it been two years ago or three when they had been expecting him momentarily and he had called from Brazil with the simple explanation that the Amazon had beckoned? Last October he had brought her a purse from Tibet. Early on in their four-year friendship, she'd determined that the world divided itself naturally into two categories, everybody else and Roger. She'd long since given up expecting him to behave in a predictable way.

"Then it *does* check? Yes, Evergreen. CUSP, the letters of an organization, Operator."

She peered around the bathroom door and saw him seated on the edge of the bed, grasping the receiver with both hands, as though fearful the operator would abandon him. Vicky sat sprawled in the middle of the bed, bent over

156

her merry-go-round. She still refused to go outside, and there was a marked absence of . . . what? Life? Energy?

She heard the receiver as Hal slammed it down, then heard his voice. "I'm going on down to the restaurant. Will you be down shortly?"

"Vicky and I will be right behind you," she called out, wishing he'd wait just a minute and walk down with them, but not wanting to add to his problems. He'd said something last night about a ruptured septic tank out at the camping area, and of course that damn boulder was still there blocking the road, and maybe Hal was right, maybe that *was* the only way, though it made them all prisoners, didn't it, which really wasn't what they'd left Boston for, and what if Joyce *had* been a victim of their—?

The front door slammed. She gripped the sides of the sink and tried to still the din in her head and felt a vibration, heard the wastebasket rattling against the tile floor.

"Vicky?"

"Mama . . ."

It ceased abruptly, except for that curious residual humming, and as she looked into the bedroom, she saw Vicky's small terrified face.

"Bed go rocky-horse."

"Yes, you stay right there, Vicky. I'm almost finished, and then we'll . . ."

Why couldn't Hal have waited for them? As Vicky, reassured, bent over her merry-go-round, Sarah stepped back into the bathroom, stripped off her nightgown, and briefly studied her own ugliness, the distended stomach, swollen blue-veined breasts, the excess in the middle causing her arms and legs to appear curiously wasted. She reached for her clothes, which lay in a neat stack on the toilet lid, oversized panties, stretch bra, and a pale-pink-flowered maternity dress left over from Vicky. It had made her feel pretty and feminine and palatable four years ago. Let's see if it could work its magic today.

Dressed, she took a last glance in the mirror. Even magic apparently had a statute of limitations. She looked for all the world like a pink-flowered, misshapen circus tent, and surveying the ugliness, she decided then and there, no more. Either Hal could get his tubes tied or wear a rubber, or she'd go on the pill. But no more of this.

I was always afraid I'd give birth to something misshapen, something which stumbled going up the ladder of evolution.

"Vicky, come on, let's go. Daddy's waiting for us, and maybe Inez will fix you some French toast."

As she extended her hand to Vicky, she thought, no, she didn't have the heart to ask Inez to fix anything. She'd do it herself in the restaurant kitchen. Then she'd leave Vicky with Hal and stop by Mina's just to prove to herself how silly she'd been. Mina had not intended to alarm her.

"Ready?" She smiled down.

Vicky nodded, though she made no move to leave the bed. "Don't want to go," she whispered.

"Of course you do," Sarah chided.

157

Vicky shook her head stubbornly.

What now? "Look," Sarah said, reaching for some loose pennies which Hal had left on top of his dresser. "These are for the gumball machine," she bribed, "*after* breakfast."

The lure proved irresistible. Awkwardly Vicky crawled off the mussed bed, scooped up the pennies from Sarah's hand, pocketed them in her jeans, then led the way out of the bedroom.

Forgive me, Dr. Spock, Sarah muttered, lifting her eyes to the ceiling, then hurrying after her daughter.

About an hour later, Sarah stood alone on the porch of Hal's Kitchen, breathing deeply of the cool, pine-scented mountain air, wondering where in the hell the pain in the top of her head had come from.

Behind her, even with the door closed, she could hear the hum of male voices. The road crew, working on mountainous stacks of pancakes, had apparently spent a placid night in the bunkhouse behind the restaurant, more than willing to pass a few days in idle gluttony. And miracle of miracles, Inez was back at her old stand before the stove, her eyes only slightly swollen and red-rimmed, insisting that Sarah leave Vicky with her and asking her to send back the Mexican boys who had gone to Mina's for an early English lesson. "See if you can somehow get through to Mina that I'm shorthanded and I didn't bring those boys up here to go to school."

Sarah moved a short distance down the street, then stopped. The discomfort was growing into pain, both at the top of her head and in the small of her back. It felt as though a single cord were being pulled tight between the two points, while at center the lump in her belly increased in weight and sat dead within her with no sign of movement.

Hurriedly she tried to push the pain out of her mind as she proceeded on down the sidewalk. All at once a curious high-pitched ringing erupted inside her head, and she walked on, ignoring it, though she felt her heart accelerate. Then there she was, standing before Mina's house, which was as shuttered and as closed as the rest of town, though she knew for a fact that the boys were here. And the young wife from the camping area, with her infant.

Before she attacked the steps leading up to Mina's front porch, she waited out a new wave of pain in her lower stomach. She grasped the banister and held on, gasping. At the height of labor with Vicky, she'd never felt this rotten. Shielding her eyes, she glanced up toward the high ridge, her attention caught by something shimmering near the Mountain Man's trailer. As the blinding reflection made a direct hit on her eyes, she bowed her head, closed her eyes, and saw the burning image of a thousand suns. It was while she was still incapacitated that she heard a warm, drifting voice.

"Well, good heavens, there she is. My dear, do come in."

She looked up through watery eyes and saw Mina framed in her front door, wearing a long red velvet robe, one hand extended, her customary warm smile on her face.

"Well, come, come, child," she urged, as Sarah hesitated and started to

158

look up again toward the high ridge and the curious mirror reflection, almost as though someone were signaling.

"No, let me help you," Mina scolded, at her side now and gently but firmly assisting her up the steps. "Oh, my, how heavy we've become," the woman sympathized. "I imagine your spine is beginning to object."

Good, thoughtful Mina. Sarah laughed. "If you want to know the truth, Mina, I feel like hell."

"Of course you do."

Inside the darkened room, she glanced about and saw it was empty as she heard Mina closing the front door behind her.

"The boys, Mina," Sarah began, turning to see the plump little woman standing before the closed door in a guardlike position. There was a peculiar expression on her face, which Sarah had just noticed. Her eyes seemed incapable of focusing on anything, and worse, there was a stupid vacant grin. Unless Sarah missed her guess, Mina Murdoch was stoned out of her head. It all would have been rather amusing if it hadn't been for the woman's guardlike stance before the door and that overpowering sweetish smell that was beginning to encircle Sarah's head. It *was* grass. Sarah remembered. Sarah remembered it well from university days.

"Well, I think you'd better send the boys back to Inez now," Sarah scolded gently, wondering how Inez would react to stoned busboys. "She really needs them."

She stopped speaking, momentarily forgetting what she was saying in her awareness of the increasing odor. My God, they must have been smoking since early morning. Now, in an attempt to hide the fact that she knew their secret, she asked, "Mina, is something on fire?"

"No more questions, my dear." The woman smiled vacantly. "Come . . ."

As she reached out for Sarah's arm, her fingers were like ice. Sarah pulled away and felt dizzy, almost stumbling over the fringed edge of the Oriental carpet.

"The young girl," Sarah asked quickly, trying to mask the awkwardness of her movements.

Mina held her position at the end of the sofa and giggled. "What . . . young girl?"

"The one Hal said had been camping out with her husband and . . . Mike delivered their baby a few days ago. The husband apparently is missing. They said you had taken them in . . ."

"Oh, that one." Mina grinned foolishly. "Indeed I did . . . last night . . . and begged her to stay, but she said she knew where her husband was and she was going to get him."

"Last . . . night?"

Mina nodded and almost lost her balance. "Impossible to keep young lovers apart, you know, my dear."

"Where did she go?"

"How am I to know? I didn't follow her into the night."

"And the baby?"

159

"What baby?"

"Hers, the one that Mike delivered."

For a moment Mina stared blankly at her. Again she giggled. "I suppose she took it with her. Really, Sarah . . ."

Something, the singsong voice speaking nonsense, the pungent swirling about her, the empty stoned eyes—all this prompted Sarah to step back. "I have to go now, Mina," she murmured. "I really am not feeling myself. Would you please tell the boys, wherever they are, that Inez is—"

"Why don't you tell them yourself?" Mina smiled. "They are in my bedroom."

Sarah had no desire to enter Mina's bedroom. "Mina, please, I just want . . ." Suddenly the room began to swirl about her. The sickeningly sweet fumes burned her throat and nose. Her already heavy body felt as if it had been filled with lead. She was aware of her own shuffling movements, and if Mina had taken away the support around her waist, she felt certain she would fall.

"Mina, I think you had better get Mike," she said softly, unable to believe that it was time. Still, it wouldn't hurt to play it safe.

"In a minute," Mina sang, and pushed open the drapes, guiding Sarah through and holding her steady, as though she knew it would take Sarah's eyes a moment to adjust to the candlelight, the shadowy outlines of the three boys seated cross-legged on the floor.

Invisible weights seemed to have attached themselves to her shoulders now, her mouth, her eyelids, and just in time she felt the security of a straight-backed chair pushing against her legs and felt Mina easing her down into a seated position.

Struggling against the stupor and the silliness of Mina's continuous giggles, Sarah tried to rise, and for her efforts fell from the chair and suffered an excruciating pain. She then felt a rush of hot water between her legs and felt as well the ominous beginnings of contractions.

"Mina . . . please. Get . . . Mike," she gasped.

Then there was movement all about her, the excitement of voices that seemed to fade, then grow loud, with Mina's voice predominant among them, stoned, drifting, bemused. "Oh, there's plenty of time yet. Help me, boys, lend a hand."

Flat on her back on the floor, she was aware of a many-armed monster working over her, the pink-flowered dress that was supposed to have made her feel feminine being stripped off, her shoes and underclothes following, until she lay naked before them and looked up into the blurred image of faces staring down on her.

The pain was increasing. "Get . . . Mike . . . please," she begged.

"In a minute," Mina scolded in an exaggerated voice. "You must trust me. I can help . . ."

Sarah tried to protest, but protest was useless as she felt hands lift her up and carry her to the bed.

"Please . . . Mina. I . . . need Mike. Get . . . him . . ." She tried to speak clearly around the pain, inwardly furious that she would have to repeat such a request.

160

But still Mina was paying no attention. The pains were terrible and grow-ing worse. She heard her own moans amplify in her ears and was aware now of strips being tightened about her ankles, her legs drawn apart and secured to something beyond her line of vision.

"No . . ." Again she tried to resist, but the many-armed monster was too much for her, and she felt the tension grow taut from her convulsive sobs and from the agonizing pain which continued to cut through from her spine to her cervix, her entire midsection in tumult.

"There," Mina said, sitting beside her on the bed, dabbing at her forehead with something wet and cold. "I think we have a few minutes left, Sarah."

"No, there's . . . no time," Sarah moaned. "Help me. Please get Mike."

Suddenly the fact of the crisis cut through Mina's stoned consciousness. "Oh, good Lord," she whispered. "Oh, good Lord," she repeated mindlessly. "Go, boys," she gasped, clearly terrified. "Get Mike, Mike, Mike . . ."

The name came out in a convulsive stream. Under duress, reason had unveiled itself for its own protection. Sarah closed her eyes to the confusion and felt something trying to escape from her womb, something ripping her in half, and hoped that reason had not returned too late.

"All right, all right," Mina murmured in terrified repetition. She disap-peared between Sarah's legs. "We can do it. I think we can do it. Did you feel anything, my dear?"

Sarah felt everything, and tried to focus on the dark low ceiling overhead and was suddenly aware of incredible heat, perspiration drenching her, caus-ing the flesh on her back to stick to the plastic sheet.

"You must go to work as well, Sarah," came Mina's frightened, taut voice from between her legs. "I'm here to help, but for a few minutes it will all be up to you. Can you push?"

Sarah heard and tried to obey. If only Mina had sent for Mike earlier. He should be here. Mike would know what to . . .

"Push, Sarah, you must push."

What was that? That new smell, like seawater, like stagnant fish-filled . . .

"You're not pushing," Mina cried. "Please, hurry. Time is . . ."

Damn you, Sarah cursed over the pain. If you hadn't been stoned . . .

Someone was crying within her, so close the sound might have come from inside her head. It was too early, only seven months, surely it couldn't live, and so far to the nearest hospital, this godforsaken place, *damn Hal, damn Mina, damn them all, God, help . . .*

"It's coming, Sarah. I can just barely see it. A little more effort on your part . . ."

She could not breathe now, and wondered if she would survive.

"Harder," Mina screamed.

Mina's fault. All Mina's fault. But maybe it would be all right. Seven months could live. Maybe she'd miscalculated.

Recklessly, ignoring the pain, she closed her eyes and pushed. And cried out. She bit her lips and tasted blood as it mingled with seawater. Now she could feel her flesh tearing.

Forcing her eyes open against the pain, she suddenly felt an overwhelming sense of release, her whole body one vast opening to be filled and emptied and filled again, another scream forming, exploding finally into something red and black, something angling out between her legs, blood and seawater, more ripping, wet, thick, stinging . . .

"Ah, there," Mina whispered. "Look, Sarah, look what . . ."

In the dim light, salt tears stung her eyes, and she saw nothing at first, only the watery outline of Mina between her legs, grasping something that was still half in, half out of her, a blood-coated infant's head attached to a scaled something, like a lizard's body and tail and four broadly placed clawing feet.

There was a sudden sharp sound, something exploding inside her head. And then a second explosion in her throat, a scream which burned holes in her lungs as Mina pulled the serpent free from her body, though it was still attached by a long entwining umbilical cord.

21

"She's a witch, you know," Lucy Hackett pronounced with conviction, rather enjoying the dumb look on Terry O'Connell's face. "She is!" she repeated. "Papa told me so. He said Mina Murdoch brought the mining people here 'cause she needed more victims."

Propped up in her papa's big double bed, in her papa's bedroom, on the north side of the house, Lucy watched Terry O'Connell's rapidly blinking eyes, then pushed down into the pillows and waited for the dumb cow to think up something to answer back.

Terry O'Connell really was dumb, and momentarily losing interest, Lucy studied her bandaged hands resting on the down comforter and wondered how long her fingers would have to be splinted. They looked awful. And worse was that hideous image which she saw again every night of Carlos sinking into the earth. She'd never told anyone. And never would.

Still, all things considered, she was rather enjoying herself. Mama had even been halfway decent to her, letting her stay in papa's room because she didn't feel scared in there. And Mama always let some kids come up to keep her company, though she might have wished for anyone in Tomis except the dumb bitch Terry O'Connell, who had the biggest tits Lucy had ever seen, but who was still a virgin.

"Well?" she demanded of the girl who sat cross-legged on the foot of the bed. "Did you hear what I said?"

Terry nodded. "I heard, but I don't believe you. My mama says that Mina Murdoch is a good woman, and anyway, when Jesus Christ died for our sins, his love was so powerful it killed all the witches."

"Shit. Don't you ever talk about anything but Jesus Christ?"

"He's our savior," Terry replied defensively.

"Yours maybe," Lucy snapped. Then on fresh breath and renewed conviction she repeated, "Well, believe it or not, I happen to know that Mina Murdoch *is* a witch. I've seen her witch room," she added, thoroughly enjoying the look of consternation on Terry's face. "All dark it is," Lucy whispered, inventing, "only candles burning, and the ceiling is painted red like blood."

"You're making all that up," Terry muttered, nervously pleating the tail of her red plaid shirt.

"Am not," Lucy denied hotly. She could take almost anything, but she sure hated to be accused of lying.

"And why do you have to talk so dirty?" Terry O'Connell added angrily. "My mama says if there are any devils around, they are in you."

"Screw your mama."

"Lucy Hackett, you say you're sorry," Terry demanded angrily.

Slowly Lucy rested her bandaged hands on the bed, pleased to have made the dumb cow so angry.

This wasn't bad after all! Here she was in Papa's big bed, still missing him, but feeling closer to him here, her mama waiting on her hand and foot, and a constant stream of visitors, all of whom she could effortlessly manipulate.

"Lucy?"

She looked up, a little annoyed to see Terry picking at her toes, like she'd gotten over being upset.

"What really happened that day?" Terry asked quietly, a stringy strand of reddish hair falling over her forehead.

No! Lucy heard the question and heard as well the voice inside her head.

"Lucy? Did you hear me?" Terry persisted, looking up at last, her dull blue eyes looking almost mean.

Lucy pushed deeper beneath the comforter and hid her hands beneath it and tried to remember when Mama had said she'd be home from the service station.

"Lucy?" It was Terry again in a singsong taunting voice, chewing contentedly on a sliver of toenail, leaning back against one of the bed posters, revealing her big flabby boobs beneath the flannel shirt. "My mama said it would be best if you talked about it, said it would be best to let it—"

"Screw your mama!"

"—all come out," Terry went on. "Everybody's talking, you know, everybody says you're taking drugs of some kind and that you're frying your brains—"

"Screw everybody," Lucy cried, and flattened herself in the bed, closing her eyes.

"Oh, come on, Lucy, you're not asleep," Terry wheedled. "Just tell *me*. I won't tell anybody else."

Like hell, Lucy thought.

164

"What were you digging for, Lucy?" she persisted. "My mama said when she saw you, you were—"

"I don't give a shit what your mama said," Lucy screamed. "Now, just get out of here—"

"Can't." Terry smiled benignly. "Your mama told my mama she'd appreciate it if I'd stay with you until she came home." Terry giggled and spit out the well-chewed toenail. "So, in a way, I'm baby-sitting you, Lucy Hackett." She giggled. "Fifty cents an hour, too."

Beneath the cover, Lucy smoldered. Shit! Since her accident, she'd thought all these people had come to visit her because they had wanted to see her. But no, they were all guards, hired by her mama to keep an eye on her.

Quickly she drew the comforter up over her head. She'd rather die than let Terry O'Connell see her tears.

"Lucy-y-y. Come out, come out, wherever you are."

"Go away."

"Can't. Tell me what happened."

In the darkness beneath the comforter, Lucy was having trouble breathing. But no! She didn't want to remember. In fact, once or twice she'd even managed to convince herself that it hadn't happened. But it had, and she'd seen it, his whole body buried and sinking deeper, the earth *eating* him, and that last awful way he'd lifted his face and cried out . . .

"Lucy, what are you doing under there? You'd better come out. Mama said I was to keep an eye on you."

In memory Lucy saw the blood running from his mouth, and the dirt covering everything. She moaned.

"Lucy! You come out of there right now. You hear? You come out or I'm gonna . . ."

What she really wanted to do was to pull Terry O'Connell's stringy red hair out by the roots. But her hands were useless, and she could feel Terry creeping up alongside her on the bed. Lucy couldn't even grab hold of the comforter to protect her concealment, and as she felt the comforter being pulled back, all she could do was shout obscenities that almost blotted out the look of triumph on Terry's face as she sat back on her heels and stared down at her.

"Mama said I could redeem your soul if you'd let me. Like Jesus Christ redeemed Mary Magdalene, but you have to want it."

"I don't want a goddamn thing from you. Now, get out of here and leave me—"

Terry went on, undaunted. "Mama says you're young yet. She says you could be a real messenger for Jesus."

"Screw Jesus!" Lucy screamed.

"Don't say that!"

"Get out! Get out and leave me alone," Lucy sobbed, tears streaming.

For a few moments there was no sound in the room except for her own sobs. Then: "Lucy, don't . . . please," Terry begged, her voice just about as soft and as kind as Lucy had ever heard it. Out of curiosity, she looked up at the girl bent over her. There wasn't a trace of meanness on her face.

"Please," Terry begged. "It will be all right. Everything . . . you'll see . . ."

Lucy couldn't see anything. Her eyes were blurred and her nose was running. But she felt Terry's hand on her forehead, a gentle cool hand. And through her tears she could just barely make out Terry's face, which appeared to be more shocked by Lucy's tears than by her obscenities.

That hand just sat there on her forehead for a minute, then gently began to move back and forth in a comforting, caressing gesture.

All right! So it felt good. Lucy would let her do it for a while, just so long as she didn't start up again with that Christ crap.

"I'm . . . sorry," Terry murmured. "I really didn't mean to make you cry." Through her tears, Lucy saw her chewing on her lower lip. She looked like a real little kid instead of someone who was almost fifteen. "We don't have to be mad and ugly to each other all the time, do we, Lucy?" she asked softly. "I mean, there's enough people around here mad at each other, isn't there? Why can't we just . . . ?"

Lucy blinked at the quivering chin and laboriously wiggled her way up to a sitting position. Without knowing exactly what she was going to do, she put her bandaged hand awkwardly about Terry's shoulders and felt kind of embarrassed but good as Terry hugged her back.

With her face resting sideways on Terry's shoulder, Lucy stared, bewildered, through the window in the direction of the high ridge. She'd never been touched and held by a friend before.

No, it really wasn't bad at all, holding each other like that. But something on the high ridge caught her eyes, a small, blinding reflection, like someone was waggling a mirror at the sun.

She'd never seen that before. Still locked in Terry's hug, she tried to look more closely. There it is, proof for Terry that something was happening on the ridge.

She started to break out of the embrace and point it out to Terry. But she changed her mind and struck a bargain at least in her own mind. If Terry didn't ask her ever again about what had happened to her hands in the backyard, then never again would Lucy scare her with the fact that there were witches in Tomis.

But of course, there were. Terrible ones. . . .

22

About thirty minutes after Sarah had left the restaurant, Hal started down the crumbling blacktop heading toward the barricaded road. He looked ahead, foolishly thinking he might still see her and regretful that he hadn't offered to walk with her to Mina Murdoch's.

He paused by the massive crater left by the boulder. *That* should be repaired immediately. It was impossible for cars to pull directly up in front of the restaurant, and with the summer traffic looming . . .

His thoughts came to a halt. *Summer traffic!* With the boulder now serving as barricade, summer traffic became a moot point.

He lifted his head and looked about to see if anybody was watching him. But all the stores were closed, most of the men either down at the barricade or taking advantage of the empty town to steal a few extra hours of sleep. Pervading all was an air of winter hibernation, of life brought to a standstill.

Sarah . . .

He glanced ahead and saw the street empty. Of course, she'd had more than enough time to make it to Mina's, and what did he want to say to her anyway, except thanks—for everything, for putting all her fears and anxieties aside, for wearing that pretty pink dress which he remembered from when she had been pregnant with Vicky, for coming with him out here and sharing his dream and making it hers as well.

As he started slowly down the street, hands in pockets, he was doubly sorry for having been so sharp with her lately. It was just that things had happened so fast, a state of siege developing almost overnight.

Midway down the street, he looked up. Where were the kids? Usually at this hour the O'Connell kids were out riding their bikes in aimless circles, waiting for Mina to open her front door, the signal that lessons were about to begin. Even the Drivers' front porch, which was usually decorated by a gangling teenager or two, was empty, as was the Lewises'.

At Mina's house he paused, thinking of going in, then decided to check on the barricade first. Ahead about thirty yards, he saw the boulder still in place, the idle crane parked at the far side of the road. Squinting into the sun, he saw several men atop the boulder, all pointing down the hill toward the parked semis and flatbed trailers.

From the intensity of their positions, he knew that something or someone was stirring, and now he broke into a run, calling ahead, "What is it? What's . . . ?"

Atop the boulder, Callie Watkins called back, "There's someone down there. Can't see what they're . . ."

Slightly breathless from his sprint, Hal lifted his head and saw several men clustered excitedly about the boulder: Tom Marshall, hands on hips, staring down the hill; Callie; old Ed Billingsly; Jim Charter; and Tim O'Connell—a ragtag front-line defense whose average age was sixty, armed with a few strands of sweet May grass on which they were sucking.

"Look!" Callie pointed from his vantage point.

At the bottom of the steep hill, Hal saw a single man astride a motorcycle, both man and machine idle, as he appeared to be studying the massive seismograph trucks.

Suddenly it dawned on Hal that a motorcycle would have no trouble slipping through the narrow passage to the right of the boulder.

"How long has he been there?" Hal asked, shielding his eyes in an attempt to see better.

"Just arrived," Tom said as he moved into position beside Hal. "I can't make out what he's doing, can you?"

When no one else spoke, Hal realized he had the youngest eyes on the scene. "Just sitting, as far as I can tell," Hal muttered, and looked more closely and saw what looked like a pack strapped to the back of the motorcycle. Binoculars would help, and Ed Billingsly lived the closest. "Ed, we need glasses. Would you. . . . ?"

Without hesitation the old man nodded, zipped up the front of his windbreaker, and started around the narrow passage on the right of the boulder.

A second request was taking shape in Hal's mind, though he found it difficult as hell to verbalize it. Maybe he shouldn't. Still, how vulnerable they were, and how effortlessly motorcycles could slip past. . . . What if that black pack contained explosives? What a simple matter it would be to dynamite the boulder, thus opening the road. . . .

"Ed, wait!"

He was aware of all six men staring at him, confused by his indecision.

"Do any of you. . . ?" he began, and could not finish.

"What in the hell is it you're trying to say, Kitchens?" Tom Marshall snapped, his nerves edgy.

"Guns," Hal said flatly, tasting the obscenity of a word even as he spoke it. "Do . . . any of you own guns?"

Five blinked back at him. One spoke. "Damn right I do." Tom Marshall nodded predictably. In a way, this had been the cause of Hal's hesitancy. He knew he'd get a yes answer from at least . . .

"What kind and how many?" he asked further.

"Two rifles, two pistols," Marshall boasted, "and all in Class A working condition."

"Get them!" Hal commanded, and instantly regretted it as he looked to see Tom already scurrying down the road which led back into Tomis. "Wait!" Hal called out.

Doing nothing to mask the expression of impatience on his face, Marshall looked back. "What now?"

"Are they . . . loaded?"

"The guns?" He shook his head as though he were dealing with a slow child. "Crap, they've never been *un*loaded."

"Then unload them now."

Slowly Tom Marshall drew back as though certain he hadn't heard correctly. "Uh? . . . Are you crazy, Kitchens? What in the hell good is an unloaded gun gonna do us?"

"They may serve better than loaded ones."

"How do you figure that?"

Hal went the short distance to meet him and tried to rein in his anger, aimed mostly at himself for bringing up the subject. "No one here but you knows one end of a gun from the other, Tom. And I don't plan to use them, just display them if we have to."

"You're crazy," Tom said flatly. "This whole thing is crazy. You can't keep 'em out forever, even with an arsenal of loaded guns. And four unloaded guns ain't gonna do you a—"

"Just get them. Would you please, Tom?" Hal tried to adopt a soothing approach, again aimed as much at himself as at Tom Marshall.

Finally the man shrugged, shook his head, and started off down the road at a leisurely pace. Obviously unloaded guns did not require the same rate of speed as loaded ones.

"And, Tom, one more thing," Hal called out, and noticed that this time the man didn't even bother to look back. "Could you . . . conceal them?"

"From who?" Tom inquired wearily, slowly turning.

"From anyone you might encounter on the way back. The women," Hal said vaguely. "I don't want to upset anyone. And bring your binoculars, if you will."

Again Tom nodded, as though the insanity if nothing else was all of a piece. Just as Hal was turning back toward the boulder, he heard a peculiar rumbling, like distant thunder, and felt the ground vibrate beneath his feet. He held still until the tremor passed, and looked up toward the stone face of Mt. Victor. Another rock slide? Surely not. They had enough troubles.

The brief tremor passed, the ground grew still, and he started toward the other men, wondering if they had felt it as well. Apparently not, for all were buzzing among themselves, still keeping a close watch on the man at the bottom of the hill.

"Where is he?" Hal asked, coming up alongside them and seeing nothing but the idle trucks.

"He's around on the other side," Ed Billingsly said. "If you ask me, he's taking pictures of some sort. Do you think we ought to go down?"

"No, we'll wait right here," Hal said.

"Is Marshall getting his guns?" Callie called down from the top of the boulder.

Hal nodded. "But they'll be unloaded."

"What's the point?" Callie asked, a look of disappointment on his face.

"Have you ever used a gun, Callie?" Hal asked, propping his foot up against the side of the boulder.

The man looked sheepish. "No, I never had much appetite for it. My pa did some quail hunting in Kansas, but I never could get with it much."

Hal nodded and said nothing, confident that Callie had answered his own question. "If we have to, we'll just display them," Hal added. "A man looking down the barrel of a gun doesn't know if it's loaded or not."

The others were listening carefully and agreeably. In fact, Hal even discerned an air of relief. Suddenly Hal heard a sharp sound, like a high-pitched scream. He saw the other men freeze and look, mystified, from one to the other.

"What in the hell was that?" Callie called down. "Did you hear it? Listen . . ."

"Wind," Ed Billingsly said flatly. "It screams like that up on the high ridge all the time, and we get the echo. You all never heard it before?"

Echo? No, Hal had never heard it, and he'd been here longer than any of them. But there was no repetition, and ultimately he too dismissed it, a little chagrined by how foreign the mountain still was to him.

"Here he comes!"

The shout had come from Callie atop the boulder and drew Hal's attention back to a sound which resembled that of a large house fly buzzing in the distance. The motorcycle was making its way slowly past the idle machinery.

"Come on, Tom," Hal muttered, glancing up toward the road. "Get your ass back here, just in case . . ."

Then there he was, as if on cue, running down the blacktop, high-stepping like a grasshopper in an effort to avoid the potholes, clasping in his arms a lumpy bundle, his weathered face flushed with the excitement of the moment.

"Here they are," he called ahead. Hal thought he'd never seen him so excited. "Look," he beamed, spreading the sheet on the ground and reverently drawing back the corners to reveal two high-powered rifles, their blue-black barrels glistening in the sun. From his pockets he withdrew two pistols, one snub-nosed, looking almost feminine compared with its companion, which on first sight and through Hal's untutored eyes appeared to be the most deadly of all.

"A German Luger," the old man pronounced proudly, holding it up for inspection. "And I ain't saying where I got it, but its owner had no further use of it."

As the men clustered around the spread sheet, Hal heard the buzz of the motorcycle growing louder. "They are all unloaded?" he asked quickly, and Tom nodded, but said nothing.

"All right," Hal said. "Ed, you and Callie take the rifles. Just hold them down at your side, but in clear sight."

Suddenly the roar of the motorcycle ceased. Hal looked down to see the man circling slowly about fifty yards away. Clearly something had stopped him. The sight of guns?

"Who are you?" Hal called. "What do you want?"

The man brought his motorcycle to a halt, braced his feet on both sides, and lifted his hands into the air in a gesture of surrender. "I'm a friend, I think." He grinned up at them.

"What do you want?" Hal shouted again, trusting no one.

"Can I come up?" the man asked. "I just want to talk, that's all."

"Why don't you let him come? It might be interesting . . ."

The quiet voice came from behind and belonged to no one from Tomis. As though under fire from that direction, Hal looked over his shoulder and saw Frank Quinton. Stunned by his sudden and unexpected appearance, Hal momentarily floundered.

"Who in the hell is *he?*" Tom Marshall demanded, and only at that moment did it occur to Hal that no one else in Tomis knew Frank Quinton, except Brian, who'd been with him the night they'd almost gone over the mountainside.

Though it seemed a bizarre time and place for formal introductions, Hal had no choice. "His name is Frank Quinton," he muttered. "He's the chief surveyor for Century Mining Corporation."

This last information caused the Tomis Home Guard to turn as one, briefly abandoning the man being held at bay on the motorcycle.

"If I were you," Quinton said, "I'd let him come up. For several reasons. One, he may have information about what's going on with the men who own that equipment, and two, he doesn't look very dangerous, don't you think?"

Without a word, Hal saw all heads turn as one toward the man still balanced on his motorcycle, resting his elbows on the handlebars now, clearly relaxed and waiting out the impasse at the top of the hill.

No, he *didn't* look dangerous. His rather long, sandy-colored hair fluttered about his face with the slight morning breeze. He appeared to be clad in the uniform of the mountains, blue jeans and Levi's windbreaker.

"If I were you, I'd let him come forward, Mr. Kitchens," Quinton repeated. "It would be no real battle, would it, all of us against him?"

Us? Hal had the feeling Quinton was laughing at them. Then he added quite casually, "I have two guns in the trunk of my car, rifles. I'm afraid my work takes me into some fairly unorthodox situations."

Unwilling to look as if he were taking advice, Hal frowned and motioned to the man on the motorcycle, who immediately came forward. For a moment, no one spoke. He was a much younger man than Hal had thought, late twenties at most, a cockiness about him in spite of his initial hesitancy to approach.

"Who are you?" Hal called out, stepping to the front of the group, more eager to dissociate himself from Frank Quinton than anything else.

"Boze Calahan." He grinned and extended a hand, simultaneously bobbing his head to the rest of the men. "I'm a disc jockey from Durango. You've probably heard me . . ." He paused as though awaiting the recognition that was due him.

When it didn't come right away, Boze Calahan went on, undaunted. "Hell, I'm the only deejay in Durango, but I'm a damn good one, if I do say so myself."

"What do you want?" Hal asked, ignoring the outstretched hand and now transferring his hostility from Quinton to the young man.

"Just sightseeing." Calahan grinned. "I was up here a couple years ago, and had a day off and thought I'd—"

"Where did you say you were from?"

"Durango, though my true destination is L.A."

"You're on the wrong road," Hal snapped, not believing a word the man had said. "Why were you taking photographs?"

The young man shrugged. "Why not? I work at the radio station in Durago and I'm always on the point for a good story—"

Quinton suddenly interrupted. "What precisely did you hear in Durango?"

Calahan grinned. "A hell of a lot of bitching, primarily. Lots of oxen down there who feel they belong behind the wheels of those machines, and they're pissed as hell over that there, blocking their way." He stabbed a finger at the boulder and looked admiringly about. "I'd say you had 'em by the balls, Mr. Kitchens, least for a while." He glanced back toward the motorcycle. "Would I be causing any offense if I took a few photos up here? I mean, you got a real live one here, Mr. Kitchens, a David and Goliath, if you know what I mean. How is a little sympathetic publicity gonna hurt you?"

"No photographs," said Hal, his anger rising. "I think it would be best for everyone, Mr. Calahan, if you got back on your motorcycle and—"

But abruptly the young man stepped closer, transferring his attention from Hal to Frank Quinton. "What did you say your name was?" he asked, peering up with a look of incredulity.

"Quinton. Frank Quinton," came the amiable response.

What now? Hal brooded.

"There was a guy named Quinton in Durango last week," Calahan went on, "connected with the mining business, or so I heard."

"At your service." Quinton smiled.

Clearly baffled by this strange alliance, Calahan stepped back and scratched his head. "Then what in the hell are you doing here?"

Quinton laughed. "Don't you see, Mr. Calahan, I'm being held a prisoner. Seriously, I can't get my car by the boulder." Then he turned to Hal. "I think he's right. A little publicity could help you."

Calahan grinned, having apparently recovered from his earlier alarm brought on by the presence of the guns. "I'd say offhand that ninety percent

172

of the entire state of Colorado would be behind you, and support like that couldn't help but serve you in the event of—"

"He's right," Quinton said quietly. "Let him take his pictures, sell his story if necessary, get someone out here from Denver. What harm, Kitchens?"

Still baffled by the man's position on the subject, Hal was on the verge of telling him to butt out when suddenly from the top of the hill he heard a familiar voice raised in an unfamiliar state of agitation.

"Hal, it's Sarah. You'd better . . ."

He looked up and saw Donna, her long hair undone, shirttail out, as though she'd been dragged out of bed and had dressed hastily.

"Hurry, Hal, please . . ." she cried again.

Sarah? What about Sarah? Torn between the cry of distress at the top of the hill and the admiring circle now enclosing Boze Calahan, Hal hesitated.

"Sounds serious," came the quiet voice from the man who now lounged against the boulder, one foot propped up behind him. "You go on, Kitchens," Quinton offered kindly. "I'll look after things here."

"Hal, hurry!" It was Donna again, gesturing wildly at him.

Helpless, suffering from the sensation of being pulled in half, he looked back and saw Calahan arranging the men in a line, with the boulder in the background, like some half-assed school outing.

"Hal!"

"Go, Mr. Kitchens. Your wife clearly needs you."

"All right, lift your guns, gentlemen," Calahan instructed as he adjusted the camera. "And look fierce, you hear? Let's see that good old American spirit."

"Hal, please!"

Sickened, Hal started up the hill, struggling against an annihilating sense of failure. The very thing he'd sought to avoid, he'd brought about. The tensions and cross-purposes and hostilities that he'd hoped to leave in Boston now flourished on Mt. Victor's plateau. He trusted no one. *No one!* And if this was another case of Sarah's self-indulgent theatrics . . .

As he dug his heels into the final incline, he heard Boze Calahan's excited voice floating up behind him: "Shit, the folks in Denver are going to love it. *Love it!* Okay, now, let's have one with three of you men on top of the rock. You know, like that famous Iwo Jima photograph. What we need is an American flag. Does anybody have an American flag?"

23

Fighting back tears, Donna stood in the archway of Mina's bedroom and decided they needed some light.

She moved quickly past Hal where he sat in the chair, face hidden behind his hands, and gently drew back the heavy velvet drapes. And instantly regretted it.

A brilliant slash of light cut through the semidarkness and revealed a room which more accurately resembled a butcher' shop.

Sarah lay on the bed, naked beneath a light sheet. And unconscious. There was a pungent smell of chloroform in the room. It was the strongest thing that Mike had that would knock her out completely. Her legs were slightly spread by the bulk of padded towels which Mike had placed in position in an attempt to absorb the blood.

Donna had arrived late, and all he'd said as he'd rushed out of the door, carrying a small bloodied bundle which had looked ominously like a dead baby, was that Sarah had miscarried, was badly torn, that Donna was to find Hal and wait here with him, and Mike would be back to tend to her.

In the brutal spill of light which she had created, Donna felt ill. On the floor in the corner she saw a piece of plastic shining with fresh blood, blood on Sarah's legs beginning to soak through the white sheet, blood everywhere, on the floor, staining the side of the bed. Coming from the kitchen, she heard poor Mina sobbing.

Donna had spoken only briefly with her immediately following Mike's departure, had at first been unable to make out anything the woman was saying. Apparently they had been having a cup of tea, when Sara had collapsed. Determining that her water had broken, Mina, with the help of the Mexicans, had carried her into the bedroom, had determined that birth was imminent, and sent one of the boys for Mike, who had obviously arrived too late.

Donna looked down at Hal, crushed and defeated and crumpled in the chair.

"I'm . . . so sorry," she whispered, and receiving no response, knelt before him. "She'll be all right," she soothed, stroking his knee. "Mike told me so."

Behind the barrier of his hands, he nodded, and she realized that he couldn't speak, was weeping, and embarrassed to be doing so.

"It's all right, Hal," she comforted, stroking back his hair, wet with perspiration. What had he been doing at the barricade? she wondered. She'd noticed a motorcycle and a man taking pictures. In her opinion, Hal had at last bitten off more than he could chew. They had created a lovely world for themselves and had enjoyed and nurtured it for four years. Maybe that was enough. In a way, she'd always known that sooner or later the rest of the world would find them and in their envy either try to join them or destroy them. It was human nature.

"The . . . baby . . ." Hal whispered behind the mask of his hands.

". . . was born dead," she said, not certain that she was being absolutely accurate. *Had* it been born dead, or had it died shortly after. . . ?"

"What . . . was it?"

"I don't know, Hal. Mike felt that he should . . . remove it, in case Sarah . . ."

He nodded strongly, and suddenly pushed back in the chair and grasped the arms as though in fear of falling, and revealed the ruin of his face.

He looked awful, his eyes red-rimmed, still weeping. "She's . . . not been . . . feeling·well," he said disjointedly to the ceiling.

"I know," Donna soothed. "The night I stayed with her, the night that Joyce . . ." *No, stay away from that.* "Well, she said then that the baby had become so quiet. She said it had been several days since she'd felt it move."

Hal nodded and appeared to be making an attempt to regain control. "Where's Mina?" he asked, looking around, dragging his sleeves across his face in an attempt to clean it.

"She's in the kitchen," Donna said, rising. "Do you want me to get her?"

He nodded as she handed him a clean towel from the stack on the table. "Would you like a cup of coffee? Anything?" she inquired further, heading toward the door which led into the kitchen. "Sarah *will* be all right," Donna reminded him softly, trying to replace the awful look on his face with hope.

Still no response, and feeling somehow that she'd wandered into someone else's nightmare, she gained the kitchen door and looked in to see Mina, her

175

head down on the table, her shoulders heaving, reflecting the depth of her grief. Donna had never seen Mina cry. Normally Mina was the rock. Standing behind her in a solicitous semicircle were the three Mexican boys. What in the hell were they doing here?

"Would you leave us for a while?" Donna suggested kindly. "Lessons are over for the day. Surely you can see that . . ."

If they could, they gave no evidence of it, and continued to stare at her with black and unblinking eyes.

Damn! She wasn't in any mood for this. *"Vamos!"* she ordered, raising her voice. *"Pronto! Pronto!"* Limited, but effective, or so she hoped as the boys straggled slowly out the back door.

"Oh, dear," Mina moaned. "Hal holds me responsible, doesn't he?"

"Oh, no, I'm sure he—"

"He does. I should have gotten help faster, but it happened so fast . . ."

Donna understood this and remembered Vicky's birth, no more than twenty minutes from first contraction to that miraculously appearing smooth round head. No torn flesh then, either. Mike had been amazed, said that Sarah was equipped to drop a dozen effortlessly.

Wrong! Apparently there had been nothing effortless about this one, and newly aware of the bloodied bedroom and grief-stricken Hal, Donna urged, "He just wants to talk to you for a few minutes, Mina, that's all."

"Of course he does," Mina murmured, and slowly followed Donna outside.

"Hal, I'm . . . so . . . sorry," the old woman began, and within the instant dissolved into fresh tears. Donna tried to lead her to a chair, but she pulled away and clung to the end of the bed. The sight of Sarah seemed to provoke even greater grief. "She was in such pain," she wept. "I've never seen anyone suffer so."

Hal lifted Sarah's lifeless right hand. "Her wrists are chafed," he said, keeping his voice low, almost but not quite an accusation.

"Of course they are chafed," Mina sobbed. "We had to restrain her so that she wouldn't do damage to herself. I can't tell you how . . ."

Restrain her? Donna closed her eyes. Poor Sarah. How frightened she must have been.

"Tell me if you will, Mina, exactly what happened." The remarkably calm voice belonged to Hal, who pushed to his feet, placed his hand gently on Sarah's brow, then moved to the window, where he stood spotlighted in a single shaft of bright sunlight.

Not again, Donna thought, and decided to leave the two to their own torture. When she came back five minutes later, Sarah was still unconscious on the bed, Hal collapsed in the chair, while Mina stood behind him, stroking his hair in a comforting gesture, though her eyes fixed on Donna with a cold, slightly bemused expression.

Please hurry, Mike, Donna prayed, and felt the smell of chloroform burn the inside of her nose. She marveled at how effortlessly the whole world had become malevolent, brutal, mindlessly cruel.

Poor Sarah . . .

There are chafed places on her wrists.

Of course. We had to restrain her. She was in agony.

A voice was crying in terror someplace deep within her. Donna turned and faced the wall and pressed her forehead against it.

24

No! No! No!

The single word exploded repeatedly inside his brain, effortlessly annihilating all his years of training. The medical landscape was cluttered with two-headed fetuses, four-armed embryos, hearts attached to the outside of the rib cage, spatulate ducklike fingers and toes, a nightmarish gallery of nature's aberrations.

But . . . *no!* Never this. No! No!

The single word seemed to set the pace as Mike carried the small miscarriage into his examination room, the outer sheet already damp with seeping blood.

Carefully he placed it on the table and stared at the red, wet sheet. For several moments he stood rooted in paralyzed shock. Two had seen it. Mina. And himself. Two too many. And what he knew and what Mina did not was that it was still alive. He'd felt a claw pushing against him as he'd carried it out of the house, intent only on destroying it before Hal had arrived or Sarah had regained consciousness.

Sarah . . . He had to hurry. She was badly torn.

Then one look. Then burn it. Perhaps in the semidarkened room his eyes had deceived him as Mina guided him to the floor at the foot of the bed, pulling back the sheet and revealing a . . .

Mike shivered and stepped quickly back as the shroud moved, a curious noise escaping from the bloodied sheet, a soft chatter like a squirrel or the rattlers of a snake.

Destroy it now, without looking, then take refuge for the rest of your life behind the safety of flawed vision and a semidarkened room.

Right. And wrong. There was the other thing as well. Joyce. What they had done had been wrong. There should have been an investigation. Clear strangulation. Not clear. Heavy grass stains around her neck and on the decapitated head. Shouldn't have been buried and forgotten. Not forgotten.

Nor would this be.

It moved again, something small, but alive, clawing at the encasing sheet.

Hurry! Sarah needs you. What will you tell them? Dead. At seven months. Umbilical-cord strangulation. Would they believe you?

One hand went forward for the end of the sheet. All movement ceased, as though it knew. Slowly he drew back one corner. A stench of seawater filled his nostrils. The soft chattering commenced again as he saw the gold fuzzy crown of a perfectly shaped infant's head, no larger than an orange, shell-like ears still caked with blood, eyes open, the neck straining to accommodate . . .

A sledgehammer blow pounded inside his temples. Reason implored him to move away. Right and wrong waged a continuous battle back and forth, both threatening, as though there were a third alternative which he'd overlooked.

Scales. Dark green, though coated with slime, a lizard's body, approximately twenty-five inches in length, four wide-splayed claws trying to support the torso, a hideous mutation, the green-scaled tail, which moved lethargically from side to side, as though trying to propel the entire organism off the table and back into some prehistoric pool, a natural habitat.

Suddenly Mike jerked the sheet over the monstrosity and backed away until he felt the cabinet behind him, never taking his eyes off the gently moving sheet, the chattering audible again, as though it did not like concealment.

Without looking, he pulled open the drawer and withdrew a hypodermic needle. One mercifully accurate injection of air and he could relegate the thing forever to his gallery of nightmares. Only two knew, and Mina would have to deal with it in her own way.

He lifted the needle and felt a sudden blast of icy air rush across his face. He inserted the needle and felt the pressure as it first encountered the scaled torso. A few minutes later he saw the tail as though in agony flip free of the sheet and heard the chattering escalate into a high-pitched shriek. For a moment he heard an infant's cry, then heard nothing, and saw the tail go limp.

He dropped the needle as though it suddenly had become hot, and tried not to focus on the small claw which fought its way through the sheet, then was still.

Now, burn it! Make it no longer to exist, and create in your own mind a

179

whole seven-month fetus, blue from strangulation, the umbilical cord wrapped tightly around a small throat, sad, so tragic. *I am sorry, Sarah, but there was nothing I could do, anyone could do . . .*

He ripped the plastic sheet from all four corners of the table, drew the ends together, and lifted it, allowing the pool of blood to form a deeper pool at center, the thing collapsing boneless in the middle. No movement now, no sound.

Hurry! Get rid of it, every trace of it before someone comes.

Holding the bundle awkwardly away from his body, he hurried out the back door, stopping at the wood shed long enough to retrieve the can of kerosene. Predictably, his eyes moved deeper into the shadows toward the rear wall, where, less than six inches beneath the soil, safely sealed in an airtight box, was his demon, a single unopened bottle of Chivas Regal.

To hell with everything. He'd see this through, see to Sarah, then before nightfall it was his avowed intention to be safely, mindlessly drunk. The only trouble was, there was only one bottle. He would have to have more, perhaps at least two a day for the rest of his life.

He stared a moment longer in the direction of his salvation, then grabbed the kerosene and matches in one hand and stumbled across the yard toward the far corner and the compost heap.

Burn it! There must be no trace. The battle, right or wrong, had called up impressive reserves. Morality, ethics, professional responsibility, normally dramatic and sobering considerations. But not now. Only two knew. Two too many.

Burn it!

The sun was high overhead in a noon position. Warm for May. Quickly he swung the plastic sheet atop the compost heap and saw the dead thing limp inside the bloodied sheet. He dowsed it all with kerosene and struck one safety match, which the wind extinguished. He struck another, accidentally dropped the matchbox, and bent over to retrieve it as he felt the sun slip behind a cloud. He looked up and saw the tail fallen free of the shroud, as though it were still alive, and struck a third match and threw it onto the kerosene-soaked plastic. He heard the small combustion and saw the flames leap high, and within seconds all was afire and burning well, a snake of black smoke climbing into the thin air.

Mike watched with dull eyes, shivering in spite of his close proximity to the flames. A new wind seemed to rush around him, fanning the fire.

He continued to watch the curling plastic edges as the fire devoured all, then for good measure tossed the empty kerosene can onto the flames and did not move until the fire had diminished and all he could see were the red eyes of smoldering embers.

Gone. It had never happened. He must convince himself of this. *It had never happened!*

A seven-month miscarriage, a male fetus, perfectly formed except for the umbilical cord wrapped around . . .

Christ, he was cold, the sun still missing behind a dark gray layer of sudden clouds.

180

A churning wind caught the smoke and blew it into his face. *He could still smell the stench of seawater.*

No!

That single hammering refutation exploded again inside his head. A mutant? Radiation? From a nuclear-power plant? Rocky Mountain Flats? All plausible. And implausible. Sarah had not left Tomis for the duration of her pregnancy. Here the air was clean and uncontaminated.

No! There was no medical or scientific reason for what had emerged from Sarah's womb. And now the evidence was gone, and if it repeated itself, let someone else deal with it.

Never again would he deliver a baby. Pregnant women in Tomis would be sent to the hospital in Durango.

There had been another infant, the young girl from the camping area, the missing husband.

Where were they? Mina . . .

Not now. Hurry! Sarah needed him.

He stepped back from the still-smoking compost heap. The fire had burned down to the moist second layer and was smoking continuously, blessedly obscuring all except the new sharp chill in the air and the persistent smell of seawater.

His hands were filthy, covered with blood. Cleanse! Everything! Hands, face, mind, vision. It had not happened. None of it.

25

Her first conscious thought was a safe one. She felt snow in the air. Four years of living in the mountains had provided her with that intuition. It *was* possible to feel snow without seeing it.

Snow? But it was May, not the season for snow. And there was the end to safety, and with the first conscious breath she smelled chloroform, and the innocuous mystery of May snow faded and was replaced with nightmare memories of pain and terror.

There were voices in the room, male voices speaking softly. And someone was sitting beside her. Again she could feel a presence without opening her eyes. The sensory perceptors in her back informed her that this was her bed— a mattress after four years fits the body like a pair of old shoes.

Then she was in her own bed, which was good, but why the strong smell of chloroform burning her nose and throat?

"I did what I thought was best, Hal."

"You had no right . . ."

"What would be the purpose in . . ."

"Sarah! She has a right . . ."

"It's over. You can have more . . ."

Hal. And Mike. She recognized both voices and tried to open her eyes, but

182

it was too much of an effort and there still was too much she had to deal with before she rejoined their world. Better to feign complete unconsciousness and deal with it alone.

She must have made a sound, for the quietly speaking voices suddenly ceased, and the near presence scolded, "Now you've awakened her. Why don't you go into the other room?"

Donna. It was Donna sitting beside the bed, though her voice sounded different, pinched, frightened.

"Is she awake?" That was Hal, standing on the other side of the bed.

Look, Sarah, it's yours, all yours.

That voice had not come from this room. That voice belonged to the nightmare, to the shadowy image working between her legs, helping her, urging her to push, drawing forth from her womb a . . .

The memory exploded within her. A sirenlike scream started at the base of her throat, and she flailed her head on the pillow in an attempt to escape it, and felt hands restraining her and for the first time felt a burning pain between her legs, her stomach flat, the infant gone.

There had been no infant.

"Sarah, lie still. You must lie still." That was Mike, pleading with her. Good, gentle Mike. *Had he seen?* Had Hal? Donna?

"Hand me my case. I'll give her another shot."

"No, don't, Mike. She has to wake up sometime and face—"

"She's too weak. She's lost blood. Push up the sleeve of her gown."

No! Mustering all the strength at her command, she forced her eyes open, determined to let them see that she was capable of making decisions for herself, and for a moment, all three seemed so surprised to see her awake that they stared down on her like guilty children.

Still holding the hypodermic needle poised in his hand, Mike spoke first, a soft inquiry. "Sarah? Can you see me?"

She could see two of him, and nodded and briefly closed her eyes in an attempt to focus them.

"Are you in pain?" Mike inquired kindly, still holding the needle at the ready.

"No . . . shot," she murmured. "What . . . happened?"

She was aware of all three exchanging a quick glance, clearly trying to appoint a spokesman.

Hal sat on the edge of the bed and took her hand in his and kissed it. "You lost the baby," he whispered, and she could feel his grief, like the snow, without seeing it, and felt guilty.

"But you're all right," he went on, "and Mike says we can have more . . ."

As she rolled her head back toward Mike, she saw him at last lowering the needle. "If you *are* in pain, I can . . ."

Weakly she shook her head and looked toward Donna and saw fear on her face. Dauntless, intrepid Donna afraid?

"Were . . . you afraid?" she asked, scarcely able to form words.

"Not until later. It was all over when I . . ."

183

Involuntarily she groaned.

"Give her the shot, Mike," Hal insisted. "I don't want her to suffer."

"No," she muttered, trying to shake her head, concealing her arm beneath the blanket. "Tell me, someone . . . what happened?"

Donna and Hal looked at Mike, who stalled as he returned the needle to the case and stalled some more as he encircled the foot of the bed, rubbing his forehead. He looked terrible. His white knit shirt bore irregular patterns of dried blood. His hands were clean, but there were dried smudges on his upper arms, and even in her semidrugged state, fighting off memory as well as discomfort, she could see his hands trembling.

"You . . . miscarried," he said, still not looking at her. "Your water had already broken and you were in labor when Mina sent one of the Mexicans for . . ."

Sarah moved her hand to her mouth to keep from crying out. Every time she made a sound, it was wrongly interpreted. Her physical discomfort was nothing compared to . . .

". . . perfectly formed," Mike went on. "Seven months, normally a chance, but . . ."

Hal still held her right hand, and now squeezed it.

"The umbilical," Mike concluded, "twisted, strangulation—nothing anyone could have done."

He was lying. She knew it and he knew it. There . . . was . . . no . . . baby, no . . .

Why couldn't she move her lips? The words were there, perfectly formed inside her brain, but her tongue wouldn't move. "No . . . baby," she stammered, and saw Mike reach back for his case and heard Donna angrily intercede.

"No, don't give her a shot. Let her talk. She needs to—"

"She's not in her right mind. Loss of blood, too much . . ."

She was aware of a scuffle in the vicinity of her left arm, Donna trying to block Mike's approach, Mike approaching anyway, Hal standing on the opposite side of the bed, looking lost and confused and tired.

As she felt the needle penetrate her arm, she saw Donna turn away. Before the drug spread too far, she had to ask one question. "Vicky . . .?"

". . . is with Inez, Sarah," Hal soothed. "Don't worry. She's fine."

"Not Mina," Sarah managed, the numbness spreading.

Donna looked quickly back.

"Sleep now," Mike urged, and drew the blanket up around her. "There'll be time for talk later, when you're stronger."

No, there won't, Sarah thought. We'll never talk again. You won't let me, for you saw it as well . . .

"My God, it's snowing."

The soft surprised voice belonged to Hal and came from the vicinity of the window.

If the two still hovering over her by the bed heard the bizarre announcement, they gave no indication of it. In a way she was grateful for the shot. She

184

had just begun to see the scene again, the small, shadowy room, the burned-down candles, the smell of seawater . . .

The lassitude extended to her brain and canceled the smell and the image, canceled everything except the throbbing pain which felt as though something with claws still was trying to get out.

26

Hal stood in the doorway of Sarah's bedroom and tried to see through the shadows caused by the single night light. He felt overwhelmed by the feelings of grief and fatigue and inadequacy which had plagued him all day. It was as though forces beyond his powers of identification had taken over, and all he could do was struggle to maintain his balance. All day he'd arrived too late, with no solution or the wrong one. God, how he hated it, this sensation of helplessness.

He'd just come from the restaurant, where he'd allowed a rescue party of five men to go out into the blizzard in search of Kate Sawyer, who, according to Brian, had become disoriented by the spring snow and had wandered away from home about forty-five minutes ago.

Hal had not expected so many volunteers. But there they had been, snowed in and helpless as everyone was, the young deejay from Durango and all four of the road crew. They'd taken different directions, and all had disappeared behind a solid white curtain of snow within twenty feet of the restaurant.

Five men. One woman. Maybe they would find her. For Brian's sake, he hoped so.

"She's sleeping," Donna whispered from the shadowy interior of the room, and Hal could see that now, his eyes adjusting to the dim light after the bright illumination of the front room.

"Will you . . . stay the night, Donna?" he asked quietly.

186

"Try to get rid of me," came the soft reply. "Is Mike . . . ?"

"In the front room. We're trying to get a call through to Roger Laing."

I don't know what you think Roger can do.

In memory he heard Sarah's voice from their conversation this morning. *Only this morning?* The day had to end soon.

"The bleeding has stopped," came Donna's toneless voice.

Something was wrong with *her*, Hal thought. She sounded different. But maybe not. She and Sarah were very close, had grown more so since Kate's distant retreat.

What was that? At the precise moment that he'd thought Kate's name, he heard it above the wind.

"Did you hear anything?" he asked quietly.

"No."

He braced himself in the door, listening. Only his imagination. He listened a moment longer. "Can I get you something, Donna, a cup of—?"

"No. Just keep Mike out of here with his goddamn needles. She has to wake up sometime. She has to deal with . . ."

Her voice broke. "A dead baby" was what she was going to say. He knew it. But out of consideration for him, she'd stopped short.

"I know," he said, and renewed his grasp on the door.

There! He heard it again, someone calling Kate's name. "Did you hear . . . ?"

He considered opening the door, then changed his mind. Whatever was happening would have to take its place in line behind his dead son, Sarah ill, the barricaded road, that blasted newsman who had invaded Tomis, Frank Quinton, the ruptured septic tanks at the camping area, and now this blizzard. And Vicky. He should relieve Inez of Vicky. And he should see if everyone in Tomis was accounted for, had enough firewood.

He leaned against the doorframe, his own shock of realization at the chaos increasing. Less than a month ago he'd thought this summer would be the easiest of all. The real work was behind them, the resurrection of Tomis an accomplished fact. Little to do now but sit back and enjoy the fruits of their labor.

The phone rang in the front room and stirred him into action. *Roger!* With a sense of guilty relief he turned his back on the two women, one sleeping, unaware, the other awake and frightened, and hurried down the narrow corridor. He grabbed the phone on the third ring, annoyed to see Mike still slumped on the sofa. *Destroyed it? Burned it? Why? It wasn't garbage. It had been his dead son.*

"Hello? Hello?" he shouted into the receiver. From the end of the corridor he heard Donna close the bedroom door.

"Hello? Who is it?" he called again, hearing only static on the line. He saw Mike look up as though he too were annoyed by the disturbance.

To hell with him. "Hello! Hello! Roger, is that you?"

More static, the sharp click of a computer. Then: "This is the operator. May I help you?"

Damn! "The phone rang here," he shouted angrily. "I was expecting a call from Evergreen, Colorado. Could you tell me if it's gone through?"

"One moment, please."

He grasped the receiver as though he wanted to strangle it, and felt a sharp chill race down his back. *Seven months. Umbilical strangulation. Not uncommon. Nothing I could do.*

"Hello? Anyone there?"

The static crackled louder.

"One moment, please."

Christ!

From someplace he heard a soft moan. Sarah waking up? Not now, please. . . .

"Operator? Are you there?"

He heard it again, a whimpering. Apparently Mike heard it as well. He raised up from his slouched position and looked questioningly at Hal.

"Hello? Hello?"

The static was a constant shriek now, so loud it hurt his ears. Then the line went dead.

Oh Christ, no! "Hello? Hello?"

Frantically he clicked the receiver. Mike was on his feet now, moving toward the door and the whimpering sound.

Hal slammed the receiver down, fully aware of the implications. The phone lines must be down.

"Don't open the door," he shouted irrationally.

Too late. As Mike pulled open the door, a blast of cold wind blew snow in, and along with it . . .

Hal stared dully forward as though somehow he had known what was on the other side of the door. A half-frozen, half-starved Copper crept past Mike in reptilian fashion, his red fur coated with beads of ice, his tail a frozen red plume.

He appeared to be having trouble standing. "Poor pup," Hal mourned. He looked ill or injured. "Come on, boy, you must be . . ."

Apparently Mike saw it first, the curious discoloration about his neck and muzzle, red drops falling onto the hard wood floor as the snow melted. Mike ran his hand along the dog's neck several times, then raised his arm, palm up, for his inspection. "Blood," he said.

Hal glanced from Mike's red hand to Copper, who now crept close to the fire, leaving a trail of red melting snow.

Mike bent closer over the dog. His voice was a monotone. "Something . . . has ripped open his throat."

An animal—foraging, hungry. These were two small thrusts of reason. But they were short-lived. There was no game, no wildlife on the plateau.

"I'm afraid he's dying," Mike said weakly. He sat back on his heels and watched along with Hal as the dog collapsed slowly onto his side before the fire, his large brown eyes staring at them, his muzzle resting in an expanding pool of melting red.

27

Evergreen, Colorado

In a state of shock and annihilating fatigue—he'd not slept more than four hours in the last two days—Roger Laing stood alone at midnight in his basement laboratory, which ran the length of CUSP House, and stared, disbelieving, at Percy Forrester's "irrefutable proof" of the H.E. Theory.

So many times in the last nineteen years Percy had made that claim, and as many times, Percy and Roger had had to swallow their disappointment, pick up what they could salvage of the failed experiment, and push on in search of more reliable data. When the call had come for him in Tomis, Roger had been prepared for disappointment again.

But not this time, and still in the state of sustained excitement and terror that had inundated him three days ago when he'd first tested the new experiment and found it beyond refutation, he almost lovingly fondled the metal edges of the carton which bore Percy's sprawled handwriting. It had come from Cornwall, or more accurately Tintagel, proof of the horrifying theory that the better part of the world would not believe until it was too late.

As despair blended dangerously with fatigue and excitement, Roger drew up one of the high metal stools close to the worktable. He sat heavily, and for a moment rested his head in his hands and shielded his eyes from the bright light overhead, and again, as he'd done hourly since the moment of confirmation, resisted the urge to call his colleagues.

There would be time, not a great deal of it, but enough. First he had to make certain that all *his* data were in order. Percy had worked on only one phase, although the most difficult. But Roger's experiments were impressive as well, and before they informed the world, he had to be absolutely certain.

Quickly he glanced over his shoulder toward the small two-burner gas stove where he'd just placed a full kettle of water. It had to reach boiling point and beyond, so there was time for a brief rest. He pushed his glasses up on his forehead and rubbed his burning eyes, glancing at the remains of the stale corned beef on rye that Mrs. DeNunnzio had brought him about noon.

Mrs. DeNunnzio. Patty. Failed daughter, failed wife, failed Catholic. Her words and condemnation, not his. As far as he was concerned, she had managed all aspects of his life efficiently and effectively for the last seventeen years.

He glanced up toward the ceiling, where in the study above he knew she was still working. For a moment he thought he could hear the tap-tap-tap of her typewriter. She was compiling Percy Forrester's latest data, preparatory to sharing it with other CUSP members before news releases and press conferences.

At the thought of the H.E. Theory finally confirmed, he found himself staring rigidly, mindlessly into space. Dear God, who would believe them?

Before him on the worktable he glanced at the dark blue CUSP folder containing every step of the experiment up until now. "CUSP," he repeated to himself, a most appropriate acronym, meaning a fixed point on a mathematical curve at which a point tracing the curve would exactly reverse its direction of motion. How many times in the last seventeen years had they had to reverse their direction of motion?

Slowly, every movement marked by fatigue, he drew a binder forward and studied it as though seeing it for the first time, the CUSP logo imprinted on the cover, a sphere resembling the earth, with the identifying words "Committee for the Understanding of Short-lived Phenomena" encircling it in a field of midnight blue. This was his brainchild, he thought with pride, formed seventeen years ago. Thirty men from ten countries, scientists, educators, economists, humanists, industrialists who met to discuss a single subject of staggering scope—the present and future predicament of man.

Out of this initial meeting the committee had grown to its present size, seventy-five men who gathered here once a year, usually in early fall, whose purposes were to foster understanding of the varied but interdependent components—economic, political, social, and natural—that make up the global system in which we all must live.

No member of the international association held public office, nor did the group seek to express any single ideological, political, or national point of view. All were united, however, by their overriding conviction that the major problems facing mankind were of such complexity and were so interrelated that traditional institutions and policies and solutions were no longer able to cope with them.

The members had backgrounds as varied as their nationalities; physicists, biochemists, naturalists. New candidates for admission to membership were asked only one question by Roger and the other members of the committee, a deceptively simple question concerning their view of man.

Was he a limited creature trapped in a purely physical universe?

It was surprising the number of highly intelligent men who responded yes. It was even more surprising that a few, a very few, said no.

Behind him on the stove he heard the water begin to purr under the duress of heat. Not ready yet. Must be a fast, hard boil. Briefly his eyes scanned the rest of the equipment he'd aligned for the experiment—the galvanized bucket filled with live brine shrimp, the large-leafed philodendron which Toby had dragged down from his office. How many countless times he'd worked this one! In a way it was the most reliable of all.

"A watched pot never . . ." he muttered, and turned back on the high stool. He heard a door slam in the house above him, and again it occurred to him to consider the layman's reaction to the H.E. Theory.

Carefully he drew the binder forward and tried to imagine what uninformed, unprepared eyes would do with the information printed there. He flattened the binder to the first page: "H.E. Theory. Phase One—Clear Identification of the Specific Components for Analyzing the Behavior and Relationship of Inanimate Objects."

Page two: "The Body of Expertise and Research Demands—Origins. Significance and Interrelationship—The Examination of Single Items in the Problematique—Five Basic Factors."

Discouraged, he thumbed through it, and on page six stopped to read a random paragraph: "Many Christian churches are built on the sites of pagan temples. The ancients believed that such places are permeated by certain nonhuman forces."

He read another paragraph: "Dowsing is a response to energies that are unrecognized by science. Levi believed that there is some form of intangible ether that carries the impulses of the will in the same way that the luminiferous ether carries electromagnetic vibrations."

No, he thought with a combination of relief and concern. A layman wouldn't have a notion what it was about. And lacking a notion concerning the problem, what in the name of God would he do with the solution?

He closed his eyes and completely obscured his face behind his hands, hearing Percy Forrester's despairing voice in his mind less than six months ago: "You think that no one but you, Roger, knows what it is like to be so absolutely certain of something, yet lacks the intelligence and technology to prove it? We are so ignorant, so *ignorant*, and yet our impulses and instincts count for nothing. We must provide measurable, irrefutable, scientifically sound proof, and even then, we frequently are not believed."

Under the weight of memory and years of frustration, he felt his bone-racking fatigue as never before, and as the large laboratory swirled about him, he held on to the worktable until it grew steady, and decided that he needed to lie down for a few minutes. Accordingly, he pushed off the stool and walked toward the stove, where the purring water was beginning to boil.

Bending over, he carefully turned down the fire. He raised up against the

191

pain of a sharp stitch in his back and walked slowly, feeling like a man one hundred years old, toward the small cubicle next to the rock room, where years ago he'd had a small couch moved in. Most evenings it was simpler to sleep here than to make the climb up to his suite on the fourth floor.

For a moment the sense of his father's mansion hovered over him. It was monstrous, far too much for one man. Now he carefully avoided switching on the light, stretched out on the couch, and looked up through the high casement windows next to the bed.

There was a perfect moon framed perfectly in one of the glass panes. From his line of vision he saw the jagged silhouette of the thick stand of fir trees which encircled the tennis courts. At a distant point on the high horizon, he noticed that black night altered and became violet-blue in color.

Beginning to relax, he folded his arms beneath his head, using them for a pillow, and felt the peace of night and earth, so peaceful, he thought, this host of ours, earth.

But most dramatic of all was the moon—large, cold, insistent, hanging against the black curtain. For a moment he stared longingly up out of the window. He'd give anything to see this globe from outer space. What was it one of the astronauts had said when asked how earth looks from the moon?

Fragile.

He stared a moment longer; then the mood was over and the practical scientist was back in control.

Get on with it. Complete the experiments, then with the last of your energies climb those four blasted flights of steps and sleep in proper fashion. Hal Kitchens had always accused him of being able to sleep anywhere.

Halfway up from the couch, he froze on the name. *Hal!* He hadn't contacted him in three days, yet he'd promised either to call or come right back. The mining threat. Tomis. As specifics from the outside world penetrated his mind for the first time in three days, he sat on the edge of the couch, his eyes blinking as though the transition were a difficult one. Tomis. What was going on there with that intrepid band of pioneers? He was fond of them all, as he was fond of anyone with the courage to follow their own compass. The Kitchenses, Donna and Mike Dunne, Brian Sawyer and poor Kate. For the last four years they had generously provided him with a kind of human laboratory of reciprocated love.

Two of the most powerful aquastats in the Northern Hemisphere encircle Mt. Victor on the Continental Divide.

As the random thought assaulted his mind, he looked around for his watch. Failing to see it, he grabbed the phone from the corner of the desk and carried it back with him to the couch. Yes, it was late. Still, he must call. In his own excitement over Percy's successful proof, he'd forgotten the mining threat facing Tomis.

He closed his eyes briefly and made a mental search for the number. He dialed immediately and waited for the familiar tone, and heard nothing. Must have made a mistake. Carefully he disengaged the receiver, broke the connection, and tried again, speaking aloud each digit of the number he'd called so often during the last four years.

He listened carefully, heard computer static, but where the reassuring buzz of a number going through should have been, he heard nothing but an ominous dead tone.

All right, then, he'd let the operator do it.

"Yes, Operator, I'm trying to place a call to Tomis, Colorado. The number is KL5-5107, to Mr. Hal Kitchens—"

With a surge of impatience he waited out the nasal voice at the other end of the line.

"I know I can dial the number direct, Operator, except I've tried and it doesn't seem to go through. Would you please place the call for me?"

He wouldn't have been too surprised if the woman had said no. There was a distinct air of imposition on the line. But shortly he heard again the metallic click of the invisible computers.

"Hello? Hello?"

Suddenly the line went dead, and the impersonal voice of the operator came on with alarming clarity. "We seem to be experiencing difficulty in that area. May I suggest that you try placing your call later."

"What difficulty, Operator?"

"Weather conditions."

"Weather—"

But then the line went totally dead and he was left with only a buzzing. Weather conditions? He glanced beyond the window to the clear dark sky. How peaceful it was here. Difficult to believe that a storm was raging somewhere.

Hurry! Hurry! Recess was over. He'd try again to reach Hal later. Spring storms generally did not last long, though they could be fierce. For now he dragged himself to his feet, tried to stretch the tight knot out of his neck, and was just passing through the door on his way back into the laboratory when he heard a familiar and very efficient step on the stone staircase.

"Thought you might be getting hungry," Mrs. DeNunnzio announced as she appeared in the door, tray in hand.

He was and he wasn't. Strangely, he was as pleased by her company as he was at the thought of food. The most difficult aspect of Percy's grim triumph had been that he'd not been able to share it with anyone. Not yet.

"Thank you, Mrs. DeNunnzio." He smiled, hoping she'd stay for a minute. She was so safe—tall, thin, dark, aging. And safe.

"It's late," she said primly, placing the tray on the workbench and lifting the silver lid on a bowl of steamy tomato soup. It smelled delicious.

"Will you join me?" he asked, dragging up the stool. "You've been working late as well . . ."

She shook her head and looked vaguely about. "I had a bowl in the kitchen. What *is* that awful smell?" she added, sniffing the air with condemnation.

Roger laughed, and ignoring the soup spoon, lifted the bowl and took a burning swallow. "Shrimp," he said, and swallowed again. "Brine shrimp, some live, some dead." He gestured toward the bucket near the stove.

"Well, I'm sure you know what you're doing," she said. It was her favorite phrase, and she looked now as though she were on the verge of retreat.

It had been so long since he'd talked with anyone. "Would you like to stay?" he heard himself ask. "One more experiment, then we both can call it a night. I think you might find it interesting."

At first he saw mild surprise on her face. He'd never issued such an invitation before.

"Well, if you're sure . . ."

"I'm sure," he said. "Come. Here, I'll arrange a ringside seat."

And he did, drawing up a second stool on the opposite side of the worktable.

For a moment a feeling of awkward self-consciousness passed back and forth between them. "Finish your soup," she said softly to her folded hands, "while it's hot."

Obedient as a child, he drained the bowl and thought how pleased he was that she had stayed, that he had asked her to stay. It would have been a simple matter for her to retire to her apartment above the garage. For seventeen years, since the formation of CUSP, she had worked around the edges of Roger's work, never insisting that she be allowed to come closer.

As he turned away from her en route to the now steadily boiling kettle of water, he moved directly to the heart of the matter. "Do you know, Mrs. DeNunnzio, what the H.E. Theory is?"

For several seconds, silence was his only answer. "Not precisely, Dr. Laing," she said honestly. "I know that you and Dr. Forrester have been working on it for ever so long."

An understatement, he thought, staring down into the boiling water. The investigation had been long and arduous. Percy had commenced it in 1952. Roger had joined him in the early sixties. And now they had amassed impressive evidence that could affect the entire world and all its inhabitants.

"In the beginning," Roger began, lifting the pail of brine shrimp and positioning it on the table, "we addressed ourselves to two basic questions first raised by the Milesians in the seventh century B.C. One: what is the real nature of the universe? And two: how is the universe as we perceive it generated by the universe as it actually is? The posing of these questions," Roger went on, "presupposes a suspicion that the universe is not altogether what it seems to be, and a consequent recognition of a difference and even an opposition between appearance and reality—"

"I'm afraid . . . I don't understand, Dr. Laing," she confessed simply, and again he was grateful for her honesty, though a secret despair took its toll of her. For a moment they stared, unblinking, at one another, their mutual bewilderment connecting them, if nothing else.

"Do you remember the paper I delivered several summers ago in California?" he asked quietly. "I called it the Theology of Ecology."

Suddenly a light altered the shadows of bewilderment on her face. "I most certainly do." She smiled. "Such a good one, though very controversial."

He leaned on the worktable and moved beyond the controversy to the paper itself. "The question raised was where precisely had philosophy and religion gone wrong in abetting bad ecological practices."

"Yes." She nodded and seemed to sit a bit straighter on the stool. "Yes, I remember it well."

"The God in Genesis, I said, did not give man a blank check when he said, 'Be fruitful and multiply, and fill the earth and subdue it; and have dominion over . . . every living thing.' Too often this has been used as a text for exploitation, reducing nature to a collection of useful objects."

Again Mrs. DeNunnzio nodded. "It was reprinted, as I recall, in several theological—"

"What I was trying to suggest," he interrupted, "was that there is a God of nature as well as a God of history. God decrees that all creation is good and holds his servant, man, accountable for what happens to it. A weak faith in the value of creation tends to undermine belief in the creator, and vice versa, and man is left only with his self-interest, which, however enlightened, will not provide sufficient motivation for ecological survival. Man must somehow come to believe once again that nature has some claim upon him, some intrinsic right to exist and to prosper."

"Oh, the letters following that one." She smiled. "Never have I—"

He held up one restraining hand. Her memory seemed to be working in the most superficial areas. Still, it was time for proof now, though what a mixed blessing this might prove to be. As he arranged his equipment before her on the workbench, he felt part child, part very old man. He wanted her interest and approval and simultaneously wanted to protect her from Percy's hard-earned proof. But this wasn't Percy's. He wouldn't test her with something so awesome as that. This was merely the first step.

"We started with a primary perception, Mrs. DeNunnzio," he began quietly. "Do dying cells send out signals to which other life responds? Alarm signals are common to all social vertebrates. All organisms consist of cells, and the existence of a system of communication among cells would provide us with some interesting data."

He felt new tension, new effort coming from across the table, and went on in spite of it. "Now, we propose that part of life's strength lies in the fact that it is precarious. The protoplasm in every cell hangs in an unstable balance that can be tipped in either direction by even the most subtle stimulus."

He paused to see if there would be an early question. There was none, and he drew forward the large split-leaf philodendron.

"There was a time," he said, caressing the glossy green leaves, "when amoeboid movement was thought to be completely random. But we know now that even the amoeba moves with intent and precision, and in the complex multicells, a miracle of organization takes place. The nerves provide a mechanical basis for electrochemical communication and promote the joint activities that give most animals direction and purpose."

He drew the large plant closer, to the exact center of the worktable. "Though plants lack a nervous system and show no transmission of impulse from cell to cell, they too demonstrate a concerted action. A touch on the end of one of the compound leaves of *Mimosa pudica* makes it fold up, and if the stimulus is strong enough, the response spreads to neighboring leaves, until the whole plant seems to cringe in submission."

He looked across to where Mrs. DeNunnzio sat with her arms braced against the stool, her mouth slightly open, her eyes blinking rapidly.

195

"Now, Dr. Forrester and I submit the proposition that the understanding of the coordination of separate cells may lie outside the bounds of normal sensory perceptions." He didn't wait for a response to that and went right on.

"A simple polygraph"—he smiled, pointing to the instrument—"a lie detector, used normally to measure the electrical resistance of the human skin. But now. . ."

He stepped close to the table. "Two psychogalvanic-reflex electrodes, known as PGRs," he said, holding up two leads for her inspection, then carefully attaching them to a leaf of the plant. He adjusted the tape, angled the polygraph around so that she could see clearly the recording pen.

"Now, watch closely, please," he invited, and reached for a large watering can and said in raised tones, as though he were speaking to a person with impaired hearing, "I believe I'll water this plant."

As he tipped the spout downward, the recording pen moved easily, steadily across the tape.

"Now," he continued in a loud voice, "I think I'll torture this plant," and he took from his pocket a kitchen match, and at the instant of this decision, there was a dramatic change in the PGR tracing pattern. The recording pen swept erratically up, then down, then up again, though so far he had not moved or touched the plant in any way.

Mrs. DeNunnzio was stirring on the high stool as though in discomfort.

Roger announced, full-voiced, "I intend to inflict harm on this plant," and he struck the match, though held the flame a good three feet from the leaf with the attached electrodes.

Mrs. DeNunnzio gasped, a sudden intake of air as the recording pen jumped in a prolonged upward sweep.

"Shall we water it again, with hot coffee?" Roger said, delighted in her response, his eyes fixed on the recording pen as again it swerved up and down, up and down, in an agitated and irregular path.

In the stunned silence, Roger said quietly, "I call it 'the threat-to-well-being principle,' a well-established method of triggering emotionality in humans."

Slowly Mrs. DeNunnzio shook her head. "I've . . . never seen anything like it."

"Now . . ." Roger continued, pleased with her response. He slipped his hands into two mitts and transferred the large kettle of boiling water from the stove to the table. The steam momentarily fogged his glasses, and hurriedly he wiped them clear.

As soon as the water had been positioned to his satisfaction, he reached beneath the table and withdrew the galvanized bucket. The odor of seawater grew stronger, a sewer smell.

With everything arranged to his liking, he took a step back from the table. "Having determined the plant's ability to perceive danger to itself, I now suggest that it will exhibit equal sensitivity to stress in other species."

He was aware, without looking up, of a rustle of doubt coming from across the table.

196

"In this pail," he said, tilting it forward for her inspection, "I have brine shrimp, some alive, some dead."

He stripped off the gloves with which he'd transported the kettle of boiling water and reached into the pail and withdrew a curling shrimp. He placed the shrimp on the table and withdrew his hand, giving her a chance to see the moving antennae, the entire curved body struggling for locomotion across the rough table surface.

Once the fact of life had been established, he scooped it up and without hesitation plunged it into the steaming water.

As the recording needle slid wildly up, he heard a whispered "No" coming from across the table, then another as the pen slid off the end of the tape, catching itself on the edge.

Roger waited until the needle stabilized; then he did it again, and for the second time the polygraph recording pen attached to the plant leaf jumped violently.

Something—either the reaction to violent death, or the taut, disbelieving silence, or perhaps both—conspired against poor Mrs. DeNunnzio. Roger saw a trickle of perspiration course down the side of her face.

In the new silence, Roger again placed a lifeless shrimp on the table. Once the fact of nonlife had been established, he dropped the dead shrimp into the kettle of boiling water.

The recording pen held absolutely steady. Then he withdrew a live shrimp and dropped it into the water, then watched as the recording pen raced up and down on the tape. He did it four times in all, and was aware of Mrs. DeNunnzio flinching visibly as each live shrimp was killed in the steaming water.

"It raises awesome biological questions, wouldn't you say?" he asked softly. "And moral ones."

She nodded slowly.

"It seems that, for the moment, on the basis of what we have seen here, we will have to assume that dying cells *do* send out signals to which other life responds."

"But why do they do so?" Mrs. DeNunnzio asked, new worry on her face, "and why should signals be perceived by a plant and not by us?"

Roger was never given a chance to answer. At that moment Mrs. DeNunnzio stood, as though she had lost interest in her own questions. "I must go now, Dr. Laing. This isn't my place. I don't know, don't really know that much about what you are. . ."

As her voice drifted, he saw her back away toward the stairs. "Sleep well, Dr. Laing," she called back, her voice almost as cheery and as impersonal as ever.

He started to call her back, wanted to call her back. Answers could be faced, must be faced. But he didn't. He listened to her diminishing footsteps until there was nothing more to hear; then slowly he sat back down on the stool. A new weariness had invaded him. Percy Forrester had been right. Even trained scientific minds would refute the H.E. Theory for the simple reason that it was unthinkable, that there was no ready frame of reference, and that, most importantly, it rendered man, the king, totally, pitifully helpless—and man would not willingly be abandoned in a universe where trees possessed brains that were superior to his.

Silence. But not the silence of failure. There was only success here, and terrifying proof.

Science no longer holds any absolute truths. In this climate of disbelief, we have begun to doubt even fundamental propositions.

He gripped the edge of the worktable. Not until he felt the muscles in his neck and shoulders object did he consciously relax his hands. Slowly he closed his eyes, his head inclined forward.

In the course of every fairly catholic education in most of the life sciences, there are many moments when the syllabus brushes up against something strange, shies away, and tries to pretend that it didn't happen.

As man exploits the resources of the world, he is going to have to rely more and more on his own.

Chaos is coming. It is written in the laws of thermodynamics. Left to itself, everything tends to become more disorderly, until the final and natural state of things is a completely random distribution of matter.

Suddenly he looked up. What if at this moment someone was caught in the reality of the H.E. Theory?

He stood rapidly in an attempt to move away from his own self-induced horror.

Ley lines awry, dizziness, disorientation, the pineal gland reacting to the heightened electromagnetic field, tremendous energies in effect, a fantastic flow of information, though none of it making any sense, total fear, panic, the whole computer the result of a senseless dance of certain kinds of atoms, stimulated and pushed by organized but meaningless energies, energy and matter exhibiting absolutely no significance, no love, no human values, no understanding, no. . .

His hands trembled. Then it was time to warn the world. But what if, like Mrs. DeNunnzio, they simply turned and walked away?

"Dear Christ," he whispered, and clung to the table, trying to still the terror newly risen within him.

28

Tomis, Colorado

It was approaching midnight, and at the very moment when he should be concentrating on the disintegration going on about him, Hal found himself thinking of the Mountain Man.

Had he taken a shot at Vicky?

"Hal, goddammit, listen to me!"

The voice, raised in anger, was Brian's. He simultaneously slammed his fist down on the table, causing Mike's empty glass to jump. Thank God it was empty, Mike passed out in drunken oblivion at the next table. So much for sobriety.

"Not one of them has come back yet!" Brian shouted, the strain taking a toll. "And Kate—we can't just . . ."

The strain broke. He turned away and walked into the large dining room, where every light was burning in the event someone, anyone, needed a beacon in the blizzard.

"Brian?" Hal called out. "There's nothing we can do now, and you know it. If five men have—"

"Where are they?" Brian demanded, as though Hal were somehow responsible.

Hal didn't answer, thoughtfully refusing to articulate what Brian surely must know, that no one could survive for six hours in that storm without shelter.

At the next table, Mike groaned in his drunken sleep and said "No!" clearly, then sank back into the depths of his first binge in four years.

Confronted with Brian's angry accusatory face, Hal bowed his head into his shoulders and thought that he should be home with Sarah, that Sarah and Donna should not be alone. At least he didn't have to worry about Vicky. Inez had put her to bed in her cabin behind the restaurant.

With his eyes closed, head down, he listened. He'd never heard the wind howl like that. In four years of surviving winter storms, he'd never heard that strength and velocity before. It pounded against the walls of the restaurant. He could feel the vibrations.

"I'm sorry." The subdued, repentant voice was Brian's. "About Sarah, I mean."

Hal shook his head. He really didn't want to think about it. They both had wanted this second child so much. Why had Mike . . . ?

Don't think about it. No time to think about it. Kate. The disc jockey from Durango. According to Brian, he'd volunteered to look for her. A bit out of character, but perhaps Hal had misjudged him. Whatever his character, Hal now feared the worst for him.

But he didn't say it aloud for the sake of the man seated opposite him now, his eyes lost in the shadows, fully aware that his wife probably was dead.

"I . . . don't understand," Brian muttered.

The statement was so simple. Hal gave no reply. Nothing very difficult to understand. They had imprisoned themselves halfway up a mountain, and nature was in the process of burying them beneath a capricious out-of-season blizzard. But it wouldn't last forever, and the thaw would come fast this time of year, and there would be six new corpses to report, and Kate alone would be happy, rejoined again with her dead son.

Dead son. Seven months. Strangulation. Not unusual. Then why in hell did Mike drink himself into oblivion?

The cry came from inside his head, but there was no sound save the screaming of the wind and the persistent, knifelike chill at his back.

He looked up and saw Brian rising from his chair. "Where're you going?" he asked.

"Out to search."

"No, you're not."

"She may be home by now."

"You know better."

"I have to go and see."

"I'll come with you when this is over."

"She hated it here."

This flat declaration combined with the accusatory look on Brian's face rendered Hal silent, awakening a painful sense of responsibility. It had been his idea, but the others had come willingly. No one had been forced.

At the table to his right, Mike moaned in his drunken sleep, seemed to grow angry, cried "No!" again, then fell silent.

"Please sit down," Hal ordered, his eyes closed.

Then he heard it, the angry scrape of a chair, and looked up to find tears on Brian's face. "God damn you," he said, his fists clenched on the table, his face bearing no resemblance to Brian Sawyer's, something childlike about him, as though he were incapable of reason. "They're both gone now, my son, my wife. Is there anything else you want, Kitchens?" His head sagged slowly over folded arms. "Oh, my God, someone, help us!"

Hal looked across at him. "It's all right," he whispered uselessly. And finally the sobs dissolved into sharp spasms and his fists seemed to relax, his head sank lower into his arms, and though his face was obscured, Hal suspected that he had eased into some safer realm, not precisely sleep, but a state of semiconsciousness where he would not have to think about anything, at least for a while.

With the new silence came a lingering sense of unreality. Through the door he saw the large dining room ablaze with light, though empty of people. To his right was Mike, who continued to groan in his sleep. To his left was Brian, the echo of his voice raised in anger still filling Hal's head.

God . . . damn . . . you. . . .

He should go home. He should stop by Inez's and pick up Vicky and take her home. Sarah probably was awake by now. She would want to hold Vicky.

As he bent over, he suddenly felt an excruciating pain in the top of his skull and saw two Brians, two Mikes. He grasped the edge of the table with both hands, fearful that as the dizziness increased, he would fall.

Suddenly, over the whine of wind, he heard the front door open. A blast of arctic wind raced across the floor and up his legs.

"Who is it?" he called out, scarcely recognizing his own voice, and at first saw nothing; then finally the tall gaunt scarecrow figure of Frank Quinton became visible, peering at him from over the cash register, his hair covered with snow, more caught in his eyebrows, the collar of his sport coat turned up in protection against the blizzard.

"The phones are dead," Quinton called across the length of the restaurant in an angry voice.

Hal gave no response. Of course the phones were dead.

"I must have a telephone," Quinton announced, the perennially passive and objective smile gone from his face. "It is absolutely imperative that I have the use of a telephone."

"Sorry," Hal called back. "It could take days for the phone company to . . ."

The man started toward him across the restaurant at a fast pace, bringing all his anger with him, the snow in his hair dripping down his face, giving him the peculiar appearance of a man melting.

"You've got to get us out of here, Kitchens," Quinton demanded. "We must have some contact with . . ."

At that moment he caught sight of Mike and Brian. "What's the matter with them?" he asked, suspicious.

"One is drunk and the other is sleeping," Hal said quietly, trying to focus his eyes, seeing two of Frank Quinton now. *What in the hell was happening?*

He started to rise but found he could not. His knees were shaking, and he felt a sudden heat on his face. At the same time, he saw Quinton stumble toward the door and reach for the doorframe, his stump trying to provide him with support and failing, and ultimately he slumped to one side and might have fallen if it hadn't been for his good hand, which grasped the door. "We've got to get out of here," he whispered on diminishing breath. "It's . . . happening . . . again. . . ."

Hal looked up. "What is it, Quinton? Tell me . . ."

But the man shook his head and flattened himself against the doorframe and held on as though the entire restaurant had become a ship in rough seas.

Hal struggled to his feet, and at first movement felt new pain explode in the top of his head. "Quinton, tell . . . me what is . . ."

But abruptly the man half-stumbled into the large dining room and sat in a far chair before the large pane-glass window, with his back to Hal.

"Quinton . . ." Hal gasped, and suddenly felt vibrations beneath his feet, the outline of every object in the room blurred, every sharp edge fuzzy.

He knew *that* sensation, had felt it before, the night of the rock slide, the massive boulder which had come . . .

"Quinton! Do you feel it?"

The man nodded, still seated rigidly in the chair. "It's . . . happening . . . again. . . ."

By propelling himself along from table to table, Hal tried to make his way to the door. But halfway across the restaurant, as the tremor increased, his hands jarred loose and he felt himself falling, feeling helpless, and astonished that this solid-looking structure was in the grip of such force.

Flattened on the floor, he gripped two table legs, closed his eyes, and waited for the impact. The vibrations increased to the extent that the tables began to move, accompanied by a roaring and whistling sound. *Earthquake?* Perhaps. There had been recent earthquake activity in Colorado, but nothing of this size.

"Quinton?" he shouted above the roar. "Mike? Brian? Are you . . . ?"

But no one answered, and the vibrations were so strong now that he could not lift his head. He heard dishes crashing in the kitchen, a thunderously loud crash of plate glass shattering, the rumble of buckling earth. His ears hurt, his teeth, his bones, like the earth was dancing.

Move quick! Sarah . . .

Would everyone die? Would the roof hold? Would it never cease?

Then it did, though slowly at first. From his position flattened on the floor, he concentrated on one rubber-capped chair leg. It was still jerking, though not as hard now, and the table above him was growing steady and the wind was dying, though he was freezing.

"Quinton?"

He flattened his head against the floor and felt the diminishing vibrations. He looked through the forest of table legs and saw Quinton still seated by the window, his back toward Hal, his legs spread and relaxed, his arms hanging limp by his side, the left stump swinging back and forth.

"Quinton, are you . . . ?"

Then Hal saw something else, a steady dripping of blood which fell from the man's stump and which increased even as he watched it. Quinton was hurt. What about the others? "Mike? Are you . . . ?"

"What in the hell was . . . ?"

Relieved, he looked toward the drunken voice and saw Mike leaning against a table. "Roller coaster," he slurred, grinning. "Old buddy, I didn't know you had a roller . . ." He aimed for a chair and missed and sat flat on the floor, his head wobbling. "Where's Donna?" he mumbled. "Need Donna." Then he passed out again and fell boneless to one side.

Hal started to his feet, his attention splintered between the blood dripping from the man by the window and Brian, who apparently had been dragged out of his despair by the mysterious tremors.

"Kate . . . h-home now," he stammered, his face drained of color. "She has to be . . . h-home."

In spite of the pain, which felt as though someone was driving an ice pick into the top of his skull, Hal pulled himself to his feet. "Brian, wait!" he called out as the man started in a wide circle around him, heading toward the door.

"Kate's home now."

"She's *not* home!"

"What happened?"

"I don't know. Quinton's hurt. . . ."

Still using the tables for support, Hal made his way slowly toward the man seated erect in the chair, legs spread, arms relaxed at his . . .

Christ! No!

Without looking, he sensed that Brian had waited, was now seeing what he was seeing, Quinton impaled in the chair by a broad sharp spear of glass from the broken window. It had penetrated through his abdomen and emerged on the other side, pinning him in an upright position. A blood lake was forming on the floor and chair, though the man's eyes were open, as was his mouth, as though he were on the verge of speaking.

It's happening again. . . .

Behind him he heard Brian moan and turn away. Feeling the need to rest his eyes from the atrocity, Hal glanced toward the broken window and saw that the snow and the wind had suddenly stopped. There was an eerie stillness beyond the broken window, the street and sidewalk buried under several feet of snow.

He looked down and saw blood eddying about his boots and heard a faint commotion coming from the street, men's voices raised.

"It's Tom Marshall," Brian said from the door, "and several others. I can't see . . ."

"Don't let them in," Hal shouted, and hurriedly drew the curtains over the broken window, thus obscuring Quinton's body from anyone outside.

"They're coming this way," Brian called out.

Quickly Hal removed one of the tablecloths and spread it over the body, then hurried to the door, literally shoving Brian out before him, and closed the door behind them both.

Time. He needed time. He needed to determine what had happened. He needed to guard against hysteria, both in himself and in others.

203

"Kitchens!"

As Tom Marshall's voice cut through the new silence, Hal saw three men coming toward him—Tom, Ed Billingsly, and Callie Watkins, all dressed in their winter gear, heavy mackinaws, snow boots, ear flaps down against the bitter cold.

"Are you all right?" Hal called out, going to meet them, taking Brian with him. "Is anybody hurt?"

Even before the men spoke, he saw the expressions on their faces and knew that they knew more than he did.

Tom Marshall aimed a high-powered flashlight directly into his eyes, momentarily blinding him. "You'd better come and see this," he ordered, a strained quality to his voice which served as a warning.

"What . . . is it?"

"Come on. You won't believe it."

In a curiously rapid movement, the men encircled him, as though giving him escort, and again Hal felt a chill tugging warning. It scraped down his spine with an icy hand.

As they started down the street, he walked with difficulty through the drifting snow and recalled how foolish Quinton had looked, emerging from out of the storm in his sport coat, demanding a telephone.

All three men had flashlights, though Marshall's was by far the most powerful, cutting a sharp white path down the middle of Main Street. A few of the residents were beginning to venture out onto their porches now, the women clutching their robes about them, children peering out of curtained windows, though no one said a word and seemed content to watch the men as they walked silently before them. As they passed by Rene Hackett's house, Hal saw the woman on her porch, clad only in a flannel gown, her hair in rollers. "He'll get us all," she shouted, frightened. "The Mountain Man don't want us here, and he won't stop till he gets us all."

Hal started toward her to offer comfort, but Tom Marshall closed ranks and blocked him with a single word. "No!"

They followed the beam of the flashlight to the end of Main, and Hal looked ahead and saw another small cluster of people, all standing well back from the edge of the road, staring out into . . .

Hal blinked and tried to clear his vision. Taking Marshall's flashlight, he ran ahead, frantically shining the light, the strong beam confirming that first distorted vision.

They were all standing on the edge of a cliff. The road leading up from the valley floor was gone, the boulder was gone, the semis and trailers at the bottom of the hill were gone, there was nothing but a deep black abyss stretching down as far as the beam of light would travel.

"Dear God," someone prayed behind him.

In his desperate need to see more, he stepped too near to the edge and felt the soft crumbling snow beneath his feet and moved quickly back. It was as though the mountain had simply sloughed off the road, leaving them isolated on a pinnacle of ground. There was no way up or down.

Someone was weeping behind him. A woman? He couldn't be certain. For several minutes he shone the beam down into the collapse, which was still billowing dust. Far below, he caught sight of an upended semi, crushed, like a child's toy, the square metal cubicles labeled "Porto-Flush" scattered about like building blocks.

He listened carefully to the stunned silence coming from the group behind him. They knew what it meant as well as he. They were in the presence of an enemy, but what or who, and how to do battle with it?

"Hal?"

It was Tom Marshall, who had moved up alongside him, a strangely subdued Tom Marshall. "We ain't gonna get down from here, are we?"

"Help will come."

"How they gonna know?"

In an effort to avoid the question, he turned his back on the sheer cliff which once had been a home. "Come on, everyone," he commanded, dredging up a last ounce of calm and trying to distribute it evenly throughout his system. "Everyone get back inside where it's warm. Come morning, we'll . . ."

What? See clearly that we are stranded, that . . .

Grateful, he saw the small group turn back, no one speaking. What had happened here tonight defied words.

Sarah! He must check on Sarah. And Vicky. And the others. "Tom, wait," he called out, "and you, Callie, Brian . . ."

As the others proceeded down Main Street, he gathered the three men about him and tried to force his mind into rational decisions. "Brian, would you and Tom check on everyone, please. Make certain that no one is injured, and ask them all to stay inside their houses tonight."

The men nodded and without a word separated, Tom taking the left side of the street, Brian the right. Hal watched them. Brian seemed calm, though he appeared to be holding himself very rigid. As he climbed the Hacketts' front steps, it was as though his mind had come to terms with something, and surely his heart would follow soon. Across the street, Tom Marshall was just approaching Mina Murdoch's. Strange that Mina's house was completely dark. Yet not so strange. The tragic events of the morning had taken a toll of everyone, and Hal knew that Mina felt responsible for what had happened to Sarah.

He grasped Tom Marshall's flashlight with fingers so numb they were beyond feeling and drew close to Callie Watkins, Tomis' best amateur carpenter. "Callie, one of the windows in the restaurant is shattered. Could you board it up for me first thing in the morning, make it as tight as possible?"

"I'll do it now, Hal," Callie responded eagerly.

"No!" Hal ordered, remembering Quinton, the blood. "Not tonight. You . . . go on home. Tomorrow morning will be fine."

Callie nodded, clearly perplexed. "If it were to start snowing again . . ."

"I don't think it will."

"You all right, Hal? I heard about Sarah and the baby. I'm really sorry. . . ."

Unable to respond, Hal nodded and thought of what was just ahead for him this night, and wondered if it was almost over, or just beginning.

"You know, I'm not too worried." Callie smiled. "The mining corporation will come back up looking for their fancy equipment, and when they see the condition it's in, they'll find a way to get us down off the mountain, if they have to airlift us down, one by one."

Hal nodded and realized that the man was right. Someone would come for them. And nothing had happened that could not be logically, rationally explained. Random earthquake activity brought on by the unseasonable storm, a continental drift, the earth's plates shifting, the road built on spongy loam collapsing into the valley below. In spite of the catastrophe, it could have been worse. Tomis could have slid into the valley along with the road.

"Can I do anything else for you, Hal?" It was Callie again, cooperative and willing.

"No." Hal smiled. "You go home and get some sleep."

As the man trudged through the snow, Hal thought there was that bonus as well, the natural cooperation of people caught in the same predicament. Help *would* come.

Roger Laing . . .

There was that possibility too. Perhaps Roger was aware of their plight at this very moment and trying to reach them. The disrupted phone service would alert him.

Yes, it could all be handled and dealt with and faced.

Quinton.

Well, almost all of it. Quinton's death would have to be reported. There were too many people connected with him, all of the mining corporation for starters. Nothing to hide or fear. His death was clearly a tragic accident, and until help did arrive, Hal would remove the body to the meat locker and say nothing to anyone until he could speak with the proper authorities.

Do it! Only then was he aware of himself standing alone in the middle of the street, shivering, everyone else having taken shelter, Brian just knocking on the Hacketts' door.

Shivering continuously from the cold, he hurried through the deep snow toward the restaurant. As he entered, he carefully kept his eyes away from the far left corner. Through the tables, he saw Mike, still sprawled in the safe and drunken oblivion. Maybe he was the smartest of the lot.

Do it! Drag the body out, clean up the blood, and take Mike up the hill with him. He couldn't leave him here. He would freeze.

Standing beside the cash register, staring straight ahead into the kitchen, he told himself aloud, "Everything is going to be all right." Every nightmare had its natural conclusion. Everything had a reason. Everyone sooner or later was affected by some natural catastrophe. It was merely the juxtaposition of events that . . .

In this subtle process of self-stroking, of clinging with all his strength to reason and calm judgment, he found the courage to face the far corner, his memory prematurely filling in the specifics, the relaxed angle of the legs, the limp arm, the glass spear impaling . . .

For a hesitant moment he stood unmoving, then almost spastically lunged forward, all sense of reason shattered.

"No!" he shouted to the empty chair, the corpse gone, the blood cleansed, the tablecloth shroud folded neatly in the seat.

The rational voice was replaced by a raging one. His eyes locked in stunned disbelief on the empty chair.

"No!" he cried again, and felt something in the room mocking him as he wept.

29

As Brian Sawyer hurried up the Hacketts' snow-covered steps, he had only one thought in his mind: *Kate.*

At the top of the steps, he looked back as though he'd expected to find her standing on the sidewalk.

Dead? Probably. Kent gone, Kate gone. Christ, what now for him? In lieu of an answer, he gripped the icy banister and thought he heard thunder in the distance, saw a jagged flash of lightning, and felt suddenly very helpless, as they all were now, at the mercy of the weather, the road washed away. He couldn't win. He couldn't lose. He couldn't even get out of the game.

He watched through glazed, fatigued eyes as Hal made his way up Main Street, heading toward the restaurant with Callie Watkins. Death there as well, an epidemic of death.

Across the street, he heard Tom Marshall knocking on Mina's darkened front door, and remembered that his own mission was to check on everyone living on this side of the street. In an attempt to keep his mind off the specter of Kate dead, he lifted one numb hand and knocked. And felt nothing.

Who had they offended by coming here?

He knocked again. "Lucy? It's Brian Sawyer. Are you . . . ?"

He heard a chain sliding, then a bolt. Someone had taken care to lock themselves in this night.

The door opened a crack, no more, and beyond, he saw Lucy's pale face. The young girl had been Kent's first playmate in Tomis. Though three years had separated them, an exclusive bond had grown up between them. It hadn't been until the following spring that the O'Connells and the Drivers had arrived with their broods. He and Kate should have had more than one, the population explosion be damned.

"Lucy, are you all right?" he inquired, his manner softening under the weight of memory, seeing the little girl from Nebraska and the little boy from New England race across the high meadow.

"What . . . was it, Mr. Sawyer?" Lucy inquired, her voice no more than a whisper.

"We're not certain, Lucy," he said. "The road is . . ."

"Gone," she said flatly.

"Yes."

Off in the distance, near the top of the mountain, he heard another rumble of thunder. The darkened porch was suddenly illuminated by a jagged bolt of lightning.

In clear terror, Lucy quickly shut the door, then slowly reopened it. "Mama . . . was afraid," she said, thus avoiding the confession of her own fear. "I gave her a pill and put her to bed."

"Good girl, Lucy." He smiled. "And there's really nothing to be afraid of. It looks like we'll have a little rain now, but that will just help to melt the snow, won't it?"

He started to say more, but changed his mind. "If you're sure everything is fine here, Lucy, then I'll—"

"Don't go, Mr. Sawyer. Please don't go."

"I have to check on the others."

"Come in for just a minute. I was fixing a cup of hot chocolate. Please don't go."

In spite of her fear, she opened the door wider, and he saw her clearly now, lost in an oversized man's bathrobe, probably Jerry's, her hair loosened and tangled about her shoulders, her hands apparently healing well, the bandages gone except for the splinted broken fingers.

Hot chocolate? Why not? She was missing a father, and he was missing a family. Ten minutes. Put her at ease. No harm.

"All right"—he shrugged—"but I can't stay long. I must see if the others are . . ."

As he stepped inside the door, she moved back and drew the robe more tightly about her, pulled the cord and knotted it, and looked more childlike than ever. Rene and Jerry were both tall, yet they had produced a daughter who would fit inside your pocket.

Aware that he was staring, he rubbed his hands and looked about at the plain living room, sparsely furnished. The move to Tomis and a better life had been financially easy for some people. The Hacketts, he suspected, had sold or mortgaged everything. And for their troubles, look at them now.

"Hot chocolate," he reminded her over a new clap of thunder. Beyond the front window he heard the first pelting of rain.

"It's cold in here." Lucy shivered. "Come on out to the kitchen." She led the way, and he followed down a dimly lit corridor which reeked of old food odors and mildewed laundry. Disintegration.

Once inside the brightly lit kitchen, she closed the door behind them. "I don't want to wake up Mama," she said thoughtfully, and motioned him toward a chair at the kitchen table while she went to the refrigerator and withdrew a can of milk.

"I hate this stuff," she said, holding up the canned milk. "It always smells like it's gone bad."

As he sat, he unbuttoned his mackinaw. The room was warm. The bright overhead light hurt his eyes, and he felt a dull pain in the top of his head.

He was aware of Lucy bustling around the stove, withdrawing a saucepan and cups. She seemed more relaxed, as though she were siphoning off the tension in a burst of activity.

"You like it real chocolaty?" she asked, glancing at him over her shoulder.

"Suit yourself," he said, and rubbed the top of his head where the mild pain was throbbing. "Do you have any aspirin, Lucy?"

She looked at him with concerned surprise. "In the cupboard behind you. Help yourself. Would you rather have something cold to drink?"

"No," he said, deciding to wait for the aspirin. Maybe it was just the sudden warmth and bright light after . . .

"I miss Kent," Lucy said softly, stirring the chocolate efficiently in spite of her injured hands. "He was a good kid. I remember we used to take peanut-butter-and-jelly sandwiches up to the meadow and look for treasures. He really was a good kid, Mr. Sawyer," she repeated, and stirred quietly, the soft click of the spoon against the saucepan the only sound in the room.

Brian tried to think of a suitable reply but couldn't, and decided to let the silence suffice.

"Something weird is going on here, isn't it, Mr. Sawyer?" Lucy asked softly, not looking up.

"What do you mean?"

"What I said. First Kent, then Mrs. Marshall, then Papa. There just seems to be a whole lot of dying for such a little place."

For a second he regretted coming in. "People die," he said stupidly, and suddenly felt very adolescent sitting at the table having hot chocolate fixed for him.

Lucy's manner had changed as well. No longer shy and frightened, she bustled about the stove with maternal efficiency, arranging cups and saucers, reaching up on a high shelf for a box of graham crackers. She was talking quite volubly now. "Well, Mama's right at least part of the way," she said, not looking at him. "Someone doesn't like us here, but it's not the Mountain Man, at least not him by himself. He's getting a lot of help from someone right here in Tomis."

He didn't know what she was talking about and considered saying as much, but changed his mind. The pain in his head was increasing, and it was warm, so warm . . .

"But I'm not telling you anything you don't already know," she went on, and suddenly scraped the spoon against the bottom of the pan, causing goose bumps to rise on his arms.

He was tired, that was all. Drink the chocolate and push on. Maybe Kate would be waiting for him.

"There you are," Lucy said, and her voice sounded loud and close. "You don't look so good, Mr. Sawyer," she added, reaching back for her cup and the plate of cookies.

"I'm . . . just . . ."

"Hot. Why don't you take off your jacket?"

"Yes," and as he pushed back in the chair, he felt suddenly dizzy. The room spun about him. He lifted his head for breath and saw two brilliant suns overhead, which momentarily blinded him.

"Did you get your aspirin?" she inquired, and left the table, in the process scraping the chair so violently across the floor that it hurt his ears.

He managed to shake one arm free from his jacket, and felt so drained of energy that he rested his hands and was only vaguely aware of Lucy tugging the other arm free.

"Maybe you'd better lie down, Mr. Sawyer," she said, not a trace of fear in her voice now, more like a little girl playing mother. "There's a sofa in the back room," she added. "Papa moved it down from upstairs so he could take naps on it. Would you like . . . ?"

"No," he said, and laughed, embarrassed by his sudden and mysterious indisposition. "This will warm me up, and then I'll be on my way," he murmured, reaching for the steaming cup. He drank too fast and burned his tongue, and felt the room still turning about him.

He was aware of her seated opposite him, staring at him, a hint of a smile on her face.

"I'm . . . really sorry." He laughed, still embarrassed. "I was supposed to check on you, not . . ."

"It's all right." She smiled. "Papa and I used to have a cup of hot chocolate at night after Mama had gone to bed, before . . ."

She broke off and sipped at her cup, her eyes down. She really was very pretty.

"Feeling better, Mr. Sawyer?"

Yes. And no. The dizziness was passing, but he was aware of his own breathing, as though there wasn't enough oxygen in the room. "What were you talking about earlier, Lucy?" he began, trying to restore a degree of normality to the circumstances.

"What do you mean? Oh, about the Mountain Man. Well, Mama thinks he's the devil, which of course he may be, and she thinks he's causing all this to happen, including Papa's death, which may be true. But he couldn't do it all alone, and I know who is helping him."

The nonsense was charming, coming from the pretty little mouth. "Who?" he asked, pleased that his various discomforts were easing.

"It's the bitch-witch across the street," she said, a dark frown marring that pretty smooth brow.

He gaped for a moment, then laughed. He really was feeling better. "The bitch-witch?" he repeated. "You mean . . . Mina?"

"Yes! She's a witch, you know."

He started to laugh again, then changed his mind. Obviously Lucy was at that state of adolescence when creepy things held great appeal.

"Mina's a witch, uh?" he said, deciding to play along with her if in return she'd just let him look at her for a few minutes. She was like a newly minted coin, all shiny and unused except for her injured hands, which now she suddenly held up for his inspection, as though she knew he'd been thinking about them.

"She caused this," she said in a calm voice, "and she's done worse. She *is* a witch, Mr. Sawyer," she added emphatically.

He nodded and tried to draw a deep breath, and looked beyond her shoulder and noticed that she'd left the stove on. No wonder it was too hot, not enough air.

"Lucy, I think you'd better . . ."

"You don't believe me, do you?"

He shook his head and tried to remember that she was only fourteen. "It's a serious accusation. I wouldn't go around telling too many people what you've told me," he added, thinking he'd better leave soon.

"Why not?" she demanded angrily. "I think it's time we all knew, so that we can protect ourselves. She's very powerful and works spells all the time."

Speaking of spells, he thought wryly, and observed that in her twisting about in the chair the robe had parted and a soft mound of rising flesh was visible almost to the nipple.

As she sulked at his disbelief, he stared at the soft flesh and wondered how soon it would be before the road was repaired and he could get back to Mrs. Underwood's. Immediately he caught himself in the obscene thought and bowed his head into his hands, suffering grief and guilt.

"Are you sure you're all right, Mr. Sawyer? You're not drinking your hot chocolate."

He shook his head and felt his left leg begin to jerk reflexively, a strained nerve, muscle, something . . .

In response to her quiet admonition, he lifted the cup to his lips and saw the dark chocolate mixture trembling, his hands shaking as though palsied. He swallowed three times and thought it tasted sour. Power of suggestion. *Canned milk always tastes funny.*

Fearful of spilling it, he placed the cup on the table and looked up to see her placidly munching on a cracker, that one breast still partially visible.

"Lucy, I thank you," he said hurriedly, "but I think I'd better go now."

"There's more—"

"No, no thank you." But as he started to rise, he discovered that his legs would not support him. The left leg buckled instantly, and he fell forward against the table with such force that the cups of chocolate skittered and spilled. On his knees, he grasped the edge of the table and tried to deal with his fear. "Get . . . your mother," he gasped, and saw everything in triplicate.

Incongruously, Lucy laughed. "Oh, I could never wake her up. Remember? I gave her a pill."

212

"Lucy, please, I need help."

"Of course you do. You see? It's the bitch-witch, Mina. She's put a spell on you."

"Dammit!" he shouted, or thought he'd shouted, suddenly angry at her bizarre claims.

"Come on, Mr. Sawyer, you just need to lie down for a while, that's all. Here, let me help. It *is* warm in here, isn't it?" and suddenly, though he tried to protest, he saw her strip off the bathrobe and drop it in a circle about her feet.

"You ever played Captain Kangaroo?" she whispered, kneeling beside him now.

She's a child.

"Get . . . Hal Kitchens," he begged, and felt her arms about his waist, pressing against him.

Again he tried to stand, tried to push her away, and in the process lost what little balance he had left and fell backward on the floor, his legs twisted and numb beneath him, his eyes staring straight up at the overhead light.

Still she hovered over him, her fingers brushing down his shirt, unbuttoning it. "No," he gasped, and tried to focus on her face, so near, tried to communicate without words that she must get help.

But she wasn't paying any attention to him or to the mysterious paralysis which had invaded his will, or the fact that he was trying to draw breath and couldn't. *Heart attack? No pain. Stroke? No, he was fully conscious and felt no discomfort except the realization that he was totally powerless to stop what he knew was going to happen.*

"Lucy . . ."

"It's all right, Mr. Sawyer. No one will see us," and he felt her hands on his chest, talons extended like a bird of prey.

He tried to lift his head, but it felt as though it were filled with lead. With nightmarish resonance he heard his own heart beating, felt a slight tugging at his legs, and saw four Lucys removing his boots and then bending over him.

What was she doing? She was a child, his dead son's playmate.

At first contact, he shut his eyes and pressed his head against the floor and felt all the heat in his body rush to his groin and knew that Kate was dead and knew that he could not remain in Tomis and face everyone, and face himself.

"Captain Kangaroo," giggled a soft adolescent voice.

He felt his skin stretched taut and tried a final time to lift his head and push her away, but she was straddling him, impaling herself on him.

Then it occurred to him. He wasn't in Tomis at all. He was at Mrs. Underwood's. It was a paid whore on top of him, rocking rhythmically back and forth, though she was saying the strangest thing, saying it over and over again.

"Don't cry, Mr. Sawyer. It's a game is all. . . ."

30

You could give him a good clean battlefield any day, either Korea or the final death gasp of World War II. No matter. He'd take both willingly, compared to what was going on here. In fact, Tom Marshall functioned best when there was an "enemy" in his world. At least the gooks and the krauts had had faces and names, and *he'd* had a gun.

He knocked for the third time on Mina's door and glanced across the street. That lucky bastard Brian Sawyer had slipped inside the Hacketts' house. Nice little cunt. Tight, like playing with a doll. Of course, Rene was there now, and that would put a cramp in Lucy's style. And Sawyer probably wasn't in the mood anyway, what with his wife . . .

Jesus God damnation! Was that lightning? Damn right it was lightning, the jagged white bolt illuminating all of Main Street.

"Mina? You there?" he shouted, knowing she was. Where in the hell else could she be?

He looked anxiously up at the night sky and heard distant thunder and saw more lightning near the top of old Victor. It wasn't smart to mess around with lightning in these mountains. Chock full of iron ore, they served as ideal conductors. In the spring the Durango paper printed a lightning death every week.

"Mina! It's me. Tom Marshall. You okay?"

214

Still no answer. He shoved his hands into his pockets, though he really wasn't cold. Rain following fast on the heels of a blizzard. *What in the name of Jesus God was going on?*

He leaned close to the door, listening. Not a sound. Could the old broad have slept through everything? The road and half the mountain slid away? The blizzard? Growing increasingly nervous, he glanced toward the end of Main Street, where the intersection with the mountain road once had been. He couldn't see it in the dark, but he didn't have to see it. Earlier he'd seen it all too clearly, half the mountain collapsed, all those semis and trailers gone, as though they'd never existed. What in hell were they going to do now? How to get down out of this eagle's nest? Sprout wings?

"Mina, just call out if you're okay, and I'll shove off," he shouted, and twisted the doorknob, surprised to find it unlocked.

Suddenly there was another jagged knife of lightning that ripped open the night sky. For a moment the porch on which he was standing was lit up as bright as though a noon sun was shining.

Jesus, he had to get the hell out of here. But as a second explosion crackled overhead, he pushed open the door, stepped inside the darkened room, and closed the door behind him.

He started to call out again, but changed his mind. Mina might not take too kindly to such an intrusion. She was prim and proper, all right. His wife used to say that Mina Murdoch put on "airs," like she was better than the rest of them.

Well, he'd wait just a minute for the fireworks to diminish, then he'd slip out as quietly as he'd slipped in. Obviously "her highness" was sleeping soundly, and it was just because he didn't want to end up french-fried that he'd . . .

He heard something and saw a slit of light beneath the kitchen door. What in the hell? Was she awake or wasn't she? Well, he'd better call out now before he scared the living daylights out of her.

"Mina?"

Still receiving no answer, he started through the clutter of furniture, bumping noisily against a low table and cussing and wishing that he'd brought one of his guns. Not once in his life had he ever been afraid of anything when he'd had a gun in his hands.

He paused just this side of the kitchen door and smelled something, like after the fire bombings, or that day outside Cologne when half the town had gone up in smoke.

"Mina, you okay?" Quickly he pushed open the kitchen door and saw . . . nothing, though all the lights were on and the back door was open and an orange glow appeared to be coming from . . .

Jesus God! Something was on fire, something in the backyard. The lightning had . . .

He took the door running, stopped, and held his breath in his lungs and felt his eyes tearing from the smoke. He tried not to see what he saw, and saw it anyway, near the back fence—a human torch, a dancing column of flames engulfing a blackened, charred body, the blood sizzling in the flames. Mina stood in the center of the yard screaming, her arms raised to the sky. The two other Mexican boys ran past her, their faces revealing their fear, as though confident the lightning would come for them next.

Tom Marshall backed away, stumbled once on the steps, then turned and ran, thinking he needed his guns, needed to put distance between himself and that awful screeching, the howls of pain, the stench of burning flesh—worse, far worse than mere war.

31

With mixed feelings of relief and dread, Hal lifted his head, glanced out of the window, and saw the first rosy streaks of dawn. For one blessed moment his memory blurred. Nothing had happened. It had been a nightmare, that was all.

But then the single crack of dawn took on an orange hue, and he ran his hand over the grit and ashes on his face and smelled old smoke. His memory shifted and fell into place, and the mosaic was complete as he remembered Tom Marshall running down the street shouting "Fire!" the orange glow coming from the vicinity of Mina's house, Tom's almost hysterical refusal to go back, standing rooted in paralyzed shock, blocking the door.

Hal had had to push him aside, and he remembered thinking that no one would survive and perhaps it was just as well, and then he remembered stumbling once in the ruts of the road, and it hadn't been until he'd fallen on his hands and knees in the muddy snow that he'd even recognized the fact of rain.

He had a vague memory of having seen Brian walking toward the end of the road. He'd appeared to be drunk or ill, and Hal thought he'd called for his assistance as he'd raced around the side of Mina's house, heading toward the fire in the backyard.

But apparently he'd imagined all that, for he'd arrived there alone, except for Mina, whom he'd found collapsed on the back steps, her face, robe, hair, rain-drenched, incapable even of looking toward the charred atrocity, the blackened limbs still smoking, the odor unendurable.

Incoherently she'd told him that she'd sent the boys out for firewood when the storm had come up. She'd tried to call them quickly back, but lightning had struck one, and she had helplessly watched him die. The others had run off in fear.

A short time later, Mrs. O'Connell had arrived, a yellow raincoat over her robe, a large black umbrella held aloft. She had taken Mina back into the house and had promised Hal that she would stay with her until she was quiet.

As for the Mexican boy, there had been nothing that Hal could do for him then except cover the body with an old tarpaulin he'd found in Mina's garden shed, though the grisly job was facing him this morning, along with . . .

He shut his eyes to the streaks of dawn and clasped his head as though in an attempt to hold it together.

He opened his eyes and ran the palm of his hand over his smudged face and thought: I should go home to Sarah.

From where he sat at the table in the back room, he could see Mike's sprawled boots, Mike himself slumped against the wall, where he'd passed the night in safe oblivion. Hopefully there had been only one bottle in his stash.

Where was Inez? A good strong cup of coffee would be . . . *Quinton is dead . . . Quinton is dead . . .*

Like an insistent child, his mind forced that thought upon him, then, child-like, backed away from the fact of the empty chair, the shattered plate-glass window.

No, at least that much was truth.

With a moan he drew forward a crumpled memo pad and the stub of a pencil, and began to write:

1. Kate missing.
2. The road crew, possibly five men, missing.
3. The three Mexican boys—two missing, one . . .

He looked up at the ceiling, then slowly wrote "d-e-a-d."

Who else? Brian. He hadn't the vaguest idea where Brian was. And from the rigid watch that Tom Marshall was keeping on the empty street, Hal doubted seriously if he had progressed beyond Mina's house last night.

Poor Tom. He had seen it happen. Inez had yet to be told. Surely there were relatives somewhere. Next of kin, though for the time being it was a useless point.

As he tried to put his head in order with the clean black strokes of words on paper, he glanced at his watch. Not quite six. It could well be afternoon or evening before help arrived. He had no idea how widespread the storm had been, and the usual lines of communication had all been disrupted.

Several days? The thought was terrifying. Oh, there was plenty of food stored away. As for the future beyond their rescue . . . There his mind was a blank. How many would stay? How many would *want* to stay? For some it would be impossible. Brian, for one, he suspected. There would be nothing for

Brian now. And Sarah. She'd suffered irrational fears before the miscarriage. What would be her state of mind after the sedatives wore off?

He stared unseeing at the bars he was drawing on the memo pad and recalled disaster victims of tornadoes and hurricanes and floods. He'd never understood how, in the face of all their losses, they could calmly say, "We'll start all over again."

Now he did. And how dense of him not to have recognized it before! The excitement, the true excitement, was always in starting again. Nothing worse than an accomplished task, a realized dream . . .

"Mike! Come on! Rise and shine!" His voice rang out eerily across the silent restaurant, and as he hurried to the door, he noticed that his call had stirred no one. Tom Marshall continued to sit ramrod straight in a chair by the front door, and Mike apparently was still safely sedated on his hidden cache of Chivas Regal.

"Come on, Mike, old man," he called again, bending over the slumped shoulders. "Work to be done. Time to rejoin the living."

Mike groaned. One hand flailed uselessly at the air. He turned over on his side, made a pillow of his arm, and curled comfortably into the fetal position.

Hal started to prod again, then changed his mind. Coffee. That's what they all needed. As he strode across the dining room, he called out, "Tom, go get Callie Watkins. Tell him to bring his tools and board up that window. I want everyone in the restaurant this morning."

He was halfway through the swinging doors when he looked back and saw Tom, unmoving.

"Tom? You awake?" he called out, trying to keep his voice light. Fear and grief would be their worst enemies today, at least until some sort of contact could be established with the outside world.

"Come on, Tom," Hal urged, approaching the man from the rear. "Please go get Callie for me. He said he would fix. . ."

But as he touched Tom Marshall on the shoulder, the man swung up and around, confronting Hal with hollow, terrified eyes. "Ain't going no place," he muttered, his shoulders trembling.

Hal withdrew a step. "Surely you've seen men die before, Tom," he chided softly. "In battle, I mean."

"What I saw last night wasn't any battle," the man snapped, dragging his chair away from the table and positioning it closer to the window.

"I'm sure he didn't suffer for long."

"You didn't hear him screaming," Tom challenged. His voice fell. "And you didn't . . . see what I saw," he concluded in a whisper, and sat again in his chair, eyes front, shoulders straight, vigil resumed.

Hal paused, baffled. "What *did* you see?" He saw stress on the man's face, and incredible fatigue.

"A witch," Tom replied without hesitation.

"A . . ."

". . . witch," Tom repeated, apparently aware of Hal's disbelief. "And I don't give a damn whether anyone believes me or not, but I know what I saw and I ain't never seen anything like it before and I don't ever want to see anything like it again, and I can tell you one thing, she's not through with us yet, no sir, she means to kill us all, then—"

"Who, Tom? Who are you talking about?" Hal interrupted quickly, recognizing the man's growing hysteria and wanting to check it.

Tom looked over his shoulder, his face scarcely recognizable. "Her," he whispered. "Mina Murdoch, that's who."

"Look, you rest here," Hal said calmly. "I'll put on some coffee. . ."

"Don't want no coffee. We got a job to do."

Hal waited, thinking the man would say more. But he didn't, and Hal noticed his right leg twitching.

As a distant alarm went off in his head, he turned back to the kitchen, his earlier optimism only slightly blunted. Through the back door he saw a fiery explosion of morning sun and was conscious of the primitive turnings of his mind. Night was bad, morning good, and with a certain forced energy he filled the large stainless-steel coffeemaker, inserted a fresh filter, and breathed deeply of the pungent-smelling coffee.

As he plugged in the cord, he heard a sudden high-pitched ringing in his ears and leaned against the counter. He must be careful today or else his own fatigue would take a toll. That first year, on occasion they had worked for twenty-four-hour unbroken intervals. But that had been four years ago, and they all had been very much intact.

The coffeepot behind him began to gurgle. Help was on its way. All he had to do was stay calm within himself and transmit that calmness to the others. Perhaps as soon as a week from now, they all would talk about this night with Roger Laing. . .

Speaking of short-lived phenomena, my friend. . .

. . . and Roger would bring his blasted pendulums and test everything and solve nothing.

As the comforting smell of coffee filled the kitchen, Hal took three mugs from the cupboard and aligned them on the counter before him.

Frank Quinton. . .

New alarm bells sounded in his head. *No precedent.* As he turned on the spigot to test the coffee, he remembered the man's sprawled and bleeding body.

Though now he couldn't prove it, he knew that the chief surveyor for Century Mining Corporation was dead. Hurriedly he filled three cups with coffee, burning his fingers slightly in the process.

Morning had arrived. There was work to be done. If he was to keep this small band of people safe until help arrived, then he did not need to concentrate on fear or mystery. The body of Frank Quinton would be found along with the others, and it would provide its own solution.

He was certain. He had to be certain. . . .

32

No more sleep, Sarah thought groggily, and allowed her mind to crawl up onto the high ground of consciousness. At first she couldn't move her legs and imagined that she was bound at the ankles again in that shadowy nightmare of a room.

With a moan she forced her eyes open and simultaneously moved her legs, straightened them. She felt the sharp pain of stitches, and lesser pain, which coursed through her entire body. She felt battered.

Momentarily blinded by a direct ray of bright morning sun, she closed her eyes, but not before she caught a fleeting glimpse of someone curled in the easy chair beside the bed sleeping.

Donna. Where Donna was, could Mike be far behind? And it had been Mike who had wielded the needle the night before.

No more sleep! If she was to get out of this place, she had to be awake. And functioning. Whether Hal came with her or not was no longer important. She was finished with being a wife anyway. Never again would anyone impregnate her, never again would she run the risk . . .

She groaned involuntarily and watched closely the repose on Donna's face. Still sleeping. Until she was safely out of here, she must pretend that nothing had happened. She was certain that Mike had disposed of it. And she was equally certain that he would try to keep her sedated today, for his own sake. So, she must convince him of her ignorance. She'd seen nothing. She'd simply lost a baby, that was all. Then, once that she and Vicky were safely off this damn mountain, she would go to her parents' home in San Antonio and make a full report to the authorities, would tell them . . . *what?*

As the insanity exploded in her head, she quickly covered her mouth to keep from crying out, and as the hot stinging tears spilled down her face, she stared straight up at the ceiling and realized that for her own sake she must never tell anyone. Never!

A few moments later, the tears subsided and she found the courage to face the finality. It was over, and she would have to live with it for the rest of her life.

Now, could she sit up? She must have made a sound, for she heard Donna stir, heard the soft moan that always marks the passage from unconsciousness to consciousness, as though, left to its own devices, the human brain would be perfectly content to slumber forever.

Half-raised on one elbow, she glanced toward Donna and saw those sleep-glazed brown eyes staring back at her.

"Where do you think you're going?" Donna muttered, blinking her eyes rapidly in an attempt to clear the cobwebs.

"To pee, for starters," Sarah mumbled, and marveled at her new self, the powerful nightmare receding, packed away under layers of self-survival. In forty, maybe fifty years, she wouldn't even remember it.

"Here, let me help," Donna offered, rising from her chair and her cramped position.

"I can do it," Sarah insisted, and gingerly swung her legs over the side of the bed. She felt a single pain, as though a double-edged knife were being thrust up into her womb.

"Damn," she gasped, grasping the sides of the bed, aware for the first time of the thickness of sanitary napkins between her legs.

Terrific! The curse was back. "Where did you find the Kotex?" she asked of the two bare feet that now appeared in her line of vision.

"In the cupboard in the bathroom."

"Didn't think I had any."

"You've not been pregnant all your life. Here, lean on me."

For a moment Donna's kindness almost undid her, but she swallowed back the burning in her throat, accepted the support of the arm, and with one massive effort pushed slowly to her feet. She felt the floor go liquid beneath her, and held on for dear life.

"You shouldn't be up," Donna scolded softly.

"You want to go pee for me?"

"Come on, then, let's be about it."

Together they moved falteringly forward until the cold tiles of the bathroom appeared beneath Sarah's feet. As she eased down onto the toilet, Donna warned, "It's liable to sting."

"Oh, God," Sarah moaned as the warning came true, the hot urine acting like a blowtorch, her eyes watering to the extent that she saw nothing clearly. With both hands she clung to Donna's arms and vowed, "No liquid for the rest of the day."

"You should eat something."

"Where's Hal?"

"Down at the restaurant, I guess. Both he and Mike left shortly after mid-night. Something happened . . ."

"What?"

"I don't know. I've been here with you all night."

"Vicky?"

"Inez has her. It's all right . . ."

"I need . . ."

"I know. Can you hold on to the sink for a minute?"

"I can do it," Sarah insisted, and took the napkins, waiting for Donna to move back.

The bleeding wasn't as bad as she had imagined, though she noticed for the first time the dried blood on her legs and toes, silent proof that earlier there had been a deluge.

"I'm filthy," she whispered.

"No bath," Donna said sternly. "Get back to bed, and I'll bring you a washcloth."

"I don't want to go back to bed."

"You don't have much choice!"

Stunned by the sharpness of the voice, Sarah looked slowly up. Was that a new Donna, or merely a tired and frightened one? Yet what had she to be frightened of? Had she seen . . . ?

The mussed bed then loomed before her like a trap. Every nerve in her body was sending an insistent instruction. Lie down! But memory was sending a stronger one. Sit up! Take it in spells and by degrees, the ultimate goal being the clothes closet.

"What are you doing?" Donna demanded, puzzled, from the door. "You should be in bed. Mike—"

"To hell with Mike." Sarah smiled, amazed at how effective the smile was in canceling the pain. "He tried to get me to go to bed after Vicky, if you'll recall. Instead I helped you and Kate fix dinner, and we sat around the fire and took turns holding her."

Her voice drifted off with the unexpected recall. She was aware of Donna staring down at her. "*You* go to bed." Sarah laughed. "You look as though you need it more than I do."

For a moment there was no sound in the room. Sarah lifted her eyes to the window and beyond the curtains saw a winter landscape, blindingly brilliant in the early-morning sun. "Vicky can make one last snowman," she said quietly. "She'll like that."

Still no comment from Donna, though Sarah was aware of her drawing near to the bed. As though feeling the need for movement of some sort, Donna bent over and smoothed the sheets, folded the comforter across the foot of the bed, plumped the pillows.

That done, she seemed to look nervously about, as though seeking other chores that needed doing. In the past, talking to Donna had been as easy as breathing. And since Kate's illness they had grown ever closer. Now it felt as though she was in the room with a stranger, all intimacy and trust gone.

"Why don't you . . . ?"

"Would you like for me to get . . . ?"

Unfortunately they both started to speak at once, and stopped at once, and now were left with the muddled echo of their voices and an even more perplexing silence.

For that Sarah was profoundly sorry, but there wasn't anything she could do about it. Her goal was simple: to be dressed and packed by noon, only one suitcase for both her and Vicky—her limited strength would not permit more. Then, to enlist Inez's help—her battered though trusty green V.W. could get around the barricaded road as well as the blocked trucks at the bottom of the hill. Her destination was the bus station in Durango, where she would purchase two one-way tickets to San Antonio. By late tomorrow sometime, she would be safe.

"May . . . I talk to you for a minute, Sarah?" As Donna sat slowly on the far side of the bed, Sarah braced herself. In a way, she wished the woman would leave. She did not need her, nor did she need Hal, or anyone else who might try to block her escape.

"Do . . . you . . . ?" Donna began, and faltered. She smoothed something off her soiled blue jeans and tried again. "Do you remember . . . much of yesterday?"

A dangerous question. "Yes," Sarah replied curtly, safely.

"What?"

"I remember pain, great waves of it, and thinking . . ."

"What?"

She'd never seen Donna so tense. ". . . thinking how different it had been with Vicky, how simple."

Donna nodded as though she knew that much and wanted to hear more. "Do you remember anything else?"

Sarah stalled. "Not much," she said. "Nature's way, I suppose, of—"

"Mina was there?"

Sarah nodded.

"Did anything odd happen?"

"I want to get dressed now." Sarah sat up too rapidly. On diminished breath she said, "Do me a favor, will you, Donna? Go and get Vicky for me and bring her home."

"I'm not certain you're—"

"I didn't ask for your advice, Donna. I asked for your help."

"Let me get Mike first. He can—"

"No!"

"Something *did* happen, didn't it? That's why Mike's begun drinking again."

Sarah couldn't listen to what she knew was Donna's own cry for help. "I don't know what you're talking about."

"Sarah, you mustn't—"

"Don't tell me what to do!" Sarah cried. "Just leave me alone. I'm quite all right. Women lose babies every day. I will survive. Now, get out and . . ."

Perilously close to tears, she stopped speaking, grasped the arms of the chair, and listened to the soft tread of bare retreating feet.

"Shall I wait out—?"

"No!"

"You're not strong enough to—"

"I'm strong enough!" Sarah repeated emphatically, and in an effort to demonstrate her claim, she pushed away from the support of the chair and felt a grinding pain in her womb, as though something with claws was still trapped inside her.

The last thing she remembered was the siren of her own scream, the painful fall, and Donna kneeling beside her, cradling her in her arms, crying with her, yet promising over and over again, "You're safe now, you're safe . . ."

Sarah had never heard a more absurd claim.

33

In spite of the anvil inside his head and the weight of guilt on his shoulders, he had seen it all, with Hal as his guide, the rocky crumbling abyss where the road had once climbed up to the plateau. And Mike had heard it all.

By my best estimate, six are missing—seven, counting Kate.

And despite his desire to seek out only Donna and bury himself in her arms, he had helped Hal and Callie Watkins round up what was left of Tomis.

But the first word that truly registered on the scorched land that was his memory was the single word which he'd just heard spoken, coming from someone at a table behind him, a woman's voice whispering:

". . . witch . . ."

He raised slowly up from his crossed arms and glanced over his shoulder.

There were about forty people crowded into the restaurant. A few were still missing. Families seemed to be staying very close together, tables rearranged, chairs assembled to accommodate small groups.

Of course they all were frightened. What the hell! *He* was frightened, not just of the events of the calamitous night and the fact of their isolation. Mike's fears stretched back to the day before: the blood-soaked sheet, the thing inside, and the ease with which he'd finally slipped away and retrieved his buried cache. On his hands and knees digging in the dirt of the woodshed last night, he'd felt like an animal.

But how good it had been, the first burning swallow, the slow but steady descent into oblivion. As he closed his bloodshot eyes against the brightness of noon sun, he thought quite lucidly that he would perform any act, commit any crime, any atrocity, for one more bottle.

Now, what was it he was looking for? Oh, yes, the person who had whispered the word. But he heard nothing now except the low hum of whispered conversations, all of them comparing tales of how they had survived the night and discussing what was going to happen next.

At the large round corner table, he saw the Driver and O'Connell kids placidly playing cards. Next to them, the Hillses and Billingslys were sitting in a state of calm resignation. The most talkative group was at the center of the restaurant. Mr. and Mrs. O'Connell, the Allegros, Ned Wilson, and Polly Whiteside all sat together, their heads bent, their gestures alternately broad, then small, several talking at once, then all falling silent.

Through the swinging doors of the kitchen he saw Hal in earnest conversation with Inez. Below the swinging doors he saw Vicky's plump legs, standing motionless beside her father.

What precisely were they all doing here? Mike had no idea. It seemed wiser to him to let everyone go about his business as best he could. But Hal had insisted that they congregate, and here they were, growing noisy and restless and even more frightened.

Briefly he rubbed his eyes, which he knew was a mistake, as a thousand hot needles penetrated his eyeballs. He'd had coffee, but it had done little to alleviate his suffering. And he *was* suffering. He should go up and check on Donna and Sarah, and would as soon as he was certain that he could stand without having his head explode.

Then he heard it again: ". . . witch"—and at the same time heard Inez's strained voice call over the top of the doors, "If some of you women would give me a hand, we could fix some sandwiches and soup. I'm sure the children are getting hungry."

As her voice cut through the low conversational hum, Mrs. Driver and Mrs. Hills left their chairs and headed toward the kitchen.

Food! No, thank you, and as he placed his hands palm down on the table for maximum lift-off, he heard Hal behind him. "Come on. While they're eating, let's go see what we can find."

From the hushed tone of his voice and the expression on his face, Mike knew what he was talking about. Bodies. They were going to search for bodies.

"I think I should go check on Donna and Sarah first," he stalled.

"We don't have much time," Hal said cryptically.

"From where I sit, it looks like that's all we got."

"A few are still missing."

"Who?"

"Brian, and Mina Murdoch, Rene Hackett, and Lucy."

"Wrong," Mike muttered, having caught sight of a well-filled white T-shirt just entering the restaurant, one arm around Rene Hackett's shoulder. Never one to be daunted by a late-season blizzard, Lucy Hackett had dressed as

227

though it were July, and the new hush which now fell over the crowded restaurant was rife with conflicting emotions.

"Is she ill?" Hal called out, starting toward the two, his attention focused on Rene's drooping head and unfocused eyes.

"No," Lucy said quickly. "I just gave her some sleeping pills last night to help her sleep, and I guess I gave her too many, 'cause she wouldn't wake up and I didn't want to stay down there in that house all by myself, so I just got her dressed and made her—"

"Mike?"

As Hal summoned him to come forward, Mike sighed wearily, motioning his hand in a gesture of dismissal. "Ask her her name and what day it is. If she can answer, she's all right, and start pouring coffee down her."

As a diagnosis and prescription, it left much to be desired. But he watched from a distance with a degree of interest as Hal followed his instructions and assisted Rene Hackett to a near table, sat her down, got the two answers, and sent Lucy into the kitchen for coffee.

"Two down, two to go," he mumbled as Hal returned to the table. Mike saw a few of the women clustered protectively about Rene Hackett, taking the coffee from Lucy, then turning their backs on her. For a moment he felt sorry for her. She looked lost. And embarrassed.

Absorbed by the mini-drama of teenage angst, Mike slowly brought his attention back to Hal.

"Who next?" Mike asked. "Mina?"

"No!" Hal said, too quickly, then with equal speed added, "Let her sleep. She had a dreadful night."

Strange! They all had had a dreadful night. Why should Mina be left out of this bizarre fellowship?

"Damn him," Hal muttered, and Mike looked up and followed his line of vision to the center table, to the place where Tom Marshall was bending over Ned Wilson and whispering something. Several others at the table leaned forward, obviously listening with interest. He saw Mrs. Lewis press her hand to his mouth.

"Damn him," Hal repeated, then raised himself up and shouted full-voiced, "Tom, I want to see you in the kitchen."

Caught mid-sentence, Tom merely gave him a passing glance, then bent over, undeterred, to complete his story.

"Tom!" Hal shouted again.

"They got a right to know, Kitchens," the man shouted back. "Most of 'em know it already."

"Know what?" Mike asked, not certain that he wanted an answer.

It appeared that he wouldn't get one anyway, for Hal started across the restaurant at a steady stride and would have reached his destination if there hadn't at that moment been a sudden rise of voices coming from the kitchen, recognizable voices, and for the first time Mike turned about in his chair with vigor and saw the top of Donna's head over the swinging doors and heard Inez's voice raised in frightened protest, "She can't do that, the road is gone. Didn't Hal tell . . . ?"

Someone was arguing with her from the back door of the kitchen, an equally recognizable though weakened voice begging, "Please, Inez. I must leave here. If you won't drive me, let me take the car."

That was all he heard, all he needed to hear, and he was on his feet, in a race with Hal for the kitchen doors, Hal reaching them first, then stopping suddenly with Mike coming up behind him in a soft collision. His attention focused first on Donna, who looked old and mussed and frightened, then on to the back door, to a very pale and drawn Sarah, who supported herself on the near counter with one hand, holding Vicky with the other, a small traveling bag at her feet.

At their appearance, all voices fell, and Mike saw Sarah glance toward Hal with a most unwifely expression. "You . . . can't stop me," she whispered, "so don't try."

Inez stepped between them with a sympathetic apology. "She wants me to drive her down to Durango," she said. "I tried to tell her . . ."

At the stove, Mrs. Hills was stirring a kettle of soup, and looked away, embarrassed. Mrs. O'Connell, with the authority of a five-time mother, laid down a knife coated with mayonnaise and started slowly forward. "Sarah, come, my dear," she said kindly. "I'm so glad to see you up and about, but you may be pushing things a bit. Why don't you let me fix you a cup of tea, and we'll talk, that's—"

But Sarah wasn't in the mood for tea or talk. She suddenly clutched Vicky to her. "Just give me the keys, Inez," she said. "I'll leave the car in the parking lot at the bus station. You can—"

At last Hal moved, though at his first step Sarah warned, "No, don't come any closer."

"Sarah, let me take you home. You should be in bed."

"No! No bed. I just want to get out of here."

As Hal stepped forward again, Mike eased through the doors and went immediately to Donna's side and put his arm around her, and on the pretense of kissing her, whispered, "Why did you let her get out of bed?"

"How was I to stop her?" she retorted angrily.

"Come on, Sarah, please," Hal begged, one hand extended. "I'm afraid you can't go anyplace this morning."

"I don't want to stay here."

"You must. The road is out. Last night—"

"That's a lie."

"No, it isn't. Ask anyone here. There's no cause for alarm, but . . ."

Wrong! From the look on Sarah's face, there was every cause for alarm. And Mike understood why better than anyone else in the kitchen, and he tried to deal with that horrifying memory, and failed, and abandoned Donna and joined Hal.

"You really should be in bed, Sarah," he said, trying to cut through the tension, aware of the crowd peering over the kitchen doors. "You've lost a lot of blood," he went on, sorry for her. "Come on," he added, passing Hal and drawing closer in spite of the rising terror on Sarah's face. "Let me take you home. I'll give you a shot that will—"

Suddenly an ear-splitting scream escaped her lips, a single high-pitched "No!" Vicky started to cry, then suddenly broke free from Sarah's grasp and ran to Hal, leaving Sarah alone.

The collapse came as Mike knew it would, a soft, grief-ridden descent first to her knees, her racking sobs filling every corner of the now quiet kitchen.

As Hal bent over her, Mike stepped around them and pushed open the back door. "Carry her home," he said quietly. "I'll give her a—"

"No!" This strong contradiction came from Donna. "No," she repeated, coming forward. "Don't take her back up there. And don't give her any more shots. She's terrified. Can't you see that?"

"She's also ill," Mike said angrily.

"She can lie down in the back room."

He started to protest again, but in the face of defeat changed his mind. Hal had withdrawn a few steps, taking the weeping Vicky with him. Clearly torn between his disintegrating daughter and his collapsed wife, he foundered. At the same time, Donna came forward, picking up a holy alliance of the three women in the kitchen as she walked across the room. The four women closed around Sarah, lifted her gently to her feet, and with two supporting her on each arm, led her haltingly through the swinging doors and into the dining room, the curious and the sympathetic stepping back and clearing a path for them as they headed toward Hal's domain of the back room.

"Will . . . she be all right?" Hal asked softly.

Mike shrugged. "I sure as hell can't examine her here . . ." He leaned wearily against the counter. Nearby, the kettle of soup was bubbling. Beyond the swinging doors, he heard the steady hum of voices.

What, God, would you require of me for the miracle of a bottle?

Sinking into self-disgust, he turned and stared straight into an open cupboard filled with canned goods and seasonings, and near the back, the answered prayer, a large bottle of cooking sherry.

With apologies to no one, and making no attempt to disguise what he was doing, he carefully removed the smaller obstructions and with reverence lifted out the dark green bottle. He carried it back to his table, unscrewed the cap, lifted it to his lips, and heard that word again, like something hanging over him in the atmosphere, merely a whisper:

". . . witch. . . ."

34

As an anesthetic, the sherry left a lot to be desired. An hour later, his senses were merely numbed, not dead, and he was aware of everything that was going on around him, of Hal's undisguised disgust as he'd rounded up men for the body hunt.

"Count me out, old buddy," Mike had slurred, and had watched impassively as the intrepid band composed of Callie Watkins, Mr. Hills, and Hal had slipped unnoticed by the others down the steps and had disappeared into the bright sunlight on their grisly hunt.

And he had been actively aware of the hurt and anger in Donna's eyes as she had stopped by his table on one of her several trips to the kitchen in an attempt to make Sarah comfortable.

Witch! There it was again. Cry witch! Well, that was one explanation, wasn't it? As good as any to account for blizzards in May, torrential rains, disappearing roads, and half-human, half-sea-monster infants.

Quickly he lifted the bottle and drank again and saw less than a cup sloshing around in the bottom. He tenderly screwed the cap back on and cradled it in his arms.

"And I saw it," he heard Tom Marshall say, full-voiced.

Why in hell did he have to shout? Mike closed his eyes and wondered if the fire inside his head was visible to others, and hoped not, because he really didn't want to call attention to himself, and hugged the bottle closer and wondered what Hal planned to do with the bodies he found.

"She was standing there, I tell you," Tom Marshall was saying, "watching him, just watching him burn."

"He's right," came a younger, female voice, and Mike looked up through bleary eyes and saw Lucy Hackett, her young face sobered. "All this is her fault," she went on. "She even caused this to happen," she added, holding up her injured hands. "I never said anything earlier because I didn't think anyone would believe me. But now maybe you'll believe Mr. Marshall."

Oh, Lord. Mike sighed and clutched his bottle and thought: Witch hunt! Time to eat the children, light the fires, drink the blood, and screw all the women. Fun-and-games time. Welcome to the thirteenth century. Let the trial begin.

Through the confusing patterns of sun and shadow, he saw the crowded room in mysterious movement, chairs being adjusted, all gathering around for the testimony. He even saw Donna standing in the door of the small dining room, her arms crossed in a peculiarly passive stance as she listened to the madness.

Hurry back, Hal, your little ship is going down.

He should stop them now before it got out of hand, and would have if he'd had the strength to stand, and if at that moment Terry O'Connell, clutching the crucifix about her neck, hadn't joined the eyewitnesses at the end of the room. "I've known it for a long time, too," she said in a light girlish voice. "She always burns candles during class, and she hypnotizes us with the flame and gets us in her power. I didn't really know what she was doing until Lucy told me, but then I understood. She can make us do anything, once she gets us in her power."

Suddenly Mrs. O'Connell stood up. "Why didn't you tell me this before?" she demanded angrily.

"Lucy said you wouldn't believe me, Mama."

"There! You see?" Tom Marshall shouted triumphantly. "Listen to the kids. They've been around her more than any of us."

As one of the Driver boys came forward, Mike discerned a slight grin on his face, as though this all was proving to be a hell of a lot of fun. "I've never liked her," he said in a voice cracking with adolescence. "And what none of you know is that she's a real head, has some of the best grass I've ever—"

"Billy!"

The shocked parental voice had come from Mrs. Driver.

"Well, it's true, Mom. And I think it's kind of funny. We moved here to get away from the pushers in San Mateo, and Miss Murdoch offered it to us free."

This stunning announcement seemed to stir the whole room to movement. Donna disappeared from the doorway and reappeared a moment later, her arm about Sarah's shoulder as she led her slowly to a near chair in the large dining room. Clearly neither of them wanted to miss a thing.

As the scraping of chairs subsided, Mike looked about and discovered that he was in this end of the restaurant alone. Even Inez came slowly out of the kitchen, wiping her hands on her apron, her attention fixed on the speaker of the moment, the theatrical little Lucy Hackett, who probably never once in her fourteen years had enjoyed a more enraptured audience.

"My mama used to think that it was the Mountain Man," she said, her clear piping voice filling every corner of the restaurant, "and he may have something to do with it, I don't know. But it's mostly her. You all always thought that she was nice, and she *was* to your face. But once, she . . .'"

Oh, it was a skillful performance, proper pauses, her injured hands now fluttering over her ripe breasts.

". . . once she told me that everyone possesses the power for good and evil and that all her life the devil had inhabited her."

Okay, show's over, Mike thought, and quietly placed the bottle of sherry on the table and was just starting to his feet when a low, weakened, though most effective voice topped the murmurs of alarm.

"She's . . . right. Lucy's right."

The room fell silent and all heads swiveled toward Sarah Kitchens, who sat weakly in a chair, Donna hovering protectively over her, her pale bloodless face an effective match for her voice, which was just barely audible.

"Lucy's right," she repeated, and Mike held his position and wished that the room would hold still as well.

"I . . . lost my baby yesterday," she began, her ruined face bearing no resemblance to the healthy, robust Sarah of three days ago. "I was at . . . Mina's when it happened."

Would she tell everything? Mike was certain she wouldn't.

"She drugged me," Sarah was saying now, her voice rising, "and she . . . tied me to the bed . . . and took off . . . my clothes and . . ."

As Sarah slumped against Mrs. O'Connell, the other women quickly arranged a bed of chairs and gently lowered her down and watched in stunned sympathy as her hands covered her face in deep and moving grief.

"Where is she?" shouted a male voice someplace near the center of the room. "Everyone else is here. Where is *she?*"

Other voices joined in, all shouting, though Mike seemed to be hearing them from a distance, as though he were isolated. He tried again to stand, thinking it had gone too far, thinking he'd let it go too far, but the voices still were increasing and seemed to be robbing him of energy.

"Wait . . ." he called out as someone rushed past him, but he couldn't see who it was, and they didn't stop. As he was trying to gather the energy for another command, someone else ran from the restaurant, and he heard the door slam like an explosion, and somewhere near the center of the maelstrom he heard the voices of excited women, their fears surfacing, the din bespeaking a kind of relief. At last they had an enemy.

Who had left and who remained, he had no idea. With the slamming of the door, his head had exploded, and the last shred of reason along with it.

He knew what he had seen on his examining table and knew further that there was no rational accounting for it.

"I saw her levitate once. She was in her garden, and I was passing by the back fence and I saw her leave the ground. . . . She lit the fire with the tips of her fingers. I saw her. Mama said she made that big rock come down that killed Papa."

"Poor Sarah. She's bleeding again."

The voices shot up around him like startled birds screeching from the banks of a river. He heard weeping coming from all corners of the room, the women trying to comfort each other, the men standing about in stunned and angry silence.

Gone. Dead soldier. Empty bottle. The center wasn't holding. The false trappings of eight hundred years had disintegrated, and if he had not actively contributed to it, he'd not actively tried to stop it.

Still, there was time, as soon as he rejoined the scattered fragments of his head, got a reliable messenger moving from his brain to his legs. He had always been a lousy drunk, nonviolent, apathetic, lethargic.

Whatever they were planning, he could stop them. There was time. And Hal would be back soon—poor Hal, who would be so shocked by this eighth circle of hell that his dream had become.

35

"Here they come!" Lucy Hackett cried from the window, and the shout seemed to stir everyone to movement.

Donna held her position, feeling sick. From where she sat near the north wall, she looked down on Sarah, curled uncomfortably on four chairs, someone's coat spread over her, apparently sleeping soundly still under the residual influence of the shot Mike had given her the night before.

Mike . . . She looked across the restaurant. Who was that vaguely familiar man passed out at the table near the window, as impervious as Sarah to the forces which had been let loose in this bizarre courtroom? Not Mike. She had known about the hidden bottle. Why hadn't she destroyed it? The efforts and good intentions of four long years destroyed. He would have to start at the beginning again, and she doubted seriously if he possessed the courage.

Where was Hal? *He* could stop them. She *should* stop them, yet in a very real way, she had contributed to the hysteria, had urged Sarah to speak out against Mina. But Lucy Hackett and Tom Marshall had needed no help. And no one seemed to notice that one testimony was that of a hysterical adolescent, and the other a second-rate and aging male mind corrupted by a lifetime in the U.S. military machine.

She closed her eyes and prayed the nausea would pass. She *was* sick, yet she'd eaten nothing. With effort she swallowed hard and opened her eyes to the macabre sight of everyone pressed against the far windows, yet no one making a sound, as though something in the street had caught their attention and held it.

Slowly, against her better judgment she raised up from the chair and saw what it was, Ed Billingsly on one side, Ned Wilson on the other, and between them a clearly protesting Mina Murdoch, her long coarse gray hair loosened and straggly about her shoulders, her arms struggling against her stern escort, her robe dragging in the mud and slush of melting snow.

"She looks like a witch," Donna heard someone mutter from the window. And she did, though Donna had seen enough and sat quickly down.

Perhaps there was time to get Sarah out of here and herself as well. She wanted no part of what was going to happen. If she could get Sarah on her feet, they could make it to the back door and up the hill.

But as she leaned over to shake Sarah, Lucy squealed from the window, "Oh, look! She fell."

As laughter erupted on the far side of the room, Donna moved closer to the sleeping Sarah and arranged a small fortress of three empty chairs in front of them . . .

Tick-a-lock, all the way around . . .

. . . and felt childlike.

They were coming. The others were beginning to move hurriedly away from the windows, returning to their tables, like guilty children awaiting an absent teacher.

Again the large crowded room had fallen silent, the sudden scraping of a chair summoning everyone's attention to the front of the room, where Tom Marshall positioned a single chair in a cleared area and was now standing behind it. Witness stand?

"Oooh! Look at her," Lucy Hackett whispered from the window, but in the new silence, everyone heard, and heard as well the scuffle of feet on the steps outside, Ned Wilson and Ed Billingsly performing their job efficiently, silently.

Then Donna heard Mina's voice, breathless, indignant, scolding, as though the men who were giving her such rough escort were merely misbehaving boys.

"Ed, I demand to know the meaning of . . . You've no right, either of you. You might have let me dress and fix my hair. Do you know what happened last night? Oh, it was a terrible night. . . . Please, you're hurting my arm."

Once through the door, she tried to wrench free, and failed, and fully occupied with her own distress, she did not at first see the crowded, silent restaurant, everyone seated, yet every head turned, all eyes focused on her.

Then at last she saw them, and the struggle ceased, and for just a moment Donna saw the mask drop and thought: *She knows!*

A moment later her eyes were defiant as she lifted her head and tried with dignity to pull free of her captors, then gave in to them and pretended as though she were merely dealing with irascible boys.

"These two"—she smiled weakly at her audience—"quite rude they have been to me. In fact, the rudest treatment I've ever received in my life."

She gave a pitiful little laugh, and Donna felt embarrassed for her. She

236

looked away and focused on the sleeping Sarah, her face pale in a direct beam of afternoon sun.

"If someone will only tell me what's going on, I'll be happy to . . ."

As Mina's voice cut through the silence, Donna looked back toward the door and saw Ed Billingsly and Ned Wilson step away, giving Mina the freedom she wanted. The question now was what to do with it.

Her self-consciousness increasing, she gently massaged her upper arms where male hands had held her fast, and immediately thereafter made an attempt to straighten her hair. In a final flutter, her hands brushed across the front of her robe as she drew the ends together and tightened the cord, reminding Donna how very small the woman really was.

She started toward a near table, where the Drivers sat, their large brood clustered about them. "May I share your table for this town meeting, Martha?" Mina asked, her manner calm, only her voice giving her away.

But the Drivers made no response, and at the same time, Tom Marshall's voice loomed across the restaurant. "We got a chair for you up here, Miss Murdoch, saved it special."

As Donna glanced from one end of the room to the other, she noticed that Tom's ever-present ally, Lucy Hackett, had moved into position beside him, her pretty face flushed with excitement, her splinted fingers perpetually pointing.

Donna looked back toward Mina and saw the confusion on her face, saw her look quickly over her shoulder to check on the whereabouts of her two guards, as though the thought to bolt had entered her mind. Unfortunately, the two men were standing directly behind her, blocking her only avenue of escape.

"If . . . only someone would tell me what's going on," she said.

"That's what we were hoping you'd tell us," Tom Marshall said, still waiting behind the chair.

"The fact that we need to meet and talk is undeniable." Mina smiled, summoning up a degree of her old courtesy. "The dreadful night took its toll, didn't it?" Her voice broke as she bowed her head. "But we'll be all right, I'm certain of it. Help will be along, and . . ."

As though aware of her own ramblings and equally aware that nothing was being received, Donna saw her step back, clearly longing to move away from the silent, staring, hostile faces.

Feeling the need to rest her eyes from the ugly scene, Donna looked toward the far table by the window, Mike still passed out, his head cradled in the crook of his arm. Surely he'd wake up in time to stop it before it got out of hand, or Hal would return. In the meantime, perhaps Mina was due a comeuppance.

"Bring her forward!" Tom Marshall suddenly bellowed from the front of the room, and again Mina was captured, struggling mightily this time, her voice climbing high in protest, her long hair thrashing every which way as Ed Billingsly and Ned Wilson propelled her steadily through the crowded tables, people pulling back as she passed, as though she were a contagion.

"No, please, let me go. I'll sit where I like. I'll stay, only, please, there's no need . . ."

But apparently there was, and Donna felt simultaneously fascinated and sickened by the forceful way they pushed her down into the appointed chair. She watched, astonished, as Lucy produced a long blue scarf from her pocket and suggested, grinning, "You'd better tie her hands behind her, Mr. Marshall. They're witch's hands."

Donna averted her eyes and heard a scraping as though a table had been moved forward, heard the sounds of male effort, and looked back to see Mina bound to the chair, the chair itself having been lifted atop a table, her fear now visible for all to see. She twisted continuously, trying to free her bound hands, some ancient residue of decorum and caution forcing her knees together, though one side of the robe had fallen open, revealing a parchment-like blue-veined leg.

Entrapped and aware of herself as spectacle, she underwent a change of mood. No longer pleading, her darting eyes stared angrily down on her tormentors. "I demand to know the meaning of this," she said. "You have no right. What have I done? Where's Hal? Go get Hal Kitchens. He'll . . ."

As her angry voice shattered the silence in the room, Donna noticed all eyes tracking her steadily, the expressions on those upturned faces one of communal and deep fear.

Mina railed on for several minutes, part threat, part plea, calling out specific names now and then, as though to appeal to old allegiances.

"Mrs. O'Connell, please. Would you ask them to untie me? I've done nothing to . . . Polly, you'll help me, won't you? We've shared such good times in the past—remember?"

But apparently no one remembered, and at the end of her pleas for help, she fell silent. Something flickered in the depths of her eyes, then was smothered, and as she glanced down to her left and saw Lucy Hackett, her expression was one of hate now, and the only sound in the room was her heavy breathing as the seconds ticked by.

"All right, if she's talked herself out, let's begin," Tom Marshall said at last. "Charges have been leveled against the schoolteacher here. And since this is America and a democracy, the accused has a right to hear those charges and to respond to them."

Mina's head slumped forward. Her eyes were closed.

Oh, for heaven's sake, just let her go, Donna thought, though at that moment Sarah moaned in her sleep, one arm flinging off the coat which served as cover. Although she didn't regain consciousness, Donna saw a sad sight. "She's . . . crying," she murmured. "She's . . . crying in her sleep."

Someone near the back of the room shouted, "Start with Sarah Kitchens. She's suffered and lost the most."

As Donna wiped away the unconscious tears from Sarah's face, she heard Tom Marshall order, "You tell us what happened, Mrs. Dunne. You've been with her all night."

At the very moment that she wanted most to be far removed from the unreality of this time and place, she found herself thrust into the spotlight, and looked timidly up into Mina's face, merely a frightened old woman now, her eyebrows circumflex with pity as she gazed down on Sarah.

238

"How is she, Donna?" Mina asked kindly from her perch high on the table, as though nothing at all were out of the ordinary. "Shouldn't she be in bed? She lost an enormous amount of blood. I can't imagine why Hal would let her—"

"Shut up!" Tom commanded, standing directly before the chair. "You're here to listen. If you've got anything to say, you'll get your turn later."

Again Mina closed her eyes and lifted her head as though somehow she were trying to rise above it all.

"Go on, Mrs. Dunne," Tom ordered, and for the second time Donna felt the weight of all those eyes as they shifted in her direction.

She had nothing to say to such a gathering, was ashamed even to be a part of it. As she readjusted the coat over Sarah, she said as much to Tom Marshall and the group in general. "Sarah didn't talk much last night, Tom. Mike had given her something to make her sleep. And she . . . slept . . ."

"She must have said something," Tom argued. "She said enough here a while ago, about being—"

"Perhaps Mike could tell you," Donna answered. "He was with her during—"

"Mike's no good to us," Marshall grumbled. "You were there, too, weren't you, right after it happened, I mean?"

"Yes, she was," came a high piping voice beyond Tom Marshall as Lucy Hackett entered the discussion. "I saw them all from my bedroom window." She grinned, drawing close to the table on which Mina sat bound. "I saw them carrying poor Mrs. Kitchens out of Mina's house, and Mrs. Dunne was with them. I saw her. She knows more than she's telling us."

As whispering erupted from all corners of the room, Donna gave the girl a hard look and closed her eyes, seeing an image of two chairs atop the table, two women bound and humiliated.

"She said . . ." Donna began, and stopped. "Sarah . . . said that she had gone to Mina's to fetch the Mexican boys for Inez—"

"They were never here when I needed them," Inez said angrily. "I brought them up here to work, but she insisted on filling their heads with such things as—"

"They wanted to learn English," Mina said calmly, though now and then she pulled against her bound hands and tried to straighten her shoulders, as though the numbness was spreading. "I saw nothing wrong in that."

"You saw nothing wrong in a lot of things," Tom Marshall snapped. "Now, go on, Mrs. Dunne, tell us . . ."

Donna shook her head and wondered what would happen if she simply got up and walked out. "She . . . said that she went into labor while she was at Mina's, that there was . . . a peculiar odor in the air, and she felt as though she were being . . . drugged."

"No," came a soft moan from the chair high on the table. "The boys had been smoking, that's all," Mina said.

Mrs. O'Connell spoke up. "One of my boys tells us you kept drugs there."

"Not drugs, Mrs. O'Connell," Mina corrected gently, a portion of the schoolmistress returning. "A little marijuana, that's all. You have your beer,

239

poor Mike over there has fallen back into his bottle, a bit of grass is no worse, perfectly harmless."

"She put something in it and made us smoke it," Lucy said slyly.

"I did not!" Mina said in angry indignation.

"That's enough," Tom ordered, intervening. "Now, you just wait, Lucy, you'll have your chance. Go on, Mrs. Dunne."

Grateful for the brief distraction and regretful that it was over, Donna shook her head, unable to look at Mina, who looked so ridiculous up in the chair.

"When I got there," she went on, trying to dispel the image, "Sarah had already miscarried. The baby was dead, strangled on the cord, according to Mike."

She looked sorrowfully down on Sarah. "She was ·. . . on Mina's bed. Her clothes had been removed, and her legs and arms were—"

"Of course she was on the bed," Mina interrupted angrily. "Where precisely would any of you place a woman in labor? And of course I restrained her, for her own good. She was in great pain, half out of her head. I felt that if I was to help her—"

Again Tom Marshall cut her off. "I said that's enough, do you hear me? You're here to listen, not to—"

Lucy giggled. "We could gag her."

Again something flickered in the depths of Mina's eyes. She lowered her head, her long hair obscuring her face. "I'm . . . sorry," she whispered, an apology as well as a clear concession to the helplessness of her predicament and the power of her tormentors.

"Go on, Mrs. Dunne," Tom said.

"Why don't you let her down?" Donna said, thinking it would be easier and certainly fairer to confront her with these accusations across a table.

But when no one moved to act on her suggestion, she went on, determined to tell them what little she knew and leave. Mina was right on one score. Sarah should be in bed.

"She was . . . bleeding, of course," Donna went on, "and unconscious. Mike . . . took the baby away, not wanting her to wake up and see it."

"Did *you* see it?" Mina asked hesitantly.

Donna shook her head. "I had no desire to."

Mina nodded in understanding and lifted her face to the ceiling, wincing as though the discomfort caused by her bound position was increasing. Donna saw Lucy gaping upward in fascination; then suddenly she darted around the edge of the crowd and disappeared into the kitchen.

Donna watched and thought: You'd better keep *her* in sight. *There's* the true evil.

"And then what, Mrs. Dunne?" Tom prompted, drawing a chair forward and straddling it backwards, his long lean frame unwinding endlessly.

"And then . . . nothing," she said, finding energy in her anger. "Mike came back and saw to her. And we took her home. As I said before, he gave her a sedative and she slept through the night, and when she awakened this morning, she only wanted to leave here. Of course, neither of us knew about the road . . ."

240

Tom Marshall adjusted his chair until he was facing the woman on the table. "Mrs. Kitchens claims that you were responsible for the baby's death. That you refused to call the doctor until too late."

"That's absurd," Mina protested, shocked. "That's vile and absurd. Why would she make such an irresponsible charge?" Her voice broke. She lowered her head and wept silently.

Unable to watch the old woman any longer, Donna looked away, to see Lucy Hackett drawing near to Tom Marshall, carrying a broom in her hands.

"What in the hell are you going to do with that?" Tom demanded.

Lucy giggled. "Well, every witch needs a broomstick, doesn't she? And besides, you can give her a good crack on the head when you want her to shut up."

There was scattered laughter throughout the restaurant, indulgent laughter, as though at a precocious child, although Donna saw Tom take the broom, rise from his straddled position, and hold it for a moment as though it were a baseball bat.

Simultaneously she charted the change on Mina's face, who now appeared to press farther back in her chair, eyeing the simple broom as though it were a lethal weapon.

"Don't forget, Miss Murdoch," Tom said sarcastically, playing to his audience as he encircled Mina, poking at her with the broom from all angles, "I saw a piece of your handiwork for myself, remember? I was there when you set that 'nice' boy on fire, and I saw you just watching him burn."

"I did . . . not," Mina gasped. "It . . . was too late, there was . . . nothing . . ." She tried desperately to keep the man and the broom in sight as he circled behind her.

"I reached for the garden hose, remember, and you set it on fire as well, and I saw *that* with my own eyes," he said, an evangelical fervor to his voice, as though seeing it again, while still poking at her with the broom, light blows as far as Donna could see, nothing very threatening except the element of fear itself.

"Please, don't . . ." Mina whimpered as he emerged in front of her, her eyes wide, trying to gauge where the next prod would come. "You don't mean what . . . you're saying, the hose was set off by a spark. I was not in any way . . . responsible . . ."

Suddenly, with one quick lunge he thrust the end of the broom directly into her mouth. The element of surprise took her off-guard, and too late she tried to avert her face, and for a moment the chair tottered dangerously on top of the table. Reflexively Donna moved forward; then some deeper, more primitive instinct canceled the reflex, and she settled slowly back into her chair, watching passively along with everyone else as the spectacle of terror escalated before them. She saw a small trickle of blood seep from Mina's mouth where the force of the broom had apparently knocked loose a tooth or cut her lip, her mouth comically distended, her eyes lightly closed as she waited in fear.

At first the unexpected cruelty had a curious effect on the crowd. They seemed to retreat into their chairs, as though denying all responsibility; yet their eyes were fixed in utter fascination on the now silent Mina and her bleeding mouth.

"Good girl, Lucy." Tom smiled, at last aware of the unique power in his simple weapon.

Lucy, preening under the praise, moved closer, the grin gone from her face. "She tied me to a chair once," she whispered, looking up at the suffering Mina with hate-filled eyes. "She called me a whore and tied me to a chair and made me sit there while the others did their conjugations."

A soft moan came from behind the blocked, filled mouth. Mina tried to twist her head free, but Tom held the broom fast and merely followed after her, and again the chair tottered dangerously.

"She's evil," Lucy whispered, walking behind the table, shaking the chair legs, causing Mina to groan again. "Everything that has happened here, she's the cause of it. *Everything*," she added emphatically. "Poor Mrs. Kitchens lying over there, her baby dead, the storm last night, the road, my papa dead . . ."

Abruptly she came up alongside Tom Marshall, took the broom from him, jerked it from Mina's mouth, and began striking her around the head. These blows were not so light, and Mina tried to duck her head against the assault.

"No," she screamed. "Help me, someone!" She lifted her head and for her troubles received one heavy blow to her left temple, the force of which clearly stunned her as her head fell disjointedly to the right. For a moment her entire body slumped in the chair.

Quickly Tom stepped forward and relieved Lucy of the broom.

All around, Donna sensed new uneasiness hanging in the room, sensed as well a fork in the road, a collective unconscious decision being made, though not a word was being exchanged. A new rupture of blood formed on Mina's forehead, joining the blood seeping from her mouth, and as she slowly revived, her head lifted in a wobbly disjointed manner and she presented them all with her martyr's face. "Please," she begged, and tried to say more, but choked on her own saliva and let her head fall forward, weeping.

Donna watched along with the others, and in a way was pleased that they had reduced the arrogant woman to such a state. Still, let her go now. She wouldn't be so arrogant in the future, and Lucy's blanket accusations were merely the ramblings of a hysterical adolescent. Donna suddenly needed fresh air. Coming from someplace was a strong smell—of urine—and as she glanced up toward the elevated chair, she saw telltale moisture seeping onto the table and closed her eyes in embarrassment for Mina, for herself.

It was while her eyes were closed that the voices started, soft at first, all unidentifiable, coming in a disjointed sequence from all corners of the restaurant, male and female blending.

"Where's Hal? Hal knows what to do."

"Hal's gone, probably like the rest of 'em."

"She made me cry, Mama, lots of times."

"Let her go!"

"The hell you say!"

"She brought the storm, she and the Mountain Man."

242

"Lucy told me a long time ago that she was a witch."

"And she is. She killed my papa."

". . . wants us all dead, so she can . . ."

"Look at her. She's not denying it."

"Wait for Hal."

"He ain't coming back. He'd been here by now. It's up to us . . ."

Donna stared up into Mina's face and saw her eyes fixed, as though in the voices she heard some hideous finality. It had to be stopped, and stopped now, and on that determination Donna stood up to talk to them and was never given a chance as Rene Hackett shouted, "She's never gonna let any of us get out of here alive. Jerry warned me, said that—"

"She's right. None of this would have happened . . ."

"What do we do?"

"Don't yell. The children are frightened."

Donna looked around and saw Vicky clinging to Inez.

"Not here," a male voice suggested, "not with the children watching."

"Where?"

As the hysteria rose with nightmarish speed, Donna saw Tom Marshall summon several men to come forward, and before she knew what was happening, certainly before she had a chance to stop it, she saw them lift Mina's chair from the table and carry her like some aging, wounded matriarch through the restaurant, her cries for help and mercy lost in the turmoil of scraping chairs and frightened children.

Though Donna's instinct told her to remain behind, some stronger instinct told her to follow after them on the outside chance that she could still stop what she had helped to put into motion. Feeling a terrible need to keep her eyes on the pitiful Mina, she abandoned Sarah with a call to Inez, "Watch her, please. They don't know what they are doing." As she passed the table, Inez cried, "Leave them alone. You can't stop them," and for a moment Donna stared down on her as she cradled Vicky, the Driver children pushing close, the adult hysteria mirrored in their young faces.

Did Inez know what they were going to do? Surely she didn't approve.

But there was no time for answers. Beyond the window, she saw the crowd following close after the men who were carrying Mina's chair, effortlessly elevating it even higher, the fervor and zeal and elevated position reminding Donna of a religious procession.

"Mike, please," she cried, shaking him in an attempt to arouse him. "Come on, you've got to stop them. *Mike!*"

But for all her efforts he merely groaned, shifted his face away from her, and muttered one word, which sounded like "bum," as he sank into an even deeper sleep.

Then it was up to her, and casting a final glance toward Inez where she was trying to comfort the children, Donna took the front door running and looked ahead to see the curious procession heading toward the end of Main Street and the place where the road had fallen away.

As she ran through the slush and mud, she struggled for balance and heard above the angry shouts the continuous siren of Mina's screams and saw the flailing of her head, the chair bobbling eerily about in the air.

243

Twice Donna fell as her ears filled with the cries of terror in macabre counterpoint to the yelping of the crowd. Her shoes were coated with mud, and she suffered that nightmarish sensation of movement with no real forward progress. The sense of unreality was strong and growing stronger, and as she started forward again, she glanced quickly to her right and saw her own house, and beyond that, Mina's, and thought calmly: No longer her house or Mina's house; the designation of "hers" and "mine" belonged to another day, another order.

As she caught up with the crowd, she saw them gathered at the edge of the cliff that once had been a road, and saw Mina being lowered suddenly from view. Unable to penetrate to the center, she fought her way to the side and saw it clearly for the first time, the sheer rock abyss where the road had once been, collapsed now into a twisted mass of rock and rubble about eighty feet below. Also far below she saw the ruined machinery of the mining corporation. The semis lay on their sides, cabs crushed, wheels upended, their blackened underbellies shining in the high sun like monstrous dying beetles. She lifted her head and tried to digest what she saw. They were stranded on the ledge of this plateau, no way down, no way up.

"Leave her there!" someone shouted. "Close to her own handiwork."

No way up, no way down.

It could not be digested, and Donna looked toward the center of the crowd about thirty feet away and saw them moving slowly back from the edge, their voices no longer raised in anger, but their eyes rigidly focused on Mina, still bound to the chair, the chair itself placed on the very edge of the abyss, with the two rear legs already sunk in the soft and crumbling loam.

"No," Donna whispered, and started forward. Then she was running, thinking of nothing except the need to move the chair back to safety before . . .

"Stop her!" someone shouted.

When she was less than ten feet from where Mina sat, she felt something descending on her from the rear, outside the scope of her vision, two strong arms that jerked her back, a male voice strangely soothing in spite of the rigid grip on her arms, "Now, you just leave her alone, Mrs. Dunne. You hear? She's brought enough trouble down on all of us, taken lives, she has. Now, let her take a good close look at her own handiwork."

It was Ned Wilson. She recognized his voice and struggled to get out of his grasp, but he drew her arms behind her at a painful angle, and as she heard his voice, still soothing, "Hold steady, Mrs. Dunne," she looked up to find them all looking at *her*, their fixed expressions the same as when they looked at Mina.

It was the quiet that summoned her attention back. Nightmares were never so quiet. The only sound was the whistling of the wind, rising now and then into a whine, while the high hot sun made a gigantic checkerboard of the new vista, black and white patterns of snow and earth.

"Please let me go, Ned," she whispered, but if he heard her plea, he did not respond.

At last, and because she had no choice, she looked up and saw Mina, the blood drying on her face, her eyes returning the crowd's gaze with quick darting movements, though only her eyes moved, as though she was well aware of her dangerous perch.

"Please," she whispered over the wind. "If I have offended any of you, I'm truly sorry. I have no . . . powers save those we all share. You're . . . frightened, and that's understandable, but if we turn against each other now . . ."

Her voice drifted with the wind and fell silent. Donna fought back tears and looked toward the silent crowd of blank faces, trying to place them in familiar roles: Tom Marshall in his white grocer's apron sweeping the walk in front of his store, Polly Whiteside with half of her hair in rollers and one hand clutching her jacket against the cold wind, and the Billingslys, white-haired pillars of the community, which they were. And Jason and Ellen Allegro stood behind them, his arm around her in a protective gesture. And the O'Connells. And poor Rene Hackett, and of course Lucy, still holding the broom with which she had tormented Mina, holding it upright between her splinted fingers. And there were the Cobbs and the Drivers and the Charters and . . .

"Listen to me," Donna cried, overwhelmed by her mental roll call of normally kind and decent people. "I don't think any of us know quite what we are doing."

She felt Ned Wilson tighten his grasp on her wrists. That was all right. She would remain stationary, but she had to talk to them, had to remind them of their individual goodness and rationality, for she had perceived in the blowing wind a communal mind, one brain doing the thinking for all, one will carrying out the impulses of that brain.

"Look at yourselves!" she cried again. "And look at her. Can you see?" As she nodded toward Mina, she instantly regretted it. The rear legs of the chair had sunk deeper. The backward angle was growing more acute. And Mina sat with her ruined face lifted to the sky, her eyes closed, lips moving.

"We know what we're doing," someone called out. "*You* look at her. She's saying a chant right now, putting another spell on—"

"She is not!" Donna refuted angrily. "She's praying. Listen to her."

"Keep her still," Tom Marshall called out to Ned Wilson. "It'll happen any minute now."

Donna winced as Ned Wilson pinned her arms together, though in that moment she saw that their intent in letting the chair fall of its own accord would relieve them of the burden of guilt.

"No, please," Donna begged, and felt Ned's hand clamp itself across her mouth, his fingers rough and smelly, his left hand holding her wrists together.

She tried to struggle, but it was useless. His strength was superior to hers, and she had no choice but to watch the terrifying spectacle along with the rest, Mina weeping now, though her voice was raised in prayer.

Then Donna could watch no longer, and closed her eyes, slumping against the man who held her and who now commended her for her lack of resistance.

245

"None of us like what it is we're doing, but it's got to be done for the good of us all, don't you see?"

No, she didn't see, couldn't see, had no desire to see, and for several long minutes nothing was heard but Mina's tearful weeping, the incoherent words of a prayer, and the whistling of the wind.

"Well, if you ask me, she needs her broomstick."

Donna did not have to open her eyes to recognize the voice, singsong, high-pitched, petulant. But she looked up anyway, and saw Lucy Hackett step out of the crowd, wielding the broom now as it was meant to be used as she daintily swept a path through the mud and slush while heading straight toward Mina, who now viewed the approaching girl with terrified eyes.

"Bitch!" Mina suddenly screamed as Lucy grew nearer. "You goddamned little bitch. If I'm a witch, I'll come back and drag you down into hell with me."

Donna could see the tendons in Mina's neck straining to accommodate her fury. Her long coarse hair was flying every which way as she struggled against her predicament, apparently no longer caring.

Lucy stopped about three feet from the chair. She looked back at the others with a clear expression of triumph on her face. "Did you hear her?" She smiled sweetly. "She won't ever fall. The mountain won't take her. The mountain doesn't want her either."

Slowly Donna straightened up from her slumped position. She saw Lucy slowly lift the broom, the rod end pointing directly at Mina.

"Bitch!" Mina shrieked.

"Good-bye." Lucy smiled and in a delicate, almost gentle movement stepped forward and just lightly touched Mina's shoulder with the broom. *No!*

The left-rear leg of the chair slipped completely free from the loose muddy loam; the chair and its screaming cargo appeared to balance precariously for a moment in the air. Then gravity took over, dragging Mina and her unearthly screams over the side. A few moments later the screams were silenced by a soft cracking thud, distant, the sound of wood splintering, then nothing.

In horror Donna wrenched loose, and Ned Wilson let her go. Obviously now there was no reason to restrain her. She ran half-stumbling to the spot where the chair had rested, saw the caved-in earth, the sheer rock descent, and far below, a twisted leg, the other bent beneath her, her arms still bound, the red robe meshing with the jagged rocks, a discarded rag doll, no longer screaming.

Something was rising in Donna's throat. Her knees gave way, and she fell in the mud and waited for the convulsion to pass, then turned away from the edge, not wanting to look over again, and saw a pair of mud-covered sneakers, smooth shapely legs, and the end of a broom.

"I'm sorry, Mrs. Dunne," Lucy whispered sympathetically.

Through unfocused eyes, Donna looked up. How simple it would be to grab those near smooth ankles and pull her over the edge, let her join the woman she had just murdered.

But the thought did more damage than anything else, and Donna moaned as she crumpled to earth and saw through her distorted vision that everyone was walking away from her, a ragtag procession trailing after each other back into town, everybody except one, a curious comforter, a piping innocent adolescent who laid her broom down and knelt in the mud beside Donna, her hand stroking Donna's hair, whispering, "Don't cry, Mrs. Dunne. You're safe now. We did the right thing. You know we did."

36

Washington, D.C.

As he sat in the pretentious splendor of Martin Avery's Senate office, Roger found momentary distraction from his desperate mission in the parallel nature of his thoughts.

All the way over in the cab from his hotel, he'd been thinking of Tomis and Hal Kitchens. Why in hell couldn't he get through to them? Before he'd left the hotel he'd placed a call to a good friend, Alex Fielding on the Denver *Post*. Journalists had ways of obtaining information, and Alex was one of the best. And of course the thought of Tomis and Hal and Sarah Kitchens had led to nostalgic images of the place, so simple and right and honest and good.

Now surrounded by Martin Avery's accumulated junk of almost six Senate years—*"In twenty-three years, Roger, people get a chance to show a lot of gratitude"*—Tomis and its simplicity seemed a solar system away. Well, he'd try Alex again when he got back to the hotel, and tomorrow, after he'd met with Adam Krafft at CUSP House, he'd fly to Tomis and find out for himself what was going on.

For now there were more important matters at hand, and as he tried to get comfortable on the antique Louis XVI chair, he reached one hand down to make certain the large leather portfolio was still intact; it contained certain carefully chosen materials he might need in his attempt to persuade Martin

248

Avery that the H.E. Theory was no longer theory, that the entire world was on the brink of ecological disaster.

The portfolio was in place. Unfortunately, his confidence in this mission was not. The unknown quantity was Martin Avery. Four-term Republican senator from the state of Colorado, Roger had known him years ago at Princeton, although they had arrived there under very different circumstances. Roger had come from a family that had had no real economic worries for the last one hundred years, and Martin was struggling mightily to erase all traces of his father's small and failing ranch outside Longmont.

Martin had done well at Princeton, and more than once Roger had borne witness to one of the keenest intellects he'd ever seen. The year following graduation, Martin had entered local politics, running for the state legislature and leaving Roger with a sense of mild sorrow, the feeling that something potentially good was being wasted.

Now, twenty-three years later, Martin Avery was a fixture in Washington. He'd served on every prestigious committee from Foreign Affairs to Senate Banking. It was rumored that if you wanted anything done in Washington, official or unofficial, see Martin Avery. Over the years Roger had lost personal touch with him, but his public life had been so public that it hadn't been difficult to keep tabs on his rise to fame and power.

Also, with a degree of amusement Roger had watched Martin carefully cultivate the "good-old-country-boy" image that he'd worked so hard to rid himself of at Princeton. Now it was said that when Martin Avery crossed the Colorado state line on a visit home, his speech automatically flattened and hayseed sprouted in his ear, while on the floor of the Senate debating a bill that was particularly close to his heart he sounded for all the world like the Rhodes scholar he once had been.

Beyond the gold satin brocade drapes and the elegant secretary at her mahogany desk, Roger saw the glowering afternoon sky of a late-spring thunderstorm.

Where in the hell was he? The appointment had been for two o'clock. Impatient and growing more so, Roger met the secretary's eyes; she smiled apologetically and eased the single strand of pearls out from beneath the collar of her black suit.

"I *am* sorry, Dr. Laing," she said in flawless diction. "Senator Avery should be along any minute. As I said, the committee ran late and . . ."

He nodded and tried to curb his impatience. He and Percy Forrester had lived with the H.E. Theory since the early sixties. A few more minutes wouldn't make any difference.

And what would Martin's reaction be? Would he even listen? And what would his suggestions be? Someone in Washington must be notified before it was too late.

He tried to check his cynicism before it grew to dangerous proportions. Nothing new here, and he'd had nothing to do with Washington since he'd formed CUSP seventeen years ago on a private, nonprofit basis. At the time, there had been considerable pressure on him from Washington to turn CUSP into a kind of think tank for the government. But Roger had wisely resisted, and with the exception of an annual punishment in the form of a prolonged and bothersome tax audit which kept his staff of accountants busy, Washington had left him alone.

But they had a good memory here, and who would listen to him? That's why he had come to Martin Avery, and all he hoped now was that the once keen mind that he'd first spotted at Princeton was still intact, had not become eroded and corrupted by years of playing the "good old country boy"—*"Hell, when I arrived in this town, I didn't even have enough money to buy a guilty conscience."*

He did now, and it was a source of minor mystery to Roger why the voters never questioned a public servant who over the years had expanded "Daddy's little spread" into a vast cattle ranch of over twenty thousand acres.

Dear God, what *was* he doing here? Suddenly he felt almost overwhelmed by the futility of his mission. He shouldn't have come. Go now, back to CUSP House. See Adam Krafft tomorrow, his closest colleague next to Percy Forrester. Adam was a biochemist at MIT, and he at least knew the rudimentary outlines of the H.E. Theory. Yes, he would be receptive, have ideas, ways in which to—

"Roger Laing? You old son of a bitch?"

Too late. The voice shattered the quiet of the office. Even before he could turn in his chair, the voice went on. "How in the hell long has it been? Too long, and some of the boys said to tell you if you don't show up at the next reunion, well, they plan just to come and hog-tie . . ."

He was standing before Roger now, a tall man, grown heavier with the passage of years. His face was flushed with the exertion of movement, and a sharply receding hairline caused the front of his skull to resemble a large high moon. He wore an expensively tailored dark gray suit and a jackass grin.

Roger tried to rise to his enthusiasm as well as the occasion. "Martin, it's good to see you. It's been a—"

"—a hell of a long time. You're right there. Well, come on in, get moving. I got me a little bar in here with just about ever'thing God ever created to quench a man's thirst. No calls, Miss Walker. Just tell ever'body to hold their horses."

The inner sanctum proved to be even more elegant than the outer. The "little bar" ran the length of the east wall. There must have been two hundred bottles arranged in dazzling symmetry against the mirrored panels.

"What's your pleasure?" Martin grinned, closing the door behind him and simultaneously loosening his tie. "God, it's good to see you, Roger," he added, slumping against the closed door, and Roger thought that he looked suddenly very tired. Or ill.

"And you too, Martin." He smiled and angled the large portfolio down onto the sofa and shook his head to the bar and waited patiently while Martin poured half a water tumbler of Chivas Regal and carried it to his desk.

"How long has it been?" Martin asked reflectively, settling into the large leather chair and wincing once as though something hurt.

"Too long," Roger said. "I keep up with you through the newspapers, however."

"Hell, you too. There always seems to be big doings going on up in that

250

Frankenstein lair of yours. Well, what kind of snake oil are you peddling today?"

As an invitation to speak, it left a little to be desired. "I'm not . . . peddling anything, Martin," he said, and approached the desk and sat on the opposite side and fought against the splintered feelings within him. What in the hell *was* he doing here?

"Are they treatin' you right at home?" Martin demanded, and drained half the glass of Scotch in one swallow and made a face at the glass. "Shit, you just mention my name and—"

"No, no, it's not that."

"When you gonna come out to the spread for a steak? You know, Roger, I'm raising some of the best goddamn beef in the country now. It makes what they raise in Texas taste like billy-goat balls."

Roger nodded. Despair vaulted.

"Tell you what I'll do." Martin grinned. "I'll send one around, a whole fucking critter. Just tell your help to put it in your deep-freeze and—"

"Not necessary, Martin," he said hurriedly. "I'm at home so little of the—"

"Sure you don't want a drink?"

"No . . ."

Martin shrugged and started up from his chair and clung a moment to the side of the desk. Ill, yes, Roger was convinced of it, and in pain.

"Martin, you don't look—"

"To hell with the way I look. Are you gonna tell me why you come here or . . ."

He broke off and refilled his glass and took a swallow even as he was returning to the desk. "Hell, this is the best medicine in the world, you know?" he asked softly, lovingly, holding up the crystal glass.

"All right, the floor is yours," he said suddenly, on a new burst of energy, "and a goddamned expensive floor it is, so use it well. Never let it be said that Martin Avery turned his back on any of his voters, no siree. All right, Roger, tell me all."

This invitation seemed sincere, and now was as good a time as any. Feeling very much like a schoolboy making a class presentation, Roger stood and paced off the bar and waited for the right beat to speak.

"I have a colleague, Martin, in England. His name is Dr. Percy Forrester. He has recently completed a study which he has been working on since 1952. He will present a paper to the British Meteorological Society next spring. However, we have the benefit of what we might call a sneak preview, an early showing . . ."

At the far end of the bar, he stopped and looked back, expecting either a rebuttal or an interruption. Neither came. In fact, from that distance Martin Avery appeared to be listening closely.

Encouraged, Roger went on. "Now, as you may or may not know, Martin, the overriding philosophy behind the formulation of CUSP was to confront these mysteries of the world whose solutions elude our scientific minds, our technology, and even on occasion our good and logical common sense."

Still no response from behind the desk, though Roger noticed that Martin had made a tent of his fingers and positioned them before his face, obscuring everything from the eyes down. At least he was silent and continued to give the illusion of listening.

Quickly Roger reached into the portfolio and withdrew the dark blue CUSP binder which contained the H.E. Theory. "Let's start with some modern data," he proposed, thumbing through the report to the truly unbelievable material. "According to the United States Geological Survey, the last three years saw earthquake activity of far greater proportion than in the past century. Does that strike you as odd that it would suddenly and mysteriously increase?"

No answer, not right away. Martin shook his head. His eyes glazed. "I've not really had too many occasions on which to think on it."

Roger ignored the confession and read on. "The death toll for '76 alone was staggeringly high: Turkey, 5,000; USSR, unconfirmed reports of over 500,000; Guatemala, 23,000; New Guinea, 9,000; China, 750,000 . . ."

He stopped speaking and stared at the numbers, six digits, incomprehensible in terms of individual lives, men, women, and children gone in one cataclysmic—

Now, rather defensively, Martin muttered, "I'm familiar with those figures."

Are you? a voice challenged inside Roger's head. *You couldn't be and sit there calmly, sucking on your bloody Scotch.*

"What if I told you the quakes could have been predicted and avoided?" Roger countered, ignoring the voice, addressing the question directly to Martin.

"Predicted, yes." Martin nodded. "Nothing new there. Avoided? That's another matter."

Roger turned through the pages of the report, not really requiring notes. He knew the material by heart.

"Then permit me to call your attention to other data, scientific data, proven beyond a shadow of a doubt; major volcanoes occurring in places they have never occurred before, the world's climate suddenly becoming unstable. Over the last few years, record rains and floods have soaked some areas, while droughts have parched others. In '76, for example, Britain experienced the worst drought in five hundred years, while in parts of Africa torrential rainfalls spawned plagues of rats, locusts, and caterpillars."

He was speaking too rapidly and he knew it. Martin was on his third Scotch.

"Geophysicists report that the ground near Palmdale, California, is beginning to swell and bulge more and more each day. It is reported that the densely populated eastern United States is rapidly becoming recognized as a potential quake area as geologists map out deep fault systems. Places such as Delaware have already received their first recorded quakes. Even New York City has major and serious fault systems running beneath it."

He glanced down at the H.E.Theory. The words blurred. "There is no need to mention the consequences if a quake hit where our proliferating nuclear-power plants are located."

"Your point, please, Roger," Martin asked in a voice that was beginning to slur.

"A pattern of increasing geological disasters seems to have begun," he replied. "My point is that we try to understand it. These are not random occurrences. They form an awesome pattern and are directly related to cause and effect."

He was pushing perilously close to the heart of the H.E. Theory.

"Cause . . . and effect?" Martin repeated incredulously. Perhaps the mind was still intact after all.

"Yes," Roger confirmed. "There are connections," he went on, "clear, simple connections, overlooked until now because of the fragmentation of scientific perspective resulting from academic specialization."

In the interim of silence, Roger withdrew the tectonic map from the portfolio, ready to call Martin's attention first to certain other undeniable facts.

"Is it catastrophe time, Roger?" He grinned. "I've seen that map before. Armageddon is imminent. Is that what you're preaching as well?"

"Perhaps," Roger nodded. "I think it's unwise to ignore bulging landmasses, continental drifts, shifting poles . . ."

Martin drained his glass and laughed. "Where is the new coastline to be? Phoenix, right? A new Riviera, with ports in Wyoming, Nebraska, Texas, and New Mexico."

Roger waited out his good humor. "Old-hat, isn't it. But what if I told you there was a possibility that natural catastrophe could be controlled, perhaps avoided altogether?"

Silence, though not a good one.

"Controlled?" Martin repeated. "Avoided? I think you need a drink."

"No . . ."

"How? Don't tell me you are a closet Bible literalist, crying along with Isaiah, 'I shall shake the heavens, and the earth shall be moved out of its place.' "

"No, no Isaiah, Martin"—Roger smiled—"but material worthy of your attention. First of all," he began, and flattened the tectonic map on the large desk, "locate the Midwestern areas, Colorado, if you will, and look closely at the substructure."

He saw Martin lean forward, adjusting bifocals to the delicate geological shadings. "From here"— and he pointed along the eastern margin of the Rocky Mountains—"as you can see, there exists a series of underground basins, some quite large, as though at one time they might have formed an ocean. And as we know," Roger went on, "this porous substructure has in the past proved to be the most resilient to earthquake-prone areas. Fairly stable— no, *very* stable—compared to the fault-ridden California coast, and worse, the underground lake beneath the Imperial Valley."

With the top of his finger he encircled the Denver Basin and made certain that Martin had seen the *scientific fact* of the tectonic map, and for good measure reminded him, "Also let me point out that there was no significant quake activity recorded here in the last two centuries until in the mid-sixties, when the U.S. Army commenced a waste-disposal program outside Denver. Now, the material being disposed of was lethal, and they felt absolutely safe in dumping it down deep wells, then capping them immediately with concrete-and-steel sealers. Four weeks to the day after the first well had been filled and capped, Denver suddenly started to undergo its first recorded earthquakes."

He paused. "I repeat, the *first* recorded earthquakes. Seismologists at the Colorado School of Mines recorded more than seven hundred and ten earthquakes."

Martin was blinking rapidly at him. "Why in the hell didn't I hear anything about this?" he muttered, apparently unaware of the nature of his confession. "In how long a period?" he asked further, moving uncomfortably back in his chair.

"Six months."

"Of what measurement?"

"Less than five, but enough to put a scare into all of Denver, even to the extent that the building codes were changed to provide a margin of safety from the new earthquake hazard." Amazed, Roger stopped talking. "You . . . heard nothing of this?" he asked.

Defensively Martin shook his head. "I was out of the country often . . ."

Roger nodded, intent only on making it easy for him. "There was a small core of citizens," he went on, "who ultimately drew a most unscientific parallel between the deep well disposals and the new earthquake activity. Let me remind you of the times, the mid-sixties, a time of proliferating idealists, radicals, anarchists, kids, oriented or disoriented, depending upon your point of view, on drugs."

Martin nodded as though to say that he was very familiar with that scene. He fingered his empty glass and stared longingly at the bar.

Roger hurried on. "And a few of those 'dissidents' managed to spread the word of their theory, the connection between the deep well disposals and earth tremors, and in the end convinced enough others so that a few suits were brought against the Army over damages from the quakes."

"With what results?" Martin inquired.

Roger smiled. "Well, in spite of repeated and heated denials by the Army's Rocky Mountain Arsenal of any connection between their dumping activities and the quakes, and following much study, the Army reluctantly agreed to stop its disposal program."

"*Was* there any connection?" Martin asked.

"Scientifically," Roger concluded, "I must confess, no. Though I also must add that at the demise of the disposal program, the earthquakes stopped as suddenly as they had begun."

For a moment the large office was silent except for the distant thunder coming from the late-spring storm outside the window. Martin's expression went rapidly from surprise to caution. He appeared ready to refute everything he'd heard.

"In a similar situation," Roger went on, "USGA geologists in an experiment at the Rangely oil fields in northwest Colorado injected water through the field's wells and merely by varying the pressure proved that they could turn small earthquakes on and off as if by a faucet."

254

Martin appeared to be listening closely, and Roger felt a surge of confidence. "On the same theme," he went on, "a rare quake occurred in Michigan after oil drilling began there, and as we both know, the slumping of ground at the Los Angeles area oil fields has also triggered small quakes."

"What in the hell is it you're trying to say, Roger?" Martin demanded, returning to the bar and draining the bottle of Chivas Regal. "New oil fields have opened all around the world in places never drilled before; major fields in China, off-shore Japan, Indonesia, Africa, Alaska, etc., etc. Are you saying the earth is objecting to all this activity? Well, the earth may be objecting," he added, muttering, "but John Q. Public has to run his three cars and haul his boat to the lake every weekend and drive the wife and kids to the nearest theme park, and as far as he's concerned, to hell with everything else."

Roger watched the man at the bar and tried to determine if he knew precisely what he had just said.

"So *what* is your point, Laing?" Martin concluded, a degree of weariness in his voice. "We all are aware of the hazards of excessive drilling. But consumer demands must be met, and there will always be someone around ready and willing to meet them—"

"At what cost?" Roger interrupted, feeling that they were moving too fast and thus were in danger of taking the wrong theoretical turn. He had not intended this to be a rehash on the availability and exploration of fossil fuel.

"At what cost?" Martin shrugged. "I'd say from the example of the last few years, at any cost the traffic will bear. With gasoline almost two dollars a gallon now, I see no noticeable decline in this country's mobility. People eat out less in order to buy fuel, that's all."

"That's not what I meant," Roger corrected. "I was referring to cosmic cost, if you will, the cost which will accrue from a damaged, objecting, and largely uninhabitable earth."

"Good Lord, you can't be serious."

"I am. Remember that oil is not the only thing man pumps from the ground. Consider the far-reaching effects resulting from water being drawn up from underground reservoirs. Consider the high incidence of earthquakes in areas with large dams. All I'm suggesting," he said quietly, "is that there has been no scientific study on what the ultimate effects of man's increasing activity in modifying the natural environment will be."

"And how can we study a result that has yet to happen?" Martin asked.

"But it *is* happening now," Roger said with emphasis. "The proverbial forest and the trees. Water tables are dropping in certain areas, phenomena such as changes in the local magnetic field . . ." Again Tomis came to mind, the peculiar variation he'd noticed in the major ley line which encircled the plateau and directly intersected the town of Tomis. Just last Christmas the varying measurements of his pendulum had been dramatic to the point of incredibility. The black-topped Main Street had already begun to buckle. . . .

" . . . and look at the lower twenty-one miles of the Colorado River, before it empties in Mexico," Roger added, mentally moving away from the mystery at Tomis. "It will be dry soon, as the U.S. Bureau of Reclamation will no longer release water into the channel. The water is being diverted as a result of the Colorado River Salinity Control Project."

"Biologists are keeping a close eye on that one," Martin said.

"They are," Roger conceded, "but their main concern is for the wild-life."

"And you don't share their concern?"

"Of course I do, but the most severe threat will not be to the wildlife, but rather to the people in the area."

Roger was about to make his point when suddenly a buzzer sounded on Martin's desk. For a moment, both men stared at it. On slightly unsteady legs, Martin made his way slowly back to the desk and pushed the button on the inter-com. "Yes," he said. "Yes, it's all right. Thank you. I'll be along."

As he straightened his tie, he informed Roger in a soft voice that was trying hard not to sound drunk, "They're reconvening, the Senate, important budget vote, civil-service raise. Why shouldn't the poor bastards enjoy at least a taste of the good life, like we do, eh, Laing? Do-re-me, that's what it all boils down to."

"Martin, please . . ."

"Can't, Roger. Anyway, I haven't the foggiest what in the hell you are—"

"I'm saying that we now have proof that the earth is capable of retaliation against human abuse, and I'm saying that we could conceivably be facing ecological disaster unless we—"

The slow-grinning expression on Martin's face erupted into a full-scale laugh of incredulity. "You're saying . . . *what?*" he bellowed, his hilarity now propelling him around the desk and into direct confrontation with Roger. "By God, I think you had a few belts before you came in here. You can't be serious, Roger. What in hell do you want me to do with that piece of bull-shit?"

"It's true, Martin."

"True, my ass. I'm not gonna tell that to no one, no how, not even the elevator boy. If I did, word would get out that old Martin Avery was wacko."

"What . . . can I say?" Roger murmured, his sense of futility confirmed. If only he'd had more time . . .

"I think you've said enough," Martin spluttered, still laughing. "I tell you where you can spring that story next time, at our summer reunion in New York. You betcha!"

"Martin, wait . . ."

"Can't, old man. Got to run the country now. Don't really know what the poor dumb taxpayers would do without me." At the door he looked back at Roger in remarkably good spirits. "Nature . . . capable of retaliation," he spluttered. "By God, you ain't been smoking some of the kids' funny ciga-rettes?"

Suddenly, when Roger least expected it, the laugh faded. The fleshy red-tinged face resembled a poorly done death mask. He seemed to cling to the

256

door now, as though literally using it for support. "Hell, I'm dying anyway," he confessed quietly to the floor. His voice broke. "No more than eight, maybe nine whole fucking months left, at least that's what the smart-ass doctors tell me. But what do they know, right, Laing? And I ain't even had a chance to cash in all my vouchers yet. So you see, I don't give a fuck what happens to the rest of the world. I really don't. Ain't no justice . . ." Then he was gone, leaving Roger alone in the office with the echo of tragedy and surrender and derision and the sense of failure confirmed.

Slowly he gathered up his materials and returned them to the portfolio. He had thought once to stay in town and try again. But there was no purpose. Besides, Adam Krafft was due at CUSP House tomorrow. He'd know what to do, what action to take.

As he passed by the mahogany desk, the chic secretary called out, "Better wait for this to quiet, or you'll get drenched," and pointed beyond the window to the dark gray late-afternoon sky where the storm was raging. Bolts of lightning cut a jagged path across the glowering sky, interspersed with rolls of thunder.

"Don't you just hate it?" The girl shivered. "It always makes me feel that God is mad at us."

37

An hour later Roger was just unlocking his hotel room when he heard the phone ringing. Once inside, he grabbed eagerly for it. "Hello? Hello? Dr. Laing here. Who is . . .?"

He cradled the receiver close, then heard a male voice on the line, very familiar. "Roger?"

"Alex? Is that you?"

"Speaking," came the confirmation of Alex Fielding, good friend, superb fishing partner, and a superior journalist with the Denver paper. "Sorry I couldn't return your call earlier, Roger, but it's been a hell of a news day. We've got this crazy weather up on the western slope . . ."

Roger nodded. "Actually, that's what I was calling you about this morning, Alex," he said, cupping both hands about the receiver. "I've been trying to place a call to Tomis for the last day and a half . . ."

"Where?"

"Tomis," he shouted, "on the western slope, near Durango." Alex's lack of familiarity with the little town didn't surprise Roger. Settled for only four years by people who for the most part wanted to keep their presence a secret from both the developers and the tourists, it was in a way Colorado's own Shangri-la, isolated, mysterious, beautiful.

Over the static, Roger heard a rustle of paper, then Alex again. "I . . . can't see it on the map, old man. How do you spell—?"

"It's there," Roger interrupted, "a new settlement."

"New or old, they probably are buried under several feet of May snow. I sent two reporters down this morning . . ."

"You couldn't get through by phone either?"

"Not a chance, but nothing unusual there. Late-spring storms, as you know, are frequently the worst. The lines are down. It's clear to Gunnison, and beyond that."

"Have you heard from your reporters yet?"

A pause. "Not a word, and they should have been there by now. That's why I'm in the office now. I told them to find a phone somewhere if they have to come back up to Colorado Springs."

"Do you suppose the roads are . . .?"

"Oh, most likely." Another pause, during which Roger heard nothing on the line. "Alex? Are you there?"

"Yeah, I was just thinking. Something strange is going on out there."

"What do you mean?"

"Well, I don't know, Roger. I wish I did. But I had a phone call this afternoon from a stringer in Gunnison, and he says he got out just ahead of the storm, and he swore . . ."

"What?"

" . . . that there was some minor earthquake activity."

Roger stood up from the desk.

"But here's the big mystery," Alex went on. "You still there?"

"Yes."

"I called the Colorado School of Mines as well as the University of California Seismograph Center, and both informed me that there had been absolutely no quake activity within the United States during the last forty-eight hours."

Roger closed his eyes, the better to concentrate.

"Can you make any sense out of it?" Alex asked. "I was going to call you tomorrow anyway, just to hear your speculations. Roger? Are you—?"

"What precisely did your man in Gunnison say?"

"Well, he said that it had been snowing like hell and he'd been at Lake City for a few days and had started driving for home, when his car started sliding. He thought it was the snow and reduced his speed, and even stopped once, and he said the whole damn car was vibrating even in a stopped position."

"Is that the only account of tremors?" Roger asked quietly.

"Well, all we've been able to get so far. Maybe we'll know more when I hear from my boys."

"And when will that be?"

"God knows. They should have phoned in by now."

Roger nodded. No cause for alarm yet. One report did not an earthquake make. And if there had been serious damage, some word would have gotten out.

"So as you can see, I'm afraid I can't help you much, Roger. Peculiar situation. We've never been cut off from such a large area."

"Will you keep me informed, Alex? I'd appreciate it."

"Of course, as soon as I learn something. And I wouldn't worry about your friends. Mountain people know pretty much how to take care of themselves."

These aren't mountain people, Roger thought bleakly. He detected a weariness in Alex's voice and could have predicted the next suggestion from him.

"Listen, Roger, as soon as everything quiets down, why don't we take off for the high country and some trout fishing?"

"Count me in." Roger smiled. "And again, if *you* hear anything at all, please let me know."

He heard the click at the end of the line and continued to hold the receiver for several seconds. He turned slowly back into the room and thought of his senseless meeting with Martin Avery. He instantly thought of about six points he should have made—one, most important, the possibility of a direct connection between geomagnetic polarity and faunal changes, the migratory patterns of animals who possessed instincts with greater intelligence capabilities than the human brain . . . .

But his mind felt blurred with fatigue and intersecting worries, and he sank into one of the easy chairs.

He claims the car continued to shake after he'd brought it to a halt. No recorded measurement . . .

In an absentminded way he lightly pinched his leg as though he were trying to goad the mind on with minor discomfort.

After centuries of research, the earth's magnetic field remains one of the least understood of all planetary phenomena.

Thought forms—matter can be converted into energy, and vice-versa.

. . . is not yet demonstrated empirically . . .

You will call me back, Alex? . . .

The mind is energy. The form of that energy is different from that of neuronal potentials that travel the axonal pathways.

"Enough," he said aloud, and pressed his head back against the cushions, trying to still the dynamo.

Tomis . . . . He hoped they were all right. But of course they were. Hal Kitchens was a good and capable man. If the storm had caused serious damage, he'd know what to do.

And Vicky . . . . He smiled and saw the little girl clearly, her long silky hair, Sarah's eyes, blue, wide-set, a fistful of yellow buttercups in her hand.

These are for Roger. I want to give them to Roger.

Two days, Three at the most. He would meet with Adam Krafft, share the burden of the H.E. Theory, then pack a small bag and head for . . .

The thought rejuvenated him. He felt his brain shift into neutral, his eyelids grow heavy.

Three days at most. Then, what a reunion they would have.

38

Tomis, Colorado

Hal Kitchens felt, along with Yeats, that this life, this circumstance and its tragedies, seemed like the lessons of some elder boy given to a younger by mistake. He understood nothing, was ill-equipped by nature and training to face it, let alone understand it.

Now, as he hurried back from his search for bodies, he estimated that he had gone about five miles due west around the rim of the plateau. At first, once past the camping area and the sulfuric odors and half-melting sludge of the ruptured septic tank, he had resisted every protruding log which from a distance had resembled a human leg, an arm. But now, four hours later, he found himself praying, "Please, God, let me find one body." Seven had been lost in the course of the storm.

Yet where were they?

Breathless from his search, he looked up into the early-evening sky and saw a miracle, a high blue *hot* summer sky, not a trace of clouds, not a trace of the arctic blizzard from the night before. During the last two hours of his search the snow had completely melted, converting the earth to the mud which clung to his boots and splattered up onto his jeans.

A mile and a half, maybe two, to Tomis. He must hurry. Perhaps the others had . . . found bodies. Not too far ahead he could already smell the camping area. When he'd passed by earlier in the afternoon, he'd noticed that the eruptions seemed to have ceased, though the sludge was still present, an ungodly blend of mud, melting snow, and raw sewage. The only feasible solution would be to bulldoze it under and start again in a new area, perhaps closer to town.

With hands outreaching, he stumbled forward to a spot of relative dryness and sat on a soft incline where light green moss stretched in a smooth carpet up to a stand of pine. He pushed back his hair and wiped the perspiration from his forehead, looking directly up into the sun, and saw a fiery explosion of light, the normally spherical shape appearing jagged and uneven.

What was happening there? A sun storm? God, he was so confused, he didn't even know enough to be frightened, and was without even the power or energy to form a complete thought.

He looked up suddenly, as though someone had called his name. There was new grief someplace close by, new agony, new death.

He pushed up too rapidly and swayed dizzily for a moment on the sloping ground, remembering he'd eaten nothing today. There had been neither time nor appetite. He looked at the damp, muddy earth strewn with broken rock. In the unseasonable heat his dizziness increased, his empty belly complaining about the lack of fuel. As he struggled for his center of balance, he looked down on a bizarre optical illusion.

The rocks appeared to be moving.

He closed his eyes and waited for the world to grow steady, and felt a solid wall of heat press down upon him. He shook off the dizziness and was mildly amused by the illusion of animated rocks, and stumbled down the path.

A short while later, dripping sweat, he clamped his hand over his nose and approached the camping area at a run, his already coated boots slipping in the dark brown sludge, the surrounding landscape shrouded in clouds of vapors. In his slippery high-speed run he suffered the sensation that the earth was running with him, that he was in fact trying to run through waves of liquid matter, waves like sea, the earth falling, then rising.

Not possible, his mind insisted, and he pushed on, fearful that he'd been gone too long as it was. Tom Marshall's leadership was questionable at best.

Suddenly, in the distorted sphere that was now the earth, he looked ahead and saw something which resembled a pink and bobbing balloon, not large, yet clearly visible contrasted against the mud-covered ground.

He slowed his pace and instantly regretted it, trying to back away while still in the process of moving forward. His feet, confused by the conflicting impulses, tripped, and he went down sideways in the foul-smelling mud, and immediately scrambled up, running now in a wide arc around the pink and bobbing balloon, which he saw clearly was not a balloon but a human head, bloated and swollen, a young man's face once.

One of the missing had been found.

A violent paroxysm seized his muscles. He wrenched loose a cry of indistinguishable words and refused to wait out an ungainly heartbeat, running from the very sight for which he had been searching.

39

The shadows moved, but the dark never quite lifted. At times Mike Dunne heard nothing; then he heard a child whimper, a woman soothing, a floor creak, and most recently he would have sworn that he heard the distant whir of a plane.

No plane, not on Mt. Victor. Roger Laing had tried it once, a dramatic descent from the heavens, and had damn near busted his ass on Victor's stone face. Down-drafts, or some such, or so he'd said.

Whatever. . . . Safe in his fog, Mike shifted his head on the table and refused to open his eyes. Blessedly, he had contrived all day to be away from this place. No point, absolutely no point. In his stupor, he'd spent most of the day in the Scorvini Brothers' liquor store at the corner of Mass. Avenue and Copley. God, paradise, the best liquor store in Boston, in the whole damn world, Paolo greeting him in his Mafia brogue, "Take-a your time, Dr. D., the world, it will wait."

And how often it had waited while Mike had luxuriated in the blended scents of the grape and the grain, the bottles arranged across the endless shelves like shiny, marching, dedicated soldiers.

"You no rush, Dr. D. You're entitled. Come, we drink to good health in back room—Angelo, he won't mind."

And he never had, and how kind the streets of Boston had appeared after three hours in the back room of the Scorvini Brothers.

"What problem?" Angelo had thundered one day. "You drink? So you drink! Our papa, when he crossed over, he was one century plus two. He drank . . . everything. No problem. Fountain of youth—die peacefully in bed, no pain, no fear."

No fear.

Fear! Involuntarily Mike groaned and caught himself in time in the event someone had heard him and would be tempted to involve him in this madness. He should have listened to Angelo Scorvini. What he wouldn't give now for one bottle of liquid oblivion.

The child was whimpering again. Couldn't someone shut it up? Where was Sarah? No. He never wanted to see Sarah again. It was *her* fault. She had been the one who had created . . .

Move the mind away. Get it out. Come on back, Angelo, Paolo, tell me about your papa.

But Angelo was gone, and Mass. Avenue with him, the whole imperfect fabric of life from which once he'd run and to which now he'd willingly, joyfully flee back.

It was quiet all around him. Where in the hell was everybody? Donna? Pissed as hell. No mere pout this time. Donna . . . *Let me come in, honey. Let me come in where it's dark and warm and moist.*

He felt the beginning of an erection and shifted to accommodate it, feeling all his body heat rush to his groin. Slowly he lifted his head and said good-bye to the safety of oblivion and saw, to his surprise, the restaurant filled with silent, zombielike people, every family clustered together, the rearranged tables resembling private territories. What sort of unholy meeting was this? And where was Donna? Everyone else was present and accounted for.

He wet his lips and tried to produce enough saliva so that he could at least form words. He started to stand, then changed his mind.

At a nearby table he saw Tom Marshall looking much the worse for wear. His clothes were filthy, mud-splattered, a two-day growth of beard on his customarily shaved-raw face. He sat slumped in his chair, staring rigidly at the floor, his left hand clenching and unclenching on the table.

"Tom?" Mike whispered. Somehow the occasion and the prevailing mood seemed to require whispering.

At first the man did not respond, and Mike was on the verge of trying again, louder, when suddenly Tom looked sternly at him, an expression of slow-boiling anger on his face.

At first Mike was so taken aback by the harsh look that he couldn't speak. Several others, he noticed, who were seated close to Tom, looked up as well: Mr. Driver, Mrs. O'Connell, Jason Allegro, all as disreputable-appearing as Tom, all as disturbed by something.

Maybe he'd come back to the living too soon. Maybe he shouldn't have come back at all, though now that he had their attention, he really should do something with it.

He leaned closer to the edge of the table. "I . . . was . . . wondering," he began in what he thought was a fairly cordial tone. "Have you, have any of you, seen Donna? She was here, I know. Did she go home?"

"She did not," Tom said with measured anger. "Lucy's bringing her, and I warn you, she'd better shut up, you hear?"

Mike blinked at the threat. What in the hell? "I . . . don't understand," he muttered, and looked out over the crowded restaurant, realizing that their voices had attracted everyone's attention. "Lucy's . . . bringing her . . . where? Where have they . . . ? And where's Hal? Has anybody seen . . . ?"

"Here they come now!" someone said behind him, and he looked over his shoulder to see Polly Whiteside at the front door where she'd apparently been keeping watch.

Despite his confusion, he twisted in the opposite direction and saw a peculiar twosome coming down the street. Donna, her head down, stumbling in the ruts, and walking close beside her was a very solicitous-appearing Lucy Hackett, one arm about Donna's shoulders—Donna hated the little bitch—the two of them making their way slowly toward the restaurant.

As they drew near, Mike rubbed his eyes in an effort to clear them and saw Donna try to pull away once from Lucy's support, which appeared now more like restraint. He rubbed his eyes again and heard a high-pitched ringing in his ears. He felt dizzy and grasped the edge of the table with one hand, while the other hung limp between his legs.

"Here she is, Mr. Marshall" Lucy smiled from the door and removed her arm from around Donna's shoulder and left her standing by the cash register, while she returned to the door, closed it, threw the bolt, and motioned without words for Polly Whiteside to come and stand before it.

Up close, Donna looked like hell, like all the rest of them, a disintegration that went far beyond their muddied clothes and tangled hair. Something had happened here while Mike had been "visiting" with the Scorvini Brothers, something that had left on their faces the same vacancy that he had felt when he had delivered Sarah.

"Mike?" The whispered, fearful word had come from Donna, who walked toward him, apparently, in her new need, more than willing to forgive him his fall from the wagon.

He was on his feet to receive her, and eagerly enfolded her in his arms, and found the sensation pleasing. He felt her trembling, and looked beyond her shoulders at the silently watching faces.

"Come on," he soothed. "Let's go home. We—"

"No way!" Tom Marshall said suddenly, rising from his chair. "She ain't going anyplace till we find out what she's going to do."

"About what?" Mike asked, and rubbed Donna's back and felt her clinging to him.

"You just leave her alone for a spell and let's see what's on her mind."

Mike was on the verge of telling the man to go to hell when suddenly Lucy Hackett appeared from nowhere. She was joined by Mrs. O'Connell on the other side, and together these two took Donna by the shoulders and pulled her from his embrace, the force of their actions upsetting his own none-too-steady center of balance, forcing him to reach out for the table for support while they sat Donna in a near chair and kept their hands on her shoulders as though fearful that she might bolt.

Steadied at last, Mike started forward, outraged. "What in the hell do you think you're doing? You've no right—"

But he felt his own forward motion blocked by Tom Marshall, who stepped between him and the terrified Donna and eased him back into the chair where he'd passed the better part of the day.

"Just stay calm, Dr. Dunne. We ain't got no bone to pick with you, just your pretty wife there. We want to hear what she's got to say, that's all."

"About what?" Mike shouted, and the force of his voice set off an excruciating pain in the top of his head. For a moment all the faces around him turned liquid, and he felt as though he was sitting under water.

While he was waiting to surface, he heard a voice that at first he did not recognize, though certain tones and inflections were familiar, had in the past spoken to him lovingly and in good humor, had sought his approval of menus, of letters, of phone calls, of shopping lists.

"You know what I'm going to say, Mr. Marshall, all of you know," the dead voice went on, no longer frightened. "You know what you've done here, every single one of you, and what you've done is wrong, criminal, and for Mina's sake, I have no intention of letting you . . ."

The voice broke, and through glazed eyes Mike looked up and saw Donna bow her head, tears close, though held at bay by some deeper conviction.

Mina? Mike looked around. Mina was missing as well. Then Donna was speaking again. "We aren't going to be stuck forever up here on this damn mountain," she said, her voice rising as she addressed everyone in the restaurant. "Can't you see, don't you know what happened here today? For your own sakes, look at yourselves. You are murderers, every single one of you."

"You spoke against her, too," someone said from the far corner.

"Yes, and I deeply regret that and will confess to it when the time comes, as you all must."

What was she talking about? Though the liquid sensation still plagued him, as did the painful discomfort in the top of his head, Mike pushed weakly up from the table. "Donna, what . . . murder? What are you . . . ?"

Now she addressed him directly, her hands, he noticed, two tight fists upon her knees. "Mina was here," she began tonelessly, "and they blamed her for everything, and they bound her . . . to a chair and—"

"Your wife talks an awful lot," Tom Marshall interrupted calmly.

"—and they murdered her," Donna concluded, and lowered her head again, and he sensed tears this time.

Murdered Mina—the incredible words cut through his head along with fresh pain. Had Donna lost her mind? Was she aware of the seriousness of her accusation? My God, they had to live with these people. Difficult to look a man in the eye when your wife has just accused him of murder.

"Let me take her home, Tom," he said quietly. "She's . . . obviously upset and not aware of what she's—"

"I'm perfectly aware of what I'm saying," came the insistent female voice.

"If you don't believe me, ask them. Or better still, go to the end of the road and look over the side. Then you'll see—"

"Come on, Donna," he soothed, leaving the chair and drawing near to her. He'd never seen her like this.

Out of the corner of his eye he was vaguely aware of others drawing close, a solid circle of females, all witnessing this most embarrassing breakdown. "Come on, old girl." He smiled and tried to touch one of those clenched fists and saw her pull away, her anger as fierce as ever and now aimed at him.

"You bastard!" she whispered. "You drunken bastard. I tried to awaken you, but you were passed out. You might have stopped them, but no, and now you're as guilty as everybody else."

He felt a sudden heat of embarrassment on his face. Wasn't it enough that she was making a fool of herself?

"That's enough, Donna," he said, aware of the circle growing closer, all eyes watching, all ears listening. "Let her go, Lucy," he commanded. "I apologize for her, and I'll take her home now."

"Apologize!" echoed Donna's voice in rising fury. "For me? I don't want your fucking apology. I don't need it. You're just a goddamn drunk, that's all you've ever been, all you'll ever be. You should have stayed back in Boston with all your wino friends."

"Shut up!" he shouted down on her.

"Pretty high and mighty, if you ask me." Lucy giggled. "If my mama had ever talked like that to my papa, she—"

"She's your wife, Dunne. Can't you control her?"

As the voices hummed about him, he stared fixedly down on the upturned defiant face, streaked with mud, her hair a tangled mass of filthy brown hair, some gray showing. God, she was ugly. When had she grown so ugly?

"If she were mine, I'd punish her," Tom Marshall muttered. "You let a woman get by with calling you names . . ."

"Haven't you ever punished her, Mike?" Mr. Hills asked calmly. "Women's lib be damned, you got to let 'em know where you stand."

"Bastard!" she shouted up at him, impervious to the voices. "If you hadn't been drunk, you might have—"

Whether she saw his hand lifting or not, he couldn't be certain. But at the moment of impact, her head fell to one side and she would have fallen from the chair if it hadn't been for the women standing behind her, holding her steady.

Mike waited out the stinging in his right hand, the flesh alive with a million hot needles, and stood rooted in shock at what he'd done. He'd never struck her before, but then, she'd never publicly embarrassed him before. Now it was all over. Take her home, soothe her, apologize.

She looked up at him, his blow still visible on the side of her face, three red and rising welts. Christ, he'd laid a good one on her. "Donna, I'm . . ."

The dizziness was getting worse, and the scene was getting uglier. What in the name of God were they doing? He didn't want to hurt her. He didn't want to hurt anybody. All he wanted was a one-way ticket back to the corner of Mass. Avenue and Copley, to the Scorvini Brothers' paradise.

He stood up and feared for a moment that his knees would not support him.

Simultaneously, Donna stood. Was she crying?

She pushed her way past her audience and disappeared into the small back room slamming the door behind her and leaving Mike wavering on his feet, gazing at . . . nothing.

40

It was almost eight o'clock and fast growing dark when Hal, still running from the atrocity he'd only briefly glimpsed at the camping area, reached the outskirts of Tomis. Polly Whiteside's guest house greeted him first, freshly painted and pristine white, like a gentle reminder of human effort, human decency.

As he stepped up onto the crumbling blacktop, he looked ahead the length of Main Street and saw the town was deserted. Good! He'd told them to stay inside the restaurant. For the first time he broke speed and hung his head in an attempt to draw breath.

It was going to be all right. Everything was. Maybe Ned Wilson and Billingsly had found the bodies. His own fruitless search meant nothing. And neither did the mirage he'd only half-glimpsed in the fading light. He should have investigated. Probably it had only been his imagination, and as his breathing grew easier, he looked back the way he had come, as though he could see across the distance without actually making the return trip.

But of course, he couldn't, and anyway, there was no need now. His rationalization suited him, logical, precise, safe.

Growing steadier, he looked up at the gray sky and saw a cloudless, limitless dome. And heard something.

Listen! Poised on the edge of the blacktop, he turned rapidly in all directions, seeking out the distant whirring which sounded like a . . . helicopter?

Thank God! Someone had found them. It would take several trips, depending upon the size of the aircraft. But where in the hell was it? He peered up toward the summit of Mt. Victor. *That* seemed to be the direction of the sound, and he finally expected at any moment to see the rotating blades and blinking red light of a rescue party.

But the longer he stared, the fainter the sound became, and gradually his ears recorded nothing except the peculiar deep silence that had always been characteristic of Tomis. Well, still no cause for alarm. Come morning, surely help would arrive. It wasn't as if people didn't know they were here. Undoubtedly, word of the unseasonable storm had spread by now. Sarah's parents in San Antonio would be trying to call. And there was Roger Laing. Surely he had tried to get through to them.

Up ahead, in the deepening shadows, he saw the restaurant, saw three men, one standing, two slumped on the steps.

"Ned?" he called out, and saw all three look up. He recognized Tom Marshall as the one standing.

"Did you find any . . .?"

"Nothing," Ned Wilson muttered. "Not even a track."

"Maybe they found a way down the mountain," Billingsly suggested, and Hal saw the old man's face shaking with fatigue.

"Kate?" he asked.

"No," Ned Wilson repeated, "and Tom here tells us that Brian is nowhere to be found either."

Briefly Hal blinked at the news which really didn't surprise him. He'd suspected that Brian would take off in his own pursuit of Kate.

"The . . . others . . ." he muttered.

Tom Marshall studied the mud at his feet. "Okay," he said tonelessly. Then rather defensively added, "See for yourself," and gestured toward the window, through which Hal could see tables of silently seated people.

"Where's Sarah?"

Then he saw her, sitting up on the makeshift bed of chairs, her face obscured by Vicky's head as the two clung together and rocked slowly back and forth.

The sight moved him. He felt a surge of deep love for them both, sorry for what he had put them through, and the end not yet in sight. He leaned against the banister and concealed his face.

"We *did* have a spot of trouble," he heard Tom Marshall say softly. "With Mike Dunne, of all people," he added, and waited to say more until Hal looked at him.

"Mike?" Hal repeated, and stole another glance at Sarah, and longed to hold her in his arms and comfort her.

Tom nodded. "He come in about two hours ago and started abusing Mrs. Dunne pretty good."

Weak bastard, Hal thought. "What happened?"

"Well, he was feeling his oats, if you know what I mean, and saying all kinds of embarrassing things in front of the other women, and Mrs. Dunne, she tried to get him to shut up, and he just hauled off and knocked her almost into next week."

Hal closed his eyes. *Christ!* "Where is he now?" he demanded.

Tom shook his head, embarrassed.

"Donna?" Hal inquired.

"She's still back there, in that room, won't come out at all, though some of the women have tried to talk to her. She has the door locked."

Hal shook his head with a lingering sense of unreality, appalled at the account. Donna had told him many times that Mike, drunk, was a different man. In fact, the Tomis experiment was to have been his last chance. If he started drinking again, she had vowed to leave him.

"I'd better go see her," he said wearily, though halfway up the steps he looked accusingly back at Tom Marshall. "Didn't you try to stop him?"

"Sure we tried," the man snapped defensively, "but he was clear out of his mind. And I don't believe in interfering between a man and his . . ."

Abruptly the man stopped speaking, lifted his head, and froze. Halfway up the steps, Hal saw Ned Wilson do the same, then Billingsly, all three fixed now into a listening position.

Then Hal heard it as well, or thought he heard it. But as he had been deceived once before, he came slowly back down the steps, walked past the three men, and proceeded out through the mud to the center of the street. He heard it clearly now, the distinct pulsating whir of a chopper, though nothing as yet marred the flawless gray-blue sky overhead.

Suddenly, "There it is!" Tom shouted, and jubilantly pointed up to the summit of Mt. Victor. And there it was, a small, distant buglike aircraft, the whir growing louder, the eye of a blinking red light growing larger.

"Hot damn!" Ned Wilson grinned, and all four men now gaped upward at the miracle, the outside world finally conceding their existence.

"Go get the others," Tom ordered, but there was no need. The ever-increasing whir of the rotors had obviously penetrated into the restaurant, and now Hal saw the door filled with people, all of them in the middle of the street now, laughing, waving their arms, a disreputable-looking crew, Hal thought affectionately, though so grateful along with the rest of them that rescue had at last arrived.

He searched the laughing crowd for Sarah and Vicky, didn't find them, and assumed that Sarah had remained inside. No matter, he'd go to her in a minute and tell her the good news, that this time tomorrow, with luck, she'd be safe in her parents' home.

As the helicopter dropped lower, he began to feel the wind pressure of the rotating blades and looked up to see it just descending from the high ridge, sleek, gray, and very small, no more than a two-seater. Well, no matter. Whoever it was, he could take the word out, and possibly larger rescue helicopters would be here before dark.

"Is he coming down?" someone shouted.

Then above the din he heard a large amplified voice, "Everybody back. Move everyone back."

Quickly Hal went into action, as with arms extended he tried to corral everyone back under the safety of the restaurant's overhanging roof. In the

271

confusion he saw some of the other men pitch in now, ushering everyone to a position of safety, their line of vision alternating between the hovering helicopter and the gale-force wind blowing in their faces from the rotors.

"Now, stay back!" Hal shouted when everyone had reached the safety of the sidewalk, "at least until he's down."

With the street thus cleared, he ran out and motioned to the pilot, pointing out the massive indentation caused by the rock slide and waving him away from that dangerous area.

The aircraft was so low now that Hal could see the man's face, could see the strain of effort as he tried to gauge the distance necessary for the rotors, almost touching ground, suddenly lifting off about ten feet and moving away from some hazard, then slowly setting it down about twenty yards from the restaurant.

A great cheer went up as the runners made their first contact with earth. The helicopter seemed to vibrate for a moment as though pulling against its own power. The blades whined, and through the window he saw the pilot thrusting levers. At last the engines died, the wind subsided, and the pilot pushed back his helmet and stared down on Hal.

"You're a sight for sore eyes." Hal grinned as he approached the man, who still stood protectively close to the door of the helicopter. He appeared to be middle-aged, fortyish, garbed in a crumpled business suit, tie removed, his slightly bloodshot eyes surveying the scene with what appeared to be stunned incredulity.

"Hal Kitchens," Hal said cordially by way of introduction.

The man shook his head. "You . . . a ghost?"

"No, very real, I assure you." Hal laughed.

"Is it . . . the whole town?" the man asked, his stunned look beginning to dissolve into annoyance.

Before Hal could reply, the man said angrily, "We thought you all had gotten off. Hell, couldn't you see the storm coming? There was time . . ."

Hal heard the new taut silence behind him, everyone listening to the nonsensical exchange. He had the suspicion that they were in no mood to apologize for their existence.

"No," he said slowly, glancing back at Tom Marshall and several of the others, who stood as obedient as schoolchildren, all ready to file onto the aircraft designed to hold only two.

"And you are . . .?" Hal asked, stepping closer, hand extended, smiling, thinking somehow an exchange of names might make a difference.

The man gave a shrug, still staring out over the faces as though they were an optical illusion. "Jeffries," he said, taking Hal's hand, then dropping it instantly. "Paul Jeffries—I'm chief surveyor for Century Mining Corporation. We had no idea . . ."

He shook his head, and the stunned disbelief moved into awe. "How in hell did you all survive? I came up today to assess the damage done to equipment . . ."

Hope it was all smashed, Hal thought, though what he said was, "We've been surviving storms up here for four years, Mr. Jeffries. I'm afraid there was no impulse to run until it was too late." He gestured over his shoulder

272

toward the collapsed road at the opposite end of town. "Now our only access road is out, and I think it best if we all abandon ship, at least temporarily."

"Of course, of course," Jeffries said hurriedly, sharing Hal's concern for the first time. "Are there any injuries?" the man asked, stepping away from the door of his helicopter, surveying the faces with what appeared to be new respect. "Hell, I don't know how you did it, I really don't."

Hal stepped closer and lowered his voice. "No, no injuries," he murmured, "though I'm afraid a few are . . . missing."

"I'm sorry." Jeffries nodded sympathetically. "Hell, you got kids here . . ."

"We do."

"Do you have enough food?"

"Enough. Why?"

"Well . . ." Jeffries said expansively, and gestured toward his small helicopter. "I tell you what," he began with purpose. "I'll go straight into Durango and pass the word. The highway patrol can notify the National Guard. Their machines can get you down from here in no time."

Hal closed his eyes and gave a silent prayer. "We're grateful . . ."

Jeffries looked straight up at the darkening sky and shook his head. "I don't know," he began hesitantly. "The boys may not want to try it tonight."

"No, I don't think they should," Hal agreed. "We'll be all right for the night. First thing in the morning, though . . ."

Jeffries nodded. "I still can't get over it," he marveled, looking out over the silent crowd. "Don't worry," he shouted, smiling for the first time. "We'll have you down from here by noon tomorrow."

Another cheer went up from the crowd. Near the steps of the restaurant Hal saw Inez clasping the crucifix about her neck. The Drivers were hugging each other and their children. As they all broke into relieved chatter, Jeffries motioned for Hal to come closer.

"Let me make two suggestions," the man said sternly. "Keep everyone together tonight if you can, under one roof. We'll get them out of here tomorrow, then search teams can come in and look for the missing."

Hal nodded in agreement and debated the wisdom of telling Jeffries about Frank Quinton. Undoubtedly he knew the man, though now that Hal thought about it, he had a vague recollection that Frank Quinton had introduced *himself* as chief surveyor for Century Mining Corporation. Well, what the hell, so there were two chiefs.

"Also," Jeffries went on, "you might have them draw numbers tonight. That would help avoid a push, if you know what I mean."

"Good suggestion," Hal said, shivering suddenly in the encroaching darkness.

"I hate to leave you here," Jeffries apologized, growing more human by the moment.

"We'll be all right," Hal assured him. "You might see if there is a place in Durango that could accommodate all of us, at least for a few days. I think we'd like to stay together."

"Of course."

"One thing more," Hal added, stepping directly to the man and bowing his head as though in close examination of the helicopter. Before he spoke, he looked back at the crowd and saw them beginning to drift back to the restaurant.

Jeffries waited impatiently, his eyes sweeping the darkening sky. "What is it, Kitchens?" he said nervously. "I better get out of here while the—"

"I'm afraid," Hal began, "that one of your men is among the missing . . . or . . ." He'd started to say "dead," then stopped.

Jeffries looked puzzled. "One of . . . my men? I . . . don't understand. I told you, we got all our men off the mountain."

"Not quite all," Hal said, still keeping his voice down in spite of the retreating people. "There was one. Frank Quinton. He arrived here a few days ago . . ." He stopped speaking, literally rendered silent by the expression on Paul Jeffries' face.

"What . . . did you say?"

"Quinton. Frank Quinton," Hal repeated, enunciating clearly. "He was here during the—"

"What are you talking about?" Jeffries demanded angrily. "Is this some kind of a sick joke?"

"Frank Quinton!" Hal repeated a third time, and shivered in the increasing wind.

There it was again, that single expression of disbelief, tinged now by resentment and impatience. "I haven't a notion in hell what you're talking about, Kitchens," he snapped, and swung into the low seat. As he buckled the safety belt across his chest, he added, not bothering to look up, "There *was* a Frank Quinton with CMC about ten years ago, maybe twelve, '68, thereabouts. He did the preliminary survey of the mountain. I took his place."

Buckles secured, he switched on the power. The enormous blades coughed sluggishly.

The cold wind increased, aided now by the displacement of air. "You took . . . his . . ." Hal tried to repeat, and failed. "What . . . happened?"

Paul Jeffries looked straight at him. "He died, was killed in a rock slide on the other side of Mt. Victor. Crushed, one hand torn . . ."

As the rotors accelerated, Hal clung to the side of the door. "You must be mistaken," he shouted above the increasing noise, and felt vibrations beneath his feet as the powerful rotors spun around, a blur above his head. He ducked reflexively, though there was plenty of clearance, and kept his eyes fixed on Paul Jeffries, who was busily pulling switches, the copter beginning to lift off.

Hal held his position in spite of the gale-force winds. There *was* a reason, he was certain of it. Come morning, under better conditions, he'd speak the name again. Surely there was family to be notified, or maybe the man himself would turn up.

. . . *one hand torn loose* . . .

As the wind and dust stung his eyes, he thought he'd never been so cold in his life. He lifted his head and dealt with his fear in a measured response.

274

There must be some misunderstanding. Jeffries was anxious to depart, Hal eager to shift the corpse to someone else's conscience.

The helicopter, he noticed, was hovering low at the end of the road, apparently checking the damage for himself.

"Coming, Hal?"

He looked back toward the restaurant and saw Tom Marshall. Most of the others were already back inside, the lights flickering low as though some of the overhead bulbs had burned out.

Hal held his position at the center of the road and watched the endless circling of the helicopter, like an immense water bug.

The rotors seemed to be screeching too loudly, and he stepped forward in concern as he saw what appeared to be a small vapor streaming out from the top of the aircraft.

"What in the hell is he trying to do?" Tom Marshall shouted, joining Hal in the road and peering toward the wildly gyrating helicopter and the blinking red light, which appeared to be blinking faster than usual.

Then slowly the helicopter seemed to steady itself directly over the collapsed road. Simultaneously, a powerful white searchlight swung erratically about the night sky and ultimately focused its beam straight down.

Mystified, Hal started off at a trot, though he'd gone only a few feet when Tom Marshall caught up with him and placed an urgent restraining hand on his arm. "Wait a minute," the man shouted. "If he's in trouble . . ."

"Doesn't look like he's in trouble," Hal protested. "Looks like he's found something. Come on . . ."

But again Tom Marshall insisted, "No, look!"

Torn between the mystery at the far end of the street and the insistence of the man standing beside him, Hal was in the process of pulling free when suddenly he heard a new sound, a rising whine accelerating into the screech of metal on metal. Quickly he glanced up and saw the blinking red light go out, followed immediately by the searchlight, and for a moment he found himself staring into solid blackness.

Then all at once he saw the helicopter try to lift up. New vapors of white smoke were spiraling skyward. In one massive mechanical struggle the helicopter managed enough power to elevate, hurtling sideways down the mountain.

"There," Tom said, relieved. "Dumb bastard! What was he trying to do?"

But suddenly the night air went quiet about them. The abrupt cessation of the distant whirring was ghostly, as though a pulse had ceased. In the blue-black light near the horizon line, Hal saw the helicopter suddenly flip over as though a gigantic hand had swatted it down.

"No," he gasped.

Then it fell, a fluid, almost graceful descent, as though in its final moments it was no longer subject to the laws of gravity, a slow-motion plunge about a mile away, soundless, culminating in a small, almost innocuous crash, a fireball, a delayed puff of an explosion, black smoke rising immediately from the flames.

Hal stood rooted in paralyzed shock. It hadn't happened. The thing would rise again and continue on its way to Durango in search of help. But it didn't rise, and it was a few minutes before he was even aware of his shaking hands and Tom's shocked voice, asking, "What . . . happened?"

Then he heard a scream on the restaurant steps behind him and saw Rene Hackett sharing their line of vision.

As he knew it would, her screams attracted the others, and within moments the steps and sidewalk were crowded with wide-eyed and shocked faces, staring at the dying flames as though they all were gazing into some hideous finality.

The fire was almost gone now, though the black-smoke tail was rising higher into the sky.

No matter. In a way, God forgive him, he was almost relieved. Paul Jeffries, whoever he had been, had not wished them well. It had been a plot, undoubtedly, collusion on the part of Frank Quinton and Century Mining Corporation.

The people in Tomis are a stubborn lot, but we can scare them off.

"Come on," Hal ordered now, deriving strength and energy from irrationality. *Dead twelve years!*

"Come on," he shouted. "Back inside. Everyone! No cause for worry. Someone will come looking for *him* in the morning. In the meantime, we'll show them all."

As his solitary voice cut through the chaos, he saw Polly Whiteside near the restaurant door, her round plain face reflecting the horror of the others as all continued to gaze out toward the trailing black smoke.

He saw Tom Marshall close by. "Help me get them back inside," Hal muttered. "This isn't doing anyone any good."

Now the picture of cooperation, Tom began to usher them back up the steps, cajoling, soothing.

"Polly?" Hal caught the woman's attention and signaled that she was to wait by the door. He stood a step beneath her and paused a moment to choose his words carefully. "I was . . . wondering if you had seen . . . Frank Quinton? I thought he would be here with the others, but . . ."

The woman seemed unable to tear her eyes off the diminishing smoke of the crash. "What . . . happened, Hal?" she asked, her voice fearful.

Hal drew even with her on the steps and gently took her hand. "An accident, Polly, that's all. Tom and I were watching. He seemed to lose power. It *will* be all right, though. Someone will come looking for him now."

He waited for the solace to soak in, then tried again. "The important thing, Polly, is to stay calm. And together. I haven't seen Frank Quinton lately, and I was wondering if . . ."

"Who?" she asked, shaking her head slightly, as though to clear it of fear and confusion.

"Quinton!" Hal repeated, tightening his grip on her hand. "Frank Quinton. He was staying at your guest house . . ."

She looked dazedly up at him, her attention still torn. "I . . . don't know what you're talking about, Hal," she murmured. "I've had no guests this season, and now it looks like I—"

"Frank Quinton!" he repeated a third time. She was distracted, that was all, distracted and frightened, as they all were. "Think, Polly!" he commanded. "Remember a few days ago, I brought a gentleman to you, a man with one hand missing. You were a little put out, claiming you weren't ready, but you gave him a room and said—"

"Don't, Hal, you're hurting me," she whimpered, and pulled her hand away, now looking as fearfully at him as she'd recently looked toward the crash. "I . . . really don't know what you're talking about. There have been no guests this year. Maybe you're thinking of last year, but I remember no one named Quinton."

"Frank Quinton!" he shouted. "He was here last week. He ate here."

Beyond Polly's shoulder he saw Tom Marshall through the screen door, his leathery face reflecting Polly's alarm. "What's the trouble?" he demanded. Then to Hal he added, "Try to settle it later if you can. You're scaring hell out of the others."

As he jerked his head toward the dining room, Hal saw every face staring back at him, a nightmare gallery of fear and alarm and distrust.

"Come on," said Tom. "You look like you both could use a cup of coffee and a sandwich. Then I think you better listen to something Rene Hackett has to say."

Hal blinked at the quietly talking mouth, though few of the words registered with him. It *was* a conspiracy, he was certain of it, yet how far it had reached, he had no idea. The mining corporation had obviously gotten to Polly as well. How much had they paid her to betray him?

Well, he'd get to the bottom of it sooner or later.

For now the important thing was to hold himself in tight control, and hold the reins of leadership in tighter control, though at that moment he was aware of Tom Marshall leading him back into the restaurant as though he were an invalid, calling ahead, "Come on. Make room for Hal here. He don't look none too good."

277

41

Predator-prey, predator-prey . . .

Those two words in that combination assaulted Hal all night. Now, with a sense of dread he lifted his eyes and saw the sleeping bodies sprawled about the restaurant, like a morgue.

Sarah had refused to speak to him the night before, though it had been a passive, lifeless refusal, her lips moving as she'd said three times, "Don't come near me," and last night, thinking the mood would pass, he'd left her alone.

Now, uncertain of how to approach his wife, he decided to seek out Donna and see if she had any advice. He eased up from his chair and started slowly around the Billingslys' table, heading toward the locked door. As he passed, he saw Lucy move toward the kitchen. He started to say something, then realized she was probably going to use the bathroom there. Ignoring her, he approached the locked door, and to his surprise found it unlocked, the knob turning easily in his hand, the door opening.

"Donna?" he called out softly, and receiving no answer, stepped all the way into the semidarkness of the room.

"Donna?" he called again, but the room was empty. Well, maybe she had decided to find Mike and forgive him. Hal decided to go and look for them both. He wanted Mike to examine Sarah anyway.

With great care he made his way through the sleeping bodies to the door.

Outside, the crisp morning air revived his spirits. The snow had melted, not a trace anywhere, though the roar he heard would be Runaway Creek, swollen from the snow melting high in the mountains. Moving faster, he hurried down the steps.

Frank Quinton was killed twelve years ago.

Suddenly a painful muscle cramp knotted in his lower back. He leaned into the pain, caught himself in time, and slowly felt the knot relaxing. He hurried across the street, sidestepping the large ruptures and noting that some had grown larger. On this side of the street, the roar was stronger, a constant thundering in his ear. He looked up, but there was nothing but the high blue dome of the sky, so he increased his step and approached the embankment at a trot. He decided to take one quick look to see how the new timbers were withholding the onslaught of melted snow.

The roar was like continuous surf. He could feel the battering vibrations as he grasped the timber railing and peered over to see the angry churning foam, the stream swollen to three times its normal size.

"Do your worst," he muttered, staring down. There wasn't a chance for the water to break through the embankment. The stream could run amok somewhere down the mountain if it chose, but it would be contained here whether it liked it or not.

He leaned farther over the railing as a long white object caught his eye. It seemed to be merged with a heavy log. He leaned farther out. The fast-running water slapped against his face as the white mass drew closer.

One of the missing . . .

Frantically he looked around for something with which to free the submerged object, but there was nothing within reach. Carefully he swung his legs over the embankment, found a narrow ledge of a foothold, and clinging to the timbers with both hands, he commenced kicking at the log, feeling the force of the water as it drenched his boot, a sucking pressure like the tide, as though it wanted to draw everything into its vortex.

"Kitchens! What in the hell are you doing?"

He turned about and saw Tom Marshall on the sidewalk in front of the restaurant, one hand shielding his eyes against the sun, his rifle in the other.

Again Hal kicked at the log and felt a small shifting as he saw the contours of a human back, shoulders, one arm floating up, buffeted by the cascading waters.

One of the missing . . .

"Kitchens! We got problems over here. You better . . ."

Dammit! There were problems here as well, and Hal kicked furiously at the wedged log. He saw it finally slip free, and within the instant it was swept downstream as though it were a matchstick, and at the same time he saw the tumbling white water catch the body and flip it over, arms and legs clearly visible now, the face obscured by long water-washed hair, the hands appearing to move of their own volition under the pounding of the water, until at last it slipped into the pressure of a whirlpool directly beneath where Hal held himself suspended over the creek. And in the final instant before it was sucked under, he saw the face, the eyes open, staring.

"Kate! *No!*" he cried out, and as he foolishly reached down in an attempt to bring her up, he felt the force of the water pulling on his hand and would have fallen in himself had it not been for Tom Marshall, who grabbed his arm and with angry strength shouted, "Hold on! Reach up! Goddammit!"

Hal felt himself being pulled back against the embankment as Tom dropped his rifle and applied both hands to the awkward job of dragging him up over the side. He tried to stand, but his knees failed him, and he clung for a moment to the railing and looked back down into the whirlpool and saw nothing, Kate gone, though he imagined where they would find her body, or what was left of it, about five miles down the mountain, where the stream thundered over a sheer rock cliff into a picturesque waterfall, a place where campers and backpackers always stopped to take photographs.

In spite of Tom's curses, Hal sank to the ground and shut his eyes against the memory of that face.

"You gone clear out of your fucking mind, Kitchens?" Tom bellowed. "My God, that's all those hysterical folks need to hear from me now, that you went over the side of the creek and . . . What in the hell were you trying to do?"

Hal didn't answer, could not answer.

"I've heard you tell everybody a hundred times to stay away from the creek when it's running. My God, just a few days ago Mrs. Dunne almost got pulled in, would have if I hadn't been sweeping my walk and seen . . ."

Hal grasped blindly at the muddy earth.

"Kitchens?" Tom asked, his voice softer now. "What were you going after? Did you see . . . ?"

"Nothing," Hal said.

"Are you all right?" Tom inquired, squatting before him. "Sorry I yelled at you. You gave me a start. You wouldn't have a chance against that," he added, pointing at the source of the unearthly roar. "Never heard it carry on so. It'll settle down, though. It always does."

Still Hal's vision twisted in a swirling of images, blurred, unfocused except for one, the stylish, attractive woman who had surprised them all with her courage and strength in these primitive surroundings.

"Come on, Hal," Tom Marshall urged gently. "We got problems across the way. Rene Hackett is scaring the shit out of everybody." Hal took a last fearful glance at the white water. Where was he to go now? Yes, the restaurant. Someone was waiting for him. Tom Marshall. Someone was frightening the others. He couldn't remember who. Now it seemed massively unimportant. Of the six original Fox Fire Kids, three were left.

Predator-prey, predator-prey . . .

Who? Where?

"Hurry, Kitchens, trouble . . ."

280

42

It was the woman's screams that first awakened Sarah, a repetitious high-pitched wail, like a madwoman, with certain words clearly audible. "My daughter's gone, Lucy's gone." In fear Sarah sat up too quickly, felt the room whirl about her, and reached out for Vicky and drew her close.

Thus secured, she stared out over the slowly stirring restaurant and felt as if she were peering into the windows of hell. She didn't know these people, had no desire to know them. She pressed the side of her cheek against the top of Vicky's soft hair.

Rene Hackett was still screaming, moving frantically back and forth between the kitchen doors and the dining room. Somewhere a young child whimpered, "Mama . . ." but it wasn't Vicky. Vicky was locked safely in her arms.

Sarah watched as several women moved toward Rene Hackett, trying to pacify her, her screams taking on a different tone now as she sobbed, "It's him. I know it's him. He come and took her away. Oh, you've got to get her back for me. She's all I got now. Please . . ."

As the women closed in around her, the screams subsided, but the cracked, distraught voice could be heard clearly, the accusations equally clear.

Mrs. O'Connell brought her a glass of water and with the help of two others eased her down into her chair. While she sipped at the water, the room was blessedly quiet, and Sarah looked about at the others. She saw Tom Marshall, gun in hand, slip out of the front door, and noticed Hal missing and wished he'd stay gone. It was *his* fault, all of it. The hardships they had endured for *his* dream were awesome. How long they all had humored him, accommodated him, sacrificed for him. *No more!*

The cries had started again, a raucous counterpoint to Mrs. O'Connell's plea, "You must get hold of yourself, Rene. Lucy will come back. She probably just—"

"No, she's gone. The Mountain Man come down and took her away, a pretty young girl like that, and he's the devil, Satan himself. He come down before, yes he has. I smelled him last night. I smell him now."

As all attention in the room was drawn to the hysterical woman, Sarah saw them lift their heads and sniff at the foul-smelling air. There *was* a repellent odor.

Then, as though sensing that she had their attention, Rene pushed effortlessly through the women and took the floor. "If it ain't so, then where is she?" she demanded. "She was sleeping peaceful there beside me all night, and when I woke up, she was gone. So where is she?" she demanded again, and waited out the silence as everyone looked about in search of the missing Lucy.

At that moment Sarah heard a disturbance at the door and looked up to see Tom Marshall returning, his face and shirt wet. A few minutes later she saw Hal. He looked like a ghost, his face drained of life and color, his clothes drenched.

At first he seemed disinclined to move beyond the door, though she saw him close it and lean against it. He looked dreadful. In fact he seemed to give no indication of even knowing where he was. She knew that expression. She'd seen it before. Something had happened. She should go to him. Perhaps she had been wrong to blame him.

But Rene Hackett had begun screaming again, her thin, flat Midwestern voice echoing discordantly about the room. "She's gone, I tell you, and he's got her, Mr. Kitchens. You gotta believe me."

"What are you talking about, Rene?"

Sarah saw Hal moving toward the woman, his shoulders sunk with fatigue, walking in a slight shuffling motion as though he lacked the energy to lift his feet.

"It's Lucy, Mr. Kitchens," Rene said. "When I woke up, she was gone. Now, you *have* to believe me, even if no one else will." She leaned forward and grasped his hand.

He allowed the contact of her hand, though even as she spoke, Sarah saw his head moving slowly back and forth. At the first break, he patted her hand and spoke soothingly. "Lucy is safe, Mrs. Hackett. I saw her not thirty minutes ago. She went into the kitchen, I assume to use the bathroom. If you recall, I asked you to use the one in the kitchen."

"Then where is she?" Rene demanded. "You go find her for me."

With everyone else watching, Sarah saw him lift his head as though he were having difficulty breathing and move slowly through the kitchen door.

Vicky whispered, "Daddy . . ."

"Shhhh," Sarah soothed, not wanting to call attention to themselves. They all stood silently waiting.

What was keeping Hal? She saw Tom Marshall move close to the kitchen doors, drawn forward by curiosity at the delay.

"What did you find, Kitchens?" he called out, pushing open one side of the doors. Hal was moving back into the restaurant, staring helplessly at the soiled white bandages and splints which had held Lucy's injured fingers.

"Help me." Rene swooned and leaned against Mrs. O'Connell.

As several men clustered around Hal, the better to examine the curious evidence, Hal pushed past them, still intent upon comforting Rene. "It really doesn't mean anything," he said kindly. "She could have taken them off herself."

"She wouldn't do that," Rene sobbed. "Her fingers hurt her. She told me so." Suddenly a new expression moved across the woman's face. "It's him, I tell you," she whispered. "He done it to her. He hurt her hands, and now he's come and took her away. Are you ready to listen to me now?" she entreated, on her feet in spite of Hal's efforts to restrain her.

"I know what most of you think of me," she went on. "Not quite as good as you. Jerry either, just country people who don't know nothing but to fix your cars."

"Rene, please," Inez begged.

"No, you gotta listen to me now, all of you, 'cause he's up there, Satan is, Lucy saw him, she did, right up close."

"Rene, come on, sit down," Hal begged, trying to reach for her hand. But she pulled away and in a rising voice demanded a chance to talk, and Sarah saw the women shift their sympathies from Hal to Rene.

Mrs. Cobb said, "Let her alone. You're just making it worse. Let her have her say. It'll make as much sense as anything else that's happened around here."

"Come on, Rene, calm down," Mrs. Driver soothed. "Tell us what you know. You got a right, and I, for one, am interested."

The support seemed to calm the woman. Either Hal took his cue from the others or he was too tired to persist. Sarah saw him back away and look helplessly about the room. In the process his eyes fell on her. In a flood of self-consciousness, she bent low over Vicky, who was amusing herself, making ever-constant encirclings upon her knee, whispering, "Merry-go-round . . ."

By the time Sarah looked up again, she saw that Hal had settled in a slumped position on a chair near the kitchen doors, the splints and dirty bandages still in his hand.

As for the rest, they seemed as somnambulant now as when they'd been asleep, their heads propped heavily up on hands, a few dozing even in these awkward positions. It was as though they all had been drugged.

The most self-conscious of all was Rene Hackett, as though after having worked so hard for the spotlight, she really wished now that it would move on and let her be. What she said first was a curious defense. "Lucy's a good girl. She *was* a good girl when we come here, at least. I never wanted to come here,

283

you know," she added. "No, this bit of foolishness was Jerry's idea."

"Rene, please sit down," Inez whispered, her face reflecting the embarrassment they all felt.

"Ain't gonna sit, no sir," Rene said defiantly. "I been trying to tell you all for three years what this place is. And nobody would listen. Well, you're gonna listen now, 'cause you don't have a choice and 'cause ain't any of us gonna leave here alive unless someone goes up there and does what should have been done back at the beginning."

Tom Marshall bellowed, "What in hell are you jabbering about, Rene?"

"Him," she whispered, and pointed in the direction of the high ridge. "Ain't you got a brain inside your head, Tom Marshall? Ain't anyone here ever seen him before?"

"Seen him?" Tom echoed. "How could we ever see him? He don't let no one get close, and he's never come down."

"Oh, he's come down, all right." Rene nodded vigorously. "Ask any of the kids here. They've seen him. You could ask my Lucy, if she was here," she added, her anger dissipating into grief, which didn't last long and which was immediately replaced with irrational conviction. "But you don't have to ask anyone but me, 'cause I seen him one . . ."

Abruptly her voice fell. Her worn face appeared drained of color, and she sat weakly in a nearby chair.

Sarah watched and listened. Something had terrified the woman. For several moments everyone in the room waited. Sarah could feel the fear, and gently renewed her grasp on Vicky. She remembered that nightmare scene, Vicky running across the high meadow, and the man, seen through her opera glasses, taking careful aim at her with his rifle.

"I felt it," Rene was saying, "the very first time we come here, the cold—not weather—cold, but something else, something I feel in August as sure as I feel in December, and I noticed things and Jerry said I was crazy for noticing them, things like where are the critters? Over by Lake City and all them places, you can make pets out of the chipmunks. They come down and eat right out of your hand." She looked out over the quiet restaurant. "Where are the chipmunks?" she asked forcefully. "Where are the deer? This is good high-range country. Where are they?"

As Rene questioned the room, Sarah shifted on the chair in a futile search for comfort, and thought only briefly on the mystery which, true, they had never solved, but at least Roger Laing had made it comfortable enough to live with, their curious plateau, bereft of all wildlife.

" . . . and that was when I begin to suspect," Rene said.

"When was the first time you saw him?" Tom Marshall asked, drawing near in case the woman said something that made sense.

"Only saw him once," Rene muttered, clearly reluctant to talk about it now. "You see, the whole earth belongs to him, to Lucifer. God gave it to him and he chose to live here 'cause it's so isolated, or was till we come, and now he wants us to go."

"When did you see him?" Tom Marshall persisted.

But again Rene dodged the answer. "I don't want to talk about it."

"No? You brought it up. Now, you tell us. We got a right to know."

Finally, as though to get it over with, Rene said, "He made her bad," her eyes down as though she were too embarrassed to look at them. "Oh, I know what she's become since we've been here. Most of you think I don't, but I do. I hear your snickers and your gossip, and it hurts, but I don't say nothing 'cause I knew this day would come, and here it is."

"When did you see him?" Tom Marshall repeated, encircling Rene's chair now like she was on the witness stand.

"Leave me alone."

"No! If something's going on up there, we got a right to know."

Sarah heard a rustle of agreement from the others. She noticed Hal seated in the chair, his hands covering his face.

In the silence that followed, she saw Rene look fearfully about the room. She commenced a peculiar rocking movement and began to speak in a voice scarcely louder than a whisper.

"It was . . . last year," she began. "I was . . . sleeping in my room, and I heard . . . something. Well, Jerry used to prowl at night, and Lucy too, so I didn't think nothing of it at first." She rubbed her arms as though she were cold, and hung her head over.

"Then I . . . smelled him," she said. "And I knew there was something in the house that oughtn't to be there, doing something that oughtn't to be done, and I left my bed, and my teeth was chattering, and I saw something coming from beneath Lucy's door, like candlelight flickering, and I *heard* her first, my Lucy, and she was groaning and carrying on like . . ."

Rene paused. "That was the first time I heard her like that," she added almost apologetically, "and I knew she was with someone and I knew what was going on, and though the smell was awful, I was so mad that I pushed open the door without knocking, and I saw . . ."

Suddenly Rene bent over and covered her face with her hands. Sarah saw Hal look up as though he were trying to understand what she was saying.

"And saw . . . what?" Tom Marshall demanded, speaking for all of them. Sarah detected a new tension in the room.

"I saw . . . *him*," Rene gasped, and shook her head. "I've never been so scared in my life except for now. Lucy was on the bed and himself was on top of her. He musta got in by his own magic, 'cause the house was locked. He was over seven feet tall and he wasn't dressed, not in clothes, but he was covered from head to toe with hair, thick black hair, and there was a glowing underneath the hair, like he was on fire at the center and if it weren't for the hair, you could have seen the fire . . ."

The restaurant was silent, everyone straining forward.

" . . . and his hands was man's hands," Rene went on, still rocking back and forth, "with sharp long nails, but his feet were . . . hooves."

Someone was crying, not a child, and Sarah leaned forward and saw Mrs. O'Connell cross herself, then cover her ears.

But now Rene was impervious to these signs of distress, too involved with her own. "Both of them just looked up from their evil and grinned at me till I screamed and ran. He was after me, I knew it, though I never looked back till I got to my own room and locked the door and I went straight to the bottom drawer and dug out a little crucifix that my mother had give me and I knelt beside my bed and pretty soon the chill left, but I never got rid of that smell. I can smell it yet."

Slowly she crumpled forward in a soft collapse, her forehead resting on her knees. Sarah felt her heart accelerate.

"And . . . what about Lucy?" Tom asked, drawing forward a chair and sitting on the edge.

Rene shook her head. "She never said nothing, and neither did I. But she wasn't my Lucy no more. She got wild and mean and . . ."

Again the voice broke, and from where Sarah sat, she saw not one head move.

"What . . . if it's true?" someone whispered.

"Why would she lie?"

"If it *is* him . . ."

"I . . . smell something . . ."

"I saw him once, too," Terry O'Connell whispered. "Lucy took me up to the high ridge, and I saw him too. And that's where she's gone now. She told me last night that he was the one hurting us, and she was going to go up and . . ."

Sarah listened. Part of her refused to believe anything that had been said. The other part believed every word. "Last week . . ." she said, and was pleased when not one head turned to look at her. "Last week he shot at Vicky. I was . . . watching through the glasses and saw him lift his rifle and take aim . . . on a child."

"Yes, that's right," came Hal's voice. "I remember," he added, meeting her eyes in what appeared to be a belated apology. "Sarah told me about it."

Grateful for his support, she recalled how she'd wanted him to take some of the other men and go up then and bring the man down. But he'd refused, claiming the man had a right to be there.

Now she saw a different expression on his face, a look of uncertainty blended with fatigue.

Then Tom Marshall was on his feet, rifle in hand. "What do you say, Kitchens? Are you game?"

For a moment Hal stared at the direct challenge as though it had been issued by a stranger. The only sound in the restaurant was Rene's quiet weeping.

"If he's got Lucy," Tom began, the vigilante strong within him, "I mean, even if he isn't the . . ." He broke off, obviously unable to say the word. "I think we better go take a look, don't you?"

Still Hal hesitated, with the same reluctance that Sarah had tried to fight a few days ago. Cowardice? She couldn't tell, and had no desire to watch any longer. She stood slowly, thinking it would ease the cramp in her stomach, and walked with Vicky to the rear window, hoping to rest her eyes on the beauty of the high meadow.

Suddenly she was temporarily blinded by a brilliant reflection coming from the high ridge, a dazzling explosion of light. She cried out, averted her face, reached blindly down for Vicky, and found the support of the chair just in

286

time. She was only barely aware of the rush to the window, the voices whispering, "What is it? Him! It's him!"

Most of the women retreated quickly, not wanting to look upon that which they did not understand.

"I say we go up now," Tom announced soberly. "If something's going on up there, we'd better find out while there's still time."

"Marshall's right." Ned Wilson nodded. "There wasn't one good reason why that helicopter went down last night."

"And the road collapsing . . ."

Sarah looked up at the voices and saw Hal staring down on her, his expression one of sorrow and apology and love.

Although she had not planned on it and certainly did not wish it, she felt herself crying for all the grief and tragedy.

"Don't, Sarah," Hal begged, drawing near, and she responded to the shelter of his arms and clung to him, Vicky at the center of the embrace.

She would have been content to remain there for the rest of her life, but he took her face between his hands, kissed her, and promised softly, almost playfully, "Now I'll go and see who your Mountain Man is." When she didn't answer, he turned to Tom. "Come on," he said sharply. "Let's go out the back door. The rest of you are to wait here. Is that understood? No one is to leave for any reason. If the rescue helicopters come, we'll be able to see them and will return immediately."

As Tom Marshall retrieved his rifle, Inez said sternly, "That will be of no help to you at all. Here . . ." and she bent her head down and slipped off the silver crucifix from around her neck, started to hand it to Tom Marshall, then changed her mind and extended it to Hal.

When he hesitated, Rene Hackett whispered, "Take it!"

Sarah saw him take the crucifix and slip it into his pocket. Both men disappeared through the swinging doors, and as Sarah heard the back door slam, she felt deep regret. What if what Rene had said was true? Any part of it. What if Hal was in real danger?

The recent tears not yet over, she lowered her head and held Vicky close and watched that one small finger go around and around, that singsong voice repeating over and over again, "Merry-go-round, merry-go-round . . ."

43

About half an hour later, near the top of the mountain, the two men paused a moment to catch their breath, Hal still struggling to maintain some degree of interior balance as well. He felt increasingly giddy, like he always did after one of the mild drinking sprees he used to share with Mike and Brian in the Copley Bar.

"Come on," Tom said, edging through the shadows, and Hal hurried after, taking only brief note of the mud underfoot and the ground covered with fallen needles and black-green moss.

"Tom, wait—"

"Shhh!" With a massive gesture the man waved away his words, and using the barrel of the rifle as a pointer, gestured up ahead to where the Mountain Man's clearing was just visible: the weathered dome of a trailer near the disemboweled World War II jeep, and beyond that the bewildering tepeelike structure, a crudely shaped pyramid, lashed together at the top with long straps of leather, the leaning timbers joined by a dark claylike substance that had dried like concrete.

They were only about thirty feet away from the edge of the clearing and were passing through an area of aged tree stumps where obviously an ax had been at work years ago. Hal could see the dirt yard enclosed by a sagging wire fence and a few chickens pecking halfheartedly at the earth. Beyond that was a tethered goat, and beyond the goat, a jagged fragment of a mirror nailed to a tree which even now under a direct ray of morning sun glittered in reflection. At least one mystery was solved. He started to point it out to Tom, but was sure he had seen for himself.

At this moment he heard the click of Tom's rifle, the safety thrown, the gun no longer suspended uselessly at Tom's side, but held upright with both hands, at the ready.

Hal found the sight offensive and quietly suggested, "Why don't you lower that thing until—?"

"Too late then," Tom whispered. "Keep it at the ready. That's the way I was taught. Come on . . ."

Again with Tom leading the way, Hal followed after to the edge of the clearing, both of them standing exposed less than ten feet from the crude tepee structure. Between steps Hal listened and heard nothing but the reverberation of his own heartbeat. Even the wind seemed to have died down, and all that remained was a soft whistling through the tops of the pines, massive trees, Hal noticed now, a solid semicircle around the clearing, some of the largest he'd ever seen.

"Listen!"

Tom's hissed command interrupted his observations, and still he heard nothing.

But Tom was moving forward again in that ridiculous half-crouched position, and Hal watched as he encircled the curious tepee and then disappeared on the other side.

Hal hurried after and saw him just ducking his head to enter the low door which led into the interior.

"Wait," he called out as Tom disappeared inside, and there was nothing to do but follow after. He felt a curious heaviness in his head, as though everything had solidified. Why in the name of God had they chased all the way up here to check on the hysterical tale of a mean-spirited and probably unbalanced woman? He had no idea what Rene Hackett *had* seen that night, but . . .

"Tom, come on out," he called, ducking his head. "Let's get out of here."

As he stepped into the semidarkness of the interior, he smelled the musky odor of perpetually damp earth, saw slits of sunlight falling in patterns of precision on the mud floor, saw an enormous tree trunk at the exact center, its lower branches stripped, the upper reaches of the tree extending through the top of the tepee, saw Tom Marshall standing on the other side of the tree trunk, the gun still at the ready, though all his attention seemed to be fixed on the trunk, as though he were fully prepared to fire at it.

"What is it?"

Then Hal saw for himself, a small altar resting against the base of the trunk, a single misshapen handmade candle burning in a tin can, that side of the tree trunk scraped clear of bark, revealing something embedded in the exact center, a . . .

He blinked and looked again. But his eyes had not betrayed him. Imprisoned in the tree trunk *was* a human skeleton, the bones of spine and skull held erect in a standing position by the encircling wood. He looked closer and saw the sight confirmed. But still it was not possible. A tree could not absorb a human being.

"What . . . is it?" Tom Marshall whispered, his voice reflecting Hal's stunned horror.

Then Hal had seen enough. "Come on, let's go," he commanded, though neither moved, held in grisly fascination.

Then they both heard it, the solitary pressure of a single footstep just outside the door. Hal moved quickly back, flattened himself against the rough timbers of the walls, and saw Tom lift the rifle to his shoulder, its barrel aimed at the bright triangle of sun beyond the door.

For several moments the impasse held. Hal pressed farther back against the timbers, keeping his eye on the light, and saw a shadow moving over it, the substance still invisible.

Suddenly an apparition appeared in the doorway with long white hair, carrying a gun exactly like Tom's.

"Don't!" Hal shouted, but too late, as simultaneously the earth was shaken with twin explosions and a flash of red fire slammed Tom Marshall backward, a massive red stain spreading in the middle of his stomach. As Hal turned, expecting to be confronted by the Mountain Man, he realized that Tom too had hit his target. All he saw of the white-haired man was a crude pair of canvas boots lying in the door.

For several moments Hal refused to move. The echo of the twin shots resounded in his head, and the precise sunlight falling through the cracks caught on the blue-gray swirls of gunpowder and smoke. The skeleton imprisoned in the tree stared down, grinning. Hal reached out for support, found none that was trustworthy, and went slowly down on his knees in the mud.

That Tom Marshall was dead there was no doubt. Yet it had to be confirmed, and he moved slowly around the tree skeleton, refusing to look at it until he was standing over Tom, whose eyes were still open, betraying a strange exhaltation, as though the death had been a good one, precisely as he would have ordered it.

Hal waited, expecting emotion. After all, he'd lived with this man for the last three years. But there was nothing except an awareness of the body and the blood, like one of nature's secrets. He turned to leave and heard a dull groan. The grizzled white head was trying to lift, and Hal wondered if beneath the canvas shoes there were hooves. Then, shrugging off the thought, he knelt beside the man. Tom's shot had hit him in the shoulder, and he was trying to speak.

"Tried . . . to keep . . . them away. Help . . . her, please . . . before it's . . ."

Not certain that he'd heard correctly, Hal leaned closer. What was the man talking about? Was there any chance that he might live?

"Help . . . her, quick . . ." the old man repeated, more forcefully this time. ". . . over . . . there, I tried to . . . warn . . . her . . ." His eyes became two sightless ovals as the blood reached the outer edges of the long white hair, and convulsively he turned his face toward the trees, as though trying with his last breath to point a direction.

Still Hal hovered over him, listening, as though in spite of the fact of death there would be further instructions. Tried to keep them away? Help her? What her? Where? His last line of vision had been to the north, toward the thick stand of massive trees just this side of the timberline. Had there been someone living up here with him?

Hal looked down on the man. Who was he? What had brought him here? And what was the most reasonable explanation for that atrocity inside?

The fact that two men were dead had yet to register fully. The greater mysteries took priority—the skeleton imprisoned in the tree, and the old man's last words. Help her . . .

Slowly Hal rose from his kneeling position. He looked north toward the trees. He felt his pulse rate accelerate, then suddenly slow as though some intelligence already knew there was something in those trees that he should not approach, should not look upon.

Suddenly he heard a soft groan and looked back down on the man as though a resurrection might have taken place. But there was nothing. The man had not moved.

Tom Marshall? No, though perhaps he should . . .

It came again, softer, merely part of the whining wind.

Hold your position! screamed a voice inside his head. And when, a few seconds later, he had not heard the moan again, the voice went away and left him on his own to make his own decision.

Slowly he started forward and left the two dead men behind. He gained the coolness of the trees and stopped, looking ahead in all directions and seeing only the massive sentinels themselves, and beyond the trees, the rugged, crumbling stone face of the mountain's summit.

Help her!

He could still hear it, the man's rasping voice, not Satan, though his life here must have been a convincing version of hell. Then he heard it again, a clear groan, though cut short, as though something was suffering and lacked the energy for a full cry for help.

"Who . . . is it?" he called out to the silent trees.

About fifteen feet ahead, he thought he saw movement, a small irregularity superimposed on the straight line of a large tree trunk. He fixed his eyes upon the shadows and waited for it to come again. For several moments he stared numbly forward. He felt his pulse accelerate and heard a dull rattle in his throat, and realized that it had *not* come from his throat. He approached the tree slowly and thought he heard another sound, something creaking, like wood under pressure.

The voice in his mind was back, warning him: *Don't move!* The three steps that would take him around the tree to the other side should not be executed. He still had time to turn and run.

"Please, help . . ."

Indistinct sounds reached his ears, along with the roar of the wind. The effort of listening sharpened his hearing. Ignoring the voice, he stepped forward. At his first step, the mud made a sucking sound beneath his boot. With step two there was no sound at all. With the third, there was neither sound nor need for sound as he stared down at a specter which he had glimpsed in broad outline only once but which he knew he could fill in perfectly in his own mind, down to the last minute details, for the rest of his life.

"Ah, Lucy, no. . . ."

His response was no more intelligible than the horror before him, Lucy Hackett struggling inside the tree, the trunk absorbing her, holding her rigid, her arms twisted behind her, her legs scraped and bleeding, blood running from the corners of her mouth, her eyes meeting his in one terrifying moment of recognition.

Hal tried to move toward her, although she was caught and pinned, her head held upright by the imprisoning bark, which was now slowly covering her face, as though a brown-scaled curtain was going down on its own handiwork.

Then she was gone. The moving parts of the tree trunk became solid and immovable. High above his head the wind whistled through the pine needles like a cackling old man.

He broke into a cold sweat, overcome by his own imagination—*for he had imagined it*—and sank softly to his knees as though life were ebbing from him. He stared vacantly at the tree, jaw slack, and followed with eagerness each feeble surge in the brain which suggested that he rise and walk away.

But he was incapable of doing this, and cried out, one indecipherable sound of terror and rejection.

44

Evergreen, Colorado

"The data are good," Adam Krafft murmured, "until you make that one quantum leap into the fanciful, leaving behind not only scientific method, but, I'm afraid, rudimentary good sense."

It wasn't a scolding. Then why did Roger feel chastised? Still sick with worry over his friends in Tomis, he thought: See it finished and have done with it. Now he waited wearily in the cool dampness of his basement laboratory for Adam to complete his criticism, and thought: How ironic, after the minor triumphs of the morning. Adam had been impressed with the recorded and measurable *fact* that dying cells do send out signals of alarm to which other life responds. He had followed the plant and shrimp experiments with several hours of data which had proven beyond all doubt that alarm signals were common to all social vertebrates, the specific calls of sea gulls that warn their breeding colonies of the approach of predators, ground squirrels and prairie marmots with their early-warning systems that alert their colonies to the danger of air raids by birds of prey.

Of course Adam had played the devil's advocate, which was what Roger had wanted him to do, and had pointed out that the same conclusions at least regarding the vertebrates had recently been drawn and documented by Henson at Southern California. And every auntie from Bar Harbor to Tiburon

293

knew that her violets did best when they smiled at them or sang hymns to them.

Now, "Of course," Adam said kindly, "I may very well be premature in my judgments as well as my criticisms. Obviously you have something in store for me this afternoon. Otherwise . . ."

Roger nodded. Hurry! Must leave for Tomis. . . . "I mentioned this morning, if you'll recall," he began, drawing close to the large tray filled with the control objects, "the threat-to-well-being principle. Obviously by now you have determined the thesis of our research," he went on. "Our search has been for a signal which is accessible to all life, from man down to the lowest forms of life. As we proved this morning, all organisms consist of cells, and the existence of a system of communication among those cells would provide the final answer. If we could prove conclusively that such a system exists . . ."

He felt a discernible disquiet, as though Adam had found even the theory insupportable. "If such a warning system does exist," Adam asked carefully, "why would man, the most advanced form of life, with the highest degree of intelligence, be excluded?"

The question was legitimate, and Roger was grateful for it. "It's not that we have been excluded, Adam. We have excluded ourselves. I suspect that unconsciously we are every bit as aware of the alarm as the shrimp or the plants. It is established fact that even in sleep we respond to certain significant sounds: a mother will sleep through a storm but wake as soon as her child cries softly in another room . . ."

"Then you are suggesting that conditioning . . ."

"Yes," he agreed with conviction. "Conditioning, the benumbing effects of the world as we have created it, all this may be preventing us from tuning in to the universal alarm. Of course we have not yet been able to draw any hard and fast limits to the acuity of our sensory perceptions. Every new probe into their potential seems to push the limits of receptivity further and further out, and new spheres of perception are continuously being discovered."

"Then what you are suggesting"—Adam smiled—"is that if we work at it, we can become as intelligent as brine shrimp."

"That's precisely what I'm saying." Roger nodded. "The Hylozoists of Greece knew it. Thales knew it, and we knew it once, but something, perhaps our egos, developed too fast for rational control . . .

"The arrangement of every living thing in the world," Roger went on, "is that of an ecosystem, with the operation of each part being governed by the state and function of all the other parts. When things are going well, it is an infallible mechanism."

"And your theory," Adam said, tapping his pipe with bemused patience, "yours and Percy's, is that things are not going well."

"*My* theory?" Roger repeated, amazed. "No, that is neither my theory nor Dr. Forrester's. We need not 'theorize' on the state of our planet. The facts are presented to us daily in the most simple form of our morning newspaper."

Warming to the subject which was being propelled by rational as well as irrational questions, Roger drew forward his high stool and sat. "In this immense organism of earth," he began, "chemical signals serve the function of global hormones, keeping balance and symmetry in the operation of various interrelated working parts, informing the cranberry bogs of Massachusetts, say, about the state of trout in Colorado streams by long relays on interconnected messages between all kinds of other creatures. That something has gone wrong with man's receiving system is an undeniable fact. We hear nothing except that data which bring us comfort in the support of our limited and half-dead perceptions."

He paused for his sake as well as Adam's. The theory was radical, revolutionary, terrifying.

"Go on, Roger," Adam urged, no longer bemused.

Roger stood and drew the large tray closer and picked up the pendulum and for the time being looped it about his wrist and allowed it to rest out of sight beneath the worktable.

"Now, I present to you a simple scientific fact," Roger said on a deep breath, "beyond refutation. All matter vibrates, from the densest metal to the most rarefied gas. Vibration is also common to light, sound, magnetic and electrical energies, and as you know, in the relativistic world of Einstein, matter can be converted into energy, and vice versa. Now, all we have done," he went on, "Dr. Forrester and I, is take that simple fact one step further than it has ever been taken before. Human thought is something intermediate between matter and consciousness. Our thoughts are formed from psychic energy, a kind of energy that is presently unrecognized by science. Yet two years ago our colleagues at MIT in invaluable research proved that fact with direct measurement. If you will recall, the field around the heart has been found to be about five times ten tauss. This is one-millionth of the earth's steady magnetic field and one-thousandth of the fluctuating background of the earth plus typical city noises in a band width of zero to forty hertz. And though the field does vary from person to person, its existence is scientific fact."

Though it was cool in the laboratory, Roger felt a single bead of sweat course down the bridge of his nose and was aware of the effort he was expending.

"Then for the time being," he said, "I will present thought as if it were electromagnetic vibrations, and if I may point out, up until now we have had no idea what environmental-influencing information may be encoded in these electromagnetic vibrations. We can measure the magnetic field of the body or the electrical rhythms of the brain, but these say nothing directly about the meaning of the message they might be carrying."

He paused, approaching the heart of the matter.

"The electromagnetic characteristics of a person's emanations resemble the electromagnetic characteristics of the solar system. We propose that human electromagnetic fields could travel out and interact with similar fields in the environment, much like tuning forks of the same wavelength responding or resonating to each other.

"I refer to the graph on page thirty-seven of the report," he said briskly, and waited out the rustle of pages as Adam followed his direction. "There is no need to go into even a limited discussion of the science of radiesthesis—

detecting and measuring with pendulums. Suffice it to say it is an ancient form of measurement and detection, regarded by some as nonsense, though the results over the last half-century have been awesome. We still lack the kind of solid evidence that would silence every doubter. You will note on pages twenty-eight through thirty the scientific data proved in carefully controlled experiments, but unfortunately it's not the kind of data that other scientists can duplicate."

"Not the new scientific elite," Adam muttered.

"Not elite," Roger corrected. "The potential for radiesthesis is in everyone, but the sensitivity must be developed. And you will further note that all the listed data have also been double-checked with voltmeters and that the pendulum is one hundred percent accurate."

Adam appeared to be reading carefully.

"Now, I have arranged here for your scrutiny," Roger went on, pushing the tray to the center of the table, "a few of the key objects listed in Dr. Forrester's report. The rate at which the pendulum will react varies from substance to substance. Keep in mind that there are two coordinates; one the length of the lead"—and he removed the pendulum from his wrist and held up the fifty-inch cord—"and two, the number of times the pendulum swings in a circle. We will deal first with the reactions themselves."

Slowly Roger lifted the pendulum into the air from the height of its complete fifty-inch extension. He took up the slack and angled it into position over the first object on the tray, a small piece of coal. His arm held steady, and the pendulum did likewise. No discernible movement.

Speaking quietly, Roger pointed out, "You'll note on the graph that the rate for black is forty."

Using a pencil and a yardstick, he took up exactly ten inches from the lead, then again lowered it into position until the pendulum was suspended one inch over the piece of coal.

He held his hand steady and watched with Adam as slowly the pendulum began to gyrate, small limited circles at first, though a few minutes later it was swinging in a broad and perfect clockwise circle over the piece of black coal.

"You're controlling it," Adam accused. "If nothing else with your power of suggestion, you're—"

Roger nodded, ready for the objection. Quickly he drew forward what appeared to be a miniature stainless-steel gallows but what in reality was a piece of equipment which Percy Forrester had designed to eliminate the possibility of his own emotions influencing the reaction. Roger attached the pendulum to the cross bar, then, using a small pulley system, reduced the lead to the desired forty inches, then stepped back in order to demonstrate that his own electromagnetic field could in no way be affecting or influencing the pendulum. Again after a few minutes, relieved of all human contact, the pendulum started its gyrations, slowly at first, then gradually picking up speed.

"Remarkable," Adam muttered, his head circling slowly as his eyes followed the pendulum.

Roger stepped forward, removed the coal from the tray, replaced it with a small silver bowl, and referred him again to the graph. "If you'll notice, twenty-two is the rate for silver. But for the sake of demonstration, let's reduce the lead to thirty-two."

This he did, adjusting the pulley, shortening the lead, then standing back to watch as . . . nothing happened.

"Let's try twenty-eight," he proposed, and again, adjustments made, he stepped back and . . . nothing happened.

"Twenty-two," he announced, secured the proper length, anchored the pulley, and even while he was in the process of stepping back, the pendulum commenced to gyrate, the rotations small at first, then growing larger.

"Good Lord." Adam Krafft smiled. "That's one hell of a toy you've got there."

For about three-quarters of an hour Roger tested every object on the tray—sodium, calcium, gold, silver—and every time the graph proved accurate, the prescribed rate of gyration duplicated to the final turn.

Then carefully he pushed the tray aside but left the automation device in place, the pendulum still attached. "As you can read in the report, we have tested and cataloged over five hundred basic substances and several combinations of each. The success of the pendulum in detecting and identifying is one hundred percent. To test the entire data would take several months.

"The next logical step," Roger went on, "was to ask what was causing the reactions. The surface explanation seemed to be that each substance, water, calcium, gold, gave off a vibration of definite wavelength and that the pendulum somehow responded to this.

"But Dr. Forrester rejected this," he explained, "and ultimately so did I. It proved to be only a fragment of the truth, as one day we discovered that in spite of the device of automation, in spite of the Faraday screen, in spite of the lead containers into which we placed the substance, the pendulum was not responding *solely* to the substance, but to the mind of the experimenter, which, in turn, was reacting to the substance."

Adam began to shake his head slowly. "I'm afraid I need further elaboration."

Fortunately Roger could provide it. "It's a form of cryptesthia," he said patiently, "a term invented by Richet meaning hidden perception, or second sight. We had been excavating that day in an Iron Age fort in the Cambridge area," he began, his voice a monotone, "and we had gathered several stones, as was our habit, to test in the laboratory later." He looked up and took note of Adam's rapt expression and felt like the village storyteller spinning a tale to help pass a long afternoon.

"Again, as was our custom, we broke down the mineral composition. Slate was predominant, if I remember correctly, in these particular stones. And as we had coordinates for slate, we positioned them beneath the pendulum at thirty-six inches, and for the first time, we thought the pendulum was in error. The reaction rate was forty-four inches. Our first emotional response was disappointment. Then Dr. Forrester, already weary and debilitated, allowed himself an unprecedented display of anger and commenced hurling stones from unclassified cartons, expending his rage, though doing little to alleviate the frustration."

Whether it was his own embarrassment at the remembered scene or the embarrassment of his colleague in simply listening to the account of subjective rage, Roger couldn't be certain, but hurriedly he added, "The display of anger, though painful, presented us with the solution to the mystery, and in embryonic form the H.E. Theory was born."

"How so?" Krafft asked politely, and Roger sensed new distance in the politeness.

"Near the end of the tirade, I began to regather the hurled stones, which were of a totally different mineral composition from those gathered at the Iron Age fort. As I was sorting through them on the table, one accidentally fell within the range of the pendulum. Almost absentmindedly I commenced to count the gyrations. The stones which Percy had hurled in anger stopped at forty-four, the same reaction rate as the stones gathered at the Iron Age fort, regardless of their mineral composition."

"And your conclusion," Adam asked warily.

"If you will recall," Roger explained, "I mentioned that we had been excavating on the site of an Iron Age fort. It seemed likely that these stones had been used in battle, that they had retained the anger of the men who had hurled them, and that the pendulum was reacting as much to the emotion as to the mineral substance of the rocks' composition."

"You're . . . not serious, are you?" Adam asked softly.

"I'm afraid so," Roger confessed. "For the last year and a half we have done nothing but test the theory, and contrary to your present disbelief, it is sound, it is awesome."

"But proof," Adam Krafft begged, as though he wanted to believe. "Where is your proof? Percy Forrester's temper tantrum proves nothing."

Roger glanced toward the rock room at the end of the laboratory where Percy's successful experiment was stored, along with cartons of rocks which he'd collected from all over the world, classified into two categories—passive and active. They had proved repeatedly that they could artificially induce the stones to register anger by hurling them, as Percy had done initially, and even on occasion by merely concentrating on the stones and *thinking* on something capable of producing an angry reaction.

But this wasn't the proof that they required. They had searched diligently for stones similar to those found on the Iron Age fort site, which irrefutably retained the anger of the circumstance, or better still, which caused the pendulum to gyrate without any exterior stimuli whatsoever.

This was what Percy Forrester had sent him a few days ago, a dozen irregularly shaped stones taken from the site of Tintagel. "Test them for yourself," Percy had shouted jubilantly into the phone. "I swear, here's our proof." He had claimed further that he'd even picked them up with a pair of tongs to avoid "influencing" them. Every stone he had tested had produced the same results, all gathered from the same site, an environment clearly hostile to its intruders, the thousands of tourists who tramped over it daily, the archaeologists themselves, cutting deep into its rock ribs. Something not known to science was being disturbed, and the signals were clear for those who could and would receive them.

"Well, where is the proof?" Adam asked, shifting in his chair.

"In a minute," Roger replied. "The entire H.E. Theory was predicated on tests which Dr. Forrester sent to me last week, proof positive that our environment is beginning to respond to our offenses in a negative manner."

"*Our* offenses!" Adam parroted. "And just what offensives would those be? Our technology is sound, our science the most advanced in the world . . ."

Stunned by the foolish question, Roger commanded simply, "Turn to page eight," and did not wait to see if Adam obliged him, reaching for his own copy of the H.E. Theory. He commenced reading. " 'On Ski Island, in Japan, fishermen knifed one hundred and twenty dolphins to death. This year over one thousand dolphins have been sold for fat, food, or to Japanese detergent makers, not counting the many thousands slaughtered worldwide in tuna nets. Fishermen in Canada have succeeded in getting the government to lift its ban on whaling. They charge that whales interfere with their nets. The chairman of the Marine Mammal Commission testified before the Senate Appropriations Committee that 356 manatees have been killed in Florida waters within the last three years. There are only about 800 left, and the species is seriously threatened. According to the National Marine Fisheries Service, oil, sewage, and industrial chemicals are killing fish eggs off the eastern coast of the United States. The chemicals cause genetic damage to the eggs and prevent their growth. The ten thousand mackerel eggs studied suffered total mortality.' "

He paused for breath, aware that his voice was rising, along with his anger, and aware also that he was no longer interested in controlling either. The typed words of the H.E. Theory seemed impotent compared to the immensity of the meaning behind them and the incomprehensible echo of Adam's stupid question.

"Shall we move on to tanker holocaust?" he demanded. " 'The long list of tanker accidents becomes difficult to keep up-to-date. Many, of course, are not reported, and *all* are innocent and almost all the ships involved fly flags of convenience. *But* within the scope of recent history, on the Mississippi, the *Baltimore Tender* collided with a Greek tanker. The oil spill spread fifty miles downstream to New Orleans. A Soviet cargo ship pulling two barges, an empty tanker, and a filled Greek tanker piled up near the mouth of the Mississippi. A 60,000-ton Liberian tanker was set aflame by lightning in Port Neches, Texas. A tanker collided off Singapore with a U.S. aircraft carrier, creating a massive crude-oil spill, and let's not forget the Mexican fiasco and the irreparable damage still being done to the wildlife sanctuaries along the Texas coast.' "

He looked up between items and observed that Adam did not return his gaze. He appeared to be busily reading, following the data for himself.

"Item," Roger went on, his voice a staccato counterpoint to the silence about him. " 'In Niagara Falls, another chemical dump site had been discovered and proved to contain four times the waste of the Love Canal. Pesticide waste from the site is now contaminating Lake Ontario. The Love Canal is only one of nine hundred chemical-disposal sites around the country containing toxic wastes and posing a health hazard. Over two hundred people in a small Alabama town have a high level of DDT residue in their blood. The pesticide was traced to catfish caught in a nearby stream. The source of contamination appears to be a chemical plant that was closed in 1971. Laws designed to protect the public from toxic chemicals and dangerous wastes are almost always unenforced because of budget restrictions and a shortage of investigators.' "

Now he refused to look up. At some point despair had moved in and joined forces with the outrage. He could "read" the silence so easily. Ecology was not Adam's field. His research went in a different direction.

We have become a race of technologically advanced imbeciles living in a world we don't understand and don't have any real desire to know anything more about than what affects us directly and individually.

"And last," he said, beginning to suffer the physical effects of his anger, a slight trembling in his hands as he held the H.E. Theory, a distinct clouding of his scientific objectivity. " 'What I have chosen to call, as you will notice, the Nuclear Blindman's Buff. For years, in the atomic maze, the public has been groping in the dark. Before the Harrisburg incident we were told and we believed that there had never been and there could never be any major problems with nuclear-power plants. Then suddenly the Three Mile Island mishap—because it had been impossible to cover up for more than a few hours—opened our very own twentieth-century Pandora's box. Like a Middle Age public-confession ritual, from all parts of the world came news of hundreds of past close calls: 2,835 nuclear incidents in the United States alone in one year. A blaze in the Indiana plant, a radioactive leak in Grenoble and in Pienelatte, France, a severe accident in the French reactor at Gravelines—appropriately named—similar to the Harrisburg accident. Even the Russians admitted officially they had had several bad accidents, including an explosion *and* a radiation leak.' "

His voice fell, no mere pause this time, but a complete cessation of words. He stared unseeing down on the page. There was more, fifteen pages of documented offense, some more horrifying than anything he'd read aloud. Then let Adam read it for himself. Slowly he closed the report and placed it on the worktable beside the idle pendulum.

"Now, for the proof of the H.E. Theory," he said, still unable to look at him.

Slowly he stepped back from the worktable and glanced to his left, to the door at the end of the laboratory behind which his vast collection of rocks and minerals was stored.

"Do you need any assistance?" Adam offered.

"No, no," he said hurriedly, and walked down the long aisle. He pushed open the door and closed it behind him, and found solace in the cool, musty darkness. He considered switching on the overhead light, then changed his mind. He knew the alphabetized storage shelves by heart and made his way like a blind man down to the far end of the second aisle, the place where the letter T was stored, reached up for the container which had arrived a few days ago from Tintagel, and found the slot empty.

What in the . . . ? Then he found it, to the left of its proper position.

With a renewed sense of seeing it through, he swung down the heavy metal container, adjusted its weight in his arms, and moving with greater speed, carried it back into the laboratory.

Still with no words spoken on either side of the worktable, he slid the metal binders from the ends of the container, drew back the lid, and stared down into the interior. In an optical illusion brought on by fatigue and stress, the rocks looked different, larger, more of them.

Convinced that it *was* an optical illusion, he lifted one out and suffered a sensory illusion, several degrees of heat emanating from the stones, though they had been stored in the cool darkness of the rock room.

"Roger? What is it?" Adam inquired on the edge of his chair.

"Nothing."

"Are those the ones that Percy . . . ?"

"Yes."

"And according to Dr. Forrester, the pendulum will react to their abstract qualities?"

"In theory, yes," Roger replied, still handling the rocks, trying to determine their differences and the cause of those differences.

He turned a rock over in his hand, still baffled by the curious illusion of heat, placed it in a line directly beneath the pendulum, adjusted the lead to the prescribed forty-four inches, and . . .

Suddenly the pendulum shot forward, gyrating in a wildly erratic circle with such strength that it pulled against the armature of the automated device and was simultaneously accompanied by a low hum which seemed to increase as the gyrations expanded.

As the rate of the pendulum accelerated, Roger stepped back and was aware of Adam on his feet, not moving toward the table, but holding steady in stunned rigid position, his eyes focused on the astonishing sight, the pendulum seeming to lose power as it swung beyond the range of the rock, then something dragged it back with equal force in the opposite direction, the hum still increasing, like a pulse now, a discernible beat, like a heart.

Roger watched along with him in awed disbelief. This was precisely the reaction that Percy Forrester had predicted.

"Watch out!" Adam Krafft shouted as the metal armature bowed under the strength coming from the pendulum. For fear that it would break, Roger waited until the pendulum had swung wide in the opposite direction, then quickly reached in and grabbed the rock and instantly dropped it, the sensation as painful as though he'd touched a hot stove.

For a moment the rock bounced eerily across the table and came to rest near the metal container. The strange pulse subsided, though there was a faint glow surrounding the stone.

"Test another," Adam ordered, his voice constricted with tension.

Slowly Roger reached into the container and withdrew a second rock, in size similar to the first, more black than gray, as though part of its mineral composition was petrified lava.

Lava? At Tintagel?

"Go on," Adam insisted as Roger hesitated. Carefully he disengaged the pendulum, lifted the lead high into the air, positioned the rock directly beneath it, then slowly lowered the lead until the pendulum hung suspended less than an inch over the rough black surface.

This time the pendulum shot forward as though someone had pulled it, defied gravity for several seconds and held itself suspended at a horizontal angle over the rock. The mysterious hum commenced again, and as the pendulum swung down in the low shuddering gyration, Roger was aware of Adam moving back, his head rotating in perfect symmetry along with the gyrations of the pendulum.

"Christ," he whispered.

The automated device began to vibrate as it struggled against the electromagnetic field coming from the stone.

"It's going to break!" Adam shouted, and quickly Roger reached in to remove the stone. He felt heat while his fingers were still inches away, and watched, helpless, as the rod snapped, the force of the gyrations hurling the pendulum the length of the worktable, the hum increasing, then suddenly falling silent.

For several minutes neither moved nor spoke, as both focused on the black stone and observed the same glow that they had seen earlier.

Adam stepped forward, one hand extended as though to touch.

"It's hot," Roger warned.

"It couldn't be—"

"It is!"

Adam shook his head slowly and looked bereft. A death *had* occurred, the death of all previously conceived and irrefutable scientific theory, the death of man's egocentric position in the world, the death of certainty and assurance, the death of faith in man's ability to predict.

Roger waited for the sense of triumph that should have been his. The long years of hard work had *not* been for nothing. Percy's instincts first, then his own, had been directly on target. The daily front-page catalog of "natural" disasters would never again be read with the same resigned helplessness.

Flash floods in Alabama claim 146 lives. . . . Killer tornadoes sweep across north Texas. . . . Casualties in the hundreds. . . . Earth tremors recorded in Delaware. . . . Chinese earthquake most devastating in history, death toll 750,000. . . .

Adam continued to hover close to the worktable. "You say that Percy Forrester sent you these . . . specimens?" he asked.

Roger nodded.

"From an Iron Age fort, did you say?" Adam pressed further.

"No. These are from Tintagel," Roger repeated.

"Tintagel?" Adam repeated, now bending over in close examination of the label on the end of the metal container.

Roger saw Adam adjust his glasses, the better to read the small print on the label which Roger had affixed to all the cartons. "If these specimens are from Tintagel, why does the label read 'Tomis'?"

Roger nodded absently, staring at the man, his attention splintered between the broken pendulum and the curious question.

"Tomis?" he repeated, wondering vaguely how Adam Krafft had heard of the place. "Tomis? No," he repeated. "Those were sent to me by Percy Forrester. They came from . . ."

Adam shrugged and backed away from the container. "See for yourself. I'd

302

have a word with my research assistant if I were you. Careless storage. To err in something as important as . . ."

For a moment longer Roger looked at him, disbelieving. All around him there was a swirl of images, blending with the sounds in the room, the residual beat of a slow but steady pulse which seemed to emanate from the inanimate stones.

Then Roger was aware of a new sensory phenomenon, his vision blurring, unfocused, loud sounds in his ear like chaotic distortions as he tried to maneuver his way toward the metal container to see for himself.

Tomis!

No! No! It couldn't be. But in spite of the rejection, certain facts rotated inexorably in his head: the unseasonable blizzard, all lines of communication down, the powerful ley lines which encircled the mountain, the absence of wildlife, the manmade offenses, the imminent destruction of the mountain, the death blow of the mining corporation. And caught in the middle, as always, the innocent, the well-intentioned, the uninformed and untrained who would not have the slightest idea what was happening to them.

The rocks had been collected as recently as last week. He'd not thought to test them. All his inquiry had been focused on Percy Forrester and Tintagel, while right here, less than . . .

Suddenly he lifted his head as though an invisible hand had delivered a blow.

"What is it, Roger?" Adam Krafft prodded.

But there was no time for explanation, perhaps no time at all. Still, he must try. "If you will excuse me . . ." he murmured, and hurried past Adam, breaking into a run on the steps leading up from the laboratory.

"Mrs. DeNunnzio! Call Stapleton. Willie Chapman. Tell him to have the helicopter ready in thirty minutes. Auxiliary tanks filled. And call Sheriff Barker. Tell him I need a police escort into Denver. Either that or pull his cars back. Call the highway patrol as well . . ."

Her shocked face lifted, struggling to make the transition from something she was typing. "Dr. Laing, I don't—"

"Do it!"

Then he was running again, glancing at his watch as he headed toward the garage. Ten after three. Forty-five minutes into Stapleton, a little less than three hours' flying time, depending upon wind conditions. With luck he'd have approximately an hour of full light left. The plane would be quicker. But it was too dangerous to attempt to land a plane in Tomis. *What would he find?*

Suddenly a grim thought occurred to him. There were more than fifty year-round residents in the little mountain town. If disaster were imminent, he couldn't begin to get them all in his Bell 222 aircraft.

Then what? He would need at least three of the large National Guard rescue helicopters stationed at Colorado Springs. Yet he had no official clearance to make such a demand, and unfortunately, he was very well acquainted with the strangling red tape which would surround such a request.

Then he'd simply have to rely on his thirty-year friendship with Pete

303

Hampstead—General Hampstead—and be willing to face the charges if charges were filed, and reimburse the taxpayer, that too, of course.

He'd call from Stapleton. The rescue helicopters could intercept him south of Colorado Springs, and he could lead them in from there to the remote mountain community.

But what if there was no need for rescue helicopters? What if there was no one left alive and . . . ?

No! As he disciplined his thought, he looked ahead now to see a startled Troy just emerging from the garage office.

"Mrs. DeNunnzio called, Dr. Laing. She said—"

"I'll drive myself," Roger shouted. "The Mercedes . . ." and saw Troy run back to the automatic-control panel in the office.

In the eight seconds that he had to wait for the agonizingly slow ascent of the garage door, he thought back to the experiment. *How could the mistake have happened?*

Then he remembered. He had not turned on the light. The cartons had been alphabetized, and in the dark he had withdrawn Tomis instead . . .

"Is it filled?" he called out, ducking beneath the garage door even before it was fully lifted.

"Ready to go, Dr. Laing. Do you need—"

—nothing that Troy could supply him with, or anyone else. Human error, he thought as the diesel motor turned over with a sluggish roar. Human error—his own.

Apparently Troy had already called ahead to the gate, for the driveway was clear and he sped through at a dangerous rate of speed onto the canyon road, hunched over the wheel, tense, terrified that at last, in the most devastating manner possible, the Hostile Earth Theory was on the verge of becoming reality.

Dear God, let me be wrong, he prayed, ready to sacrifice a lifetime of work for the simple return to a stable, predictable, understandable world.

45

Tomis, Colorado

Hal knew. Not in any rational way, not in any way that he could share with the others. But still he *knew*, with a simple deep quiet conviction, the seed of which had been planted in that first tragedy over three years ago but which only now did he admit to: the death of young Kent Sawyer, the lower portion of his body embedded in rock—Mike had said *crushed* by rock, but Mike had been wrong, had seen only what he had wanted to see.

Now, with the almost clinical objectivity of a dying man viewing the phenomenon of blue sky for the last time, he paused at the edge of the stand of trees and knew that the journey ahead of him was treacherous, a descent of half a mile down to that safe-appearing weathered roof beneath which over fifty people huddled, people who yet did *not* know, and who still clung to the illusion of hope and rescue and tomorrow.

The journey he'd already made was awesome. There had been nothing he could do for Lucy Hackett, and in an attempt to banish the memory, he stared down at his hand, truly a unique mechanism, and released his fingers, like the opening of a flower. He would not have to remember it for long, that specific death.

It had happened before. And someone in unbearable grief had made a small shrine at the place where it had happened and had stepped out of life and had become the falsely accused old Mountain Man of the new Tomis.

Every mountain community worthy of the name has its own mountain man. He can be ours.

The Fox Fire Kids . . .

In remembering the hope at the beginning, he felt his knees give way, and slowly he sat in the cool, moist shade and gazed out at a vista so beautiful that it took his breath away.

Viewed from the distance of the moon, the astonishing thing about the earth, catching its breath, is that it is alive.

Who had said that? And alive in what sense? Vengefully alive? Capable of retaliation? Yes!

The voice was coming from inside his head. The thoughts were not his, yet in a way they calmed him, allowed him to forget the last twenty-four hours and not to think on the next twenty-four. If only he could control his trembling, he would start back down the hill. He felt certain that everyone in the restaurant had heard the shots. Everyone would be in need of reassurance, lies.

We are protected from lethal ultraviolet rays by a narrow layer of ozone, provided we can avoid technologies that might fiddle with that ozone.

Roger Laing? Was it Roger's voice inside his head? *Jolly Roger, where are you now? The idyll is over, destroyed from without and within.*

He placed both hands, palms down, in the mud and tried to push up, but lacked the strength. He heard a sucking sound and felt pressure under his hands, like the pull of an outgoing tide. Suddenly he was scrambling upward in a spastic movement, pitting his strength against the suction, and winning.

He knew!

. . . but could not understand. *They* were not the enemy. True, they had cut down some timber when they had arrived, dug the holes for septic tanks and power lines, graded and blacktopped the road. But these were simple actions they had viewed as improvements. They had taken nothing, altered nothing, destroyed nothing that they had not needed to sustain life. *Then why?*

As he walked down the steep incline, he felt slides of small rocks accompanying him, as though following him. A few struck against his ankles. One tumbled between his feet and almost tripped him, and in anger he reached down, scooped it up, and hurled it with angry strength and felt a lingering sensation of heat on his hand.

Hurry! Their only hope was to take a party of the strongest men, the ones who stood the best chance of making it, and try to walk down the mountain. Then let them deliver the cry of alarm and send the rescue helicopters back for the others.

The creation of a plan, even an ill-conceived one, had a positive effect on him, and he was running now as fast as the steep descent would permit, keeping his eyes trained on the beacon of hope that was his own roof, the steeply pitched dark brown shingles which were just visible at the center of the tall pines. It was his intention to stop for blankets and jackets, a change of clothes for Sarah and Vicky, anything that would make them more comfortable while he and three others tried to walk down the highway.

He was just starting up the steps to his cabin when he heard it, a low creaking of wood straining against itself. He froze midway up the stairs and felt the railing begin to vibrate beneath his hand. At first he thought it was the house itself, the frame shifting on its foundation, the wood still curing in the high altitude.

But suddenly he felt a strong compulsion to look up, saw one of the massive pine trees behind the cabin begin to sway, its enormous trunk moving back and forth, the rate of swing increasing along with the vibrations, a high-pitched whine erupting in his ear. He kept his eye on the huge tree, and only at the last minute did he let go of the vibrating banister as the intent of the pine became clear.

He stumbled backward as the tree, caught in its own powerful sway, cracked and fell, the entire weight crashing down on top of the cabin, slicing through the roof like a knife blade, exploding windows, timbers flying, cutting a monstrous swath, and coming to rest at last in its own division.

Hal lay facedown in the tall grass, gasping, the breath knocked out of him. For several moments his lungs refused to take in air, and as he clawed at the ground, the high-pitched shriek grew to dangerous proportions. At last he felt his lungs contract, felt a torturous explosion of air and a cool trickle of blood on the side of his face, and realized he'd been cut by flying glass.

He knew! And knew further that it was not over, and looked fearfully up at the destroyed cabin. Several yards below, coming from the back door of the restaurant, he heard a familiar voice and looked down to see Inez, an expression of terror on her face as she assessed the damage, which changed rapidly to relief as she caught sight of him.

"Hal? Hal, are you all right?"

Then she was running up the hill, pulling herself forward on the grasses. "We heard the crash," she called out. "Are you—?"

"Stay there!" he shouted, on his hands and knees. "Stay where you . . ."

But still she came, less than twenty yards now, a small determined figure battling her own fear, the steepness of the incline, and now suddenly a rising wind. He felt it blowing over him, plastering his shirt against his back, and saw the effort on her face, mingled with bewilderment as she looked up once toward the sky.

"Go back, Inez!" he shouted, and saw her slip and fall, one hand reaching out for support, the tall grasses appearing to ensnare her.

Still on his hands and knees, he started down toward her, but the force of the wind pushed him off balance and caused him to fall forward. He tumbled over and over in the thrashing grass and tried to brace himself as he drew near to the spot where she had fallen. He grabbed at the earth and stopped his fall and heard above the wind a weak cry of, "God help . . ."

He tried to find her, but as the gale-force winds whipped about him, he smelled smoke and looked up to see the cabin on fire. Apparently a gas line had been ruptured by the falling tree, and now the flames were shooting high into the air, fanned by the wind.

"Inez!" he cried. He looked back toward the place where she had fallen and saw only the back of her head, the rest of her totally obscured by the whipping grasses, which appeared to be lashing her into the earth.

He closed his eyes as her head slipped from view, and when he looked up again, she was gone, the grasses limp now under the decreasing pressure of the wind. It wasn't possible, and slowly he dragged himself forward, thinking he'd misjudged the spot, thinking she'd slipped and fallen about ten yards farther down the incline. Suddenly he was struggling to stand, the better to see, and the wind permitted him to do so now. The howling ceased as suddenly as it had begun. He looked over his shoulder and saw the flames diminishing, though a small fire burned steadily at the heart of the cabin, causing a cloud of white smoke to lift over the large trees, obscuring the tops.

Find Inez, his mind insisted.

He stared at the hillside, scanning the incline. The grasses were now blowing gently together, making a singing sound, a low, almost gentle hum.

Find Inez, reason dictated. But something other than reason suggested she could not be found, and in rising despair for knowing but not understanding, he glanced down toward the rear of the restaurant and saw every window lined with terrified faces.

Then go to them. Wait with them. Urge them not to try to understand. Take Sarah in your arms, and Vicky, and think about the times that were good and comprehensible.

For a moment longer he stood on the hillside, unconvinced. "Inez?" he called out, and received no answer.

Leave! It was an unfair battle.

The greater challenge was with the living, with trying to prepare them for what was ahead. Their debilitated systems could not endure the strain much longer. The faces at the window had already seen too much.

He had expected to be greeted at the back door by hysterical questions. But he was greeted by no one, and walked the length of the quiet kitchen and stopped before the storage room.

"We heard . . . shots," Ned Wilson said without inflection. Hal stopped at the swinging doors to see them all seated like punished children at their respective tables. Even the young people had ceased their nervous chatter and now sat slumped in their chairs, their eyes fixed unseeing on the empty spaces before them.

"Shots," Ned Wilson repeated, abbreviating his earlier question, as though he lacked the energy to complete the sentence.

Hal nodded and clung to the swinging doors for a moment, suffering from a shortness of breath.

"Who . . . was it? The shots?" Wilson repeated a third time, and Hal watched as the man rested his head on the table, as though he really didn't care if he received an answer or not.

"Tom Marshall is dead," Hal said softly, finding it increasingly difficult to draw enough air into his lungs. If anyone heard, he had no idea, for there was no reaction, and he stared out at trancelike faces.

In the far corner he saw Sarah, still at the window, Vicky pressing closer to her. The object of her focus was clear, their still-burning house halfway up the incline. Donna was at her side—thank God she was safe. Slumped a small distance away he saw Mike. But it was Sarah who needed him.

He must go to her. She appeared to be on the verge of collapse.

"Sarah." He called her name as though to let her know that he was coming, when Mrs. O'Connell reached out for his hand. Her eyes glittered unnaturally bright in the semidarkness of dusk.

She was nodding all the time she was drawing him close, as though for a whispered intimacy. "Inez will be back in a minute," she whispered. "She said she just wanted to go check on something—Mina, I believe, yes," she added, her face brightening.

"Of course." He smiled reassuringly.

Two tables away, old Mrs. Billingsly spoke. Without looking to the right or the left, simply addressing the air, she said, "I really should go and fetch my violets. They won't know what to do either."

Hal caught Ed Billingsly's eye and gently shook his head, and as her husband offered reassurances, Hal found himself hearing again that curious last word: They won't know what to do *either*.

Again he looked out over the restaurant, pleased that no one felt compelled to demand an explanation. They knew now, he was certain of it, knew further that it was only a matter of time before . . .

But there his mind stopped, the instinct for life still strong within him. It was not too late for rescue to come. Once safe, they could deal with the phenomenon itself. Only by clinging to the hope that understanding was possible, that there *were* reasons, that someone could say to them, "Look, this is why and this is how, and both are because . . ."

He tried to draw deep breath and felt his lungs hungry for more, and looked down on one of the Hills children and saw her eyes fixed and staring, a faint blue tinge coating her lips.

No oxygen, not enough oxygen, and suddenly he understood the trancelike states. They were slowly suffocating.

"Sarah," he called gently, and as he moved toward the far corner, he saw her collapsed in the chair now. Still she held Vicky close beneath one arm, the child's head in her lap.

Quickly he bent over and felt of Vicky's neck. Still a pulse, though faint. He stood up and tried to raise the near window. It stuck, and without thinking he grabbed a near chair and hurled it at the glass, and quickly lifted his arm to shield his face as glass shards fell about his feet.

He felt a new coolness upon his face, a faint breeze, which he tried to drag into his lungs. He reached back for Vicky and lifted her into his arms and held her before the open window and heard the child protest the rough treatment, pushing softly back into his arms, where she might sleep, uninterrupted.

"No, Vicky," he scolded. "Open your eyes. Wake up."

But again she pushed against him and nestled her head on his shoulder and murmured, " . . . go . . . round," and went back to sleep.

"No use," Sarah whispered behind him, and before he turned back, he looked up through the shattered window at the gray sky and thought hopefully: It's light still, still a chance. . . .

Others now had lowered their heads to the tables, the inertia spreading.

The flare of hope which had given him strength earlier, the chance of a few walking out, fast faded. Something was draining all their energies, and he viewed the short distance to Sarah's side as though it were a journey of impossible length.

"You're . . . hurt," she murmured as he collapsed beside her, and only then did he remember the flying glass.

" . . . nothing," he replied, and lifted one arm, which felt as though it had been filled with lead, and drew her close.

"It's too late, isn't it?" she asked with quiet resignation.

"Not . . . yet," he replied. It was necessary to first think the words, then force the lips to form them.

He came back to awareness with the feeling of her hand on his leg. "Is . . . everyone dead?" she asked simply.

"No, leave them alone. It's best . . ."

"I love you."

He felt her hand tighten and covered it with his own and tried to lift his head against the grief that was cresting inside him.

"I'm . . . so sorry," he whispered, and rested his face atop her head.

Someplace, someone was weeping. Rene Hackett. He should have told her . . .

She knew. All of them knew.

" . . . can't breathe," Sarah gasped.

His pulse was racing at an unbelievable speed. He tried to count the heartbeats and couldn't.

Count the dead! Count the dead!

No!

"Sit up, Sarah," he scolded, holding Vicky in one arm, trying to raise Sarah to an upright position with the other.

" . . . can't . . ." she murmured, and slumped against him.

He felt her defeat as though it were his own, and felt it invade the place where his will resided. They would not leave this place alive. None of them. Now he knew that as well. The mountain not only did not want them here. It wanted them dead.

46

Roger Laing was as familiar with the inner and outer workings of his Bell 222 helicopter as he was with his own body. He was intimately acquainted with the potential of each, the limitations of each.

Shortly after he had lifted off from the helicopter pad at Stapleton, he'd checked the controls, set a continuous cruise speed at 170 mph, double-checked the high-altitude gauges, radioed in for confirmation of an air route and corridor, then tried to settle back and let the remarkable helicopter do its job, regretful in a way that it did not require more of his skill.

Inside the small cabin he found a final maintenance check on the control panel, then in the quiet of the compartment he realized that all he could do now was wait and try to control his fears and hope that Pete Hampstead got his helicopters in the air in the next twenty minutes. Roger would not take the time to go down for them. He feared that he was out of time.

As he cruised over the jagged outskirts of Denver, he grasped the control lever and held it steady, aware that the aircraft was performing perfectly. *He* was the one in need of balance, and because it was easier to concentrate on what he could understand, he double-checked both hydraulic systems, nagging superficial details at work in every corner of his mind: Had he told Mrs. DeNunnzio where he was going? No. Or *had* he? Stapleton knew. Willie Chapman had his flight pattern.

Abruptly he closed his eyes in an attempt to still the turmoil. The helicopter

311

hit an air pocket and shuddered softly, drawing his attention back to the control panel. For several moments he concentrated on the dials, the slim black needles fixed on proper readings, everything working as it should. He checked the map against his visual sightings below, skirting the foothills of Mt. Evans, passing over the Idaho Springs area, then heading toward Colorado Springs. It was his intention to cross the Continental Divide at Loveland, then, keeping to the extreme western edge of the divide, make his way south past Gunnison and on down into the La Garita Wilderness and ultimately to Tomis. ETA 1900 hours.

The plane would have been faster. But no safe place to land.

Though his instinct was to increase his speed, prudence dictated otherwise, and again he made a conscious effort to still the fear within him, the fear that, in all respects, the H.E. Theory was correct, and voiced the intense prayer that it was not.

For a few minutes the dazzling blues and greens of the mountains below provided him with brief distraction. Seen from this limited height, the terrain was indescribably beautiful, like a piece of heavily veined green marble, benign-appearing, man's personal property, part garden, part zoo, part energy source, existing for his unique and personal use to be devoured and exploited as he wished.

No! The rebuttal inside his head was swift and filled with conviction. Man was master of nothing. The illusion that he was had persisted for centuries. But it simply wasn't so. It was impossible for man to have a life of his own without concern for the ecosystem in which he lived, not in mastery, but in complete interdependence.

Now, viewed with the echo of that thought, the placid, idyllic scene below appeared less placid.

We cannot continue to walk rough-shod over the face of nature without doing damage to ourselves.

This had been the fervent and driving motivation behind the H.E. Theory, proof that human mastery *was* only an illusion, and tragic proof that all things were alive and therefore capable of retaliation when abused.

He looked out and down again and suffered a sudden shock. The greens and blues had disappeared. In their place he saw a sepia landscape, deeply cut and blackened arteries twisting in snakelike fashion around a dark crimson central core, like an open wound. The afternoon sun caught and reflected on vast metal roofs, endless boxcars lined up on a rail siding, four large tanks containing bloodred water, yellow smoke billowing from three massive smokestacks, a dismal satanic place, the Climax molybdenum mine near Leadville, the nation's second-largest hard-rock mine.

He brought the helicopter lower, the better to see. Straight ahead he caught a glimpse of the giant tailing pond, a red-brown inland sea edged by poisonous-looking white foam, stretching ahead for miles, cutting deep into fresh green waterways.

With new awareness he recalled Howard's words from *The Treasure of the Sierra Madre*: *We have wounded this mountain and I think it is our duty to close its wound. The silent beauty of this place deserves our respect.*

The wounds were clear even from this distance, and the irony of the moment was not lost on him: the technology that enabled him to skim as gracefully as a water bug over such ugliness and condemn it was made possible by the ugliness itself. He was at the moment flying the very mineral that had left the earth a scarred and bleeding place.

For a minute, confronted with such ugliness, he was unable to deal with the irony, the fact of his dependence, along with that of everyone else, on the exploitation of earth.

The contradiction would have to be reconciled. For himself. For others. Priorities altered. Life-styles replaced by simpler, less expensive values, as they were trying to do at Tomis, the preservation of original fabric, as Hal had said, life simplified and enhanced.

Tomis. . . . There was an irony as well. Why would the H.E. Theory manifest itself first at the very place where people were trying to relearn basic lessons of mutual respect and inter-dependence?

Energy implies life, life implies will, but will does not imply reason.

One of the basic premises of the theory. He knew it by heart and in his heart. Retaliation would be capricious, whimsical, as lacking in "intelligence" as the tornado that levels one side of the street and leaves the other standing intact.

He looked back and down for a final glimpse at the mine and thought of the vast new mineral exploration that had been planned for Tomis and Mt. Victor.

Then he turned about in his seat and did not look back again, though for several minutes he continued to see the scarred landscape before his eyes. His direction was straight ahead, down the western slope of the divide, keeping low to the foothills. The earth below had turned green again except for an occasional broad gray ribbon of highway.

It would be awesome, terrifying, he heard Percy say in memory, the retaliation of nature, every benign object, trees, grass, suddenly weapons to be used against us.

Roger stared unseeing at the instrument control panel. It could not last for long, such a retaliation. The shock of horror, of the unexpected, of the unknown, would be massive. Something in the human will would shrivel and die. Even the extraordinary characteristics of courage and perseverance would be short-lived. For a while it would be possible to resist that which one did not understand. It would be impossible to resist that which one did not see or suspect.

"Come on, come on," he whispered aloud, for suddenly the small helicopter felt plodding and archaic, like a slow milk truck when he needed an express train.

But maybe not. And as the gargoyle of hope surfaced in his mind, he thought how absurd he was going to feel in less than an hour when he touched down in the high meadow above Tomis and saw a very mystified Hal and Sarah and all the others hurrying toward him, asking of *him*, "Is anything wrong? Where's the Jolly Roger? And no luggage? Poor Roger, you need a keeper, you do. Let him catch his breath, Vicky, before you show him your merry-go-round."

He heard their voices so clearly, and effortlessly envisioned past scenes of good fellowship: the small hearth in Hal and Sarah's house; the simple dining room of Hal's Kitchen, out of which crept the odors of heaven; Inez Fuentes' strikingly handsome face, its concealed sorrow giving it its beauty. And Mike Dunne would be there, wisecracking about everything, like a stand-up comic. And patient, beautiful Donna, and good, practical Brian, trying to deal with Kate's grief in loving attention, and the whole assortment of mismatched, eccentric, hearty souls who voluntarily had turned their backs on the urban nightmare and—

Abruptly his reflections ceased. Everything went out, his memory of sight and sound and sensation.

He shook his head in an attempt to dispel the frightening feeling, and in most uncharacteristic fashion rejected that which he could not understand as he hurled himself into a useless double-check of all instrument readings, purposefully forgetting the small built-in computer that was doing the same job better, more efficiently than he could ever do it.

Suddenly, radio static interrupted the quiet of the cabin. He picked up the mike, identified himself, and heard a distant voice: "We're waiting for your directions, sir."

He leaned forward and scanned the broad windshield and at last saw them, three enormous dark green National Guard choppers, flying in formation at twelve o'clock. He owed Pete Hampstead a tremendous favor.

47

Hal lifted his head. And froze. Mike did the same, and for several moments they stared at each other over the darkening restaurant, eyes hopeful, fearful.

"Listen . . ." someone whispered.

Though Hal's head was throbbing, he started up from the chair, taking Vicky with him. At the window, he shut his eyes, the better to listen.

"Is it . . . ?" someone whispered behind him, and could not finish.

Then he heard it clearly, the rotors of a helicopter, still distant, but lightly splintering the silence with a hum of hope.

"It is!" a voice cried out, and he looked over his shoulder to see them all struggling to their feet, drawing on the last of their energies, a few of the women crying, all pushing toward the front doors and in the process trampling over the ones in the lead, whose energy source had been depleted and who now fell and became stumbling blocks for those still on their feet.

"Wait!" Hal cried, seeing the disaster seconds before it happened, the passage to the front door totally blocked.

The sound of the rotors was growing louder, coming in over the high meadow. He was certain there was more than one. Although he could not see them, they were there, dropping lower, like miracles from the slate-gray sky. And the crush at the door was increasing as well, everyone screaming to get out, no one remembering that the door did not push out, but instead drew in.

Hal tried to shout over the hysteria, and felt a new fear move in. Failing to see any sign of life, the helicopters might just leave. Hurriedly he reached back for Sarah, roughly lifted her to her feet, slipped a supporting arm around her shoulder, and drawing on strength he didn't know he had, he shouted toward the others and pointed toward the back door, still an open artery which in their hysteria they had overlooked.

As they hurried through the kitchen, Sarah stumbled and almost slipped from his grasp. Donna assisted him on one side, while Mike tried to guide the others.

They had just cleared the door when he looked up and saw one helicopter descending over the high meadow. It looked so small.

The others pushed past him, waving their arms as they looked up toward the sky and the tiny encircling aircraft.

Vicky stirred in his arms, and with a surge of hope he renewed his grip on Sarah and dragged her forward as if to squeeze back into her wrist the last impulse of life.

48

Precisely at his ETA of 1900 hours, in the flushed light of a dazzling red dusk, and with the three National Guard choppers following behind, Roger caught a glimpse of Mt. Victor's rocky summit, that implacable old man's face that he'd first seen as a boy more than fifty years ago. What delight he'd taken in telling them all that he had camped on this very plateau long before most of them had been born, had poked about the old ruins and pondered the mystery, never dreaming that a town would grow up on his boyhood haunt.

There it was, and he brought the helicopter around in a northerly direction and looked straight into the mountain's face and thought he saw human features, deep-set rocky eyes, the bridge of a nose, a stern pursed mouth at timberline, and . . .

As he guided the helicopter carefully around the eastern slope, he looked down on the high meadow and saw . . . nothing. Surely they had heard the rotors by now. Sitting up straight in the seat, the better to see, he guided the helicopter lower and made a skimming pass over Main Street and looked out of the window to his left and saw . . .

He looked back, unable to believe . . .

The access road leading up the mountain had collapsed. A sheer rock abyss now loomed where the road had once been, and farther down the mountain he saw what appeared to be the jumbled and crushed remains of mining equipment.

317

The helicopter began to rock from lack of a steady hand on the controls. With one firm grasp he anchored the lever and brought the dipping under control. Yet every place he looked he saw new disintegration and felt the blood pumping faster through his veins.

Something had happened, and for a moment he allowed the helicopter to drift over Main Street as he took careful note of the violent ruptures in the blacktop, the heavily rutted ley lines pushing up with awesome strength. He saw a few cars along Main Street, although all were on their sides, pushed over by a force coming from beneath the surface of the earth, and near the far end of the street, in the direction of the camping area, he saw enormous geysers of steam shooting upward like rigid white fingers. Convulsively he gripped the controls and brought the helicopter about for a second pass, searching, always searching for a moving speck of humanity.

The visible disintegration pounded off the rim of his consciousness, and his pulse increased. Still no sign of life, and now he felt the hairs on his arm bristle. He hovered over the deserted town, the data from the H.E. Theory crackling through his brain.

Someone! There had to be someone . . .

Suddenly, to his left, at the back door of the restaurant, he saw a small figure, then two—*life!*

He lifted the craft, skimmed the top of the restaurant, and angled it back over the high meadow, all the time keeping the moving specks within his line of vision, more now, ten, fifteen, scrambling up the steep incline, some falling back, others still coming out of the door.

Quickly he established radio contact with the three National Guard helicopters that were just coming into view; the static was bad, and getting worse. Still the pilots followed his directions and one by one angled their large cumbersome craft down onto the high meadow above the town.

The pounding of his pulse grew louder, hammering at a speed too rapid to be gauged. People were still streaming from the restaurant, clearly terrified, their mouths open in cries he could not hear over the vibration of the helicopter.

As he descended, he hurriedly drew down the window, thinking to warn them to move back. Many were directly beneath him now, their hysterical faces upturned, their clothes windblown into distorted angles by the force of the rotors.

Frantically he waved his arms at them, but either they didn't hear or refused to obey, and suddenly he felt new vibrations and quickly lifted up, thinking that now they would understand that he had to have a place to touch down.

In the slow-rising ascent, he looked back and saw some of them shaking their fists at him. A few of the women appeared to have dropped to their knees in the high grasses, their hands covering their faces. Through the open window he felt the wind turning colder, and as he came back around for a second pass, he saw an isolated figure—no, several—just starting the difficult ascent up the embankment. A child was in the man's arms, something clinging to . . .

318

Hal!

Thank God, Roger prayed.

Suddenly a muffled pounding jolted the helicopter, then another, then a steady shuddering, as though unwittingly he'd entered a field of powerful electromagnetic force. For several seconds his full attention was focused on the aircraft as he struggled to bring it under control, lifting and falling erratically, thinking: air pocket? down-draft? though neither was powerful enough for the present buffeting.

Only by lifting up several hundred feet could he restore the craft to a degree of equilibrium. Then slowly he tried the descent again, and this time settled more easily to earth. Once down, he considered shutting off the rotors, as the noise was deafening. Then he saw Hal and Sarah—dear God, what had happened to her?—and Mike and Donna Dunne hurrying toward him, and something in their appearance, in the terrified expressions on their faces, suggested that it was necessary that they leave now.

Without abandoning the controls, Roger pushed open the small side door and extended a hand to Hal. "Are you all right?" he shouted above the noise. "I should have come sooner—"

"Oh, God, it's good to see you," Hal shouted back, and Roger thought he detected an unprecedented break in the man's normally strong voice. And he looked like hell, as they all did, gaunt, somehow, bad color; Vicky's lips, he noticed, had a bluish tinge.

Well, time for examinations later. For now, get them out of here.

Apparently Hal's thoughts were running along the same track. "Can they go with you?" he shouted above the rush of the wind, gesturing toward Sarah, who leaned heavily on Donna.

Roger nodded. "Of course, though hurry . . ."

Then Hal shouted back at Mike, who still was trudging up the incline like a man twice his age. "Get them inside and stay with them," he ordered. "I'll see that the others are loaded aboard . . ."

He didn't stay to finish the command, but apparently Mike understood, for he seemed to double his effort on the incline, and arrived at the helicopter, gulping in deep breaths, his hand shaking visibly as he reached out for Roger's grasp.

"Jolly Roger." He smiled weakly, a sadness and defeat in his face that Roger had never seen before. "Welcome to hell," he quipped, and around the dark edges of the joke and his voice, Roger sensed the truth.

Still keeping a firm hand on the controls, Roger reached back to assist them as best he could, relieving Sarah of the burden of Vicky and lifting the child effortlessly into the front seat with him. The child's face was absolutely bloodless, and she appeared to be shivering continuously, and he wondered what, if anything, he could say to comfort and soothe her.

Suddenly he heard a sharp cry coming from behind, and craned his neck about to see Sarah on the verge of complete collapse, now literally being propelled forward by Donna on one side and Mike on the other.

"Is she ill?" Roger shouted, concern vaulting.

"She . . . lost the baby," Donna said, and Roger saw tears in her eyes.

319

Hurry, Hal, Roger thought. Time was of the essence, in more ways than one, and he leaned far out of his craft and saw Hal, a distance away, herding the last few stragglers into the large helicopters.

From some unknown source came another mysterious jolt, not connected in any way with the vibrating aircraft.

"What in the hell was that?" he shouted, and looked over his shoulder at Mike as though for illumination. The man sat crammed in the small rear compartment, Donna on one side, staring out of the window, weeping silently, Sarah on the other, her head back against the cushion, eyes closed.

"Come on, Hal, dammit!" he cried, and looked back to see the three large helicopters lift off simultaneously, the roar deafening, Hal bent double against the gale-force winds, his arms laced over his head in protection against the flying dust and grit.

All right, it was their turn next, and accordingly Roger turned back around in the seat and tried not to see the faces of grief and despair and terror surrounding him. He made a quick adjustment on the fuel injector to be sure of enough power to lift off, tested the rotors, sent them into a high-pitched squeal, and saw Vicky in the seat beside him cover her ears and start to cry.

Later, he'd have to offer comfort. Later. *Hal?* He looked back again and saw the National Guard helicopters slipping safely into the horizon. Destination? He had no idea. At least they were safe. Now, where in the hell was . . . ?

Again he felt a severe jolt, and looked down to the ground and saw what appeared to be a macabre illusion, the ground shaking so that water came bubbling out from the center of the earth, then everything becoming liquefied, the tall wind-lashed meadow grasses resembling waves.

"No," he whispered, rejecting what he was seeing, that most rare and cruel natural phenomenon of all, the violent shaking of earth which resulted in poorly consolidated sediments liquefying and turning to quicksand. It was reported to have happened in the '64 earthquake at Niigata, Japan. There had been only a few survivors, thousands of others simply drowning in an earth vibrated to the point of failure and liquefaction.

Hal . . .

Mike leaned up. "What in the hell is . . . ?"

"Got to lift off," Roger shouted.

Sarah screamed, "Hal . . ."

Less than thirty feet below, he saw Hal, his face streaked with grime, his entreaty clear in spite of the distance. He had fallen to his knees, though he looked up, one hand reaching, and Roger heard his cries as the solid earth beneath him turned to liquid and he fell to one side, thrashing futilely, his head twisting to avoid the suffocation of drowning.

Behind Roger in the cabin, Sarah was screaming continuously. No one attempted to soothe her. All were frozen on the horror below. Roger saw Hal now trying to avert his face from the wind force of the rotors, a force which Roger noticed was causing the earth to ripple as though he were hovering over water.

320

"We're going down," Roger shouted. "Mike, get on the other door and open it."

Within the instant, Mike perceived Roger's intention. Twenty feet lower, and Hal could be saved. Reflexively Roger pushed the lever forward and felt the slow vibrating descent to fifteen feet, then ten, trying to keep everything within his sight, Hal up to his waist, the expression on his face reflecting the pain and horror and urgency.

At five feet from ground, Mike threw open the door. Still too far. Vicky in her fear was thrashing wildly in the front seat. In the back, Donna and Sarah were clinging to the opposite side of the craft in an attempt to maintain a degree of balance.

"Lower!" Mike shouted.

Then lower to four feet, then three, then two, the rotors hurling liquefied earth in all directions. Hal's face was so clear beneath them now, a look of sad inquiry in his eyes, as again with one final effort he thrust his arm up, and in the same split second Mike reached down, suspending himself with one hand on the back of the seat, grasping the upraised arm, missing, reaching again, and without looking, tightening his grip about it and slowly dragging Hal into the compartment.

Within the instant, Roger lifted up and was aware of the others scrambling for balance within the craft, Mike falling back exhausted into the rear compartment, Donna now clinging to him, both women weeping, while in the front Hal drew Vicky into his embrace in spite of his wet, mud-covered clothes. The reunion was sweet, fate defied, with Vicky clinging to him, crying "Daddy" over and over again.

For a second Roger concentrated on clearing his vision, and was aware of nothing but the now empty high meadow, the blowing of the cold wind through the still-open door and the slow pounding of the vibrations. Staring feverishly at the phenomenon, he felt a burning behind his eyes and found that for a moment he could neither exhale nor inhale air. What they had seen was not possible. He looked up toward Mt. Victor, washed in the dull rose of dusk. The wind was dying, as though the anger had spent itself.

"What . . . was it, Roger? What . . . happened?" Hal asked quietly.

Roger refrained from answering. He would tell them later, when they all were warm and safe and dry, though he wondered if they would believe him.

Suddenly, coming from the town they saw a small explosion. It seemed to center in the restaurant, though quickly it was followed by others, gas lines ruptured by the vibrations, the entire street ablaze within minutes. Roger could feel the heat, and this, combined with Vicky's terrified screams, brought him back to himself, and quickly he closed the door and lifted higher.

Shut it out! Shut it out! he thought. But it could not be shut out, and as he circled upward away from the fire, his hands began to shake and he felt a blind rage at the frailty of the body.

These people were not the enemy, a voice raged inside his head.

They hovered over Tomis for almost twenty-five minutes, with no one speaking, until the fires had extinguished themselves, and below, the whole length of Main Street, they saw nothing but charred and smoking rubble, new ruins for some young boy to discover a hundred years from now.

Suffering a wrenching anguish, Roger circled low over the high meadow. The liquefaction was over, the earth grown hard and reliable again.

He sank back and drew a long shuddering breath. How could the authorities explain what had happened today? An earthquake? Most likely. Though he knew all too well that if he were to call the nearest seismograph center, there would be no measurable recording of earthquake activity. What had happened here *could* be explained and understood. But he had failed to fully explain it to Adam Krafft. What would the farmer, the truck driver, the steel worker do with the H.E. Theory?

They took a final wide pass over the small plateau and stared numbly out of the window.

Wearily Roger glanced at Hal, counting on a simple question, a simple answer. "Where to?"

Hal shook his head as though trying to shake off a stupor. "Durango. I want us to stay together. I feel . . . responsible. Authorities must be . . ."

Notified? Ominous, that. Well, Roger would stay with them and help them in any way he could. And if anyone asked and appeared genuinely to want to know, he was prepared to tell them that nature was capable of retaliating against human abuse as long as man continued to act as though the world were his own private garden, until ultimately . . .

The "ultimate" thought died for lack of impetus. Roger maintained a death grip on the controls. Behind him, someone wept softly. He wasn't certain who, and he didn't want to look, for he had nothing to offer in the way of comfort.

The question occurred: *Isolated incident? Or portent?* But in the fires below, the explosions, the liquid earth, there had been no comforting answers.

At last he sealed the window and locked it and secured the cabin for the short run to Durango. The only sound came from Roger's right, from Vicky, who, clutched between her father's legs, stared down with frightened eyes on the destruction and in a self-comforting gesture made small slow circles on Hal's knee with one grimy finger, all the while whispering, "Merry-go-round . . ."